Just Loving You

FREDERICK WILLIAMS

Just Loving You

FREDERICK WILLIAMS

Jaed Publications
Los Angeles, California

This is a JAED Publication

Printed and bound in the United States of America
by OneTouchPoint-Southwest

Williams, Frederick
ISBN 978-0-9976552-1-6

This novel is dedicated to my beautiful wife, Venetta, because I enjoy Just Loving You!

Acknowledgements

Like every other author, I owe a debt of gratitude to a number of people who assisted me in this endeavor. First and foremost, I must thank God who is the inspiration behind all that I have done and will do from now on. I would like to thank a very dear friend, Addie Armstrong who was the manager of the Carver Library in San Antonio, Texas when I first wrote the original version of this book. I would like to thank Maureen Smith who is a top-notch writer in her own right, for encouraging me to take on the challenge of writing a love story. A special thank you to Ms. George Anne Byfield and Ms. Terry Sherrell of OneTouchPoint Printing for the beautiful cover design and the layout of the text. I must also acknowledge my publisher, Jaed Publications for working closely with me to complete the book in its revised format. I would like to extend a very special thank you to Ms. BernNadette Stanis for the endorsement and kind words on the back cover. And finally, as always, a very special thank you to my wife Venetta Williams who is always there for me, sticking by my side when I get these new ideas to write. As I sit, locked in my study, I know she is only a room away and is always there to lend me the support every author needs. Thank you for being there all the time and that is why it is so much fun Just Loving You.

Chapter 1

2004—Los Angeles, California

Jason Mitchell's BMW sports convertible shot around one of the many sharp curves on the 110 East Freeway. He had left his Los Angeles apartment in Leimert Park at 7:20 sharp, giving him plenty of time to make it to the Pasadena Courthouse before Judge Henry Hutchinson gaveled his courtroom into session at nine o'clock. Jason anticipated the traffic would be heavy on both the 110 and 110 Freeways that early in the morning, but for some reason it seemed to be heavier than usual. Probably because this morning he had to be somewhere at a specific time. It took over an hour to get to the 110 and that left very little time for the rest of the trip. Before leaving that morning Jason had removed the top off his BMW and the sun felt good beating down on him. The smog hadn't set in yet, and he could feel a slight breeze which made his ride that much more enjoyable.

As wonderful as the morning felt, he still couldn't rein in his anger toward Angela. What did she expect? He paid her eight hundred dollars a month in child support and now she wanted more. He figured it wasn't really the money, but her need for revenge. She'd been all set to get married and load him down with a house full of kids. Along with kids, a wife, and a mortgage went a nine to five job with his father's company, managing a bunch of knuckleheads who worked only because they had to. He did the job thing for a few years after graduating from the University of Southern California's business school. He went that route at the insistence of his father. Big Casey Mitchell had built his multi-million dollar construction company with only a high school education. He claimed he'd sacrificed for Jason and his other children so they would never have to suffer the indignities that he had. His father assumed, with Jason being the oldest, he would take over the mantle of leadership and continue to build the company. Disciplining employees, doing balance sheets, and bidding on jobs were not Jason's idea of the good life. He had something very special and different: he was an artist.

After struggling through business school and working for his father for three years, he finally decided he had to confront Big Casey and let him know he wasn't cut out for that kind of life. At the same time, he had to also put some distance between Angela and him. She also graduated from the University of Southern California and her family mirrored his perfectly. Her family was upper-middle class and would never admit affirmative action played a large role in their success. That's where Angela's folks differed from Jason and Big Casey. They both knew set-aside contracts had been the assistance Big Casey needed to reach such a high level of success.

There was drama when Angela got pregnant. Both families, especially Hazel, Jason's mother, insisted they make it right and real soon. Initially Jason agreed because he felt obligated. But their problems started big time when he quit his job and told Angela he was going to write. When she laughed and told him he wasn't going to be the next Richard Wright or James Baldwin, he responded by telling her that he would be better than both of them. She insisted that he not quit his job so he moved out of their three bedroom home in the Meadows in Pasadena and leased an apartment in the Leimert Park area of Los Angeles. He loved their daughter Julianne to death, but couldn't believe it would take more than eight hundred dollars a month to raise a three year old child. That's why they were in court. He planned to fight any increase in his monthly support payment.

Jason shot up the Orange Grove exit and headed down the boulevard to Walnut. It was 9:10 and he could only hope Lincoln Murphy, his attorney, could provide the judge with a sufficient explanation so he wouldn't sanction him for being late. He took a couple curves going over seventy in a thirty-five mile per hour zone. He needed to slow down. If the Pasadena Police stopped him, that would add to his tardiness. He cut his speed back to fifty.

At the corner of Walnut and Garfield, Jason pulled into a parking garage next to the courthouse, paid the attendant eight bucks and hurried inside. Just as he cleared the metal detector and started down the long hallway to Courtroom 75, his cell phone went off. He grabbed it from inside his jacket pocket, hit the voice activation button and stopped right outside the courtroom.

"Hello, mother."

"Jason, what happened?" Hazel asked.

"Nothing so far. I haven't gone inside yet."

"You're not there yet!" Hazel's voice shrieked. "I thought you were supposed to be there by nine and it's already close to nine-thirty."

"I know what time it is, mother, and I know I'm late."

"I just don't understand why you can't be on time for something this important."

"Okay, mother, I'll try to explain it to you later on. But I do have to get inside."

"Jason, don't forget I need you over here right after you get out of court. You hear me?"

"Yes, mother, I hear you and I'll be there," Jason finished and hung up the phone.

Rushing through the courtroom door he spotted Lincoln standing in front of Judge Hutchinson, obviously making excuses for his tardiness.

"I'm giving him five more minutes and if he's not here I'm issuing a bench warrant for his arrest," Hutchinson scowled at Lincoln.

"I'm here, Your Honor." Jason jogged to the front and stood next to Lincoln. His attorney gave him a disdainful look.

"Mr. Mitchell, you were supposed to be here at nine o'clock, not nine-thirty. In the future show the proper respect for this court and be here on time." Hutchinson looked over the top of Jason's head at Angela and her attorney standing behind them.

"Mr. Edwards, do you and your client want to come forward?"

Jason turned and looked at Angela as she and her attorney approached the bench. In his haste to get to the front, he hadn't noticed her standing off to the side. But as she came forward, he glared at her. She looked exquisite and beautiful. Why did he ever give her up? Jason checked out her lawyer, a young good looking brown-skinned brother with a clean shaven head. Henry Edwards looked like a million dollar man of success in his Brooks Brothers suit.

"All right, isn't there some way we can work this out?" Hutchinson asked.

"Your Honor, my client feels there should be an adjustment to her child support payment based on Mr. Mitchell's ability to pay," Edwards said. "We don't believe he has provided us with all his financial resources."

"What are you looking for?" Lincoln asked. "At the time of the settlement we gave you all his financial records including his tax returns."

"That was almost a year ago and we still aren't satisfied that you were completely honest with us," Edwards rejoined. "Furthermore, my client has decided to place their daughter in a private preschool and the tuition is six hundred dollars a month."

"A private school!" Jason practically shouted. "She's only three years old and we've never talked about a private school before."

"Mr. Mitchell, you know the rules in the courtroom," Hutchinson said in a raised voice. "You have an attorney. Let him speak for you."

"I'm sorry, Your Honor," Lincoln said. "It won't happen again." He turned and gave Jason a hard stare. He then looked back at the judge. "Your Honor, we provided Attorney Edwards with all my client's financial records. He still is not working full time."

"How does he make a living?" Hutchinson asked.

"He works part time for his father's construction company."

"And therein lies the problem," Edwards said. "We have no way of knowing exactly how much his father is really paying him. We would like a court order to examine Casey Construction's financial records."

"That's absurd." Lincoln's voice now rose a couple decibels. "There is no basis for such an order. Casey Construction is not a party to this dispute."

"If the records they provided us during the initial hearing are not a correct representation of what Mr. Mitchell is making, then they've done something wrong," Edwards retorted.

"That's a witch hunt!" Lincoln shouted.

"Counselor, we don't need you to shout," Hutchinson said. He glared down at Edwards. "That's a little extreme right now," he continued. "You folks appear to be reasonable people. I want you all to come up with what you feel is a suitable increase. I'll give you all a month and then come back and see me. If you can't settle then the court will get involved and find a settlement. You both understand?"

"Yes, Your Honor," both attorneys answered.

"Go see what you all can work out. You're dismissed. And Mr. Mitchell, don't ever come into my courtroom late again or I'll hold you in contempt."

"Yes, Your Honor," Jason said.

"Why don't we meet in the lawyers' room and see if we can work this out," Edwards suggested.

"I don't know why we have to meet," Jason said. "I don't have any more money to give right now." He looked directly at Angela. She looked away. "You can't look at me because you know you're doing wrong, don't you?"

"Mr. Mitchell, please don't address my client," Edwards quipped. "She's made it quite clear that she wants all conversation to go through me."

"That's ridiculous. Why can't you talk to me, Angela? Am I going to have to go through him when I want to see my child?" Jason pointed directly at Edwards.

"Cool it," Lincoln said. "Let's talk in the lawyers' room." He grabbed Jason by the arm and pushed him toward the exit.

Jason and Lincoln sat on one side of an oblong conference table while Angela and Edwards took seats on the opposite side.

Damn, she was looking good with her long black hair flowing over her shoulders, fantastic full lips and long thin neck. But he couldn't afford to think in those terms. He'd made the decision to end it.

"Mr. Mitchell," Edwards broke Jason's concentration. "We all can save ourselves a lot of money and time if you'll agree to increase the child support to twelve hundred dollars a month."

"What are you talking about? I don't have that kind of money. You all seem to forget that I don't have a full time job."

"And why don't you have a job?" Angela finally spoke up. "Because you decided you're going to be the next Walter Mosley of the world."

"Angela, don't go there," Jason shot back at her. "We've had this conversation and it's just not going to accomplish anything."

"Okay, I think we all need to calm down," Lincoln said as he placed his hand on Jason's arm. "You both know that's a little unreasonable for only one child. The average child support for one child in the state of California is about six hundred. My client is already paying more than that."

"Your client is not the average run-of-the mill person," Edwards retorted. "He's the son of one of the most prosperous Black businessmen in Los Angeles County."

"What does his father's success have to do with my client?" Lincoln asked.

"We know that Casey Mitchell is taking care of his son while he pursues this writing career of his."

"You don't know that for a fact." Lincoln pushed down firmly on Jason's arm, an indication for him to remain quiet.

"If he doesn't still have him on his payroll, then you shouldn't have any problems with a court order to examine the company's payroll records."

"Big Casey would shoot the first person who showed up at his office and tried to examine his company's records," Jason admonished.

"Then he'd have bigger problems, wouldn't he?" Edwards rejoined. "Look, why don't you guys come back at us with an offer? We don't need to be fighting like this."

"Give us a couple weeks," Lincoln said.

"Okay, today is the second of June. Can we meet at your office, Lincoln, on the 16th?"

"That'll be fine."

"How about you, Angela, is that good for you?" Jason asked.

Angela looked away and Edwards answered instead. "That's just fine with my client." He and Angela got up to leave.

"What's wrong with you, Angela? Can't you speak for yourself?"

"Screw off, Jason!" Angela shouted. "Is that good enough for you? You walked out on me and your daughter and you want me to be kind to you. Well just get ready to increase that monthly check because I know you have the money. Let's get out of here." She turned and walked out the door. Edwards followed closely behind her.

"That's an angry young woman," Lincoln said as he and Jason got up. "You really hurt her and she's going to make sure you pay."

"She didn't want to support me, and I don't mean with money. She was turned off by my dreams."

"You know her anger is because she still hasn't given up on you."

"Yeah, well she'll just have to get over it."

"Has she seen you with any other women?" Lincoln asked as he opened the door and held it for Jason.

"No, because I haven't been with any other women."

"Be prepared, my brother."

"For what?"

"For all hell to break loose when she does find out you have somebody else." Lincoln smiled and patted Jason on the back. They both walked out of the room and down the hall.

Chapter 2

Jason pulled up to the electronic gate at the end of the long driveway leading to Big Casey and Hazel's six bedroom, two story, brick home in the Altadena Hills overlooking Los Angeles. He punched in a set of numbers, the gate swung open and he drove inside, continuing the two hundred yards to the front of the house. As he brought his BMW to a stop he glanced to his right at the guest house where he once resided. He had many good times in that small, private bungalow. If Hazel only knew the number of young ladies he'd entertained there, she'd never forgive him. Those were the days before Angela. That kind of lifestyle was fun at the time but now he'd set out on a much more serious pursuit in life. Nothing, and especially no one, would interfere with his goals.

According to the deal with Big Casey, he had two years to write and publish his first novel and after that he'd be on his own. During those two years Big Casey agreed to cover all his expenses, including his child support payment to Angela. If he failed as a writer Jason agreed to return to the business and take over the daily operations, allowing his father to retire. Essentially they had a bet. Jason enjoyed the challenge and was determined to win. No matter how pleasurable the memories of the good times he experienced behind those doors, he had to steer clear from that kind of activity now. It meant no complicated relationships for the next two years. Even with Angela, no matter how good she looked he had to stay on track. But Jason wasn't fooling himself. As a healthy 27 year old man, he recognized sex was awfully important in his life. But the kind of relationships he would have for the next two years would be non-binding ones. His close friend Elliott would often say, "All you want right now is sex for fun." Jason climbed out of the car and headed inside the house.

Big Casey loved to refer to his large ornate home as the Black Palace. It had been built right to his specifications and his company completed part of the construction. Friends and visitors to their home referred to it as the magnificent edifice. Jason could recall his father working eighteen hour days to build his company. He had vivid memories of the insults Big Casey endured from the large white construction companies who refused to subcontract any of their work to him. Then in the late seventies and early eighties federal government set-aside contracts opened up the market for minority contractors. The state, county, and local governments followed suit. Big Casey played the political game the right way, won the contracts, and in a period of five years had a multi-million dollar company. That's when he set out to build his dream home.

Jason unlocked the front door, sauntered through the foyer by the spiral staircase and to his father's study. He swung the door open and Big Casey, sitting behind his large oak desk, looked up at him.

"Hey, Mr. Novelist, I didn't know you were coming out this way," Big Casey said in his deep baritone voice.

"Your wife caught me on my way to court and said she needed me over here this morning." Jason sat down in one of the beige leather chairs in front of the desk. "Do you know what she wants?"

"No, don't get me to lying. I sure don't know what your mother wants."

"You mean you can't give me a heads up? Give me a little warning of what I'm walking into?"

"I'm afraid not, son. You're on your own on this one." Big Casey pulled out a large cigar from inside his desk drawer. He removed the wrapper, ran the cigar along his mouth, and lit it.

"Dad, when you going to give those things up?" Jason asked.

"When I have to give up all the pleasures of this life, then it's time for me to move on to the pleasures of the next life. With this diabetes I can't eat half the food I want. I can't drink Scotch anymore. But at least I can still have a good old cigar."

"Yeah, but those things don't help. And you know darn well you haven't given up the Scotch. I bet you have a bottle right there in your desk."

Big Casey sucked on the cigar and slowly let the smoke trickle out of his mouth. "Well, my boy, you don't always do what's good for you either, which brings us to your little trip to court this morning. How'd you make out?"

"Angela's just bitter. She's pissed off because her little scheme didn't work."

"Oh it worked if that's what it was, a scheme."

"How you figure that?" Jason asked as he leaned forward in the chair and waved the cigar smoke out of his face.

"She got you so you didn't wrap that thing between your legs. Now she's going to get a check for the next eighteen years."

"If you look at it that way, you have a point. And now she wants more."

Big Casey tapped the ash from his cigar in a large gold-plated ashtray on his desk.

"How much does she want?" he asked.

"Twelve hundred," Jason replied. "But she won't get it. I'm going to fight her."

"How much is your daughter worth to you?" Big Casey asked.

"Why are you asking a question like that?" Jason didn't want to answer that question because he knew a trap was waiting for him.

"You can't answer it?" Big Casey shot back at him.

"Sure I can, but I know you."

"What you mean you know me?" A big smile spread across Big Casey's face.

"You used to do that to me when I was a kid. And before I knew what happened I was tricked into something."

Big Casey's smile widened. "No trick at all. Just a simple question that calls for a simple answer. How much is your daughter worth to you?"

"Okay, I'll bite. The world."

"I was hoping you'd say that. So here's what I'm going to do. I am going to pay that extra four hundred for you and in return—"

"No, dad," Jason interrupted. "You can't do that. She's money hungry and she's just trying to get even."

"Who, your daughter Julianne?" Big Casey asked.

"No, you know I'm not talking about her."

"But that's who I was talking about. I didn't ask you how much you loved Angela, so why you drag her back into the conversation?"

"Because the money's going to her."

"Yeah, but you can't afford to look at it that way." Big Casey put the cigar down in the ashtray and leaned across the desk. "You have to believe that every penny you give is for your daughter and you have to leave it that way. Otherwise you're going to be miserable for all the years you have left to pay child support. When you write the check think of Julianne and not Angela."

"I can't keep taking money from you like this."

"You want to give up your little writing project and come back to work for the company?"

"You know I don't want to do that."

"Then don't be tripping on all this stuff. Take the money, do your thing for the next year, and let's see how it all works out." Big Casey picked up his cigar and relit it. He stuck his big hand across the desk. "If we have a deal, let's shake on it."

Jason grabbed his father's hand and vigorously shook it.

"The only stipulation to this agreement is that you won't fall in love and you'll keep it wrapped up until you're published. Can you live with that?"

"No problem," Jason answered. "There's no way I'm going to fall in love with anyone. She could be the goddess of all eternal beauty and there still wouldn't be any happenings."

"Be careful," Big Casey admonished. "Don't let your mouth get you in trouble. I know there is some woman out there who could steal Jason Mitchell's heart."

"I don't think so. In fact, I know that can't happen because I have a goal and nothing's going to get in my way."

"We'll see," Big Casey smiled and he looked up just as Hazel made her way into the room.

Hazel was a small woman, standing 5 feet 2 and weighing all

of 110 pounds. Big Casey stood 6 feet 4 and weighed at least 275. The two made quite a contrast in both size and demeanor, Big Casey being more laid back and relaxed. It was very difficult to make him angry. But you could do it if you messed with any one of his four children. Hazel, however, was much more feisty and hot-tempered. People who knew the two also claimed that she was more of a snob and had a tendency to dip into her children's business far too much. They had been married for thirty-two years and in all Jason's years with them, he could only remember them having one serious dispute.

She frowned and waved the smoke from in front of her. "You need to stop smoking those nasty things," Hazel said looking at Big Casey. "You know the doctor has warned you. But you're so hard-headed." She now turned her attention to Jason. "How'd it go in court?" she asked as she kissed him on the cheek and stood over him.

"It went okay," Jason answered.

"Well it's just a shame that you all have to drag that poor baby through all this legal mess," Hazel continued. "I don't know why you had to go off on this crazy tangent about being a writer."

"Okay, mother, we've been through this a hundred times. Can't we let it rest?"

"No, I'm not going to let it rest," Hazel's voice raised a couple decibels. "Your daddy paid all that money for you to go to USC and now you don't even want to use the degree it cost us so much money to buy."

"Mother, you didn't buy my degree. I earned it."

"You all just cut it out," Big Casey intervened. He'd been intervening between those two for years. Jason and his youngest sister Theresa had always been the two that challenged Hazel, and Big Casey usually would have to intervene in order to keep the peace. "We all agreed that Jason would do this writing thing, and we'd support him. So just leave everything else alone."

"You didn't ask me over here just to find out what happened in court," Jason said, playing on his father's attempt to change the subject. "What's up?"

Hazel's expression changed. She seemed to soften up somewhat. She reached over and placed her hand on Jason's arm. "I need to talk to you in private," she said.

"What do you mean in private?" Big Casey asked. "Why can't you talk in here?"

"Because I need to have a private conversation with my son," Hazel answered in a stern tone. "Do you mind?"

"I do, but it won't make any difference." Big Casey got up and walked around the side of his desk. "One minute you fussing with him, then the next minute you have to talk with him in private. You can use my office. I need to make a bathroom run anyway. Two cups of coffee run straight through me."

Hazel and Jason watched Big Casey as he limped over to the door, opened it, and then left the room.

"Why is he limping?" Jason asked. "And why isn't he at work today? Something has to be wrong because that man never misses work."

"I know and he's starting to worry me. It's his diabetes and his blood pressure. You know he won't go back to the doctor. He was supposed to go back over a month ago. But he's stubborn and it's going to kill him one of these days. I give up trying." Hazel let out a big sigh and then changed the subject. "Your sister's the reason I called and wanted you to come over."

"Theresa, what's wrong with her?" Jason asked.

"Not Theresa, Jacqueline," Hazel corrected him.

"Miss Perfect Jacqueline's got problems?"

"Don't get smart and yes she does," Hazel admonished. "It's not really Jacqueline, but her husband."

"What's wrong with Arthur?"

"I'm not sure and that's why I called you."

"Wait a minute. You don't want me to get into their business, do you?"

"Better you than Big Casey. If he finds out that Arthur may be abusing his daughter I guarantee you, he'll kill him."

Jason sat straight up in his chair. "What is it you want me to do?"

"Go over there and find out what's happening. Jacqueline called late last night crying and talking about leaving Arthur because he hit her. Last week she called at four in the morning crying because he hadn't come home."

"Mother, I don't think it's in Arthur's nature to hit a woman."

"Will you just go and find out before this gets back to your father?"

"Okay, tomorrow I'll drop by and find out what's going on, if she'll talk to me. You know how Jacqueline can get."

"Why can't you go by there tonight?"

"Because I have something else I have to do tonight. I'll go by in the morning."

"You promise?"

"I promise I'll go by there tomorrow first thing in the morning."

Big Casey walked back into the room. He grabbed a domino set, opened it and placed the dominos on his desk. He then looked at Jason.

"Got time for a game so I can whip you real good?"

Jason scooted in close to the desk and said, "You wish, old man. I'm going to put a good whipping on you."

"You all have fun with your games." Hazel got up and walked toward the door. "I have real work to do. Remember tomorrow, Jason. You promised." She finished and closed the door.

Big Casey arranged the dominos on the desk and gave Jason an inquisitive look. "What was that all about?"

"Just my mother being my mother and your wife being her usual self."

"I don't know what kind of answer that is and because you're so flippant with your response, I'm going to whip you even worse."

"Go for it, old man. Go for it."

Chapter 3

Big Casey had put Arthur Hannon, his son-in-law, in charge of the construction project at the Los Angeles International Airport when the company won a small set-aside contract to build an auxiliary parking lot in the southwest portion of the airport. A year ago Arthur lost his job as a computer programmer with the state of California. Arthur never told Jacqueline the reason he was let go. And since he did have past experience in construction and was married to Big Casey's oldest daughter, Arthur received the position at the expense of the veteran employees of the company. Big Casey's seasoned workers complained that his son-in-law knew very little about running a construction project. Furthermore, he was arrogant and unwilling to listen to others who could assist him. But they were no match against Jacqueline and Hazel, who both insisted that it would be much too degrading to make Arthur work for one of the other men. He'd already suffered through the humiliation of losing his job and it would be damaging to his fragile ego if he had to go to work for his father-in-law as a common laborer. It bothered Big Casey because Arthur couldn't provide him with a reasonable explanation for his dismissal from the job with the state. He told his daughter that people just didn't get fired from civil service jobs unless they did something terribly wrong. But Jacqueline's tears and Hazel's badgering won out. With great reservations Big Casey made Arthur the foreman.

Arthur knew he'd gotten the job because of his wife and that had now become a sore spot with him. It put him in a position of weakness. If he pissed her off she could get him fired. He didn't like that at all. Arthur had to carve out his own piece of the action and figure a way to break loose from Big Casey. But for now, he had to do his job. Sitting in the trailer at the construction site, staring out at the men laying the foundation for the long runway, he just couldn't get his thoughts off the young dancer he'd met at the Black Zebra Gentlemen's Club last night. She had to be one of the finest Black women he'd ever laid eyes on. After three drinks, she told him she'd be dancing that afternoon and if he could break away from work to come on by the club and continue their party from last night. He glanced at the clock on the wall. A little past two o'clock. She would start dancing at three. But Arthur had promised Jacqueline he'd be home right after work. She'd been totally pissed because he didn't get in until two-thirty in the morning. Jumped in his face and he'd slapped her. Not hard, but just hard enough to let her know he wouldn't stand for that kind of disrespect.

Arthur stepped outside the trailer and watched a jumbo jet soar out of the sky to land. He could smell the hot tar his men laid on the runway. The tar smell and the exhaust fumes from the jet seemed to make the temperature much hotter than it already was. It had to be over ninety degrees in the shade. His crew consisted of poor Blacks and Mexicans. How they could take this heat and the smell of hot tar was a mystery to him. And to think Big Casey would have started him out as a crew member if it hadn't been for his wife and Hazel.

What he needed was to spend an afternoon with that fine dancer he'd met last night. The day was almost over and no one would miss him. He took off his hard hat and headed towards his Mercedes Benz.

"Stephen, can I see you for a minute?" Arthur called out to one of the crew members.

"Yes, Mr. Hannon," Stephen said as he hurried towards the Mercedes.

"Take over," Arthur instructed him. "I have to take care of some personal business before the bank closes. If Mrs. Hannon calls tell her I had to go by the bank and then I'll be on home." He finished his instructions and drove off.

The Black Zebra was located right off the 110 Freeway and Avenue 26 in the Northeast portion of the city. Arthur discovered the club after he and some friends had gone to a Los Angeles Dodgers/San Francisco Giants baseball game. They partied until it closed. Since that time, Arthur frequented the club at least twice a week. He was known as a regular. He would mess with a number of the dancers. He actually dated one girl for about four months. Lately, he'd been seeing a white girl who used to dance there and now was his private property, available to him whenever the urge arose. She'd stopped dancing just before this new girl began. But after meeting Dominique last night, he knew he would definitely dump the other lady as soon as he could expose the new girl to all his charm, including the charm that swung long and thick between his legs. He would have a piece of her no matter what the cost. He pulled into the parking lot next to the club, locked his car and headed inside. He couldn't wait to lay his eyes on that chocolate brown princess he'd met last night.

Arthur paid the ten dollar cover charge and then hurried inside. The dimly-lit club smelled of smoke, sweat, and perfume. There were three stages and each one had a dancer performing her seductive movements. A number of men stood at the foot of each stage with dollar bills in their hands, waiting to place them inside the garters that snugly hugged the bare thighs of the dancers. Arthur checked out all three stages but did not see Dominique. He found an empty table and sat down. He figured she was probably in the back. He had nothing but time. The waitress approached his table and he ordered an Absolut and tonic with a twist of lime, then reared back and waited for his dream woman to appear on stage.

u

At ten o'clock in the evening, after sitting at his computer for two hours, the plot just wasn't coming together. When Jason started writing, he knew where he wanted to go with this scene, but for some reason the movement had stalled. He suffered from writer's block and didn't know why. Jason leaned back in his chair and placed both hands across his forehead. He needed to concentrate on the task before him. The day's activities had blocked his creative ability. So much negativity ran counter to his nature. He didn't need the problem with Angela and felt guilty about accepting additional money from Big Casey. Someday when he'd made his name in the literary world he'd repay his father. Now he had to deal with Jacqueline's problem. What the hell bothered Arthur? The man had it made. A boat load of brothers out there would love to take his place, being married to a beautiful Black woman, whose father happened to own the most successful Black construction company in LA County. And he wanted to act a fool and beat up on his wife.

Jason got up and walked out of the bedroom where he did all his work. He had a small apartment, with his desk and computer and a small shelf full of books on how to write in his bedroom. There was a regular size bed and a combination radio CD player with two small speakers. In his living room he had a leather couch, two chairs, and a 27 inch Sony TV that sat on a small table next to another CD player. A counter separated the living room from his small kitchen, with three bar stools lined up next to the counter. That's where he usually ate while watching the news. Jason disciplined himself to watch no more than two hours television per night. That got kind of tough during basketball season when the Lakers would be playing. Or when Elliott would come over and insist on watching some ridiculous musical videos on BET.

Jason opened the refrigerator door and grimaced as he looked at all the empty space. He did miss Angela's cooking. She loved to prepare gourmet meals and there would always be plenty of leftovers. When they lived together he never had to worry about finding something to eat. He could picture her Cornish hens, with rice pilaf and string bean casserole. She would always tease that her favorite desert to prepare was banana pudding, and her favorite desert to deliver was in the bed. This time there was nothing but a couple cans of Sprite, some milk, a package of bologna, and some cake he'd gotten while at his mother's house. He grabbed a piece of cake and a Sprite then sauntered back into the bedroom and sat down at the computer. Jason had decided to write a historical novel about slavery. It had been close to thirty years since Alex Haley's Roots shocked the American conscience with its vivid description of the cruelty of slavery, and practically a half century since Margaret Walker's Jubilee. He figured it was time for another novel on the same subject but with a different twist. He had made good progress identifying his main characters and creating their dilemma in the novel, which was quite simply how to escape. One possibility was to have them somehow come in contact with Harriet Tubman who would help them escape. But he decided that would be too easy. There had to be more intrigue. His three main characters had to escape on their own. This evening he'd planned to write the scene where the plantation owner rapes one of the female slaves. But for some reason it just didn't flow right. Jason took a big bite of the lemon cake and chased it down with a gulp of Sprite.

Just as he visualized the scene, the phone rang. He was tempted not to answer but instead got up, walked over to the night stand next to the bed and lifted the phone to his ear.

"Yeah, who is it?"

"It's your main man, and I have a couple of ladies who'd like to stop by and socialize," Elliott said.

"You know this is my time to write. Why you want to mess with me this way?"

"Because I know, better than anyone else, that you need a little recreation in your life. We're right around the corner. We'll be there in five." Elliott finished and hung up.

Oh shit, Jason whispered as he walked out into the living room and glared at clothes strewn all over the place and dirty dishes in the kitchen sink. He picked up the clothes, tossed them in the bedroom and closed the door, then started for the kitchen. Before he could get over there the doorbell rang. Damn, that was fast. He opened the door and Elliott, along with two very attractive sisters, smiled at him.

"Come on in," Jason greeted the three. "That didn't take long."

Elliott and the two women strolled into the living room and Jason closed the door behind them.

"My Brothah, Mr. Novelist, and writer extraordinaire, how you doing?" Elliott held his hand up for a high five.

Jason faintly slapped his hand and gave him a very hard stare. "I'm fine. What are you all up to this evening?"

"We just came from a poetry slam around the corner at Evelyn's Coffee House," Elliott answered. "You should go some Friday. They have some great poets reading their stuff."

"That's wonderful, but I'm not that deep into poetry. I'm long winded. I go for the full story." Jason raised his eyebrows and dipped his head in the direction of the two sisters.

"Oh, my bad," Elliott apologized. "This is my friend Denise and notice I said my friend." Jason reached out and shook her hand and Elliott continued. "And this is Denise's friend Raquel, and isn't she luscious?"

Jason placed more emphasis on the handshake with Raquel a very attractive, tall, brown- skinned woman with sharp features and long black hair. She looked like she could be a model.

"Have a seat. Sorry I don't have anything but soft drinks to offer you."

"That's all right, I brought the libations." Elliott pulled a bag from inside his coat pocket. "You have the cork screw, I have the wine."

After pouring drinks for everyone, Jason sat in the love seat to the left of the sofa. The other three sat on the sofa with Elliott in the middle. Jason wasn't sure what his friend had in mind. But he didn't have a lot of time to socialize. He had to finish writing the rape scene.

"What's up with you all this evening?" Jason asked.

"Like I said, we just enjoyed listening to some original and creative writing by some fine sisters," Elliott reiterated.

"There weren't any brothers reading?" Jason asked.

"Only a couple," Elliott answered. "Just seems that the poetry scene is dominated by sisters."

"Why do you think that is?" Jason took a long sip from his wine glass.

"Because sisters are much more comfortable in expressing their emotional side than brothers," Raquel said. "Poetry is quite emotional, and I might add quite real."

"You don't think brothers can display emotions?" Jason turned his attention towards Raquel.

"I wouldn't say that," Denise now spoke up. "Elliott has written me some beautiful poetry and I can assure you he's all man."

"Hush, woman, don't reveal my secrets," Elliott said with a smile. "Why keep something that good a secret?" Denise leaned over and kissed him on the cheek.

"All right, don't start that mushy stuff in here," Jason also smiled. He gazed over at Raquel and she stared back at him. He took another gulp of his wine.

"I feel you all connecting," Elliott said and an even larger smile spread across his face.

Elliott's bold move made Jason a little nervous. He hadn't been with anyone since Angela and had managed to keep his mind on his goal. But he was a man and she definitely was fine. Raquel broke the silence.

"How long have you been a writer?" she asked.

"I've been working on my first novel for about nine months. But I feel I've always been a writer since I wrote my first short story when I was in seventh grade," Jason answered.

"How wonderful," Raquel smiled and took a sip from her wine glass. "I find that so exciting. I'm in the company of a future novelist. Can I ask you what you're writing about?"

"It's an historical novel. Takes place during slavery." Jason's attention was now riveted on Raquel. He knew Elliott had planned to set a trap. He was on him all the time to get a woman and loosen that energy. He took another gulp from the wine glass. Raquel had moved right up to the end of the couch and crossed her legs, exposing brown thighs.

"We have tickets for the play Sunday night at the Ebell Theater. I have a couple of extras," Elliott said. "So if you're free I'm offering them to you and Raquel. What you say?"

"I don't know, that's up to Raquel. I'd love to go, but she might have something else to do."

"I'm free and I'd love to go with you," Raquel said with no hesitation.

"Hey, well that sounds like a deal," Elliott said. "Why don't we plan on getting together and just make a real night of it? In the meantime, I have to get these ladies home. My baby has to work in the morning."

"Don't remind me," Denise said as she straightened out her clothes.

They stood and walked to the door. Jason unlocked and opened it. Raquel pulled a card from her pocket and handed it to him.

"Please call me. I'd love to talk to you about your writing," she said.

"He's going to do better than that. Sunday we're all going to hang out," Elliott said as he and Denise walked out the door.

"But there's still tomorrow." As Raquel strolled past Jason she kissed him lightly on the lips. "Isn't there still tomorrow?"

"There certainly is," Jason answered with a wide smile. He watched them as they headed for Elliott's Buick Century. Before she got in the back seat, Raquel turned and looked back at Jason, returning his smile.

Chapter 4

It was after ten o'clock in the morning when Arthur woke up to an incessantly throbbing headache. His mouth was dry and he felt nauseous. He couldn't remember much about last night, but did recall Dominique dancing so seductively right in front of him and then joining him at his table after she finished on stage. That's when he lost track of place and time. How did he get home? Damn, he was lucky not to get busted. He already had one drunk-driving conviction and the judge warned him that he would take his license if he got another.

Arthur raised his aching body and sat up on the side of the bed. If the headache would just subside he'd be okay. He bent over and placed his head between his hands. His problem was that he always had to be concerned about what Big Casey would think. Why should he care what another son of a bitch felt about him? He'd become so damn dependent on the Mitchell family he could no longer act as his own man. When he told Dominique his problems she even agreed that he needed to break loose from those strings. At least that's what he thinks she said. He was so drunk he couldn't be sure what anyone said or did. It was time to stop that kind of behavior.

Forcing himself up, he stumbled out of the upstairs master bedroom into the den. Arthur slid back the glass door, stepped on the balcony and took in the ocean breeze. Their Malibu townhouse had a clear view of the Pacific Ocean. He could see dozens of sailboats floating peacefully in the water, and a low-flying airplane had a banner strung out behind it welcoming the surfers to "Malibu's 2004 Annual Surfers' Contest." He plopped down in one of the chairs on the balcony and closed his eyes. Where the hell was Jacqueline and why hadn't she been upstairs to check on him? Oh shit, she had to be pissed off. He'd promised to get home early, but didn't get in until after four in the morning. It was at least that late because the club closed at three and he faintly remembered having stayed until that time. Damn, over ten hours in that place. How much money had he spent? Arthur had gone in there with over six hundred dollars and should still have about three left. Despite the throbbing headache, he got up and went back into the bedroom, grabbed his crumpled pants off the floor, and searched in all his pockets. No money. Frantically he looked inside his wallet and again no money. Arthur knew damn well he hadn't spent six hundred dollars in a club. He ran out of the bedroom with his head still throbbing and shouted downstairs.

"Jacqueline, did you take money out of my pockets?"

She didn't answer so he increased the volume. "Jacqueline, damn it, did you take money out of my fucking pockets?"

Still, no answer. Arthur grabbed the handrail and bolted down the stairs. "Jacqueline, where the fuck are you?" He looked in the living room, the kitchen and the family room. She had to be in the downstairs bedroom. She probably got pissed off last night and slept down there. He swung the bedroom door open and said, "Jacqueline, did you take..." She wasn't there.

She'd never up and left before. Even though they had problems she would always stay and deal with them. Arthur rushed back upstairs and threw open the closet door. Thank God all her clothes still hung there. She hadn't left him. But what if she'd gone to Big Casey's house and told him everything that happened between them? Big Casey would probably fire him. He grabbed the phone determined to call Hazel and explain his side of the story. Hazel liked him and would intervene on his behalf. On second thought, that was a dumb idea. Big Casey might answer the phone and then Arthur would have to deal with his wrath. Actually he could do nothing but wait this out. No matter how angry Jacqueline might be, she would eventually come back home and then he could make everything right. Use his charm, his good looks, and his exceptionally pleasing sexual skills to make her happy. Arthur went over to the refrigerator, grabbed a beer, and headed back upstairs. The best way to fight a hangover was to drink a beer or two. He would do that, take a shower, and then wait for his wife to come home so that he could right the wrong done last night.

u

The shrill doorbell snapped Jason out of a good sound sleep. After his company left last night, he had concentrated on his manuscript and actually finished the rape scene. He didn't get to bed until after four o'clock. So when the doorbell rang at a little past ten, he felt he'd just gone to sleep. He slid out of the bed, yawned and made it into the living room. Jason peered through the peephole and was surprised to see both his sisters standing on the other side. He unlocked and opened the door. His expression changed from surprise to shock when he saw Jacqueline's puffy and discolored face.

"What happened to you?" he asked Jacqueline as he motioned them inside. Jason could read anger all over Theresa's face. He detected Jacqueline's fear and pain. The two sisters sat on the couch. Jacqueline reared back and closed her eyes. Theresa scooted forward with her body right at the tip of the couch.

"That sorry excuse for a man hit her again," Theresa fussed.

Jason's assessment of Theresa had been correct. She was angry.

"Can you believe that sorry bastard hit our sister?"

"I can tell he did by your anger and her face," Jason replied. "But you need to cool it. You're more upset than Jacqueline."

"That's because she's weak to that bastard and thinks she's in love with that pretty boy," Theresa continued at an even higher pitch. "Why is it these wavy-haired, white-looking Negroes think they can treat a Black woman any way they want to?"

Theresa had always been the most militant of the four siblings. Big Casey often told her she'd been born one generation too late. She belonged to the Black folks of the 1960s. Theresa, with her Afro, would have fit perfectly into the Angela Davis liberated Black female movement. She and Jacqueline were exact opposites in temperament, lifestyles, and in choice of men. Whereas Jacqueline could be dominated by her man, Theresa dominated all her relationships. Hazel always made her angry when she told her that's why she was alone most of the time. Theresa would retort by telling her mother she'd rather be alone than totally submissive to some sorry son of a bitch who didn't know the proper way to treat a woman. And then the battle would be on between Theresa and Hazel with Big Casey ultimately having to intervene, always on the side of his baby daughter. This time Jason had to intervene in order to cool her off.

"Have you had breakfast?" he asked.

"Hell no. Who can think about eating right now?" Theresa scowled.

"Jacqueline, are you hungry?" Jason again asked, this time ignoring Theresa.

"Yeah, a little," Jacqueline answered faintly.

"I'm hungry too. Why don't we go over to Cafe Soul on Slauson and grab some breakfast," Jason said. Cafe Soul was one of the more popular eating places in Leimert Park. If you wanted true southern cooking that's where you went. It's where Jason ate a lot of his meals.

Theresa practically jumped off the couch. She turned and pointed to her sister. "Look at her face. She doesn't want to go anywhere. In fact, she doesn't want to go anywhere for a while."

"What do you mean she's not going anywhere for a while? You're not going back home, Jacqueline?" Jason asked.

"No, she's not going back home until that fool gets out of her house and out of her life," Theresa said.

Jason's patience was about to reach its limits with Theresa's belligerent attitude. "I think I was talking to Jacqueline," he said staring Theresa down.

"She's in no condition to make that decision right now,"

Theresa continued, undaunted by her brother's stares. "Just look at her face. Why do you think she'd want to go back to that son of a bitch?"

"Theresa, shaddup!" Jason's voice rose. "I'd like to have a conversation with your sister if you don't mind."

Theresa jumped up from the couch and stomped toward the kitchen. "You two talk about that sorry bastard. I'm going to see if I can find anything to eat."

Jason got up and sat on the couch next to Jacqueline. She still had her head tilted back and eyes closed. He took her hand and she jerked forward. "My God, Jacqueline, has he messed you up that badly?"

"Jason, I don't know what's happening to him." Jacqueline began to cry.

"Is it the drinking?"

"Yeah that's part of it. He came in so drunk last night he couldn't hardly make it up the steps. I don't know how he made it from wherever he had been."

"The brother needs his ass kicked," Theresa shouted from the kitchen. She'd opened the refrigerator and looked inside.

"Theresa, chill with the drama, please," Jason shouted back at her.

"I'm hungry and there's no food in this refrigerator. I'll go and get us some carry out." Theresa came back in the living room. "Cafe Soul does have carry out?"

"Yes, they have carry out," Jason answered as he stood up, reached in his pocket and pulled out a twenty dollar bill. "Get me eggs, grits, and sausage with whole wheat toast. What you want, sis?" he asked Jacqueline. But again she had drifted off. "Bring her whatever you get." Jason handed Theresa the twenty dollars.

"See you in a few," she said and disappeared out the door.

Jason sat back down in the leather chair and glared over at Jacqueline who still had her head back and eyes closed. He had to question himself as he watched the disappointment on his sister's face. Had he done the same to Angela that Arthur did to Jacqueline? Did she carry on like this when he first broke off their relationship? But his situation was different. He had ambition and goals that Angela didn't share. He never tormented her the same way Arthur did Jacqueline. And his reason for leaving had nothing to do with other women, booze, and a good time. Last night was the closest he'd come to desiring a woman since breaking up with Angela. His state of mind was drastically different from Arthur's. He needed to find out, however, exactly what Jacqueline wanted to do. Theresa didn't speak for her, but she would always back down to her more aggressive sister.

"Jacqueline, you have to talk to me," he said. "You can't let Theresa talk for you because only you know what you want to do."

"I want my marriage and I want my husband," she said, head still tilted back.

"Even if he treats you the way he's been doing since...I don't know how long this has been going on?"

"Since he had to ask daddy for a job," Jacqueline answered.

"Well if that's his only problem, he can quit and go find his own job."

"Where's he going to find a job making the kind of money daddy's paying him?"

"He can't have it both ways. If he likes the money then he's going to have to accept the fact that he gets it because he's married to the owner's daughter."

Jacqueline had composed herself. She moved up closer to the edge of the couch. "I think Arthur would be okay if he was working at corporate headquarters instead of out in the field. Jason, you know he's used to wearing a suit and tie. Not overalls and a hard hat."

"But he's not going to make as much money at the main office." Jason got up and finally took the four wine glasses and the wine bottle from last night off the coffee table and into the kitchen. Jacqueline got up and followed him. She stopped by the counter.

"He will, if you'll talk to daddy," she said. "Please, Jason. Big Casey will listen to you."

"Jacqueline, what is it with you and your father? He'll do it for you quicker than for me. Why do you lack the confidence to talk to him like Theresa does?"

"Because she's always been his baby and everyone understands she can get anything she wants."

"That's crazy, girl," Jason shot back at her. "You're his oldest daughter and he hasn't ever denied you."

"Please, Jason," Jacqueline pleaded with her brother. "Do this for me."

Jason glared at his sister and began to understand why she was so submissive to Theresa and in some ways to him also. Jacqueline really did believe that Big Casey played favorites and she didn't think she was one of his favorites, despite the fact that he spent over ten thousand dollars on her wedding.

"Okay, I'll talk to him."

"Thank you, Jason," Jacqueline shouted. She walked over to her brother and hugged him.

"Not so fast," Jason said. "First I have to talk to Arthur."

"Why?" Jacqueline asked and backed away from him.

"To make darn sure he isn't going to keep using you as some kind of punching bag,"

"No, you can't do that."

"Why can't I tell this man to stop beating on my sister? In fact, Hazel asked me yesterday to talk to him. She was concerned when you called her the other night."

"No, you just can't. Forget everything," Jacqueline walked back and sat on the couch.

Jason followed her and sat on the leather chair.

"Okay, don't get upset. I won't talk to him this time. But if he ever puts his hands on you again, you're not going to be able to stop me. As a matter of fact, I'm going to get your brother down here and we might have to whip some ass."

"Don't even talk like that," Jacqueline rejoined. "I know after he gets transferred downtown he'll be all right."

"I hope you're right," Jason said. He heard Theresa, got up and let her in.

"Plenty of food for everyone." Theresa strolled right by them and to the kitchen. "I hope you all are hungry because I brought back a little bit of everything." She started to take the containers out of the bag. "You sure look a lot better," she said looking at Jacqueline.

"I think Jason and I worked it out." Jacqueline joined her sister at the counter. Jason also joined them.

"Does that mean you're going back to that asshole today?"

"Yes it does and please don't refer to my husband as an asshole."

"Oh heaven help me, I'm too through," Theresa shouted. "What'd you do to turn this thing around?" she asked Jason.

"Let's all eat and chill out for a little while," Jason said.

"Yeah let's do that because I'm just too through." Theresa handed Jacqueline and Jason their containers.

Chapter 5

Like her older sister, Theresa had decided on an oceanfront apartment. However, an affinity for the ocean was all she had in common with Jacqueline. Instead of living in the exclusive high rent Malibu Beach community, she resided in the Bohemian environment at Venice. Late that morning after Jacqueline dropped her off, Theresa headed to her favorite spot, a small beach area where very few people wandered. After the drama with her sister she needed some quiet time. At the cove she could relax her mind and concentrate on the pleasant aspects of life. A slight ocean breeze whisked across her face, and the sun found its way around a bevy of clouds. It radiated some energizing heat.

She tossed off her sandals, held her head high toward the sky and walked gracefully, but briskly along the edge of the water. She decided to walk the mile down to the pier and then back as an antidote for all the negative energy she endured that morning with her older sister and brother. Theresa's life had not been free of its own drama. But long ago, when she first entered Spelman College, she'd decided to rid herself of anyone who caused her to function in a negative space. If only she could get Jacqueline to adopt the same standards then all this bullshit niggah drama over some man, so hung up on his own inequities, would be eliminated.

Theresa managed her life so that most of the time she could avoid hassles. In the past her problems had been with Hazel. She glared at the dozen or so sea gulls that hovered above ready to strike the unsuspecting prey in the ocean. The sun seemed to gleam against the birds, accentuating their whiteness. As she watched a sea gull dive down to the water and snatch a fish, then fly away, her thoughts ran rampant, something she loved to let happen. Free thinking opened the doors to creativity which in turn carved a path to independence. She cherished her freedom and independence above all other things. One reason she loved to wander the ocean side was because of the always present breeze. The wind represented a form of freedom that no one could ever capture and control. It had its own essence, blowing all the time, somewhat like infinity. One never knows when it starts nor where it goes and when it ends. That made a perfect paradigm for her life, and because she refused to be pigeonholed it had always caused severe problems with Hazel.

Her rebellion began ten years ago when she refused to participate in that ridiculous ritual specifically designed to trap young girls into a certain kind of lifestyle. The Cotillion Ball ostensibly represented a coming out announcement for young girls when they turned sixteen. Subtly, it served as a wedge to separate the upper class morally correct daughters of the Black bourgeoisie from the masses of Black people. The girls of the Cotillion Ball represented the best of Black America and separated them from the immoral, degenerate 70% who dared to have children out of wedlock. Hazel felt it important that each of her daughters participate as a clear statement that the Mitchell family had risen above the masses. Just as their mansion sat high above the poverty-strewn areas of Pasadena, so did her daughters excel over the young girls at the bottom of the hill.

When Hazel insisted that Theresa follow in her sister's footsteps and participate in the Ball, she refused. Hazel adamantly insisted that Theresa participate. She told her that a refusal to come out as a proper young lady of society would be an embarrassment to her parents because it would be an admission that she was no longer a virgin. Theresa couldn't tolerate the snobbishness so she, in a moment of anger, blurted out that she was no longer a virgin and therefore had no right to participate. She had lied, but didn't care. She just wanted Hazel off her back. That definitely got her off her back for a very long time. Hazel insisted that Big Casey find another place for her to live. She had insulted the integrity of the family and needed to be placed in a boarding school where she could re-discover her moral responsibility to herself and family. Even though he shared his wife's anger with Theresa, Big Casey refused to force his daughter out of their home. The turmoil lasted for only a few months. Theresa at sixteen graduated from high school and left for Spelman that fall. An entire year passed before she came home, choosing to spend holidays with Big Casey's sister who lived right outside Atlanta. That next summer, when she did finally come home, she was no longer a virgin.

Her first year at Spelman was a defining period in her life. During that year she went from being a young and rebellious girl to a mature and determined lady. The boy's name was Cleveland Jackson. He possessed all the qualities that Theresa sought in what she considered would be her soul mate for life, as well as into the next one. She opened her heart and legs. The next month she was elated to learn she was carrying their child, conceived not through sheer passion, but through love. Cleveland crushed her enthusiasm and love when he insisted that a DNA test be done on the child. How he could even think that the baby would be someone else's was foreign to her. Afterwards, he apologized, but it was too late. He had broken that sacred trust that, even at seventeen, Theresa believed existed between soul mates. She concluded that he was not for her. She dropped him and secretly had an abortion.

After that experience, Theresa plunged all her energy into college, majoring in Sociology, with a minor in African American studies. She received a Bachelor of Arts Degree in three years. Theresa then went on to Howard Law School and graduated with Honors. She'd fallen in love with both cities, Atlanta and Washington, D.C. because they represented cultural capitals for Black folks, but settled on Los Angeles because of her love for the ocean. Hazel had long forgotten about their fight over the Cotillion Ball and now bragged on her all the time. They did have a brief skirmish when Theresa graduated number one in her law class and Hazel insisted that she go to work as Big Casey's legal counsel. She loved her father and was grateful for all he'd done for her over the years, but informed both parents that she had a different kind of law in mind. She didn't want any part of commercial law, instead decided to take a job with the poverty law program in south central Los Angeles. Hazel again exploded, but soon got over it. She seemed to realize just how far she could push her daughter. The year Theresa refused to come home evidently had an effect on Hazel. Big Casey agreed with his daughter's decision. He paid the first year's rent for an apartment in Venice. He didn't care what kind of law she practiced, he told her. He was just happy she decided to come home where she belonged. After all she was his baby daughter. And she looked just like him.

Theresa dug deeply into the wet sand and found a shell. She meticulously cleaned off the sand, placed it to her ear and listened to the roaring sounds. She had always been intrigued by the sounds inside the open end of practically every shell. It was so deceptive because you could hear it, but you couldn't see it. Theresa smiled as she thought of the significance of hearing but not actually seeing. All part of the mysteries of the universe that constantly made her want to gaze into the past and simultaneously prepare for the future. The connection was quite apparent, you knew the past because you had lived it, but you could only try to prepare for the future with no guarantees. But one issue that she could not leave to chance and that was Arthur's violence toward her sister. She recognized that Jacqueline was too weak to do anything about it and Jason too absorbed in his own problems. Cedric had escaped to San Francisco doing his own thing, whatever that might be. Therefore, Theresa had to deal with that cowardly bastard. In her day to day work, she interacted with many men and women who would have no problem helping her out for the right reward if she had to call on them. Spotting her apartment straight ahead, she pledged that Jacqueline would take no more beatings from Arthur. Because the next time it happened she would make sure he never did it again.

Chapter 6

The Leimert Park Writers Group met every Saturday evening from seven to nine in the back of an old theater on 6th Avenue near Crenshaw Boulevard. Jason had been meeting with the group for the past year. He'd started going even before beginning his first novel. The group consisted of over forty aspiring writers as well as some who had already been published. Elliott turned Jason on to the group when he first told his friend of his plans to start writing. Elliott attended the sessions because the group studied all forms of fiction as well as poetry. He loved to read his poetry at the meetings whenever possible. The group's primary purpose was to critique different works in progress. They also discussed the most important and pressing issues the Black novelist confronted at the time. On this particular night they would discuss the image of Blacks in contemporary fiction.

Elliott showed up at Jason's apartment at six-thirty and they drove around the corner to the theater in his Buick. Jason suggested they walk since the theater was right around the corner from his apartment. Elliott told him he planned for them to make a run after the session and therefore needed the car. They found a parking place right in front of the theater, parked the car and went inside.

Devon Bartlow, President of the Group, had gotten an old oblong conference table donated from a law firm downtown. The chairs had come from an accounting firm in Beverly Hills. They could squeeze in a good thirty people at the table. And if they had a full house of all forty members, the other ten could squeeze in as close as possible. Since it was only six forty-five when they arrived, Jason and Elliott had no trouble finding a chair. They had fifteen minutes to wait, so Jason took out a pocketbook copy of Evelyn Palfrey's Dangerous Dilemmas and began to read.

"So what do you think of her?" Elliott asked.

Jason knew that would happen. Every time he went out with Elliott and they had some time to kill, he would start with the small talk.

"Who are you talking about?"

"Brothah, please," Elliott said. "I'll take that book away from you and beat you all up side the head with it."

"Damn, aren't you getting a little belligerent with the threats?" Jason kept reading the novel.

"If you don't put that book down and answer me I'm going to call Raquel and tell her you a down low brother."

"Oh man, you're sick," Jason said. "All right I think she's fine."

"Good, 'cause I do believe she's going to give it up tomorrow night," Elliott whispered to Jason and smiled.

"How do you know what she's going to do?"

"'Cause I listen to those treacherous women talk. And you have to be able to read between the lines when you messing with women who always got sex on their mind."

"Why do you say that?" Jason asked.

"They're women, aren't they?" Elliott smiled. "See man, I accept that you're pretty much a rookie when it comes to the scandalous shit a bunch of women will do. And you have to listen closely to pick up all the nuances to what they're saying."

"And what did you pick up last night?" Jason put the book down. Elliott had awakened his curiosity.

"At what point in the evening? When you all were making love through word games, or after we left and she was panting over you to Denise?"

"Anybody ever tell you that you have a sick way of viewing women?"

"But it sounds good, doesn't it?"

"What sounds good are the words that say you're sick," Jason said and smacked Elliott on the arm.

"Yeah you tell me that when you're riding that thing about

midnight tomorrow."

"I don't ride that thing. I make love."

"Yeah, yeah, whatever."

Other writers strolled into the room and took seats next to theirs. That ended the conversation as Jason returned to reading Palfrey's novel. Finally Devon made his way to the front of the table and took a seat. The room filled up with other writers. Some of the people Jason recognized, but the others he'd never seen before. He knew a lot of potential authors resided in Los Angeles, but he thought they all wanted to be screenwriters. Given the standing room crowd in here, evidently Los Angeles had its share of novelists.

"Good evening, my fellow geniuses of the pen," Devon began. "Later this evening we're going to critique the first three chapters of Monique Johnson's romance novel, In Need of Love. I hope you all have had a chance to read the chapters we handed out at the last meeting and have some positive feedback for the sister. Before we get to that I want to discuss our topic of the week and that is how should we handle images of Blacks in our writing?" Before Devon could finish his sentence a number of hands shot up.

"All right, let's start with Sistah Elizabeth Gray."

A sister with a short Afro and long red nails spoke first. "I think we ought to stick to positive images only. We sistahs need to stop putting the brothahs down in our story lines. I mean Terry McMillan's game is about worn out."

"Amen, sistah," a number of brothers shouted out.

"But wait a minute," a sister at the other end of the table spoke up without raising her hand.

"Sistah Shirley, you have to raise your hand, please," Devon admonished.

"I know, Devon, but I have to make this point real fast. You other sistahs and brothahs don't mind, do you?"

"Well, I did have my hand up before you, Sistah. But if what you have to say is that important go ahead," another woman said.

"Thank you, Sistah," Shirley rejoined. "But you can't stymie creativity in that fashion. If my thoughts take me on a trip where I have to write about some dog brothah, then that's what I have to do."

Jason now shot his hand in the air, but Devon recognized the sister who had been cut off by Shirley. "Go ahead, Dorothy," he said.

"I write about my experiences. Some have been good but most of them have been bad 'cause these brothahs out here aren't about anything. And to tell Black women that they shouldn't portray the image as they see it is to suppress us just like white men have suppressed all of us."

"Oh, that's bullshit," a brother at the opposite end of the table from Jason shot back. "We're not trying to suppress your voice—"

'Vernon, man," Devon interrupted, "you have to wait your turn. I believe Jason Mitchell had his hand up first. Jason, the floor is yours."

Jason leaned forward in his chair. "There's something wrong with all these negative images of brothers. Either sisters feel compelled to put down brothers in their writings because of their negative experiences, or the white man is telling them that's all he's going to publish. Either way brothers are going to get a bad rap from you sisters."

"Yeah, and the beat goes on," Elliott added his comment.

Devon ignored Elliott and pointed at Vernon. "Go ahead," he said.

"I don't think brothers are consumed with how you all write about us. But if you do have to knock a brother down why don't you try picking him back up some time?"

"All right, brothah," a number of the men said. They clapped their hands as a sign of support for Vernon's comments.

Ten different women shot their hands up in the air. Jason began to get a feeling that this session would soon be out of control. Devon acknowledged the one that had put her hand up first.

"Yes, my good Sistah Mattie, have at it."

Mattie jumped to her feet. "I don't think as writers we should take this personally. A writer has to reflect what's on their mind. And I'm going to tell you, brothahs, you some scandalous mothahfuckahs." Mattie smiled and looked all around the table, then sat down.

All the women burst out cheering and applauding Mattie. Elliott leaned over to Jason and whispered, "Man let's get on out of here. This ain't going nowhere but to a nasty argument."

"Just a couple more minutes," Jason replied. "I want to see how much trouble I'm in with my writing." He shot his hand back up again.

"Okay, Brothah Jason, it's your turn again," Devon said.

Jason adjusted his body in the chair and leaned forward, placing his elbows on the table.

"What you all aren't addressing is that the white man is still controlling what we write. And that means things haven't changed since the Harlem Renaissance days when they also controlled those writers."

Hands from every direction shot up in the air.

"Sistah Shia had her hand up first." Devon acknowledged a light-skinned sister with dozens of braids falling all over her face.

"Brothah, I don't know what you're talking about, but our brothahs and sistahs back then wrote the way they wanted to," she said, with a tinge of irritation.

"They wrote the way Carl Van Vechten suggested they write often using his novel Nigger Heaven as the prototype, so they could sell their manuscripts to the white publishing houses," Jason shot back.

"Who the hell was Carl Van Vechten?" a brother to the right of Jason asked.

"He was the patron saint for the Black writers in Harlem. Check it out, he would give parties and invite agents and Black writers. He had a special relationship with the editors at Knopf. And every Black writer wanted to get published, so they bought into the program."

"This brothah's crazy," Sister Shia shouted.

Momentarily, Jason considered Elliott's advice. Maybe they should have left because these brothers and sisters were getting awfully angry with him.

"Are you saying Langston Hughes wrote the way white folks wanted him to?" Sister Shia wouldn't quit.

And neither would Jason. Her belligerent tone irritated him. "As a matter of fact, Langston wrote during his early years in a manner to appease his supporter, an old white lady named Charlotte Osgood Mason. That old white woman took care of Langston and he called her godmother. She also supported Zora Neale Hurston with all her stereotypes done just to keep that white woman happy."

"Brothah, you cracking on Zora Neale Hurston now?" another sister at the opposite end of the room shouted. "Devon, where did you find this brothah?"

"You all don't have to get all bent out of shape with me because you haven't read your literary history," Jason's voice rose a couple notches. "If we're going to make a difference we have to understand what's gone before us."

"The brother's got a point," a tall dark skinned brother with a bald head and earrings in both ears spoke up. "The images of Black men over the years haven't been positive ones. I just caught The Color Purple on cable the other night and that movie's almost twenty years old. They still like to throw that shit in our face. Black men having sex with their daughters and holding their women hostage is not a Black thing. We Black men can be accused of a lot of shit, but incest ain't one. In my community a nigguh get his ass kicked good he start talking about having sex with a little girl or boy. That's the white folks' stuff. But you ain't seen no white movie still showing regularly twenty years later about a white man doing that kind of shit. No, they still showing us Gone With the Wind, where the white man is the hero." The brother paused and looked all around the room. Jason had the feeling the brother was showboating, but that was all right, he was defending his position and Jason needed the support. The brother continued. "The first real movie about a Black man in a positive role was Malcolm X and Spike Lee had to beg other men in order to get it distributed. On the other hand, you got Oprah Winfrey putting a punk ass nigguh who screws other men on her program for an hour, and that brother makes a million dollars selling that shit. And then the whole world thinks that's typical of Black men. Somebody needs to get that nigguh and other nigguhs like him and beat their asses."

"Okay, brothah, we're getting a little off topic," Devon said. "Let's keep it on the image of Blacks in fiction."

"Let me get my final point in," the brother refused to be cut off. "I don't care what you say, those nigguhs who been giving AIDS to sisters need to be lined up and put on an island and just let them deal with each other. They give the rest of us brothers a bad name, not to mention they're killing our women."

"Okay, my man, we got your point," Devon continued.

"You brothahs know you have issues and you love to lay that dirty linen on a sistah," Sister Shia said as she became more aggressive.

"Yeah, but you sistahs, that's all you want to write about," asserted another Black man who was speaking up for the first time. "Check out Brighton Press. That's all they want to do is sign a sistah to a contract who's going to write that negative shit about a brothah. You grab that chump change they're going to offer you as an advance and you give them all the dirt they need. You're selling out the brothahs for chump change. You're whoring to the white folks so that you can see your book tucked back in aisle 99 at Barnes & Noble."

Sister Shia jumped from her chair and shouted at the brother. "Watch it, you didn't have to go there."

"Easy, easy," Devon said in a calm voice. "See this is what happens when we try to have a decent discussion about our craft. We have to get ugly." He paused for a moment and looked to both ends of the room. "We need to keep the rhetoric down." Devon looked at his watch. "I tell you what, let's take a ten minute break and get back to the real reason we're here. We'll discuss and critique Monique's first three chapters. During the break let's all kiss and make up. After all, we're all in this for the love of the art." Brothers and sisters jumped out of the chairs and headed out of the room, many of them continuing the conversation that had precipitated the friction.

Jason scooted back from the table and stretched his legs. Elliott jumped up and turned his body from side to side as if exercising.

"Man, this is too much drama for me," he said. "You novelists are some complicated people. We poets don't go through all these changes."

"The brother went a little too far, but he was making some sense to me," Jason said.

"Okay, but that's enough. It's time to leave," Elliott said.

"I kind of want to hear how they critique Monique's work."

"Why? All she going to do is defend her stuff. And heaven forbid any of those first three chapters is about a negative brother and it's going to be on all over again."

"I know, but I'm going to submit my work for critique next month. I'd like to get a feel for what to expect."

"Man, you're talking about two different kinds of writing. She's romance and your work is historical. Now unless you're writing historical romance, which I know you're not, then you can't compare how they'll critique yours with hers. Now let's get out of here before they get started all over again," Elliott said with some impatience in his voice.

"All right. Why you in such a hurry? Where you want to go?"

"Since you all been talking about brothers being trifling and dogs, let's go do something doggish. Let's go look at some titties and asses."

"What?" Jason' voice rose even higher. "Where do you want to go?"

"There's a club over off the 110 Freeway has some of the finest women that LA has to offer. Better than Hollywood." Elliott glanced at his watch. "It's only eight-thirty, so we should be able

Chapter 7

Arthur sat in the lounge chair on the balcony and stared out at the sun as it began to disappear behind the ocean. It was already after eight o'clock and Jacqueline hadn't come home, nor had she called. That wasn't like her. No matter how angry she'd get, Jacqueline always came home. He figured he'd really messed up this time. He remembered striking her the other night, but was too drunk to recall his behavior last night. If he'd hit her two nights in a row, then she probably was hiding out over her sister's house. And that uppity bitch would advise her to stay away and get a divorce. Theresa needed to mind her own business and leave his alone. Get herself a man to lay some loving on her.

He watched as the waves crashed against the shoreline and a light fog began to cover the sky. He held his head up and the breeze struck him directly in the face. Arthur had gotten over his hangover and could better enjoy the evening. He loved his townhouse just across the Pacific Highway, with its clear view of the ocean. While growing up in south central Los Angeles, he always dreamed of moving out of that hell hole to either the mountains or the ocean. He would go where the white folks loved to live. They always had the best of everything in the city and for that matter in the country and all over the world. His mama was white and his father Black. Why the hell couldn't she have married someone white and then he wouldn't have had to deal with this in between shit? And also wouldn't have to suffer the indignities associated with being a Black man in America. Arthur was more fortunate than most other Black men. At least he was half-white and therefore had those features that attracted Black women. His good looks, straight hair had definitely attracted Jacqueline. And to top it off, he possessed the ultimate weapon, a gigantic-sized pleasure maker between his legs. Arthur chuckled as he thought of the women who'd looked on in shock at the size of his weapon. After the initial jolt they attacked it like it was something good to eat. To many of them, it was.

As the wet, cool, freshness of the sea breeze continued to brush against his face, Arthur felt reinvigorated. That morning he'd been a mess with a terrible hangover. But since then he'd showered, shaved, and rubbed Calvin Klein Obsession for Men body moisturizer all over his body. He topped it off with Calvin Klein aftershave lotion and then slipped into his silk lounging set with the top left open halfway down his chest. He felt good, smelled good, and damn sure looked good. Now all he needed was his wife so he could make up to her the right way. He glanced at his watch again. A little after eight-thirty and still no sign of her. Why worry, no matter what he'd done, Jacqueline would come home. She needed him and she very much needed his sexy body. Maybe if he smoked a joint, the time would go by faster. It would relax him and he would really be in the mood to give her the kind of loving she needed in order to forgive him.

Arthur went back into the apartment to the bedroom, pulled a shoe box from under the bed and opened it. He loved the smell of good green marijuana. It had a strong and invigorating smell. He took a cigarette paper and rolled a joint. He'd cut down on the amount of smoking since he took the job with Big Casey. Even though he worked for his father-in-law, he still had to keep a pretty level head at work. That's what had happened with the state job. Too much smoking and he'd lost his cool and went off on his supervisor. They'd forced him to take a drug test and he failed. He'd learned his lesson from that experience. Too much indulging was detrimental to his future. But a joint every now and then wouldn't hurt anyone. Jacqueline knew he smoked, but she didn't. And she didn't try to stop him. Reason being is that the sex got so damn good when he was high she didn't want to give that up. Arthur went back into the den, put on an Etta James CD and turned it up loud. Then sauntered out on the balcony and lit his joint. He'd bought an outstanding bag of weed the other day. A couple hits and he could feel his body lighten up and his thoughts become more pleasurable and coherent. He took another deep hit, slowly blew the smoke out into the ocean breeze and smiled as Etta James sang I'd rather be a blind girl than watch you walk away from me.

He watched as sea gulls swooped down near the water and then took off toward the sky. The music and the weed took him out there also. That urge was coming down on him. He could relate to Etta James' melodic words. His Jacqueline felt the same way about him. She'd rather be a blind girl than see him walk away. Because, as Etta said in her song, he had those kisses and that other thing. Jacqueline needed to come home now. He had created a mood in that apartment with the ocean breeze, the weed, and Etta James.

Suddenly his mind drifted back to the club last night. A vision of Dominique standing on stage right in front of him seemed so real. She possessed the perfect body and the most beautiful face he'd ever been that close to. If he could just get her up into this atmosphere with the ocean, the weed, the music, and his sweet-smelling body, she'd make love to him until they both fell out. He could picture himself going down on her and tasting and smelling her precious juices. The weed had his mind romping wild through his fantasies. No longer did the six hundred dollars matter. In fact, he hoped that she'd gotten it all so she'd know he wasn't cheap. Arthur glared out at the sun as it finally disappeared beyond the horizon and under the ocean.

He got up, leaned against the railing, took one more hit from the joint and then put it out. Where the hell was Jacqueline? If she didn't get in within the next hour, he would get dressed and go back to the club. They had a back room for private dances. He'd take Dominique back there and see how far he could go. Damn, why did she have to be so fine? It would just be a matter of time before he'd get to her. He could imagine her going down and wrapping her soft full lips around his big thick weapon. That would be ecstasy and he'd be willing to pay good money for that thrill.

Etta James had just broken into her rendition of At Last when he heard the door open. He turned, rushed back inside and down the stairs to meet Jacqueline. When she got inside the door, he took her by the hand and began to dance slow and close. Etta served his purpose quite well. He wanted to get Jacqueline's mind off the negatives and concentrate only on the positive, and that positive was him.

Jacqueline tried to break away from his grip. "Arthur, I don't want to dance," she said.

"Ssh baby," Arthur whispered as he held her tighter. "Remember when we first heard this song? Leave the negativity outside the door. Come on to your pleasure palace, baby. 'Cause I got nothing but pure unadulterated pleasure waiting for you. Both with my tongue and with what you like best."

Jacqueline relaxed in Arthur's embrace and they both moved in place to Etta James and the music.

Arthur lowered his hands and placed them on Jacqueline's soft butt. He pulled her closer to him so that she could feel the full effect of his erection.

"No, Arthur, I don't want to do this," Jacqueline pleaded faintly. "Please..."

As he moved his lower body seductively to the music, Jacqueline responded. Etta James kept the mood at a high crescendo, with her seductive voice.

Arthur gently blew in Jacqueline's ear and nibbled on the lobe. That drove her crazy. He felt her temperature rising. Finally Etta James' voice faded away, but Arthur continued the slow dance. Jacqueline was now like putty in his hands.

"Let's go upstairs, leave the balcony door open and make love while listening to the ocean and feeling the ocean breeze." He was on a roll and loved it. He was throbbing and knew she was aching to satisfy his throbs.

"Arthur, I love you, baby. But you can't keep hurting me," Jacqueline whispered to him as she followed his lead up the stairs and into the bedroom.

"I love you too, baby, and I'm sorry. But let's leave yesterday alone and enjoy this moment."

"You have to promise me, baby, that you won't hit me anymore."

"I promise," he whispered.

They laid together on the bed and he pulled her body close to him. They kissed passionately. He could feel the warmth of her mouth as she opened it and sucked on his tongue. Arthur removed her blouse and bra and caressed her breasts with each hand. He teased the nipples with his tongue until he had both of them erect and hard. Arthur then slid her pants and panties off, placed his hand right at her pleasure palace and felt the wetness flowing from within. He worked his tongue down the front of her body, stopping to kiss her on the navel, then on both thighs.

He finally began to suck right at the top of her love canal. Her body tensed for the pleasure about to come. His tongue slowly played around the front of her treasure palace and slipped inside to find the spot. It didn't take him long to find it and began a soft sucking motion, while also licking on the tip. He could feel her building toward a climax. Just as Jacqueline screamed with pleasure Arthur knew the time was right. While her love flowed and muscles throbbed, he lifted his body on top and directed his erection inside her. He whispered, "I love you, my princess, and ain't nothing ever going to come between us."

"Oh God, Arthur, just shaddup and fuck me. I want to come again."

With his head to the side of hers, he smiled and said, "You will, baby, I promise."

Chapter 8

Elliott was wrong. By the time he and Jason arrived at the Black Zebra there was a full house. They found an isolated table in a corner far away from the three stages where the ladies danced. Elliott ordered a rum and coke. Jason ordered cranberry juice and soda. Less than five minutes after they sat down a young lady wearing her most seductive outfit, a bra and G-string, approached the table.

"You men want some company?" she asked.

"Not right now," Elliott answered. He pulled out a dollar and slid it between a black garter and her soft milky white leg. "Check back with us later and we might be in the mood."

The young lady turned her body toward Jason and put her leg between his. "You got something for me, baby?"

"Oh yeah," he said. Jason pulled out a dollar bill and slipped it under the garter.

"Thank you, baby," the young lady said and then moved on to another table.

"You don't have to feel obligated to give every one of these begging women a dollar every time they come up to the table," Elliott said. "They just like a bunch of hungry birds. They see you throw a crumb to one, they all going to come flying over here."

"I know how to handle myself." Jason watched a dancer on the stage twist and turn her body for maximum exposure. "I've been in these joints before."

"Excuse me, man about town," Elliott said grinning. "I thought all you ever did was write."

"Be serious," Jason retorted. He glanced back at the stage as the ladies rotated from one location to another. A tall blonde with blown-up breasts left the center stage and crawled on the stage closest to them. She lay on her side chatting with an older man who had followed her from the center stage.

The disc jockey, from his elevated post to the right of the bar, hollered, "All right get ready for the luscious Ms. Tina on center stage." He started the music and a short woman, also with blown-up breasts, glided out on stage and began her dance. A couple of men jumped from their chairs and rushed to the stage with plenty of dollar bills. They waited for her to come closer. When she did, they held up the dollar bills. She danced her way over to them, knelt down and pulled each of their heads between her legs. She teased each one for a couple of minutes and then put her leg out so they could place the money in the garter.

The waitress finally showed up with their drinks. She placed them on the table and said, "Ten dollars, please."

"Ten dollars," Jason practically yelled. "For a cranberry juice and one rum and coke?"

"Chill, man." Elliott pulled out twelve dollars and gave it to the waitress. She leaned over so that he could place the money in her bra. She also seemed to have blown-up breasts.

"Thank you, honey," she said to Elliott.

"You got it, baby," Elliott acknowledged her. She then strutted over to another table. Elliott watched her all the way. He then turned and glared at Jason. "Man, what's wrong with you?" he asked, but didn't wait for an answer. "Don't front me out like that, dawg. You can't come in here and go for cheap. You won't have any fun at all. These ladies will put a label on you so that you'll never get any play."

"You got to be kidding," Jason shot back at him. "Who the hell wants to get play from this bunch of losers?"

"Dawg, you definitely need an attitude adjustment. You ain't here to judge anybody. You ain't here to fall in love. You can do that tomorrow night. But tonight you here to party, talk shit, and if you're lucky, walk out of here with an easy, but good piece of ass."

"You are sick," Jason said as he watched the young lady on stage three continue to work her body. "I'm not going to dinner, let alone to bed with one of these losers."

"Why do I bother?" Elliott asked rhetorically. He got up, walked over to the stage, and placed a dollar under the dancer's garter. Then stood there while she gave him his own dollar's worth of a private dance.

Jason reared back in his chair, took a drink from his glass and chuckled at Elliott. One thing his friend didn't do was hold back on having fun. Finally the dance ended, the music stopped, and Jason could hear himself think. It's a wonder that all these dancers in here night after night didn't have hearing problems.

"And now on stage one, everybody's delight, everybody's delicious piece of fantasy, Ms. Dominique," the disc jockey called out.

Jason was watching Elliott run his game on the dancer who had left the stage when he caught a glimpse of Dominique out of the side of his eyes. He immediately turned and stared at her as she gracefully moved in a beautiful flowing motion toward center stage. Absolutely gorgeous, he whispered. She couldn't have been any more than 5 feet 7 with a slim waistline, full breasts, and perfectly shaped legs. She had the prettiest glowing cocoa skin that he'd ever seen, along with ebony eyes and long coal black hair. Her angelic face and curvaceous body seemed too perfect for anyone to possess. He had to look at her from a closer view. Jason started to get up, but then sat back down. At least ten men rushed to the stage as she made it to the very front and began to swing around a long pole extending from the ceiling to the floor. As he sat back down Jason knew he had to get to know this lady at all costs. Before the night was over he would spend some time with her.

"Damn, man, that trifling woman didn't want to give me any play," Elliott said as he sat back down at the table and took a sip from his drink.

Jason didn't notice him, and what he said didn't register. His eyes remained riveted on the lady on center stage. The music stopped and most of the men returned to their tables. Dominique leaned back against the full length mirror at the back of the stage, slowly rocking from side to side. She had to know he was staring at her and pick up his emotions because they were so strong. Finally, she glanced in his direction and did a double take, stared back for a moment and then smiled. He practically melted. She had a broad, animated smile, somewhat coquettish, even angelic, but tinged with some naughtiness.

"Say, man, you hear me talking to you?" Elliott asked.

Jason still didn't answer. He felt spellbound at this point and didn't know how to react to her smile. But then it dawned on him that she did that with everyone. That was her job, to get men to spend money. Why would such a beautiful woman be a dancer? She probably was a part-time actress trying to break into Hollywood. This was only temporary until she got her big break. Halle Berry had nothing on her.

"Man, what's wrong with you?" Elliott asked. "Hey earth to Jason, what's happening to you?"

"Who is she?" Jason asked still not taking his eyes off her. "I have to find out who she is."

"That's Dominique," Elliott answered. "You're in good company if she's getting you excited. She does it to half the men in this club."

Finally another song began and she moved to the center of the stage. She leaped up on the center pole, wrapped her long legs around it and slowly slid back down. A dozen men jumped from their chairs and headed to the stage with dollar bills in their hands.

"Give me a couple dollars," Jason said to Elliott. He held his hand out across the table while keeping his eyes on Dominique.

"You don't have any dollar bills?" Elliott asked. "I have to keep the few I got for my own use."

Jason dug in his pocket and found a ten dollar bill. He started to get up.

"You're really going to give that woman a ten dollar bill?" Elliott asked.

"No you're right," Jason dug back in his pocket and this time he had a twenty. "She deserves more than a lousy ten." He finished and started toward the center stage.

"Don't be a fool," Elliott shouted at him. "Don't give her a twenty dollar bill."

Jason didn't look back at his friend but just kept moving toward center stage. He stopped a couple feet back and waited for an opening. A Black man in a business suit turned from the stage and headed toward his table. It was the opportunity Jason wanted. He swiftly moved to the open spot before anyone else could get there. Dominique had so much money in her garter it was falling to the floor. She continued to dance her way around the front of the stage, kneeling in front of every man that had money in their hands. After they placed the dollar under her garter she kissed them on the cheek. Jason waited patiently for her to get around to him. But before she did, the music ended, also bringing an end to her dancing on center stage.

Along with the other disappointed men, he turned and headed back to the table. Some of the men followed Dominique to another stage where she would continue her dancing. Jason decided to wait until she made her way to the last stage, which was close to his table. Maybe by that time the other men would have tired of chasing her and he would have her all to himself. As he walked by the stage closest to his table, he glanced at the lady up there dancing. No comparison to Dominique. The lady looked like she should be a dancer. Dominique had the appearance of a princess or someone from nobility. No one else could match up to her.

"I know you ain't about to give that woman twenty dollars?" Elliott said as Jason sat back down at the table.

"I'll give her anything she wants and everything I got," Jason answered. "That is the most beautiful woman I've ever seen." Excitement tinged Jason's words. "Elliott, I have to get to know her."

"Yeah, you and every other man in this place," Elliott said. He took another sip from his drink. "Everybody in here has tried to pull her, but from what I understand there ain't no happenings. Last time I was in here a couple brothers must have spent five hundred dollars on her. Brothah got mad 'cause she wouldn't give him any play and the bouncer had to put his ass out. Another time I heard some brothahs say that she was gay. She doesn't like what we have to offer."

"A lesbian dancing in here?"

"Where you been all your life? Half these women in here are lesbians."

"Well, she just can't be," Jason said. "No way in the world someone that pretty and fine is going to be sleeping with another woman."

The music ended and Dominique strolled toward the stage closest to where they sat.

"Here's your chance to find out," Elliott said. "If you give that woman twenty dollars she's going to want to give you some play."

"I guess I'm going to get the play."

Jason positioned himself right at the center of the stage. Within a couple of minutes the music started and a dozen men with dollars in their hands surrounded Jason on both sides. Dominique moved to the center of the stage, swaying from side to side, while also gliding forward. The beat of the music increased and she glided to the far side of the stage like a princess. She finally stopped in front of an older man, put her long leg forward and leaned back resting on her outstretched arms. Dominique moved her hips from side to side. The man moved his face forward so that he was only inches from having his mouth parallel to her pleasure palace. She remained in that position for a few seconds and pointed at the pink garter belt snugly hugging her shapely thigh. The man smiled, then reached up and tucked the dollar inside the garter.

Dominique blew him a kiss, then got up and moved on to the next man. She repeated the same maneuver until she finally reached Jason. She moved in close to the edge of the stage and smiled at him. A very encouraging sign since she hadn't done that with anyone else. Or maybe she had caught a glimpse of the twenty dollar bill. Jason didn't care what the reason. He could feel his body tense up as she knelt down in front of him.

"You're beautiful," Jason said as he tucked the money inside the garter.

"Thank you and you're quite a gentleman," Dominique replied. She then bent closer and kissed Jason on the cheek.

He thought he would melt. She had an aura about her that made him want to take her in his arms and wrap her up in his love. Instead, he forced himself to remain composed and said, "Is it possible you could join me at my table when you finish dancing?"

She smiled, placed soft hands on the sides of his face, and said, "I have a couple regulars I have to sit with first. But don't go anywhere. I'll make my way over to your table." Dominique got up and moved on to the next admirer waiting to tuck money in her garter.

Jason watched as she made her way around the stage. She didn't have to dance, just gracefully prance around and collect the money. As he watched her, he wondered what chance he would have with her. She could rein in any man with big money. But she said she'd make it to his table. With her words of encouragement Jason turned and headed back to the table.

Elliott had disappeared to one of the large lounging chairs in the back corner of the room. Jason spotted him relaxed and reared back, while the young lady he'd been after earlier was draped all over him, moving up and down his body to the rhythm of the music. Jason smiled, shook his head and sat down. A fresh cranberry and soda sat in front of him. He took a sip and then turned to look at Dominique. But the song had ended and she'd already left the stage. Now it would be a waiting game. It didn't matter how long it took. He'd stay there until she kept her promise and made it over to his table.

Chapter 9

"**D**amn, she never did make it over to my table," Jason said to Elliott on the phone Sunday morning. He'd just gotten up a little after eleven and was preparing to go to Cafe Soul for breakfast when the phone rang. "I watched her go from table to table, but she just kind of ignored me."

"And you gave that trifling dancer twenty dollars. What did I tell you about these women out here? They'll use your ass to death," Elliott said.

"Don't refer to her that way," Jason shot back at Elliott.

"Man, don't tell me you getting soft on a dancer. You sure need to get you some."

"Why you have to make everything sound so crass and ugly?"

"All in your perspective," Elliott rejoined. "Look, brothah, I have to go. I'm doing a poetry slam this afternoon and I have to get ready. If you're not busy you can join me."

"No, I have to pick up my daughter and take her to spend the afternoon with her grandmother."

"That should be interesting. You talk to Angela since you went to court?"

"My attorney told her lawyer that we would have them covered for the extra money."

"There you go again, brothah. This shit with these women always boils down to the dollar bill. I keep telling you they're treacherous. I don't care if it's a dancer or a school teacher, they all after one thing, the money."

"And what are we after?" Jason asked.

"No doubt about it, the loving. You know that, my brothah. And that's the game. Can we get the good stuff without giving up the money? And for them it's can they get the money without giving it up. Life's major dilemma between man and woman."

"Boy, you're sick but I love you just the same. I have to get out of here."

"All right, we'll see you at six this evening so you can get you some loving instead of just imagining it."

"Later, man."

u

Jason pulled into the driveway at the home where he once lived, got out of the BMW and hastily made it to the front door. He knew Angela would have an attitude. He was supposed to pick up Julianne at 12:30 after they returned from church. It was nearly two and Angela would claim he deliberately messed up her plans for the afternoon. He rang the doorbell and braced for the battle. After a couple of minutes, the door swung open and Angela glared at him through the screen door.

"As usual you're late," she said.

Jason forced a smile and said, "Can't you at least say hello before you start fussing?"

"You were supposed to be here two hours ago," Angela snapped at him. "What if I'd had some plans, Jason? Don't you think I also have a life besides waiting for you to get here and see your daughter?"

"I'm sorry," Jason said softly. "But I stayed up half the night writing and overslept."

"Sure you did," Angela continued. "Your butt wasn't home at ten-thirty because I called to remind you to be on time."

"You going to let me in?" Jason asked

"Daddy, daddy," Julianne shouted as she ran up to the screen door.

Angela finally unlocked the door. Julianne bolted past her and jumped into Jason's arms.

"Hi, baby," he said. "How's my baby girl?"

"Okay and I want to see grandma and grandpa Casey." Julianne squeezed both arms around Jason's neck.

"We're going to do that, baby," Jason said as he put Julianne down. "You'll probably see your Aunt Jacqueline and Aunt

Theresa too."

"Good," Julianne said. She began to pull Jason by the hand in the direction of the car. "Let's go, daddy."

"Have her back here by seven," Angela said. "She has a busy day tomorrow and I want her in bed by eight."

Jason suddenly remembered that he had to meet Elliott at six. That meant he'd have to let Hazel or one of his sisters bring Julianne home. That would also set Angela off.

"Something's come up tonight, so I'm going to have to let her grandmother or one of the girls bring her home."

"Why can't you spend the time with your daughter when you have her?" Angela shot back at him. "It's not like you get her that often."

"Okay, cool it, will you? She doesn't need to hear this."

"Why not? She needs to know her daddy doesn't have time to spend with her."

"Daddy, you don't have time to spend with me?" Julianne asked while pulling Jason's arm.

"That's real smart, Angela."

"It's your own fault," Angela rejoined as she flung her arms in the air. "Whatever, Jason! Just don't let Theresa bring her home. She's always got a funky attitude."

"Why don't you stop that kind of talk?"

Suddenly Julianne began to cry and grabbed at Jason's pant leg.

"See what you've done now!" Angela shouted.

Jason ignored her. He picked Julianne up, kissed her on the cheek and she immediately stopped crying.

"I'm sorry, baby," he said. "Come on, let's go see grandma." He hoisted her up in his arms and then looked at Angela. "This animosity has to end."

"Just have my child back here by seven and I don't care which one of the Mitchell clan brings her home. Make sure she's here on time." Angela slammed the screen door shut and glared at Jason.

He started to say something, but then stopped. Why continue

the hassle? Instead he wiped Julianne's tears and said to her, "Tell your mother bye-bye."

Angela pursed her lips, gave Jason one final hard look, and closed the door.

u

When Jason pulled into the driveway he saw both Theresa's and Arthur's cars parked out front. That meant the whole gang was inside. Kind of strange that Arthur would accompany Jacqueline to the house especially if he knew Theresa would be there. Evidently he was kissing a whole lot of ass to get back in good with his wife, and especially with Hazel. Jason parked his BMW right behind Arthur's Mercedes, picked up Julianne and headed inside.

When they got inside Julianne jumped down and ran to the dining room where they all sat eating lunch. She ran right into Big Casey's arms. He snatched her up and kissed her on the cheek.

"How's grandpa's little girl?"

"Okay, grandpa," Julianne answered as she got down, ran over and this time jumped into Hazel's lap. "Grandma, I want something to eat."

"Aren't you going to speak to your aunts and your Uncle Arthur?" Jason said as he shook Arthur's hand and then took an empty seat at the table. "How's everyone?" he aksed and noticed Jacqueline's swelling and discoloration was gone. Evidently an excellent job with the makeup. He watched Julianne make her rounds, hugging and kissing her aunts and her uncle. She finally ended up back in Hazel's lap and grabbed a piece of sandwich off her plate.

"We're doing fine," Big Casey finally answered Jason. "We were just discussing the Williams sisters. Arthur thinks that Venus is really the best tennis player. But the father who controls both of them has made the decision that Serena should get the limelight, so Venus doesn't play as hard against her and deliberately loses." A big smile spread across Big Casey's face. "Would you agree with his assessment?" he asked Jason.

Jason immediately recognized this as one of Big Casey's traps. He loved to pit one person against the other. He never did it maliciously, but only because he thrived on competition. When Cedric was home he used to taunt the two brothers. He never realized that Cedric couldn't handle it and that was one of the reasons he moved to San Francisco and never came home. Jason glared over at Arthur and detected his discomfort.

"I don't know," Jason answered cautiously. "He might have a point. I don't see that same aggressive nature in Venus when she plays her sister. She certainly has the speed and the reach to beat Serena, so Arthur might have a point."

"That's bull," Theresa said. "Serena is so much better than Venus, and there's no way either one of them would throw a match just to satisfy their father."

"What's this little sisters sticking together syndrome?" Big Casey asked. "I guess if I had raised you all as tennis players, you'd have figured you could beat Jacqueline."

"Daddy, please," Jacqueline said. "Why are you always trying to start some mess?"

"I ain't starting nothing," Big Casey said with an even larger smile all over his face.

"Yes, you are, Casey," Hazel said. "Now leave these kids alone."

"All right, you all ain't no fun. I'm going to get some sunshine." Big Casey got up and started for the side door.

Jason got up and followed him outside. He held his breath that Arthur would not follow behind them. He needed to talk to Big Casey about the transfer to the main office and he couldn't very well do that if Arthur went outside with them. He didn't. Just as Jason figured. He stayed sitting under Jacqueline and near Hazel. Sometimes he appeared to be such a wimp. Why the hell Jacqueline took his shit just didn't make any sense. Big Casey stopped by the wet bar and poured himself a Scotch and soda.

"You want one?" he asked Jason.

"You know I gave all that up," Jason replied. They continued out the door and took seats around the patio table next to the swimming pool. Off to their right was a full tennis court and to the left, a built-in barbeque pit. "And you know you need to stop drinking too. How's your blood pressure?"

"It's up some. But what the hell, I'm not giving up everything cause of blood pressure."

"Dad, you don't give up anything. You're way overweight and you're drinking. A perfect combination for disaster."

"If I die tomorrow I can say I lived a full life," Big Casey said rather philosophically. "There ain't much I haven't done that I wanted to do."

"Well I want you around when I have my first best seller," Jason said.

"Don't worry, I don't plan on going anywhere." Big Casey lifted the glass to his mouth and took a long gulp.

The sun beating down made little beads of sweat break out on Big Casey's face. Jason got up and adjusted the awning, cutting off the direct impact of the sun. He sat back down, leaned forward and folded his hands on the table.

"What do you think of Arthur as a worker?" he asked.

"He's a real lazy son of a bitch and he hides up under my daughter's dress."

"That's being pretty blunt. If you feel that way why'd you make him foreman on the airport project?"

"To keep harmony in my daughter's marriage." Big Casey took another swig from the Scotch glass.

"What if I told you that he's not happy being a foreman on a job in the field?"

"What you driving at, Jason?" Big Casey stretched his legs straight forward and reared back in the chair. "What has Jacqueline put you up to this time?"

"She wants Arthur to be transferred to headquarters," Theresa said as she walked up next to them and took a seat at the table.

"Damn, Theresa, you have a big mouth." Jason looked back towards the door to make sure it was shut.

Big Casey sat straight up in his chair. "She wants what?" he asked looking at Jason.

"She thinks he'll be happier downtown and it'll make their marriage more harmonious," Jason said.

"What do you mean more harmonious? Every time they come over here, he does nothing but sit up under her. Can't get more harmonious than that."

"Yeah, but you're the one that always said things aren't always what they appear to be," Jason retorted.

"What's going on with them?" Big Casey asked and then took another drink of Scotch. He held his glass out to Theresa. "Get me some ice, will you please?"

"No, daddy, I won't get you ice to go into a drink," Theresa answered. "I will not participate in the slow death of my father. I love you too much."

"If you love me so much, get the ice," Big Casey said with a raised voice.

"Daddy, I cannot tell you no, but I don't want to." Theresa continued the battle.

"Please get the ice, Theresa," Jason practically shouted. He wanted to resolve the Arthur issue before they all came outside.

Theresa gave him a long, hard stare, snatched the glass from Big Casey and stomped toward the door.

"So what's going on with them?" Big Casey repeated his question.

"Nothing, really," Jason felt a tinge of guilt. "It's just you know how Jacqueline is. She gets all bent out of shape if Arthur stubs his toe."

"Did she ask you to talk to me?"

Jason hesitated while he watched Theresa stomp back to the table and thrust the glass down in front of Big Casey. She then sat down and stared out over the pool. "Don't let me bother you. Just continue," she said tersely.

"Yes she did," Jason finally answered.

"What's wrong with that girl she can't talk to me herself?" he asked. "She's just like your brother always keeping some distance between us, but always wanting something."

"She's just selfish and spoiled," Theresa said. "She gets everything she wants and now she wants that creep of a husband to get everything."

"Look who's talking about being spoiled," Jason said as he looked directly at Theresa.

"At least I'm not living off daddy while I write the great American novel. I go to work Monday through Friday."

"That's a pretty low blow even from someone like you," Jason said.

"Okay, this ain't about you all so let's not get off track," Big Casey said and took a large gulp of Scotch. "If I do this who'll run the airport project?" he asked.

"Stephen's quite capable of filling in," Jason answered.

"Bringing Arthur in puts one more person on overhead."

"But it's worth it for your daughter, isn't it?" Jason asked.

Big Casey stared out at the tennis court. He took another drink and then glared at Jason. "You kids going to break this business. I have to carry you while you become the next Walter Mosley and now I have to carry Arthur 'cause I sure to hell don't know what he's going to do in the office."

"Let him make coffee, go out and get lunch, and answer the phones," Theresa said.

"Give it a rest, Theresa," Jason shot back at her. He didn't need her negative and sarcastic comments. Dealing with Big Casey on this matter was difficult enough.

"All right, let's not say anything today," Big Casey said. "I'll call him on Monday and offer him the job at the head office."

"One other thing," Jason continued as enthusiasm crept into his voice. "You can't let him know that Jacqueline had anything to do with this."

"Oh, my God, I think I'm going to be sick," Theresa scowled. "Now we have to feed his ego."

Jason shot a hard stare at her. "Why don't you go back in the house and visit with your mother?"

"Why don't you drop dead?"

"Do you ever get along?" Big Casey asked. He didn't wait for an answer. He again stretched his legs straight out, grabbed his Scotch, and took another drink. "I don't want to hear the answer to that question 'cause it will just cause a prolonged argument and frankly I ain't in the mood."

Jason watched as Big Casey closed his eyes. He knew his father would be sleeping within a few minutes. He glanced at his watch. It read 4:30. He had accomplished his mission for Jacqueline and now it was time for him to head back across the freeway. Even Theresa held her head back in a relaxed position. He got up and headed back inside the house. As he walked into the dining room he winked at Jacqueline who smiled back at him.

"Mother, can you take Julianne home?" he asked.

"Why can't you take your own daughter home?"

"Because I have something to do this evening and Angela won't be home until seven."

"We'll take her," Jacqueline volunteered "After all, I do owe you."

"What do you owe him?" Arthur asked.

"Just a private thing between brother and sister," Jacqueline answered.

"Thanks sis," Jason said. He walked over to Hazel who was still holding a sleeping Julianne. He kissed his daughter on the cheek and then kissed Hazel on the forehead. "I wish my other sister was as considerate as you."

"You just can't manipulate me the way you do Jacqueline," Theresa said walking back into the room.

Jason decided he didn't want any more confrontations for the day. He'd done his good deed and now it was time to take care of his needs.

"I love you too," he said to Theresa. "I'm out of here." He finished and headed toward the door. He was on his way to an evening of pleasure with a beautiful and intelligent woman. But he couldn't get real excited about his date with Raquel. He still had Dominique on the mind.

Chapter 10

Elliott managed to get center stage tickets in the second row at the Wilshire Ebell Theater for the New York-based play Brother Take Your Game and Shove It. The original New York cast was appearing in tonight's opening performance. Reviewers claimed the play was an off-shoot of Terri McMillan's Waiting to Exhale. For that reason, Jason hadn't been that excited about seeing it. They arrived at the theater fifteen minutes before the curtain went up. Sitting next to Raquel, Jason couldn't help being taken aback by her beauty. Her long black flowing hair and perfectly applied makeup were only matched by the silk low-cut blouse and skirt she wore. When they sat, she crossed her legs, exposing her firm and fully developed thighs. Jason also caught the scent of her perfume which added to his excitement. It had been awhile since he'd been with a woman. His mind was not on the theater or the play. He could feel an erection rising as he imagined what could possibly happen later on that evening.

"You comfortable?" Raquel asked.

"Yeah, I'm fine. How about you?" Jason replied.

Raquel reached over, grabbed his hand and locked it in hers. She then rested it in her lap. "I feel wonderful."

"Okay, you two ease up now," Elliott said. He sat to their far right with Denise next to him.

"Mind your manners and your business," Jason rejoined.

"When's the last time you been to a play?" Raquel asked Jason.

"Over a year ago."

"This boy's been locked up like a hermit." Elliott again invaded their space. "He's so determined to write the great Black American novel he can't find time for anything else."

Raquel squeezed Jason's hand and said, "Maybe we can do

something about that starting this evening."

"Maybe we can." Jason smiled at the prospect.

The theater lights went dim, an indication that the play was about to begin. With his hand still resting snugly in Raquel's lap, Jason relaxed so that he could try to enjoy one more episode of Black man bashing by sisters.

As the play progressed, Jason's tolerance level diminished. After a while, he didn't care how good Raquel looked or what was in store for him later that evening. His anger was ignited at the theme of the play and how the plot was carried out. Four hard-working wonderful Black women and an equal number of scheming lazy Black men, who had to be treated with kid gloves because of their sensitivity. They had been mistreated all their lives by the white man and so they had to take their frustrations and aggressions out on the women in their lives. In the end, the four women got just retribution and all ended well according to the rules of the game that seemed to be set by sisters. When the curtain went down the females in the audience, including Denise and Raquel, jumped to their feet and gave the performers a standing ovation.

After the play, Elliott suggested they stop by Jackie's Nightspot for a snack and a drink. When they arrived at the restaurant it was crowded with other couples who had been in the theater. The hostess sat them in a booth next to a window looking out on Wilshire Boulevard. Raquel squeezed in close to Jason. Elliott and Denise sat close together across from them. As they waited for the waitress, Denise broke the silence.

"Well, Mr. Novelist, what's your opinion of the play?"

"I wasn't too impressed with it at all," Jason replied.

"You weren't," Denise continued. "I thought it was wonderful. I really do think it captured the essence of the Black female's struggle with all the insecurities that Black men have."

"What about the Black man's struggle with all the crap they always have to take off Black women? Shouldn't that get an equal airing?" Jason asked.

"Well, aren't we an angry man," Denise shot back. "Some

sister must have gotten under your skin."

"That's not it at all," Jason said. "I mean we've been inundated with all this bullshit about how the poor Black woman has been so mistreated. You read it in novels, and you see it in movies and plays. All some distraught sister has to do is write about her trials and tribulations with the mean, insensitive Black man, and white folks going to make sure it gets prime time."

Raquel took her arm and wrapped it inside Jason's. He could feel her soft breast resting against his arm. It felt good, but he wasn't going to be distracted.

"Don't get so upset," Raquel said. "It was only a play, something for entertainment."

"That's right," Elliott added. "That play ain't going to change the condition of Black people in the real world. Black women going to continue to dominate us no matter what." He paused, leaned over and kissed Denise on the cheek. "But for what we get in return when they want to be sweet and loving, I say dominate as long as you want to."

"Ease up, sweetheart," Raquel advised Jason. "You getting all uptight and worked up about something that isn't even real."

"Not real?" Jason asked. "It is real because it effects how the world views us in our relationships. Bunch of white folks come and see that play, then they go away saying no wonder there are so many babies born out of wedlock in the Black community. It plays right into their stereotype."

"Okay, I'm sorry," Raquel apologized. "I didn't mean to upset you." She snuggled closer to Jason.

Finally, the waitress showed up at the table. They ordered wine and hors d'oeuvres. As soon as the waitress moved away from the table Elliott pulled Denise into his arms and squeezed her. "I don't care what those folks write about. I know this is my baby."

Elliott and Denise's cuddling and kissing made Jason nervous. He felt out of place, because no matter how fine Raquel was, he didn't want to carry on with her in that manner.

"You all right?" Raquel finally asked.

"Yes, I'm fine." He wasn't really, but he didn't want to let her know that. He knew his problem was that he was suffering from the after effects of last night. Visions of Dominique danced in his head. He wanted to get back over to the club and see her. It made him uncomfortable knowing that she was cuddled close dancing all over someone else's body. That it bothered him was rather ridiculous. He didn't even know the woman and felt that way. And she's a dancer. He must be losing it. Here he was cuddled close to a beautiful woman, who also had a reputable profession as a teacher, and was ready to jump all over his bones, and his mind wandered to a woman who made her living serving as a sex object for any man who had a couple dollars in his pocket.

"Say, brothah, you all right?" Elliott now asked.

"Yes, I'm cool," Jason answered. "Who wouldn't be with a beautiful lady sitting next to him?" He figured it was time to lighten up.

"Just checking," Elliott said. He stared over at Jason with that look in his eyes that said "man, don't you start no shit tonight."

Finally the waitress brought the drinks and hors-d'oeuvres and they turned their attention to eating.

When they finally made it to Elliott's two bedroom stucco apartment in West Hollywood, it was already after one o'clock. And Jason couldn't help wondering what Dominique was doing right at that moment. Raquel sat down on the love seat and signaled for Jason to join her. Jason plopped down next to her. Elliott took Denise by the arm and led her toward the bedroom.

"You all have the run of the place," he said. "Me and my baby got a lot of private business we getting ready to transact." Denise disappeared into the bedroom. Elliott pulled the bedroom door almost shut. "I hope you all enjoy yourself and we'll see you in the morning. Take care of your business, brothah." He smiled and closed the door.

Raquel kicked off both shoes, folded her legs up on the couch and rested her head on Jason's shoulder. She stayed in that position for a few seconds, then pulled Jason's arm up and cuddled against his body.

"You seem tense," she said.

"Why you say that?" Jason asked.

"I don't know. You just don't seem relaxed."

Jason took his free hand, placed it on her chin and turned her face towards him. He then leaned toward her and pulled their lips together. It started as a slow, dry kiss. But her lips were soft, and the flavor of her lipstick in his mouth excited him. He opened his mouth and she followed. She laid in closer to him and put both arms around his neck. Now his tongue was exploring the inside of her mouth. Their long, wet and seductive kiss started his sensuous juices flowing. Raquel slid her hand down the front of his body until she reached his erection. She began to rub the top through his pants. She also began to suck his tongue, wrapping her lips tightly around it and pulling it further into her mouth. They had practically slid off the love seat. Jason slid his head down and placed his mouth on the top portion of her soft breast. They slid further down the love seat. He stopped and finally said, "We can get much more comfortable than this."

"I thought you'd never make the suggestion," Raquel said while pulling her body up on the love seat.

Jason smiled at her. "You know you could've made the suggestion yourself."

"I know, but that wouldn't be ladylike."

"How long you going to remain ladylike?" he asked as they both got up and, with his arms around her waist, started toward the bedroom.

"Only until we get in the bed. Then I'm going to show you just how unladylike I can be."

"I can hardly wait." They went into the bedroom and he closed the door.

Elliott turned the corner onto 7th Avenue and pulled up in front of Jason's apartment. "Damn, man, you sure had that woman hollering. What were you doing over there?" Elliott asked.

"I know a little something," Jason said, smiling.

"Shit, the way she was carrying on, I guess you do."

"You got to know how to hit the corners. It's not always the length of the ship. But it's the motion of the ocean," Jason couldn't stop smiling.

"Bullshit, man, that wasn't a conventional holler. That was the tongue being introduced to the magic wand holler. You know the one that sends them into ecstasy if you know how to lick and suck. Brothah, you told on yourself last night. You did what brothahs claim they don't do. I just hope it was reciprocal."

"Believe me, it was. That lady has skills."

"Yeah, well, I guess you going to follow up on that?" Elliott asked.

"I will," Jason answered. "But you know I'm on a mission and I have a deadline. I can't afford to get all hung up behind a beautiful woman."

"That don't mean you can't hit it every once in awhile."

"I'm not about hitting it," Jason said. "That's a disgusting term."

"Wasn't so damn disgusting last night when you had your head buried down in that pleasure palace."

Jason flung the door open and jumped out of the car. "I don't guess you're ever going to change."

"I just make it real, my brothah," Elliott replied. "Anyway, aren't you going to thank a brothah for hooking you up?"

"Yeah, thanks."

"I'll take that acknowledgement even though I know there isn't much sincerity in it. What's up this evening? You going to see Raquel?"

"I don't think so. I haven't written anything in almost a week. I'm going to catch a couple hours sleep and then get busy on the manuscript."

"All right. I'll talk at you later. I'm hoping to hear from New York on the book fair this week. They have my tape with my poetry. They should be making a decision any day now if they're going to let me read. I'll be home all day. Give me a holler when you take a break."

"You got it." Jason closed the door and headed toward the

Chapter 11

Arthur held his head high and allowed the hot steamy water from the shower to fall over his body like a waterfall cascading down on a statue. He took the soap and covered his body from head to toe. He was extremely proud of his recent accomplishment. Big Casey had promoted him to an administrative job in the main office in downtown Los Angeles. Once again he could dress in a suit and tie and not that common laborers' uniform at the job site. No more hard hats for him. He'd always had doubts about his father-in-law. The man never seemed to warm up to him. Because of the excellent job Arthur had done managing the work site at the airport, the man had no other choice. Big Casey deserved credit for recognizing outstanding talent.

He finished rinsing suds off his body and stepped out of the shower. As he dried off, he could hear Jacqueline downstairs preparing his breakfast. They'd both gotten up at five o'clock. Arthur wanted to make sure he was on time. The drive from Malibu to Los Angeles took about an hour. That should put him downtown by eight o'clock, an hour before he was to report to work. He wanted to make a good impression on Howard Bagley, the Vice President for Operations and the man under whom he would be working. The two men didn't like each other because word had gotten back to Arthur that Howard fought for someone else to head up the airport job. Obviously, the man was jealous because Arthur had the connections, being married to the boss's daughter. But he could tolerate Howard for a while. Eventually though, he would have Howard's job and someday when Big Casey was no longer around he'd run the entire operation.

Arthur slipped into his blue pinstripe Armani suit with his white shirt and grabbed a blue tie. When he first considered marrying

Jacqueline he didn't think he'd have much of a chance to manage the company some day. Jason had just graduated from USC and was working for his father. But then he got on this silly kick about being a writer and that changed everything. His other brother-in-law, Cedric, never hung around long enough to be considered for the head job. He was too busy chasing some wild ass dreams in San Francisco, or possibly something else. The best thing that ever happened to him was the fact that he lost that job with the state, and both of Big Casey's sons turned out to be frivolous chasers of wild dreams. It left the head position open for him when Big Casey finally stepped down, and this was the beginning. It pissed him off when they first stuck him at the construction site. He'd always wanted to be at headquarters. Yesterday when Big Casey told him that he was bringing him on board downtown, a sure sign Arthur was on his way to the top.

He moved in front of the full length mirror inside the closet door and started to tie his knot, but stopped and stared at his body. What a hell of a good looking man, with his olive skin, long black wavy hair, and thick moustache. In fact, women often told him he looked like Billy Eckstein. And what made him even more dangerous was his big ass weapon. It had always gotten him over. And it always worked with Jacqueline. How the hell could she ever stay angry with him when he yielded such a potent weapon of sheer pleasure? As he continued to knot his tie he pictured Dominique taking it all in someday. Good thing about being downtown was that it put him much closer to the Black Zebra. He could even go over there for lunch. What a wonderful thought, eating lunch while staring at Dominique's luscious body. He smiled, grabbed his suit jacket and started down the stairs.

Jacqueline had the kitchen filled with the aroma of bacon, eggs, and coffee. She had the table set for Arthur.

"Hey, baby, it smells delicious in here." Arthur sauntered up next to Jacqueline and kissed her on the neck.

"It's ready." She touched him on the arm. "Sit down, baby, and let me serve it to you."

"Why all this special service?" he asked while at the same time taking his seat at the table. "Wouldn't be because of that bomb I laid on you last night, would it?"

"Don't be so cocky," Jacqueline said as she brought the plate over and placed it in front of him. She then poured his coffee.

"You got to admit I've been in rare form the past couple times."

"I think I hold my own, Mr. Hannon," Jacqueline rejoined.

"You do, baby, and I'm not interested in any other woman but you."

"You'd better not be. If I ever catch you cheating on me, I'll do like that woman did her husband back East. I'll chop it off."

"Ouch, don't even kid that way."

"Who's kidding?" Jacqueline had fixed her plate and sat across from Arthur. She smiled and said, "But I'm so happy for you, baby. I know you're going to do a superb job at the main office."

"Yeah, and the best part about it is I did it all on my own. Big Casey recognized real talent and he rewarded me."

"You go, baby," Jacqueline said and smiled. "I'm going to fix you up with a special meal tonight." She got up, walked over to Arthur and hugged him.

"And after that I'm going to give you a treat that's going to make you holler for joy." Arthur smiled back at her.

"We'll see about that. We'll see who's going to make who holler tonight." She kissed him again and then returned to her chair at the table.

"I do believe Big Casey's got more trust in me than he does in his own sons," Arthur continued. He finished his eggs and bacon and took a drink from his coffee cup. "What is it with your brothers? They don't realize what a good thing they got going for them. Usually the ones that have it so easy don't appreciate what they got."

"Never mind them. You just go take care of business like I know you can."

"You're right. I don't have to worry about anything but doing my job and doing it right." Arthur pushed the plate back, got up, grabbed the coffee cup and gulped down the rest of its contents. "I'm out of here. Don't want to be late the first day."

"Arthur, it's only seven o'clock. You'll be there in plenty of time."

"I know but there's nothing like being a little cautious." He kissed Jacqueline and headed out of the apartment.

"Call me and let me know how your first day's going."

"You got it." Arthur closed the door and started to his car.

Arthur pulled out into the traffic on Pacific Coast Highway and headed toward the 10 East Freeway. He peered to his left and smiled as the morning sun sent its orange rays over the top of the mountains, then glanced off to his right and stared at the ocean waves with their large white caps crashing in against the coastline. To top it off the sky was a radiant blue with no clouds in sight. Could anything on earth be more beautiful and invigorating than an early morning ride up the coastline on a clear day?

Arthur turned the stereo to the KJLH morning show. The disc jockey had just jumped off into a monologue about those things couples take for granted in their marriage. He turned the volume up in order to take in every word.

"Men and women get so they take each other for granted," he said in his very distinct tone. "Act like they don't have to do the same things they did when they was trying to impress each other. Women go to bed with their hair in rollers and men don't brush their teeth. They don't think about cuddling no more. The man leaves the toilet seat up and gets in the bed and turns on his side so his back is to his woman and he so close to the end of the bed, if she just gave him a slight nudge he'd fall out. But she ain't going to do that, 'cause she's also hugging the other end of the bed."

A broad smile filled his face as he related what was said to his own situation. In many ways Jacqueline takes him for granted. She doesn't wear curlers to bed, but sometimes she does get in with socks on her feet. How unromantic is that? And she also felt comfortable passing gas in the bathroom so that it can be heard in the bedroom. She also released deep, long, nasty sounding belches. She didn't do any of those things before they got married. So, like his fellow brother behind the mike explained, she took him for granted. That's why he needed to pursue the dancer at the Black Zebra and also had someone on the side. He had to bring some excitement to his life.

He followed the traffic onto a large ramp that fed him onto the 10 East Freeway, headed toward downtown Los Angeles. His new work location would place him less than twenty minutes from the Black Zebra. He could picture himself having a thick and juicy steak for lunch while Dominique fluttered her big ass right in front of him. In fact, as a reward for his promotion, he'd cut out a little early today and spend a couple hours at the club. He wouldn't stay too long since Jacqueline planned to prepare a fancy meal and he'd promised her some loving out of this world, at a level only he could deliver.

After a half hour, he finally pulled into the underground parking facility at the Arco Building, parked his car, strutted into the lobby of the ornate edifice and took the elevator to the 35th floor. As he rode the elevator up, he reflected that there was no stopping him now. He opened the hughe, oak double doors with two large golden door handles and strolled into the empty reception area. Evidently he was the first one into the office, which was a very good sign. It was a little after eight o'clock and the rest of the staff would arrive aound nine and he knew he would be immediately escorted into Big Casey's office, and then given an office right next to the boss.

Arthur could feel his temperature rising after sitting on the big leather couch in the receptionist area for over two hours. The receptionist knew who he was and she'd told Big Casey that he was there. Big Casey told her to have him meet with Howard Bagley. Arthur viewed that as a direct slap in the face. He was Big Casey's son-in-law so why couldn't he meet with him? After he thought about it for a few minutes he figured that was simply protocol. There was no reason for him to get all bent out of shape because Big Casey followed office procedure. And anyway, he didn't want any special treatment or favors just because he was a member of the boss's family. For a while that perspective worked just fine, but after sitting for two hours waiting on a man whom he didn't like and assumed didn't like him either, his objective perspective began to shift. Why would that son of a bitch keep him waiting that long? And why hadn't Big Casey found a minute or two to come out and greet him? Surely he deserved a simple greeting. Again, he found room for rationalizing his behavior. They probably got caught up in some emergency matter and hadn't found time to break loose in order to deal with him. That would be him in a couple of weeks. Important people would be there to see him, but he'd be tied up in some sort of important meeting. He had to maintain his composure because the day was still early. Besides, the receptionist was super fine. She kept looking up and staring at him. She knew a fine ass Black man when she saw one. That would probably be a problem he'd have to deal with there at the headquarters. Big Casey had an affinity for hiring fine women and undoubtedly they would all want to get next to him. He could handle that kind of situation as long as he could get out of there some afternoons and head over to the Black Zebra.

Finally, Howard opened the door leading to the back office area and hurried over to Arthur. "My goodness, I'm so sorry," he said. "We had an emergency out at a job location and I had to deal with it right away." He extended his hand to Arthur.

Arthur stood up and shook Howard's hand. "No problem at all," he said.

"Let's go to the back and I'll get you all set up in your new office."

Arthur followed behind Howard. Before exiting the receptionist area he shot a glance at the young lady behind the desk. She was looking the other way. That didn't bother Arthur because women had to play their games. She had to be interested in him. Arthur continued behind Howard, all the time looking inside other offices they passed to see what kind of view they had out of their windows. He'd be getting a prime spot near the boss and with a perfect view of the mountains. That would be a clear indication of his status with the company.

"Hold up for a minute," Howard said as he stopped in front of a large well-furnished office with a perfect view of the mountains. "I need to get some paperwork for you." Howard hurried over to his desk, grabbed some papers and came back out.

They continued down the corridor and past Big Casey's office. Finally, they reached the end of the hall and made a left turn. Arthur followed behind Howard wondering when he was going to stop. According to his calculations, they were going away from a view of the mountains and back towards the offices that looked out at the freeway. What the hell was that all about? Clearly his status meant more than an office overlooking the freeway. At the far end of the hall, Howard stopped, grabbed a key off a chain of keys and unlocked the door.

He swung it open, moved to the side and said, "This is it, your new home."

Arthur walked inside and his jaw dropped. No way this could be his office? You couldn't even consider it to be small. It was tiny. The furnishings consisted of a small wooden desk, a swivel chair, and two plain old chairs in front of the desk. He had a view of the freeway and some old buildings beyond.

"Get settled in and I'll be back later to go over what you'll be doing," Howard said.

Arthur could swear a smirk spread over Howard's face as he spoke.

"We'll get your computer in here this afternoon," Howard continued. "Then I want you to start on some account reconciliations. I understand you can do spread sheets. That'll really be helpful to us. So get comfortable, read over this material and we can get together for lunch." Howard handed Arthur the papers he had stopped by his office to pick up.

"I thought I'd be having lunch with Mr. Mitchell," Arthur said.

"No, he's already gone out to the work site where we're having problems. But he'll probably say something to you when he gets back. In the meantime, enjoy and I'll see you later." Howard ended the conversation and hurried out of the office.

Arthur tossed the paperwork Howard gave him on the desk and plopped down in the swivel chair. He spun it around and looked out the window. The smog had started to thicken so all he could see was the freeway filled with cars, trucks, and buses heading into downtown Los Angeles. What a hell of a mess this turned out to be. He swung back around just as two men entered the office with his computer.

"Where do you want us to put it?" one of the men asked.

"Hell, you don't have much of a choice," Arthur answered. He pointed to an area on his desk and said, "This will do."

The two workers put the computer and the console down on the desk and one of them turned and headed out of the office. The other one began to assemble the computer. Arthur sat there staring at the man, still in shock. He finished assembling the computer and said, "Is there anything else you need, Mr. Hannon?"

"No, that'll do for now," Arthur answered and smiled. That was a good sign. The man already knew his name. It meant the staff recognized that he was someone they would have to deal with. After the man closed the door, Arthur rubbed his hands together, then opened up the paperwork and began leafing through it.

He couldn't concentrate because his thoughts wandered to the Black Zebra and Dominique. She was just too close for him not to go and see her. If Big Casey wasn't back by 4:30 he'd sneak out and head over to the club. In the meantime he needed to absorb the material in front of him. After all, his journey to the top, and eventually to Big Casey's office had just gotten started and nothing was going to stand in his way.

Chapter 12

The shrill sound from the alarm clock on the night stand jolted Jason awake at eleven o'clock in the morning. It was the day after his date with Raquel and he still struggled to get back to his high energy level. He took his pillow and covered his head for a few minutes, but then realized that would not help at all. Jason forced himself to get up, sit on the side of the bed and smile as he recognized that his problem was due to over indulgence in sex. It had been over six months since he'd been with a woman. His encounter left him rather exhausted. He needed to get back in shape, which meant spending a little more time with Raquel.

Jason swung his legs out the side of the bed and sat there trying to decide if he should turn on the television and catch the late news report on CNN. After a moment's hesitation he decided against that. He needed to shower, eat and get right on his manuscript. That afternoon he planned to write the chapter on Sally the slave woman who was forced to have sex with the plantation overseer. In this chapter Jason would carefully craft the tragedy Black women faced every day they were trapped on the plantation. This was one of the most important chapters in the entire novel because it represented an opportunity and an obligation for Jason to dispel a myth that Black women actually did love the plantation owners and willingly entered into sex with them.

The biggest myth of all being that Sally Hemings loved Thomas Jefferson. Jason always wondered how that love could be determined given the fact that Sally was a slave and really did not have the free will to decide if she wanted to be with Jefferson. That's what he would address in this chapter: the absence of free will for the Black woman. Nothing is more demeaning than denying a woman the right to determine with whom she will have a relationship. Essentially it is rape, absent the right to freely engage in the act. Jason smiled as he considered the impact his novel could have on the literary world.

He finally pulled himself out of bed, scrambled over to the bathroom, turned on the shower, dropped his underwear and started to get in when the phone rang.

"Damn," he whispered and hurried over to the nightstand. He snatched the phone out of its cradle and snapped, "Yeah, who is it?"

"Damn, dawg, you don't have any better phone manners than that?" Elliott asked.

"Hey man, I was just about to get in the shower," Jason replied.

"I won't keep you long, but I had to call and share my good news."

"What's that, you find out Denise is pregnant?"

"Now why you want to go there, dawg, when I told you I wanted to share my good news, not my nightmare?"

"Sorry, brother, go ahead. What's the good news?"

Elliott shouted into the phone, "I just heard from QBR out of New York and they want me to read at the Harlem Book Festival."

"What?" Jason also shouted into the phone. "Man, that's fantastic. You know how many literary giants are going to be there?"

"That's a rhetorical question 'cause you know damn well I know how many are going to be there. And it's my chance to shine and get discovered. Just like Christopher Columbus discovered America, well some publisher going to discover my Black ass."

"When is it?" Jason asked.

"It's in two weeks."

"That sure is late notice. Somebody must have canceled on them and they needed a substitute."

"There you go bursting my bubble."

"No, man, you know I don't mean to do that."

"It don't matter to me how I got a chance to be on center stage at the Shomburg Theater in the Langston Hughes Auditorium. I'm going to be there and these people going to hear the new

Langston Hughes reading poetry in the auditorium named after the master."

"We're going to have to make this a real outing," Jason suggested. "You know, do the whole works."

"What do you mean? You're going to go?" Elliott shouted.

"You know I'm going to go and see my main man outdo Langston Hughes in his own auditorium."

"You going to take anybody with you?"

"I hadn't really thought about that, but since you mentioned it—"

"I'm going to scrape me some extra money and take Denise," Elliott interjected. "Or maybe she'll pay her own way if I play on her independent nature. You know these women love to do their own thing."

"Not when it comes to spending money."

"It's worth a try. I keep my money and still get the honey."

"Don't you ever stop?"

"Why? You know it's just natural for me to be a poet. And I'm going to Harlem to perform in the main poet's auditorium." Elliott was shouting again.

"All right, it's a plan. But I have to get off this phone and get to work."

"You got it brothah. I'll be by that way about six so we can go to the joint and celebrate."

"I don't know about that. I need to write all day and into the night."

"Man, give a brothah a break. Step out with me for a minute tonight and let's look at some naked bodies."

"You know you're going to have to change your filthy ways if you're going to perform in Langston Hughes' auditorium."

"He won't mind. He was asexual anyway. Are you with me this evening? Your dream girl might be there and just might act a little nicer this time. All you have to do is increase your tips from twenty to fifty." Elliott laughed.

"Real funny. Yeah I'll hang out with you for a minute."

"Good show, dawg. Then I'll holler at you later." Elliott finished and they both hung up.

What a hell of a break for his friend, Jason mumbled as he returned to the shower. He stayed under the water for a good ten minutes and during that time his mind wandered. He loved the prospect of going to New York and walking in the shadow of the great literary giants of the past. Later on that day he would call Raquel and invite her to go along. The trip would put a dent in his savings but being at the Harlem Book festival with his friend and new lover would make it worth the expenditure. With a wide grin, he finished in the shower, dressed and headed for his computer.

A half hour passed and he still hadn't written a paragraph. Jason stared at the monitor, but just couldn't make the connection and it bothered him. The greatest fear of all was writer's block. That couldn't be happening to him. The first part of the novel had flowed so well. He just needed to concentrate more for the middle part to come together. Maybe he should do like many other writers and draw up an outline. But that all seemed so deliberate and planned. Good writing flowed from the passion the writer felt for the story. You can't outline the flow. You just have to let it happen. He needed to write the scene about the slave woman Sally's tragedy.

Jason took in a deep breath and slowly released it. Too many outside interruptions blocked his concentration. And the most bothersome was the image of Dominique twisting and undulating on the stage. Maybe it was best she hadn't made it over to his table the other night. Any involvement with her would impede his ability to concentrate on his work. That's one headache he didn't need and if she were at the club later on he would ignore her. Right now, in his life, Raquel was enough. With that settled, Jason turned his attention back to 1836, the plantation, and Sally.

He could now visualize the tragic scene and began to type but just as he reached the flow, the doorbell rang.

"Damn," he shouted. He pounded his open hands down on the table, got up and headed for the door. Jason swung the door open and his jaw dropped as he stared at his brother Cedric standing next to a man Jason had never seen. He hadn't heard from his brother in over a year. After Cedric had fallen out with Big Casey, he'd claimed that he'd never return to Los Angeles. He hadn't called and now a year later, shows up at Jason's door with another man who looked almost as feminine as some of the dancers at the Black Zebra. Jason glared hard at his brother and thought this couldn't be. Big Casey would kill him if what he suspected was true.

"Well, brother, you going to invite us in?" Cedric asked.

"Oh, yeah, come on in," Jason replied. He couldn't take his eyes off the other man who strolled past him and gave him a contemptuous smile. Cedric sat on the couch and his friend sat right next to him. The man then took Cedric's hand and held it between his.

"What the hell's going on?" Jason asked as he took a seat.

"This is Aaron and he's my lover," Cedric answered. Aaron lifted Cedric's hand up to his lips and kissed it. He then held his hand next to his cheek.

"Hello, Aaron," Jason said dryly. "I guess I should say I'm happy to meet you. But with the turmoil this is going to create I'll withhold any joyous response to knowing my brother is gay."

"I love Cedric," Aaron said in a very soft tone.

The man is feminine all the way, Jason thought. Thank God my brother's taken the masculine role. "Well you wanted a clean break with your family and Big Casey," Jason said. "It looks like you got it."

"Does that include you too, brother?" Cedric asked.

"You're in the apartment, aren't you?" Jason replied.

"I can gather from your tone that you really don't approve," Aaron said with his voice rising.

Jason got up and walked to the opening into the kitchen. "I don't have anything to drink but some juice. You're welcome to it."

Cedric also jumped up and hurried over next to his brother. "Can we talk in private?" he asked.

"What about your lover boy here?"

"He'll be all right," Cedric answered.

Jason pointed toward the bedroom. "In there," he said. Cedric headed toward the bedroom and Jason hesitated. He glared at

Aaron, shook his head, and joined his brother in the bedroom.

"What are you thinking about, Cedric?" Jason shouted his question at his brother as they both sat on the side of the bed with the door shut. "Big Casey is going to disown you. He's not going to allow you within a mile of his house. And you know what that's going to do to your mother?"

"I can't help who I am," Cedric said. "I've known for a very long time that I was gay. I just withheld my natural feelings because of Big Casey."

"How long you been doing this thing?"

"It's not a thing," Cedric said defiantly.

"Okay, you know what I mean. Let's not get defensive."

"After I got to San Francisco I met Aaron and we hit it off."

"How many others have there been?"

"Does it matter? I don't want to know how many women you've been with."

"Okay, that's fair. It doesn't matter. And I guess if you're happy that's all that counts. Although I don't see how you can possibly be happy lying next to a man."

"That's because you don't know the absolute joy and fulfillment I get with Aaron."

"Spare me, please," Jason said as he bolted off the bed and walked over and leaned on the side of the dresser.

"I thought you could handle this," Cedric shrieked as he also got up. "I was wrong. Evidently you don't love me enough as your brother to accept who I am." He started toward the door. "Sorry, Jason, I'll get out of your apartment now."

"Sit back down." Jason grabbed Cedric by the arm and led him back to the bed. They both sat on the side. Jason wanted to slap his brother who had a defiant "I don't give a damn look" on his face. He'd known a number of gay brothers at USC and it seemed that they had a chip on their shoulder. Always bitter and angry and that's how Cedric appeared to him.

"Now that you've found yourself, what do you plan on doing?" Jason asked.

"I'm moving back down here to Los Angeles," Cedric answered.

"What! You're going to do what?"

"Why does that surprise you? After all, this is my home."

"Since no one has heard from you in over a year, we just figured you were pretty much content in San Francisco."

Cedric shifted his body to the left. "Actually it was Aaron's idea." A smile spread across his face. "He wants to act. You know he's handsome enough to make it in Hollywood and I want to help him."

"You have to be kidding? You know how many pretty boys are in Hollywood trying to make it in movies? Thousands of them."

"Aaron's different," Cedric again took a defiant posture. "He's not only handsome but he's good. He was in a number of plays in San Francisco and all our friends encouraged him to come down here."

"Does he have an agent?"

"No, he doesn't. But as soon as we get settled he'll find one."

"Have you lost your mind, Cedric? Better still what have you been smoking up there?"

Cedric jumped up and leaned against the dresser to look Jason in the eyes. "I resent that. Have you been smoking something to believe that you can be a great writer?" he asked sarcastically.

"Since you've come out of the closet you sure have gotten temperamental."

"Jason, I didn't come here to fight with you. I thought maybe you'd be the one person in the family that I could depend on to help us."

"Okay, cool down. What is it you want me to do?"

Cedric hurried back over and sat on the bed. "You can loan us some money. You know, just enough to cover our down payment, first month's rent and food," he said.

"You mean you came down here without any money?"

"We have a little. Enough to get a motel for maybe a week and for gas. I would ask Big Casey, but you know I can't do that."

"If you're going to be down here, at some point you're going to have to confront him. And what about Theresa and Jacqueline?"

"Theresa already knows. Didn't you kind of wonder how I had your address and knew you were writing?"

"Well it did cross my mind, but there were more pressing issues at the moment. How about Jacqueline?"

"Please don't tell her. She's too much like mother."

Jason shook his head and stared for a moment at his brother.

"Okay, I'll get you the money. But at some point you're going to have to face your family. Especially if you're going to live down here. Los Angeles is a big place, but not that big. It'll be worse if Big Casey or Jacqueline or even your mother happens to run into you somewhere."

"I can't do it right now, Jason. But I promise you sometime in the next two or three months I'll call mother and tell her the truth."

"How much money you think you're going to need?"

"A couple of thousand will take care of us. And I promise we'll pay every penny of it back."

Jason got up and walked over to his desk. He pulled out his checkbook and wrote out the check. "I want my money back as soon as you all find work," he said as he handed the check to Cedric.

"You mean as soon as I find work." Cedric folded the check and stuffed it in his pocket.

"What do you mean?" Jason asked. "Pretty boy out there isn't going to work?"

"His name is Aaron," Cedric snapped. "And no, he's not going to work. How could he possibly work and pursue his career also?"

"With a great deal of determination."

"You don't work while you're pursuing your career."

"Don't compare your friend to me," Jason shot back at Cedric. "Not after I just loaned you two thousand dollars to take care of his sorry ass."

Suddenly the door swung open and Aaron walked halfway into the room. "Cedric, I don't want to sit out here alone any longer," he said with a grimace. "Haven't you all finished your business yet?"

"Don't do that again."

"Do what?" Aaron asked.

"Open my door without knocking," Jason replied.

"Hmph," Aaron grunted, turned and walked back into the living room.

"Do you have to be so rude?" Cedric scowled. "He was only checking to see how long I was going to be. And he knew damn well he wasn't going to walk in on anything."

"I hope he knew that," Jason quickly replied. They both walked back into the living room. Aaron had sat back down right at the edge of the couch.

"I'm sorry, I didn't mean to snap at you," Jason conceded. "Since you're going to be with my brother, let's try to get along."

"That's fine with me," Aaron said dryly. "Is our business finished here, Cedric? If so I'd like to go."

"Yes, we're finished," Cedric answered with a smile. He walked over to Jason and forced a hug on him. "Thank you, brother. And I'll make sure you get every penny back."

Jason jerked back a little when Cedric put his arms around him. Flashes of the many times they hugged and wrestled when they were young shot through his mind. They had even taken baths together as little boys. Now all of a sudden he felt uncomfortable hugging his brother. He would have to work hard to overcome this new obstacle placed between them.

Aaron and Cedric walked to the door and started out. Cedric turned and looked at his brother. "Tell Theresa that I'd like to see her. And if she's comfortable with this I'd like for Aaron and me to spend some time with her."

"Why don't you call her yourself since you've already talked with her?"

"Please do this one last favor for me and I won't ask you for anything else."

"Yeah right, okay. I'll call her."

Cedric again started toward Jason to hug him. But instead he abruptly stopped when Jason jumped back. He held out his hand and the two shook.

"I love you, brother," Cedric said.

"Yeah, I love you too."

"I'll call you when we get settled."

"You do that."

Jason watched as the two men headed toward their car. He shook his head as he imagined the turmoil this new revelation would cause in the Mitchell family.

Chapter 13

Arthur found an empty parking space near the front entrance to the Black Zebra, parked his car and headed inside. Finding that space near the front of the building was a good sign. His luck had just improved and that meant he'd have a lot of success with Dominique. He'd felt a little upset when he left the office at 4:30 because Big Casey hadn't come back yet, so he never had the opportunity to talk with him. As Arthur headed into the club he glanced at his watch. It was 5:30. He had four good hours to get better acquainted with the dancer. He stopped at the money machine and got three hundred dollars, enough to spend on her in one of the private rooms in the back. But he might not have to spend any money if he could just get her to feel on his enormous weapon. He'd probably have her for nothing. He smiled at that prospect as he found an empty table close to the center stage. A skinny girl with raisins for breasts danced on the stage in front of him. Two other girls who didn't look much better than the one on center stage were dancing on the side stages. He had the perfect table for viewing the dancers and getting Dominique's attention when she came out. Yes, his luck was running quite good.

After four dancers and two drinks Arthur wondered if Dominique was working that night. Then she appeared on center stage. He glanced at her as she slowly made her way forward. He watched as two men shot out of their seats and rushed up with dollar bills in their hands. Arthur also jumped up and headed for the stage. Damn if he was going to let those white boys beat him to the punch. She would spend time with him if he had to give her all three hundred dollars then and there. She stopped in front of one of the white men, kneeled down and let him put the dollar inside her garter. She did the same with the other three men and then finally made her way over to Arthur. She smiled at him and leaned down.

Arthur took a one dollar bill and gently tucked it inside the garter, making sure he rubbed her soft thigh as he pulled his hand back.

"You remember me?" he asked.

"How could I ever forget a good-looking guy like you?" Dominique replied.

Arthur found a twenty dollar bill and placed it inside the garter. "There's plenty more of that if you'll just be good to me," he said.

"For that kind of money, I'll be real good to you." Dominique smiled as she spoke.

"Think we can make it to one of the back rooms?"

"We'll see."

Arthur took another twenty dollar bill and put it inside the garter. "I'm on a tight time schedule tonight. Could you make it earlier rather than later?"

"I think I can do that for a gentleman like you." Dominique kissed him on the cheek and then moved on to the next man waiting in line. Arthur returned to his table excited about what would happen in the back room.

The small private room behind the main stage had only a love seat and a small table. Music was piped in from the main area of the club. A sign on the wall in large black letters stated the rules for behavior in the room. "GIRLS ARE NOT TO BE NUDE! MEN ARE NOT ALLOWED TO REMOVE ANY OF THEIR CLOTHES! ORAL SEX IS PROHIBITED IN THIS FACILITY!!! ANY ONE CAUGHT BREAKING THESE RULES WILL BE REMOVED FROM THE PREMISES!!! Arthur read the warning, chuckled, and reared back comfortably on the love seat while Dominique stood in front of him. She wore only a bikini top and a G-string. Arthur stared at her perfectly shaped body and then glared up at the warning letters on the wall. He had no intentions of obeying the rules. They were put there to appease the police. He definitely planned on taking something off, and most definitely planned on some oral sex. In fact, he knew once Dominique saw the length of his private parts she'd be all over him.

Finally Dominique removed her top and said, "Each dance back here is fifty dollars, sweetheart."

Arthur pulled out a number of bills and counted out three twenties. He handed them to Dominique and said, "I have ten dollars credit on the next dance. But if the first one is good enough we'll just consider the extra ten your first tip."

"Aren't we generous," Dominique whispered in a soft seductive tone.

The music began with a slow tempo. Dominique moved in very close to Arthur so that her large firm breasts were parallel to his mouth. She slid her whole body down the front of his and stopped just when her face was half-way down. She then turned and slowly moved her full and firm butt close to his penis. He could feel his erection coming on. If he lifted his body up she could also feel it. He started to make his move, but the first song ended. Dominique stood straight up and smiled at Arthur. "You know the exercise, sweetheart. If you want another dance you have to pay the piper."

He pulled out 3 twenty dollar bills and gave them to Dominique. "Damn, baby, you're good."

"Thank you," she gave him a warm and seductive smile.

This time the music had a much more upbeat rhythm and that disappointed Arthur. He liked the slow stuff. He leaned back on the love seat and Dominique stood over him moving her body to the rhythm of the music. She leaned over him and positioned her breasts close to his face. He tried to kiss them but she quickly moved away. Again she turned her back to him and slid her butt near his erection, but did not make contact. He knew he was getting to her now. She couldn't resist him. They were at the point when he could make his move. He spread his legs to give her more room to work. She placed a hand on each of his thighs and continued her movement close to his penis.

Arthur wanted her and most of all he wanted to feel her full, wet, and soft lips around his erection. He had to let her know that he expected a lot more than what she was offering. Before he could make his move the music stopped.

Dominique again rose up and stood over him. She moved her body slowly from side to side. "We going again?" she asked.

He would pay this bitch one more time at sixty dollars, but then he'd expect her to get busy. Arthur pulled out another sixty dollars and handed it to her.

"Yeah, we're going again," he said, "but this time why don't you take off the bottoms?"

"I can't do that, sweetheart. You read the sign and you know the rules," she said while also pointing to the sign.

"Bullshit with those rules," Arthur said. "They don't mean shit. We can do what we want to back here."

"No we can't and I don't plan on going to jail," Dominique replied. "Now are we going to behave or are we going to have problems?"

Arthur relaxed back on the love seat, and spread eagled with both arms extended along the top. "I'm yours, darling, take me."

The music began and Dominique again came close to his body. She started with her breasts right in his face and then began to slide down the front of his body as she had done before. This time Arthur took his hands and began to rub her back. Her skin was smooth and soft. That excited him and she didn't resist. She now had her breasts between his legs. Now was the time for action. He reached down and unzipped his pants and his erect penis shot out right at Dominique.

She jumped to her feet and moved away from him. She then turned her head away. "Cover up and get out of here!" she shouted at him.

"Come on baby, you know you want some of this. Shit, this is twelve inches of sheer pleasure," he said smiling.

Dominique snatched her top and fastened it around her breasts. "Well you take your twelve inches of sheer pleasure and get out of here before I call security."

"Are you serious?" Arthur was now shouting. "I thought this was what you really wanted?"

"Believe me that's not what I want."

"What the fuck, you a dyke bitch?" Arthur rose up on the couch.

"Don't matter what I am, you just broke the rules of the club. You have to leave."

"Fuck you, bitch, you didn't finish my last dance."

Suddenly the door swung open and a very large Black man walked in.

"Everything all right, Dominique?" he asked.

"Yes, everything's all right. My guest was just getting ready to leave." She took the last 3 twenty dollar bills he'd given her and threw them back at him. "You're right, I didn't finish your last dance. Here's your refund. In the future if you come in this club tip the other girls and not me."

Arthur hurriedly zipped his pants and sat up on the love seat. He took the money and stuffed it in his pocket. "You're a real snotty bitch, aren't you? Or better still you're not a bitch at all. You're probably a fucking dyke."

"Watch your language." The bouncer moved toward Arthur.

"Whatever I am, you'll never get close to me again, you perverted son of a bitch," Dominique strolled past the bouncer and out of the room.

Arthur got up and headed out of the room. He gave the bouncer a disdainful look and said, "You all need to teach these bitches some manners."

"Keep on going," the bouncer said. "You can come back when you learn how to be respectful."

"Respectful to whores. What a joke." Arthur hurried to the door and out of the club.

Chapter 14

By the time Elliott and Jason pulled into the parking lot at the Black Zebra it was already full. Elliott had to park his car around the corner from the club. They walked back, paid the ten dollars to get in and found a table in a far corner away from the main stage. Just as the two sat down a waitress approached them and took their orders. Elliott ordered rum and coke. Jason again ordered cranberry juice and soda. Jason's eyes wandered from one side of the club to the other. He wondered if Dominique was working. What if she'd decided to take the night off? Or what if she had quit and moved on to another club?"

"Say, dawg, you looking for somebody?" Elliott asked with a wide grin all over his face.

"You know damn well I am," Jason replied without looking at Elliott. He continued to look around for Dominique.

"Brothah, you'd better take it slow. Seems to me you getting a hard on for a woman you don't even know. But that's okay here in the club. You're allowed to get a hard on without a personal relationship."

"It's not about all that," Jason shot back. "I just know what I want in this place. And if she isn't here then I won't be here long."

"Well I sure hope she's here 'cause I plan to have some fun tonight."

The waitress approached their table and placed the drinks in front of them. Elliott paid and gave her a five dollar tip.

"Thank you, sweetheart," she said with a smile. "Is everything okay with you men?"

"As a matter of fact," Elliott spoke up, "my friend here was wondering if a certain woman was dancing tonight."

"Don't tell me her name," the waitress said. "It must be Dominique."

"I'll be damned, how'd you know?" Elliott asked.

"That's not a hard one at all. Most of the men who come in here looking for a special dancer are usually looking for Dominique." The waitress paused to look at Jason. "You're not alone in admiring her. She is dancing tonight. But she had to take a break. Earlier this evening she had an unpleasant incident in one of the private rooms. The manager told her to skip a couple of dances and get her head together. Not that she needed to take a break 'cause can't nobody rattle that woman. She should be out in about ten minutes." The waitress finished then turned and headed over to the next table.

Elliott took a sip from his drink and smiled at Jason. "You're too late. She already made her money for the night in the back room."

Jason ignored Elliott as his mind wandered through all kinds of machinations. If she went into one of the back rooms with someone, did that mean she had sex with them back there? Or did she give them a blow job? What a cheap slut, and he was crazy to ever think he could get involved with a dancer. What a loss of perspective. He needed to get out of there, go home and write. Jason snatched his glass, took a large gulp and started to get up, then she strolled onto center stage.

Excitement built in his body as he glared at her dressed in a white outfit. It looked so sensuous against her chocolate brown complexion. All of a sudden leaving was no longer an option. Jason took another drink from his glass, got up and hurried over to center stage. He found a spot at the corner of the stage and watched as she made her way from one man to another collecting a large number of dollars.

Finally Dominique danced directly in front of him. She smiled as she looked down at Jason. Dominique had already discarded her top. He stood there stunned at the beauty in front of him. After dancing in front of Jason she then knelt down and extended her left leg so that he could put the money inside the garter. Jason selected a ten dollar bill.

"Thank you, sweetheart," Dominique whispered and then

started to get up.

"Why'd you stand me up the last time I was in here?" Jason quickly asked before she could move on.

She leaned back down. "When were you in here?"

"About a week ago. Remember, the man who gave you the twenty dollar bill?"

"Honey, you're going to have to tell me something better than that to remind me of who you are," Dominique said.

"Why's that?"

"Because I get twenty dollar bills on a daily basis."

"I'm sorry, I didn't know you were so popular." Jason started to move away from the stage.

"Hold on a minute." Dominique touched him on the top of his shoulder . "I do remember you. I tell you what, as soon as I finish this set, I'll come over and we can talk."

"Like you did before?" Jason asked.

"I promise and that's something I don't do too often in this place."

Again Jason felt excitement building inside him. But he didn't want to reveal his emotions to her. He took out another ten dollar bill and slipped it inside her garter. "We'll see," he said with a smile. She smiled back, got up and danced toward another eager man waving money to get her attention.

Jason strolled back to the table and sipped on his drink. He continued to keep eye contact with Dominique as she finally finished her set on all three stages. She left the stage and headed toward the dressing room, stopping at a number of tables to talk with the customers and to pick up additional tips.

"Look back," he whispered to himself as she neared the exit. "If she looks back then she just might be interested." Just as she was about to exit, she looked back at him and smiled.

"Yes," he shouted.

"What's wrong with you?" Elliott asked

"Not a thing, nothing at all."

An hour had passed and Elliott had taken off to one of the back rooms with the dancer he'd talked with the last time they were there. Jason had finished off three cranberry and sodas and his patience was wearing thin. This would be the second time this woman had lied to him. He wasn't going to sit there and drink cranberry juice all night long. He didn't want to pay for lap dances from any of the half dozen women who'd approached him, and he refused to let Dominique make a fool out of him for a second time. He glanced at his watch. A little after ten o'clock and he probably could catch a cab out front. It would cost him a small fortune to get from that side of town to his apartment, but it would be worth it. Maybe he could still call Raquel and if she wasn't busy, go over to her place.

Jason started to get up and again she came strolling through the door and looked over in his direction. They made eye contact and she smiled. Jason sat back down and followed her movement toward his table.

"Sorry, sweetheart." Dominique sat down in the chair next to Jason. "I had an incident in here earlier with a real creep and I had to fill out a report. That's why I'm late." She grabbed Jason's hand and smiled. "Did you miss me?"

"I missed you to the point that I was getting ready to leave," he said.

"But now you're glad you didn't, aren't you?" She squeezed his hand then began stroking the top of it.

"Yeah, I guess you can say that." Her hands were soft and warm. "Do you want a drink?"

"Yes, I'll take some champagne."

Jason signaled for the waitress and she hurried over to the table. She smiled and said, "I see you finally got who you been waiting for all night. Girl, this man sure got a thing for you."

"You like me, baby?" Dominique whispered. She and the waitress chuckled at Jason's reticence. "Bring a glass of champagne, Jennifer."

"You got it," Jennifer said and headed toward the bar.

"Don't tell me I have a shy man on my hands," Dominique said.

"I'm not shy," Jason responded defensively. "I guess I'm a little quiet when I'm around someone I could really like."

"Now that's a new one." Dominique smiled and squeezed Jason's hand.

"What's new? The fact that I'm quiet or that I could really like you?"

"Those aren't the first words a girl expects to hear working in a place like this."

Jason moved to the edge of his chair and relaxed. "Why is it that someone as pretty as you would work in here?"

"That's not a new one." Dominique released his hand and also relaxed in her chair. "I hear that same line at least ten times every night."

"Do you ever give an answer?"

"I guess I could turn that around and ask you why a guy as handsome and polished as you seem to be is in a place like this? It seems to me that you'd have plenty of women to keep you busy and out of places like this."

"Do I hear you putting down your place of work?" Jason took a sip from his drink.

"No you don't hear me doing that. A girl has to make a living and that's all this is, a way to make a living. And a rather good one at that."

Jennifer placed the champagne on the table. "Five dollars, please," she said.

Jason gave her the five dollars and another two for a tip.

"Thank you," she said and walked away.

"So what happened earlier with the man back in the room?" he boldly asked.

"Nothing really. He was a real pervert. He thought that if he exposed himself that I'd go wild for him and do whatever he wanted."

"And you didn't?"

"Not at all. That's not my thing. I dance and on occasion make you feel good. But I am not a whore. I don't sell my body."

"What if I wanted some time alone with you?" Jason asked.

"If there's a room available let's go," Dominique answered

pensively. "But I can't handle two perverts in one night. It's only strictly dancing back there. You understand that?"

"Let's go."

Dominique took his hand as they both got up and headed to the back of the club where they found an empty room and went inside. Jason sat on the love seat and Dominique stood close to him.

"In here, each dance is fifty dollars and, remember, no crazy stuff."

Jason pulled out a fifty dollar bill and handed it to her. "That guy earlier must have really shaken you up. You keep reminding me what I can't do."

"Like I said, I don't want any problems."

The music started and Dominique removed her top. She began to dance right over Jason's outstretched body, but he stopped her.

"You don't have to do that," he said. "Let's talk instead."

"What? You want to talk. For what?"

"Because you're more than a dance. You're a very intriguing woman with all the beauty in the world, and I want to know you."

Dominique put her top back on and squeezed next to Jason on the love seat. She laid her head on his shoulder. "What are you, my beautiful Black prince in shining armor?"

"Is that what you're looking for?"

"No, not really. That kind of person doesn't exist."

"That sounds rather negative and pessimistic. Not the same person that strolls out on the stage and exudes confidence."

Dominique rose up and tilted her head backward. "This is a business," she whispered. "It's how I survive in this crazy world."

"Have you ever done anything else?" Jason asked.

"Not really. A long time ago I figured out the easiest way for me to make a lot of money in a short period of time was by playing on most men's weakness and that is their ego and their overbearing need to be with a beautiful woman."

"So that's your initial assessment of me?"

"It's my initial assessment of all men."

The music ended and Dominique gave Jason a look that told him it was time. He went in his pocket, pulled out another fifty dollar bill and gave it to her.

"It can get pretty expensive back here," he said.

"You men have to pay to play." Dominique tucked the money inside her garter and asked, "Are you ready for a dance?"

"No, I'm fine. I like talking with you."

"Are you gay?" Dominique pulled back away from him.

"No, I'm not gay. Believe me, I'm not gay," Jason said with a chuckle. "Do you believe that you're so desirable that a man couldn't be alone with you and just talk?"

"This is not the place you come to talk. But anyway it's your dime. If you want to talk that's what we'll do."

"Are you from Los Angeles?" he asked.

"No. East St. Louis."

"How long you been here?"

"Going on three years. I mean really what's up with you? Why you asking me all these questions? If you think we're going to get together outside the club you can forget it. I don't date customers that I've danced for."

"That means I'm still in the running because you haven't danced for me."

"I guess you're right." She smiled.

"So would you at least consider it?"

"Consider what?"

"Seeing me outside the club and before you say no, please just think about it. I don't need an answer tonight. Me and my friend are going to New York. When I get back you can give me an answer."

"New York." Dominique's voice rose. "Oh, I've always wanted to go to New York."

"Come on and go with me," Jason said.

"I can't do that, not just yet."

"That sounds encouraging."

"I'm sure you have a lady or maybe two or three or more."

"No, I don't. At least no one I'm committed to. You think I

would ask you to go to New York with me if I was in a serious relationship?"

"It happens all the time."

"But not with me."

"Look, I need to get back out front because this is getting too deep for me." Dominique stood up.

"So you're going to leave me hanging?"

"You have a pen?" Dominique asked.

Jason handed her a pen and she scribbled a number on a napkin. "Here's my number. Please don't turn out to be some kind of freak. Call me when you get back. Now to make sure you're on the up and up, you know like not really married or living with someone, give me your number and make sure it's really your number."

Jason took the napkin and stuffed it in his pocket. He then grabbed another napkin on the table and scribbled his number. He handed it to her and said, "You've made me the happiest man in all of Los Angeles."

"Did you hear what I said about the freak and pervert?"

"I did and I'm not. You don't have to worry."

"Good, now let's get back up front."

When Jason made it back to the table Elliott was sipping on a rum and coke. Jason didn't sit down. "I have to get out of here," he said.

"What the hell, what happened to you? She shoot you down again?"

"No, not at all."

"I got myself taken care of pretty good and I was just waiting on you." Elliott finished his drink and got up. "What's going on? What happened?"

"Paradise, my friend. Unadulterated pure loving paradise," Jason answered as they started for the door.

Chapter 15

"What the fuck was wrong with that bitch," Arthur fumed while driving the Pacific Coast Highway on his way home. It pissed him off that a low-life dancer turned him down when he made it apparent that she could spend some quality time in his company. She had to be a dyke. Just a bitch who didn't recognize a good thing when she saw it. He'd spent over two hundred dollars on her sorry ass and all he'd gotten was a hard on. That added insult to injury. She walked away with the money and he got nothing. He'd wait a couple weeks or maybe a month and then go back there and somehow even the score with that tramp.

He snapped to his senses as a highway patrolman came up the other side of the highway. He glanced at the speedometer. It read ninety miles an hour. The patrolman signaled with his bright lights and Arthur slowed down to seventy. He'd been drinking quite a bit and didn't need to get pulled over for speeding and end up going to jail for intoxication. The officer had given him a courtesy signal and he'd best heed the warning. Arthur checked the speedometer and it registered seventy miles per hour, then looked in the rearview mirror and all was clear. Feeling confident that he wasn't going to be pulled over and busted on a DWI, his thoughts turned back to the Black Zebra. There had to be a way to get even with that lowlife bitch.

Arthur finally turned off the highway and headed toward his town house. His thinking shifted to Jacqueline. She would be angry since he promised to be home right after work and it was now after eleven. Jacqueline cramped his style and it was her fault that he'd struck out with Dominique. If he hadn't felt rushed he could have taken more time. His approach would have been different. Not quite so direct and to the point. But no, he had to worry about getting home at a decent hour just to pacify Jacqueline. She'd be upset, but pulling into their garage he really didn't care.

Arthur entered the townhouse through the garage door leading into the kitchen. Every light in the place was out and dead silence. He flicked on the light in the kitchen, went to the refrigerator and grabbed himself a beer. He looked over at the dining room table and the plates, glasses and food that sat there. The dumb ass bitch left everything there where she knew he'd see it when he walked in. She was playing silly games with him, however, there was no need to lose his cool. He needed her because he needed his job. And anyway Dominique had made him horny as hell and Jacqueline was at least some loving if not the loving he wanted. For that reason he'd be nice and have sex, all the time imagining that she was Dominique.

He climbed the stairs but instead of going directly to the bedroom he strolled over to the balcony, opened the door to a brisk and invigorating ocean breeze. He leaned against the railing and momentarily closed his eyes. After a few minutes he went back inside but left the door open. He heard no sound or movement from the bedroom but knew damn well that Jacqueline was awake. She never slept when he stayed out late. No sense in delaying the inevitable. He walked into the bedroom, turned on the light on the table next to his side of the bed, then sat down and began to undress.

"Please don't undress in here," Jacqueline whispered.

"What do you mean don't undress in here? This is my bedroom," Arthur shot back.

"No, Arthur, I don't want you in here," Jacqueline turned to face him. "In fact, I really don't want you in the house. So I sure don't want you in here."

"Jacqueline, I know you're upset and baby I'm sorry for—"

"Just shaddup, Arthur!" Jacqueline screamed. "How could you be so fucking insensitive?"

"Jacqueline, don't curse at me. That's not your style." Arthur continued to undress. He figured her anger would pass in a few minutes. "Now are you going to let me explain why I'm late?"

Jacqueline reared up in the bed. "No I'm not going to let you lie to me, Arthur. Now get the fuck out of my bedroom."

"Your bedroom? Where do you get off thinking this is your bedroom?" Arthur's voice rose a few notches. "This happens to be both our bedroom."

"No, Arthur, you're only here because I allow you to share it with me," Jacqueline continured to scream.

"I don't know what the fuck you're talking about! I pay the rent here. I'm the one who gets up and goes to work every day. Not you."

"That's just my point. You get up and go to work at my father's business because you are married to me. If you weren't my husband, there's no way in God's creation you'd have that job."

Arthur jumped to his feet, rushed over to Jacqueline's side of the bed and stood over her.

"So what you're saying is I'm beholden to you?"

"What I'm saying is that you need to try being a decent husband to someone who has helped you make it in this world. You know damn well you wouldn't be doing as well as you are if it wasn't for my family."

"We're going through all this just because I'm a little late getting home? Well I'll be damned, I don't need all this bullshit." Arthur stomped back over to his side of the bed and sat back down.

"Arthur, you're always late and you're always disrespectful." Jacqueline now sat way up in the bed and rested her body against the bed backboard. "Let me ask you something and I want you to be completely honest with me. Were you with another woman tonight?"

"No, Jacqueline, I swear I wasn't." He reached over and tried to grab her hand, but she snatched it away.

"Do you love me, Arthur?"

"Why would you ask that?" Arthur again reached for her hand and this time she didn't pull away.

"Because love is important to me and I don't want to be in

a relationship with a man who doesn't love me and who I can't trust."

Arthur slid in the bed and moved over close to Jacqueline. Again she didn't pull away so he figured he had it under control. He really didn't want to tell Jacqueline that he loved her because he wasn't sure that he did. But it was something she needed to hear and if it would help get him out of this dilemma then he would say it. He placed his arm around her neck and pulled her close.

"You know I love you," he whispered.

"Then why do you treat me the way you do?" she asked, but didn't try to pull away from him.

"You want me to be quite honest with you about what happened this evening?" he asked.

"Yes, I do," Jacqueline's head still rested on his shoulder.

"I have to admit I was really disappointed when I got to the office this morning."

"Why, what happened?" She pulled out of his embrace and stared at him.

"It's kind of silly and something I should be ashamed of."

"Tell me, Arthur. What happened?"

"I thought I'd be treated better than what I was. Big Casey wasn't there to greet me and welcome me to the main office. In fact I didn't see him all day." He paused to put his arm back around Jacqueline's neck and pull her in closer to him. "And then they gave me the smallest office in the entire building. I mean it's not much bigger than a broom closet and it overlooks the freeway." While he talked, Arthur slid off his pants and his underwear. "So I guess I just got a little frustrated. I went over to the fraternity house and had a few drinks. I'm sorry, baby." He slid Jacqueline down in the bed.

"Arthur, I'm not sure I want to do—"

"Quiet, baby. You know I'm sorry. And you have to know I love you and I'd never cheat on you."

"You sure?"

"You have my word. In fact, I promise you that if I ever get to the point where I need to cheat, I'll give you the opportunity to leave me first." Arthur began kissing Jacqueline on her neck. "You know I love my baby and you're the only woman I want to be with." He could feel her weakness. He slid the bottom of her pajamas off and slowly moved his middle finger inside her. He kissed her lips and then slid his head down and kissed her breasts. He could feel her wetness. "All this belongs only to you, baby."

"Arthur, I do love you but you can't keep treating me this way."

"Which way?" he asked. He climbed on top of her and slid his penis inside her. "This way?"

"Oh baby, hell no. I love this."

"You love what, baby?" he asked as he moved inside her.

"I love this big dick inside me, baby. I love it. Don't you ever give this big ass dick to anybody else. You hear me?'

"I hear you, baby. Never will that happen." He increased the up and down motion inside her as he thought to himself that this should have been Dominique tonight instead of this jealous ass woman who had the audacity to think that all this could belong only to her.

Chapter 16

United Airlines Flight #667 from Los Angeles to New York City circled around the large buildings in Manhattan, giving Jason a clear view of the city. The pilot illuminated the fasten seat belt sign and the attendants collected all cups for the final landing. Raquel reached over and grabbed Jason's hand as the pilot began his final descent into La Guardia Airport. Jason had the window seat and Raquel the middle one. Elliott and Denise sat in the seats in front of them. Jason squeezed Raquel's hand while looking out the window at the Empire State Building and then the Statue of Liberty. Finally the plane touched down and taxied to the terminal.

"I'm so excited," Raquel said. "And I'm so glad you asked me." She kissed Jason on the cheek. "I'm going to make sure you don't regret choosing me among all the many women you could've chosen."

"Don't flatter me," Jason said, smiling. "I live a pretty boring life."

"We're going to take care of that starting this weekend. Just wait until tonight, boy."

"I hear you all talking nasty back there," Elliott said.

"Mind your business," Jason said. The plane stopped at the terminal and they headed for the door.

They followed the crowd off the airplane, down the corridor and took the escalator to the luggage area. Elliott and Jason stood at the carousel and waited for the luggage.

"So far so good," Elliott said.

"What'd you expect, the plane to crash or something?"

"No, not at all. I just meant that we're off to a beautiful weekend. We have two beautiful ladies, who also happen to be freaks, and we're in New York about to go to the greatest book festival in the country."

"Yeah, brother, and you're getting ready to imitate Langston Hughes."

"Imitate my ass. I'm getting ready to outdo the master himself right in his own house."

"That's a pretty tall order. You think you can handle that?"

"You know I can."

"You got it." Jason raised his arm in the air and the two slapped hands.

"Just think next year we'll be coming back here for your book signing," Elliott said.

"I don't know about that."

"Have confidence and believe you're the best. That's the only way you will be."

Jason looked at Elliott and smiled. The red light illuminated and the conveyor belt started to move. They both looked at the opening through which the luggage would come.

"If I keep taking trips like this and wasting time back home, it might take me two years to finish." Jason spotted their luggage on the conveyor belt.

"Then let's make a deal," Elliott said as they both moved up to grab their luggage. "After this trip, no more wasting time. No more trips to the Black Zebra and no more Dominique."

"I don't know if I'm ready to go that far," Jason said. He grabbed his suitcase and then Raquel's.

"I can't understand the attraction you have for her. I mean she's not even in the same league with Raquel and here you are thinking about her." Elliott finished and grabbed two bags for Denise and him. They turned and walked back toward the women.

"You brought her up, not me," Jason demurred.

"I won't do it again, at least not during this trip. But that woman ain't nothing but trouble."

"Let's just leave it alone for right now," Jason shot back. "I'm content with who is with me right now and I'll worry about the other when we get back to Los Angeles."

Raquel and Denise walked up next to them and the four made it out of La Guardia Airport.

Elliott wanted to rent a car, but Jason nixed that idea. It made no sense to fight the New York traffic and pay the extravagant parking fees when none of them knew their way around New York. The city wasn't like Los Angeles where you were forced to drive. They waited their turn in the taxi line and finally were waved over to a Yellow Cab.

Denise, Raquel, and Elliott climbed into the back seat and Jason sat up front. It took them over a half hour to get to their hotel in Manhattan. Jason paid the driver and they hurried into the Biltmore. After checking in they rode the elevator to the 34th floor where they had adjoining rooms. They stopped in front of Elliott and Denise's room while Elliott unlocked the door. He opened it and placed the luggage inside. Denise went in, but Jason and Raquel remained in the hall.

"You all coming in?" Elliott asked.

"No, we're going to get settled in," Jason said.

"Oh yeah, I know what's up," Elliott said with a smile.

"What time you all want to get some dinner?" Jason asked, deliberately ignoring Elliott's comment.

"About seven sounds good," Elliott answered. "Oh, and a friend of mine told me about a Black-owned restaurant called Jezebel's. Told me the food and the ambiance were outstanding."

"Sounds like a winner to me." Jason picked up the two suitcases. "We'll be at your room about six-thirty."

"Let's do it," Elliott said, "and you go do it."

"Watch your manners, boy." Jason and Raquel turned and walked toward their room.

Jason stretched out on the bed while Raquel disappeared into the bathroom. He grabbed the remote, turned on the television and flicked the stations until he came to a channel that had the movie Best Man playing. It was on the scene in the hotel when Lance discovered that his bride to be had sex with his best man. Jason smiled as he thought how unrealistic but enjoyable the movie was to him. He'd seen it when it first came out years ago and enjoyed the acting but found the plot to be absolutely unrealistic with a first time novelist having Oprah Winfrey read his novel and chooses it as her book of the month choice. Of all things, a story about a best man who screwed the bride because she wanted revenge. And then the groom getting all upset because she wasn't still a virgin. Virgins are an anachronism in this day and age. But all in all, it was a pleasant story with some great acting.

Lance was about to throw his best man over the balcony from at least twenty stories up when Raquel strolled out of the bathroom, opened her suitcase and removed a tube of lotion. She lay on the bed close to Jason.

"You comfortable, sweetheart?"

"I feel pretty good," Jason said still watching the scene on the television.

"You like the Best Man?" Raquel asked.

"It's a little unrealistic, but yeah it was a pretty good movie."

"I liked it a whole lot," Raquel said.

"Why's that?"

"Because it showed Black people in a different light. It wasn't about struggle and it didn't show us in the ghetto and committing crimes. It showed us in an upper middle class setting for a change. It let the world know that we can plan beautiful weddings and that we make beautiful brides and handsome grooms who by the way have money."

"Is status important to you?" Jason asked as he turned his attention from the movie to Raquel.

"No, I wouldn't say status. But if you're asking me do I like nice things, well the answer is yes."

"Do you think that movie's a realistic depiction of Black life in America?" Jason was now more interested in Raquel's answer than watching Lance practically beat his best man into oblivion.

"Who wants realism all the time? We all live the tragedy, why do we have to see it in a movie? And yes I do think some Blacks live in that world and quite frankly it's good to see."

"I don't know," Jason said. "Movies like that leave a false

impression of what it really is like to be Black in America."

"But that's my point, sweetheart. We know the tragedy, why do we have to also make it part of our world of entertainment? We want to be entertained, not depressed." Raquel kissed Jason on the lips. "Now why don't you slip out of these clothes and let me entertain you?"

"What?" Her abrupt change caught Jason off guard.

"Yes, mister. Let's take off all these clothes, lie on your stomach and I have a real treat for you."

Jason smiled as he took off all his clothes and lay on his stomach. He felt the wet lotion on his back and then Raquel's soft hands moving in a circular motion starting at the base of his neck. She slowly and methodically worked her hands down his back. It felt wonderful and as she began to rub between his legs, he couldn't control his excietement. She continued down both legs and then his feet. Jason forgot about middle class living, night club dancing, and allowed Raquel to smoothly take him to ecstasy.

The maitre'd at Jezebel's escorted Jason, Raquel, Denise and Elliott to a table near the tuxedoed musicians softly playing jazz. The lights were dim and each table had a lace tablecloth and a lit candle. After they sat down, the tall, handsome maitre'd gave each of them a menu and said, "Your waiter will be with you shortly. Please enjoy your meal and your evening here at Jezebel's."

"Thank you," Denise said in a soft voice. "We will do just that."

The maitre'd smiled at Denise, turned and glided away.

"What's up with him and why you smiling at him?" Elliott asked as he looked directly at Denise.

"I was just being nice," Denise replied. "Quit acting insecure. It doesn't fit your style." She picked up her menu and began reading it.

"That's right," Jason chimed in. "I know you're not showing signs of jealousy. Not Mr. always got it together Elliott Jackson." Jason smiled at his friend.

"You know where you can put it," Elliott rejoined.

The waiter approached the table and took their orders for drinks. He then hurried away.

"You seem to be in a rather rough mood tonight," Jason continued, "nervous about tomorrow?"

"No way," Elliott answered. "Man, I'm so ready for tomorrow. I practiced this evening at the hotel. That is until I was interrupted by some sounds of passion from the other room."

Raquel now put the menu directly in front of her face.

"You're embarrassing the lady," Jason said as he reached over and took Raquel's hand.

"I see the two of you are clicking pretty tight as a couple," Elliott commented. "Doesn't take long to forget, does it?" he asked with a smile and looked directly at Jason.

"Don't pay any attention to him. He's just being cynical," Jason retorted. The waiter placed their drinks in front of them.

"Are you all ready to order?" Jason asked. They placed their orders and the waiter left.

"This is what I was talking about back in the hotel room," Raquel whispered to Jason.

"No secrets," Elliott said. "No whispering. You have to share your thoughts with all of us no matter how intimate."

"It's nothing really," Jason said. "We were talking earlier—"

"Talking," Elliott interrupted. "Damn brothah, I thought you were screaming."

"Will you get serious for a minute?" Jason shot back at him.

"Yes sir," Elliott answered and bowed his head in Jason's direction. "Serious it will be. What is it you all were discussing?"

Raquel placed the menu on the table and said, "I think it's a sign of progress when Black people can share the finer things in life. Being here in New York and eating at a first class restaurant owned by Blacks is a sign of progress."

"But tomorrow when we get to Harlem you're going to see the other side of that coin," Jason said.

"I know but does that mean we shouldn't enjoy this life?" Raquel asked.

"Black people don't want to help themselves is the real problem," Denise joined in. "All these young girls having babies and with no way to take care of them and some trifling nigguh who has no idea what it means to be a father."

"Hey, easy, girl," Elliott said. "Someone listening to you might think you listen to Rush Limbaugh or Bill O'Reilly. You know those two idiots who claim the only problem with the Black race is that the women have babies out of wedlock. As if these white bastards had nothing to do with Black poverty."

"I don't listen to Rush Limbaugh and I don't know who the other guy is. But I do know that we have to accept responsibility for part of our condition," Denise continued.

"And we have to stop knocking those that do make it," Raquel added. "Just because someone wants to better themselves, doesn't mean they're a cop out. I like going to nice places to eat and taking trips, staying in fine hotels."

"But we still have a responsibility for the collective good. In many ways our plight is directly tied into the struggle of Black folks with less than we have," Jason said.

"I feel you, my brothah," Elliott agreed. "That's what I'll be addressing through poetry tomorrow. Black folks can't afford to get all caught up in class structures 'cause that just leads to class warfare. That's white folks' crap, not ours."

"I still say you don't have to be caught up in class because you enjoy good things," Raquel said.

"I agree," Denise added.

"It looks like it's the men against the ladies," Elliott said. "How are we going to resolve this difference?"

"By not worrying about it," Jason answered. "At least not this weekend. For the sake of solidarity I suggest we call a truce and I'll concede."

"You have a point there," Elliott said. "At least for tonight. But this will be revisited tomorrow when we get to Harlem and you hear my poetry."

"Until tomorrow." Jason held his drink in the air. "Here is a toast to us, to Harlem, and to our poet friend Elliott Jackson."

Chapter 17

The taxi, with Jason up front and Elliott squeezed between Raquel and Denise in the back, pulled up to the corner of Lennox Avenue and 134th Street in Harlem. The three piled out of the back seat, Jason paid the driver with a twenty dollar bill and got out without waiting for the change. Taking Raquel by the hand, Jason started up Lennox Avenue. The street had been closed from 134th to 135th for traffic. Instead row after row of booths with brightly colored canvasses, representing all the major publishing houses in New York City and a few of the smaller Black publishers, filled the street. All sorts of books by Black writers and dealing with every possible subject lined the counters of the booths. At the end of the row, where they had exited the taxi, a large platform had been erected, with a microphone and an array of speakers. Later on in the day, writers would stand up there and read excerpts from their works. Since one of the purposes of the Festival was to merge the beauty of the written word with the genius of Black music, there were two very large speakers to the left and right of the platform, blasting out loudly the words "People get ready, there's a train a'comin" by Curtis Mayfied.

People of all races, ages, and genders crowded the street. But mostly there were Black folks with corn rows or bald heads, wearing ear rings and dashikis. Some pushed babies in strollers and others on canes struggled to make it up the row. Vendors shouted out their wares, from posters depicting Harlem, to tee shirts with jazz artists, blues singers, and messages that expressed the freedom Blacks felt belonged to them while in Harlem. Curtis Mayfield's voice seemed appropriate for the cause. Curtis sang as a prohpet of hope, faith, and a future for all the Black folks who had gathered in Harlem to celebrate their past and build for the future.

Jason smiled as he felt in the presence of Langston Hughes, Claude McKay, and Countee Cullen all around him. What an opportunity to walk down the same boulevard as did Zora Neale Hurston, Nella Larsen, and Jessie Fauset over a half century ago. He imagined some of the conversations they must have engaged in walking right down this same street. Much like the discussions he had at the theater in Leimert in Los Angeles. They had to discuss the nature of their writing and the impact it would some day have on future writers.

"Jason, you with us?" Elliott jolted him back to reality. "Man you were way out there."

"I know," Jason said. "This is where it's at. Black America in all its different manifestations."

"This is exciting," Raquel said as she now placed her arm inside of Jason's. "Harlem's such an exciting place. I think every Black person should visit here at least once in their lifetime."

"And every white person too," Denise added. "It'll teach them how to loosen up."

"There was a time when they did come up here to loosen up," Jason said as the four of them started walking toward the Shomburg Theater right at the corner of 135th and Malcolm X Boulevard. "Problem was they still wanted to treat us like shit with all that holier than thou bullshit."

"Okay, today is not about white folks," Elliott jumped in the conversation. "Today is about our folks and only our folks."

"You got it," Jason said as he slapped hands with Elliott. Just as they started into the Shomburg Theater Jason heard Curtis Mayfield again fill the air with, We're a winner. Right at that moment, with close friends and the people he loved most, and with the sun shining brightly on the day, Jason did feel just like a winner.

He escorted Raquel and Denise to the seats reserved for Elliott's guests right down front near the stage. An usher escorted Elliott through a side door and into the back of the theater. The auditorium quickly filled up. Jason recognized Max Rodriquez, the man who had the vision for a Harlem Book Fair, being interviewed by C-Span. Jason figured that at some point during the day he'd introduce himself to Max. He definitely wanted Max's magazine QBR to review his novel once it was published. Raquel took Jason's hand and placed it in her lap. He looked at her and smiled. He really liked her. She was exciting and quite intelligent. Even though they disagreed last night she impressed him with her ability to intellectually defend her position. And she had succeeded in keeping his mind off Dominique. Maybe something serious would develop from this relationship. Raquel definitely had one of the major criteria for a serious relationship, and that was some very outstanding love-making skills. She turned and stared at him just as though she knew his thoughts. She raised his hand and softly kissed the top of it. They smiled at each other and then turned and looked at the stage as the host was about to start the program.

"Ladies and gentlemen, welcome to the Shomburg Theater," he began in his deep baritone voice. "We are pleased to welcome you to the Harlem Book Festival and to our first event of the day, our poets' salute to Black culture. We have with us some of the finest poets in Black America. Brothers and sisters dedicated to capturing the essence of our culture trapped for over three hundred years in the ugly vise of another man's culture. So sit back and relax as we take you to a new level of excellence in our rich and fabulous heritage here in America."

The first poet, a tall, brown-skinned brother with long dreadlocks, strolled out on the stage. Jason moved up to the edge of his seat in anticipation of this brother's message. With good cadence and decent symbolism the brother spoke through verse of poverty, inner city struggle, guns and prison. Nothing really dynamic about his performance and Jason knew that Elliott would put him to shame. When the second poet approached the microphone, Jason tried to conjure up in his mind some of Elliott's poetry he had heard in the past. He just couldn't put it together, but nevertheless, knew his friend would be better than any one of these Langston Hughes wannabes. After a couple more poets, the announcer took to the microphone and said, "Now straight from

Los Angeles, California, a last minute addition to our program, a brother with immense talent, Mr. Elliott Jackson."

Elliott ran up to the microphone and adjusted it up for a proper fit. Jason, who had relaxed back in his chair, now leaned forward. If widely accepted by the audience, Elliott would be on his way to a book contract. Jason took in a deep breath and slowly released it. Raquel moved forward in her seat and rested her hand on Jason's leg. He looked over at Denise and she reared back in her seat and smiled up at Elliott. He whispered, "Give them your best and lay it on them."

Elliott unfolded the paper and momentarily stared at its contents. He then pushed the paper away and began.

> "I know feelings that
> Lie deep inside the soul of Black Folks
> That make you explode with anger
> That make you hide from fear
> I know frustration that lies
> Deep inside
> The soul of Black folks
> That makes you hate
> With contempt
> That makes you scream
> For revenge
> I know emptiness that
> Lies deep inside
> The soul of Black folks
> That makes you covet
> With envy
> That makes you kill for love
> But
> I know beauty
> That lies deep inside
> The soul of Black folks
> That makes us whole
> Creates us unique

Our existence
In a world filled with
Anger, hate, contempt, revenge
And envy
And death
For
We are the soul of Black folks
With
Our beauty, love, heart
To counter
To defeat
Their anger
We are the soul of Black folks
Of Douglass, Tubman, Truth, DuBois, Garvey
And Malcolm
And Martin
We are the beauty of the world
For we have suffered
Their fear, contempt, revenge, envy and death
The ugly side of God's world
And we shall always be
The best because
We
Conquered the worst!"

The crowd jumped to its feet and gave Elliott a two minute ovation, far more than given any of the other poets. Jason also stood and clapped as did Raquel and Denise. Elliott seemed to be in a trance as he stood there staring straight out at the crowd. Jason knew his friend loved every minute of the adulation. Finally the crowd sat down and Elliott read two more poems. He left the stage to a standing ovation and there was no doubt his debut had been an overwhelming success.

Jason, Raquel, and Denise waited outside the theater for Elliott. After five minutes he came bolting out of the building with a wide smile on his face.

"They want me for a poetry slam next month, all expenses paid," Elliott said enthusiastically.

"Congratulations," Jason said. "I have to admit you were awfully good."

Denise threw her arms around Elliott and echoed Jason's remarks. "Baby, you were the best and I just love you so much." She kissed him on his lips.

"Easy, woman," Elliott said as he broke out of her grip. "I have a reputation to maintain," he added with a smile.

"Yeah, I got your reputation," Denise rejoined. "Don't get no ideas just because you a star now. Remember I knew you when."

"Let's go celebrate," Jason said.

"Yes, this calls for a wonderful celebration," Raquel finally chimed in.

"I'm all for that," Elliott added. "But first let's check out some of these writers." He pointed down the row of booths being manned by Black writers, all prepared to sign and sell a book.

"This is your show and we're just along for the ride," Jason said.

"Let's not take too much time." Denise grabbed Elliott by the arm. "This is New York, my man just outshined everybody, and I have a real treat for him."

"I heard that loud and clear," Jason took Raquel's hand. "Let's get this show on the road."

They headed down the row of booths at the Harlem Book Festival.

Chapter 18

A surge of energy shot through Jason's entire body when he entered his apartment Sunday evening a little past nine o'clock. Three hours earlier they'd landed at Los Angeles International Airport, grabbed a bite to eat, and afterwards Elliott dropped off Denise and Raquel, then drove Jason home. They talked incessantly about the Harlem Book Festival and how they needed a comparable festival in Los Angeles. A festival that concentrated specifically on West Coast writers just as Harlem seemed to feature New York artists. Jason felt challenged and enthused to finish his novel and see it in print. He sat down at his desk, more determined than ever before to finish the novel in the next two months.

The next two chapters were critical. He'd already created his mystic character Hula Jack for the purpose of recounting the story of the Prophet Nat Turner. The story time is in the year 1836 and the Nat Turner rebellion had already occurred. Nat Turner had become a mystical character, representing the hope of salvation and freedom for slaves throughout the south. A number of slaves are sitting around the fireside passing on tales about great Black people and events larger than life. Jason juxtaposed the white man's version of Nat's rebellion with his own. He'd read William Styron's The Confessions of Nat Turner when he was in college and it left him both angry and frustrated. The fact that the literary world gave Styron a Pulitzer Prize in Literature for that garbage angered him most. How could a white man get inside the head of a Black man and one that was a slave at that? Jason searched the library to see if he could find a novel by a Black man about some famous white person. No such luck. That's when he decided he had to write this novel and present the account of Nat's rebellion from the point of view of a

Black man. It surprised and disappointed him that the prominent Black authors had failed to do that.

Jason stared at the blank screen on his computer and tried to get his thoughts together for the version of Nat's rebellion he had to now write. He took a sip from his glass of cranberry juice and reared back in the chair. For some reason his thoughts weren't flowing just right. He was probably too hyper from the New York trip to write. Images of the rows of booths, manned by representatives from all the major publishing houses, dangled in front of him. The majors had opened their doors to a large number of Black writers. That was a good thing. But he couldn't help but wonder would these houses have accepted the same number of writers if they wrote about something other than romance and relationships. They had even stepped off into erotica. The same old shit. White folks loved it when Blacks were depicted engaged in sex acts.

He took another large gulp from his glass, got up and walked over to the window. He pulled back the blinds and stared out into the darkness. It looked like it might rain, something the city could use. Jason loved it when it rained. There was something about the rain that brought out the romance in people. His mind raced back to the times he and Angela would stay in bed most of the day making love when it rained on the weekends. Damn, he hadn't been to see his baby girl in over two weeks. He had to call Angela in the next couple of days and get by there. He also hadn't been to see Big Casey, something he usually did once or twice a week. Jason could feel all these obligations moving in on him. No wonder writers escaped to secluded places. Sometimes that seemed like the only way a person could get something accomplished. But after New York he had a renewed inspiration and a reinvigoration of energy to plunge straight ahead.

Jason stared at the cars as they sped up the street. Everyone seemed to have somewhere to go, but probably in reality were going nowhere. In a way he envied these faceless individuals as they sped up and down the street. Most of them didn't have a clue that they were racing to nowhere. Sometimes that was a good thing, but he could never do it. When he deviated away from his goal, like the past weekend, that voice somewhere in the center of his consciousness would tell him to put it all down, out of the way, and get back to writing something. That's what he needed to do right at that moment. Jason closed the blinds and sauntered back over to his desk.

Hula Jack, Hula Jack. He had the character all laid out in his head, now he just needed to write the scene. But for some reason he wasn't connecting. He really did suffer from a little writer's block. Rushing right in and trying to write just wasn't the way to get his story done. Maybe he should call Raquel and head on over to her place. That would cool him out. Jason smiled as he recalled their lovemaking when they got back to the hotel after visiting the festival. They were out of their clothes five minutes after they got back in the room and didn't bother to put anything on until the next morning when it was time to check out. She referred to Jason as her personal stud, and said he could service her needs when the urge hit him. He looked over at the clock. It was ten thirty and he felt the urge rising, but had to fight it because he must write. Jason chuckled to himself thinking maybe he should switch directions and write a sex scene. Maybe that would be sufficient for the night. Get off vicariously through one of his characters.

He realized his imagination was only distracting him from what needed to be accomplished. With a renewed determination, he decided to write instead of type. He snatched his pen from the table, grabbed a yellow legal pad and, just as he began to write, the phone rang.

"Damn, now what," he whispered as he got up and hurried to the phone. Probably that crazy Elliott wanting to go to a strip club. He would tell him no tonight. Much as he would love to see Dominique, he would refuse. Jason grabbed the phone on the fourth ring.

"Yeah, what's up?" he asked, knowing that it would be Elliott on the other end.

"I'm sorry, but I was trying to reach Jason Mitchell. Is this his number?" a warm, soft female voice asked.

Jason heard the voice and his body stiffened. He recognized the caller, but couldn't really believe it would be her. "You have the right number and this is Jason Mitchell."

"Oh good. How are you, Jason? This is Dominique from the club. I hope I didn't catch you at a bad time."

Jason plopped down on the side of the bed. He could already feel an increase in his heartbeat. "Yes, I'm fine, and how about you? How are you doing?"

"A little tired," Dominique answered. "I tried to work a double shift today and I'm just plain worn out."

"Sorry to hear that. Is there anything I can do to help?" Jason asked.

"As a matter of fact there is. I am so tired I can hardly stand up. I know I can't do another round on the stage. And if you don't dance they don't want you to hang around."

Jason gripped the phone even tighter knowing where she was going with this conversation.

"My ride has to stay until 2:30 and if I stayed that long tonight, I'd be too tired to do anything tomorrow," Dominique continued. "So I was wondering, if it wouldn't be asking too much, would you mind terribly coming and getting me and taking me home? I can pay you for your time and gas."

It happened. She really did ask him to pick her up. "No problem at all," Jason said as he tried to maintain his composure. "I need a break from this writing and this is a perfect time to take it."

"I want to make it clear," Dominique said in a stern voice. "I only want a ride home and this is no kind of advance on you. Like I said, I'm willing to pay you."

"Dominique, you didn't have to say all that," Jason shot back at her. What arrogance! "I didn't agree to pick you up thinking that anything was going to happen between us. You're assuming I'm interested in you that way."

"I know you are," Dominique casually said. "You wouldn't have agreed so quickly to pick me up if you didn't think there was something in it for you. I just want to make it quite clear that this is nothing more than a ride home."

"You act like I'm forcing myself on you." Jason was now getting a little irritated. "You call here and ask me to do you a favor and then make it sound like you're doing me a favor. You sure you want me to pick you up?"

"I'm sorry, but in this world I live in you have to establish the ground rules on your terms or you'll get destroyed. I know you're doing me a favor and I do appreciate it."

"What time would you like to be picked up?" Jason asked dryly.

"How about in an hour?"

"I'll see you then. And don't worry. I'll even drop you off a block from your house so you won't have to worry about me knowing where you live."

"I don't mind you knowing where I live. In fact I'm pleased you'll know," Dominique said in a softer voice. "But you sure you don't mind? And are you sure you don't want me to pay you?" Her tone now was all business.

"No, I don't mind and I'm sure I don't want to get paid. I'll see you in an hour." As he placed the phone back in its cradle he didn't know if he should be pleased by her call. It seemed that he was about to deal with a woman who has absolute control over her emotions. The ability to control emotions always gave a person one upmanship in a relationship. Just maybe the woman he saw and admired at the club was not at all what he imagined her to be.

u

The Black Zebra parking lot was full when Jason pulled in just a little after eleven. He drove by the front of the club and looked to see if Dominique was standing outside. There was no sign of her so he continued searching for a parking space. It struck him as rather interesting that so many people would be frequenting a strip joint that late on a Sunday night. No doubt the money in this kind of business had to be good. Jason finally found an open space, quickly zipped into it, and headed into the club.

He pushed his way past a line of men waiting to pay for entrance into the club. When he reached the door a large man blocked his way inside. Jason didn't plan on paying ten dollars to get in just to find Dominique and then leave. Surely the bouncer would understand that his only purpose there was to pick someone up. With that in mind he approached the man at the door who refused to move. He could hear some of the men standing in line grumble as he hurried past them.

"What's your problem, pal?" the bouncer shouted at Jason. T

Jason stopped in front of the man and said, "I'm here to pick up one of your dancers and take her home. She called me and said she wasn't feeling good. She couldn't wait for her ride so I came to pick her up."

"Yeah, yeah, sure, what's her name?" the bouncer asked, still not budging.

"Dominique," Jason answered.

"Well you're too late," the man replied.

"What do you mean too late?" Jason could feel his heart drop She wouldn't really do that, would she?

"What I mean is that she left about fifteen minutes ago. Seems as though someone else was more available than you." The bouncer smiled.

The man had to be lying, had to be kidding and any minute Dominique would come walking out of the club. The joy he felt hearing her voice when she called, the exhilaration that came over him when she asked him to pick her up, and the personalizing of their relationship couldn't end like this. Jason smiled at the bouncer who had just shattered his dreams and said, "You sure you're not mistaken? Do you mind if I go in and look around?"

The man again smiled at Jason and said, "Go ahead, brother. I'll give you five minutes. If you ain't back here in five minutes then I'm coming after you for a cover charge." The bouncer swung the door open and Jason rushed through it and into the club.

He first looked at the three dancers on the stages, then to the back of the room where half-naked women were giving men table dances. There was no Dominique. He then glanced at the women sitting at tables with customers having drinks. Still no Dominique. He spotted one dancer who just seemed to wander from table to table trying to hustle a table dance from any man willing. No one seemed to be falling into her trap so Jason rushed up to her and said, "Here's five dollars. Will you go check in the back to see if Dominique is back there?"

The girl gave Jason a long hard stare, snatched the five dollars and disappeared into the back. He had three minutes before the bouncer would come stomping into the club and throw him out on his ass. After another minute he glanced at his watch. Two minutes left and no Dominique. Finally the young girl came back out by herself.

She hurried toward Jason and said, 'Sorry, man, she ain't back there. In fact one of her friends, the one she usually rides with, said she caught a ride about a half hour ago and left. Claims she wasn't feeling good." The young dancer moved in closer to Jason. "But if you want the real thing, someone much better than Dominique, come on and go to a back room with me. I'll give you a treat I guarantee you'll never forget."

"No thanks, sweetheart, but I appreciate the offer," Jason said, quite despondent.

"Why the fuck does everyone always want Dominique?" the girl asked rhetorically as she turned and stomped away.

Jason had less than a minute before the bouncer would probably seek him out and insist on the ten dollars cover charge. He didn't need that hassle so he headed toward the door. Before opening it, he turned and took one more look around the club, as if Dominique would suddenly appear. No such luck so he swung the door open and the smiling bouncer moved out of Jason's way to let him pass by. Once outside Jason took in a deep breath and released it. A smile then crossed his face. He had been taken by a damn stripper. That's how vulnerable he had become. His thoughts instantly snapped to Raquel. She would

Chapter 19

Theresa sat across from her sister Jacqueline at a table set to accommodate four waiting for their brother Cedric to show up. Cedric's telephone call to Theresa on Tuesday evening had set off a domino effect. He told her that they should meet for lunch because he had good news to share with her and also had someone special for her to meet. Since she had a relatively light schedule at work that week, she agreed. Theresa then called Jacqueline and shocked her with the news that their brother was back from San Francisco and living in Hollywood. When she told Jacqueline dead silence followed from the other end of the phone. She finally responded with anger. She couldn't understand why Cedric hadn't called her. After all she was the one who in the past had practically raised him and often protected him from the bullies in the neighborhood.

Theresa chose not to deal with Jacqueline's insecurities. Instead she invited her sister to join them for lunch and told Jacqueline that Cedric had some very good news to share with them. Someone he wanted them both to meet.

Theresa picked a restaurant near the UCLA campus. She still loved the college ambiance despite the fact it was a long ways from her office in south central Los Angeles. While they waited for Cedric and his friend, they both ordered drinks. The waiter placed them on the table.

"Would you ladies like to order now?"

"No, we'll wait for our other party," Theresa answered.

The waiter sashayed over to another table.

"Do you think he's gay?" Jacqueline asked as she sipped on her vodka martini.

"Who?" Theresa asked.

"The waiter, silly. Did you notice the way he just swished his little butt away from our table?"

Theresa frowned and glared at her sister. "What difference does it make?"

"None really. Not to me. But I just think this city is so full of those horrid people that you don't know who you can trust."

"What are you talking about, trust? Why do you think gay people can't be trusted?"

"Because that's a filthy habit. It's a sin against God. And they always want to compare their plight to that of Black folks in America."

Theresa wasn't sure she should pursue this with her sister or just change the subject. But since she did have a pretty good idea what Cedric had planned to share with her, and she'd invited an unsuspecting Jacqueline, maybe she should find out her sister's feelings on the matter.

"There are many similarities between the Black struggle and their struggle," she said.

Jacqueline took a pretty heavy gulp from her martini. "How do you figure that? They had a choice. Black folks didn't have a choice. Their sexual act is a sin against God. Being Black is not a sin against Him since He's the one who made us Black."

"But you would admit they've been discriminated against?" Theresa asked, assuming a lawyer's posture.

"For a good reason. They're sick and they're trying to pass their sickness on to other people."

"They're not trying to convert people to be homosexuals. And the way you're talking about them now is just how people used to talk about us."

"They had no right to treat our people the way they did."

"Are you saying they have a right to treat gays badly?"

"Certainly, because they're bad people." Jacqueline took another gulp from her drink, then waved to the waiter and ordered another.

"Their behavior doesn't touch your life so why would you want to judge them if it doesn't affect you?"

"I'm afraid it does affect Black people. What about all these brothers on...what do they call it, the down low or something like that? It's frightening to think that you or I could have gotten involved with one of those brothers and know nothing about how sick and dangerous they are."

Theresa now took a sip from her Chardonnay. "Those brothers don't consider themselves gay," she said. "They're in denial and, therefore, they are dangerous. But gays don't deny who they are and have been very careful with their sexual behavior since the AIDS epidemic."

"What do you call them if they're not gay? They're making love... oh no that sounds too good, men and women make love. They're fucking each other in the ass and that is some sick ass shit. That's why they're catching AIDS. God is punishing them for their perversion."

"Come on, Jacqueline, you telling me you haven't done anything that's just a little perverted?" They stopped talking while the waiter placed the drinks in front of them, gave them a hard stare and then walked away.

"What was that all about?" Jacqueline asked.

"Maybe he knew we were talking about him,"

"He couldn't have known, could he?" Jacqueline asked, looking in the waiter's direction.

"Girl, ease up." Theresa reached over and tapped her sister on the arm. She then smiled at her. "You're getting all uptight too early. Your time is coming to get uptight real soon."

"What are you talking about?"

"You'll see." Theresa needed to change the conversation knowing darn well all hell would probably break loose when Cedric arrived. "How is everything with you and Arthur?" she asked.

"Just fine. Since he got that job downtown, he's like a new man."

"You know that you owe Jason for that."

"I know. Do you think Jason approves of Arthur?"

"Girl, I don't know. Your brother is a hard one to read. What do you think? You were always much closer to him than me. So you should be able to read him."

"I thought I knew him pretty well until he went off and did this writing thing. What's that all about anyway?"

Theresa glanced at her watch and then looked up the street for Cedric. There was no sign of him. That little chicken had better show up. They needed to get this all out in the open and decide how they would deal with Cedric's sexual preference with Big Casey and Hazel. Big Casey with a gay son is like a racist with a Black son-in-law.

"Theresa, where's your mind?"

"I was just wondering what was taking Cedric so long. Maybe we got our restaurants mixed up."

"You know I'm just a little pissed off with him. Not contacting me when he got back in town. Do you know if he's talked with Jason?"

"I'm not sure." She knew Cedric had been over to Jason's apartment but had no reason to share that with Jacqueline and anger her even more.

"What's he been doing all this time in San Francisco? Do you know if he has a girlfriend?" Jacqueline paused for a couple of seconds and then placed both hands on her cheeks. "Oh God in Heaven forbid. I pray he hasn't gone gay."

Theresa almost choked on her wine. Maybe the idea of surprising Cedric by inviting Jacqueline wasn't such a good one after all.

"What if he is gay? Would it make a difference with you?" Theresa asked.

Jacqueline again took a gulp from her martini. She hesitantly said, "Well...well not really. I'd still love him. But I'd feel compelled to try to save him from his sinful ways."

That was the exact answer Theresa did not want to hear. Jacqueline irritated her with these sanctimonious platitudes.

"I can't believe you're so self-righteous all of a sudden. I remember when you used to sneak out of the house to spend time with that little hoodlum Hazel didn't approve of. And don't try and tell me you guys were studying history."

A broad smile broke across Jacqueline's face just as if she was recounting a pleasant experience from her past. "Girl, that boy was the bomb. You're right, we weren't studying history. I'm going to tell you he was phat. His thing was hung long and thick. Ump I get warm just thinking about him."

"So when did you become this godly person that can't tolerate other people's sexual ways?"

"That's when I was young and dumb. I have matured since then. And certain behavior is no longer acceptable. Being gay and cheating on your spouse is not acceptable."

"You've never cheated on Arthur?"

"Heavens no, girl. I would be stepping down a notch if I did. That is one well endowed man."

"I'm starting to get the idea you choose your men according to the size of their private parts."

"That way you'll always be satisfied."

"But not happy." Theresa perked up. Cedric and Aaron turned the corner and headed toward the restaurant. Her heart sank when she saw that sweet-looking white man holding Cedric's hand. She looked at Jacqueline as the two men approached from behind her. When Cedric saw the back of Jacqueline's head, he came to an abrupt stop. He glowered at Theresa and just stood there. Aaron turned and looked at him. He jerked at Cedric's hand and they slowly approached the table. Theresa feared that this time she'd overstepped her bounds and wished Jason was there to help bail her out of this one.

Cedric walked right up to the table and still holding Aaron's hand spoke to his sisters.

"Theresa, how are you?" He looked at Jacqueline. "Goodness, Jacqueline, you're looking good."

Jacqueline's jaw practically dropped to the ground. Her eyes riveted in on Cedric and Aaron holding hands. She turned and stared at Theresa.

"Aren't you going to speak?" Cedric asked with more defiance in his voice. Aaron jerked on his hand and cleared his throat. Cedric pulled his hand away from his lover and continued, "This is my friend Aaron Fitzpatrick. These are my sisters, Theresa and Jacqueline."

"My pleasure," Aaron said and reached out to shake Theresa's hand. Theresa took his hand and shook it briskly. He reached for Jacqueline's hand. She did not reciprocate. Her eyes stayed on Cedric.

"Please join us," Theresa said.

"Thank you." Cedric and Aaron took the two seats across from each other at the table.

"You have to forgive my sister," Theresa continued to carry the conversation and Jacqueline continued staring at Cedric. "It'll take her a little while to get used to seeing you again."

Cedric turned and faced Jacqueline square up. "Sister, if you're uncomfortable with this we can leave. Believe me I had no idea that you would be here." He confronted Theresa. "Why'd you do this? You know neither one of us was ready for this."

Awkwardly Jacqueline picked up the menu and stared at it.

"Cedric, is there something wrong?" Aaron asked.

"No, not really. It's just going to take my sister a little time to get used to seeing me again. It's been over a year."

"Oh well, you work this out." Aaron picked up the menu and began reading it.

"What the hell do you think you're doing?" Jacqueline shouted and slammed the menu back down on the table. The other three jumped from the abruptness of her actions.

"Easy, Jacqueline," Theresa warned her sister.

They got a moment's reprieve as the waiter approached the table and took drink orders from Cedric and Aaron and another round for Jacqueline and Theresa. Jacqueline watched as the waiter walked away. "Now I know the reason for the questions," she said looking directly across at Theresa.

"Look, you two," Theresa started in. "I guess I should have said something to both of you, but you are brother and sister and remember what you said earlier, Jacqueline."

"Yeah sure, that's before I knew my brother would show up with the fairy queen."

"That's enough!" Cedric shouted at Jacqueline. "You have no right to talk about my friend that way. I think we should leave." Cedric sprang out of the chair and Aaron did the same.

"Wait a minute," Theresa pleaded. "Come on, we're family. Let's talk this out."

"When my sister can learn to respect me and be polite to my company, then we can talk."

"I'll always love you, Cedric, because you're family, but don't expect me to respect your lifestyle and that thing that is with you. And by the way, please stay away from sisters. It's you brothers screwing these white boys that's giving AIDS to our sisters."

"Jacqueline, stop!" Theresa shouted. People sitting at the other tables began to stare.

Cedric leaned down and kissed Theresa on the cheek. "I guess like father like daughter." Still holding hands, he and Aaron walked away.

Theresa watched as they disappeared around the corner. She then looked over at her sister.

"Is everything all right?" the waiter asked. Theresa was so angry she hadn't seen him walk up to the table with the drinks.

"Yes, everything is fine, but I don't think we'll be having lunch today. And you can take those drinks back. I'll pay for them. Just bring us the bill."

The waiter turned and walked away.

"You mean you can't have lunch with me just because I don't condone that filth?" Jacqueline asked with some anger in her voice.

Theresa snapped her head around and zeroed in on Jacqueline. "That was absolutely unnecessary."

"How can you tolerate that kind of behavior from our brother?"

Theresa watched as the waiter headed inside the restaurant. She then gulped down the rest of her wine. "When Arthur was beating up on you and you wanted family to be there, we were.

Both Jason and I were there to support you. Now when your baby brother needs you, look how you act. He's reaching out to family because that's the way we were raised. Hazel and Big Casey would be ashamed of you because of the way you treated your brother."

Jacqueline now tossed down the remainder of her martini. "They'd be more ashamed of their son, walking down the street holding hands with some white faggot."

"Jacqueline, stop, please, before I get up and walk away from you."

"Maybe that's what you need to do. Remember I am the oldest and you'd better stop right now."

The waiter hurried up to the table, dropped the bill right in the center then practically ran the other way. Theresa picked it up, pulled out forty dollars and tossed it on the table.

"Whatever you do, don't tell mother about this," she said to Jacqueline in a more somber tone. "She'd tell Big Casey and then all hell would break loose. I think we all need to wait awhile then get with Jason and figure out how to break this to them."

"I agree, but you do know that they have to be told. At some point Cedric has to come back into the family," Jacqueline said, also having cooled down.

"Let's get out of here." Theresa stood up and Jacqueline followed. "I need to get back to work." The two sisters hugged but with some distance between them, turned and went their separate ways.

Chapter 20

After one week of doing nothing but inputting numbers into a computer and taking very long lunch breaks, Arthur finally decided to confront Big Casey. His father-in-law was avoiding him and Arthur began to wonder if he'd been transferred to the main office because of his talent or because he was married to Jacqueline. He was excluded from the front office where all the big shots were housed and the decisions made. He doubted that they even knew he was there most of the time. As he sat at his desk drinking a second cup of coffee and staring at the traffic on the 110 Freeway, he made up his mind that Big Casey would see him or else. In the meantime he needed to make sure everything was set for later on that afternoon. He snatched his cell phone and dialed a number.

The phone rang three times and finally a female's voice on the other end said, "Good morning, Arthur."

"Elizabeth, how you doing?"

"Fine now that I've heard your voice. You know I'm getting a little fed up with you having to get up in the middle of the night and always go home."

"I know, baby, but right now you have to understand that other woman is the reason I can pay your rent and keep you in pretty things."

"I don't care about that bitch, Arthur."

A smile spread across Arthur's face. He loved the idea that women would probably fight for his treasure piece.

"I don't like it no more than you do, sweetheart. It won't be long now."

"You keep saying that, but you don't do nothing but come over here, fuck me, and run home to her. I know you ain't fucking her when you get home. Not the way I wear your ass out."

"You right about that." Arthur again smiled. "Ain't no way on God's earth that I want her after laying up with you." Arthur heard footsteps outside the door. He knew it probably wasn't Big Casey but why take the chance? He lowered his voice and continued, "Look, sweetheart, I'm leaving out of here about three o'clock. So I'll be there before four and we'll have a few quality hours today."

"You know I need some money, don't you, Arthur?"

"Yes, you told me last night. I'll have a few dollars for you."

"Few?" Elizabeth's tone suddenly changed. "It better be more than a few."

"You know what I mean. I never just bring you a few."

"I know you don't, sweetheart." Elizabeth's voice again softened. "I'll see you about four. And be ready cause I'll be well rested."

"Damn, I can hardly wait."

By eleven o'clock Arthur had made five trips to the front, peering in Big Casey's office to see if he was in and if he could catch his attention. Each time he failed to even catch the attention of the secretary. On the sixth trip he charged up to Dorian's desk right outside Big Casey's office. She looked at him with a rather startled expression on her face. She spoke first.

"Is there something wrong, Arthur?"

When he first charged up to the desk Arthur knew exactly what he wanted to say and accomplish. But now confronted with Dorian's dour expression he backed off.

"I was hoping that I might have the chance to talk with Mr. Mitchell."

"Is there some particular reason you need to see him? And have you talked with Mr. Bagley? I understand he's your immediate supervisor."

"No I haven't!" Arthur shot back at her. Why was she trying to irritate him? He shouldn't have to report to Howard or anyone else. He was Big Casey's son-in-law and that should count for something. "This is a matter I'd personally like to discuss with Mr. Mitchell."

"Mr. Mitchell has two representatives from Martin Marietta in his office. They're talking about using us as a major subcontractor on an overseas project. After the meeting they're going to lunch and I just don't know when he'll be back in the office. I can set you up for a meeting with him tomorrow morning at nine-thirty. But I'll have to inform Mr. Bagley of the meeting in case he wants to sit in."

"Never mind. I'll use another way to see him," Arthur said smugly. He didn't want to play the family card in front of Dorian, but she'd pissed him off.

"I'm sure you will," she replied and returned to her typing.

Arthur stomped back down to his office, his temperature rising as he thought about Big Casey meeting with business representatives from Martin Marietta and not including him. He probably had those white boy flunkies in there with him. But he ignored the brother when it came to including staff in meetings that could result in million dollar contracts. Typical of all these damn minority contractors. They use their minority status to get the contracts under the guise they're going to hire minorities, but give all the lucrative and important positions to white boys. Big Casey wasn't anything more than a front for white boys who really controlled the company. Arthur sat back down at his desk and banged his fist on top of it.

He swung his chair around and again stared out at the freeway. The traffic was still backed up as far as he could see. Sitting there staring out at the traffic congestion depressed him. Is that what his future with the company would be, running fucking numbers into computers and staring out at traffic and smog all day long? He understood why Big Casey's sons bailed out on him and did their own thing. Maybe that's what he should think about doing. But no company would pay him the kind of money he made there. What the fuck, why should he complain? He really had it made. Push the numbers. Stare out at traffic and make good money. Not a bad life at all. So why was he tripping? Arthur glanced at his watch. Eleven-thirty and if he left now no one would even know he was gone. Last night he'd picked up a bag of weed that was the real bomb. He'd rolled four joints before he left that morning. He figured he could sneak out of the office and spend the afternoon with Elizabeth. Make her earn that free rent money she collected from him every first of the month. Arthur bounced up and headed out of the office. If Big Casey and the other members of management treated him with such disrespect, he would at least get some compensation for their contemptuous behavior.

By twelve noon the smog was so thick Arthur couldn't see the San Gabriel Mountains tucked tightly behind Pasadena. He sped along the freeway on his way to Elizabeth's. On days like this he was glad he lived in Malibu with a fresh ocean breeze all the time. Arthur was determined to never live anywhere but near the ocean. The only drawback, he couldn't have his other women friends over to his place in Malibu. What a hell of a playboy's apartment his place would make. But there was Jacqueline with her "do you love me"ass. Hell Arthur wasn't sure who he loved, but damn well knew what he loved and that was good sex on a Monday afternoon and a good joint in between the sex. Elizabeth was the perfect piece for that afternoon. An afternoon of wallowing in sexual ecstasy.

Arthur finally reached the entrance off Wilshire Boulevard to Elizabeth's apartment and pulled his Mercedes into the empty stall he paid an additional hundred dollars a month to have available whenever he showed up. He'd already smoked a joint in the car and the weed had taken him to another level. Right then and there everything was alright with him as he climbed the ten steps to her second story apartment and pushed the buzzer. His entire body felt mellow and he knew how good the loving would be once Elizabeth took a couple hits of the joint. Damn, it was taking her a long time to answer the door. Momentarily he entertained the possibility that she might have company. Even though they never discussed that possibility, he had to acknowledge she was single and forced to spend a lot of time alone. There was always the possibility that she had someone else.

Arthur straightened up and this time leaned real hard on

the buzzer. After all he didn't call and give her warning he was coming over early. But why the fuck should he have to? He paid the rent there and, for that, could expect a certain amount of loyalty. Despite the mellow mood from the marijuana he was getting pissed off. Not so much from the possibility another man might be in the apartment, but because that would screw up his afternoon and definitely destroy his high. Finally, he heard someone stirring inside. He felt relieved. Now he could relax and get back into his mood.

"Who is it?" Elizabeth called from the other side of the door.

"It's me, Arthur!" he shouted.

"Arthur, what are you doing here this time of the day?" she asked still not opening the door.

"I'll tell you if you open the damn door."

Another pause and then he heard the lock turning and finally the door swung open.

"Hi, baby," Elizabeth whispered as she opened the door all the way and let him in.

A smile covered Arthur's entire face as he stared at Elizabeth in a black negligee that clung to her milky white skin. Her long blond hair flowed down over her shoulders and her full breasts were partially exposed.

"Damn, baby, you look good," Arthur whispered and then kissed her. "But why you take so damn long to answer the door?"

"I was busy."

"Doing what?"

"You'll see. Come on back into the bedroom." Elizabeth grabbed him by the hand and led him through the living room into the bedroom.

He reached the bedroom door and came to an abrupt stop. Another female smiled at him from her position on the bed, wearing only black panties and a black bra. She had short black hair and caramel skin with beautiful hazel eyes. He glared at the woman on the bed and then at Elizabeth.

"Don't look so damn surprised," Elizabeth said. "Surely you didn't think that I spent all my days just sitting here watching television?" She grabbed Arthur by the arm and led him over to the bed. "Arthur, this is Indria, my very dear friend. You haven't seen her at the club 'cause I don't believe you've been back since she started dancing."

Arthur didn't know if he should extend his hand to her or just jump right on her and go to work on one of those luscious breasts protruding out of her bra. Instead he did nothing but continue to stand there somewhat dumbfounded.

"Arthur, are you all right?" Elizabeth asked. "I thought it was about time I brought a little reality to this relationship and let you know who I really am."

Arthur had regained some of his composure. He stared at the woman on the bed. She adjusted her position so that her back leaned on the backboard and her legs were spread eagle.

"I have to say this is a hell of a lot of reality," Arthur finally said.

"Can you handle it, baby? It's all good and it's going to be especially good to you." Elizabeth loosened Arthur's tie and unbuttoned his shirt. "Get out of these clothes, baby." She unbuckled his belt and unzipped his pants. "I told Indria about that big ass thing you got between your legs. And she sure wants to see it."

Arthur allowed his pants to fall down to his ankles. He then unbuttoned his shirt and tossed it on the floor. The thought of things to come brought his penis straight up and bulging in his underwear. He'd done a lot of crazy things in his thirty-three years, but he'd never had two women at the same time. He dreamt of doing it, but for some reason it had always escaped him. He smiled as he thought, not this time. Arthur remembered he'd rolled four joints. Nothing would be better than to smoke another joint and roll on the bed with two super fine freaks, one white and one black.

"Come on, baby, you going to get with us?" Indria seductively whispered. She crawled on her hands and knees to the end of the king size bed. She turned on her side and smiled at Arthur.

"You get high?" he asked Indria. He already knew Elizabeth did.

"You bet I do," Indria replied. "Makes the loving that much better. You have something to smoke?" she asked as she sat up in the bed. Elizabeth sat down next to Indria and began to suck on her breast. Arthur was now hard as a rock.

"Yeah, I brought some joints," Arthur said nervously.

"Joints?" Indria shot back. Elizabeth now slid her head down between Indria's legs, pushed her panties to the side and began to suck her. "Damn," she said leaning back on her arms and extending her legs in the air. She smiled and looked directly into Arthur's eyes.

Arthur wasn't sure what he should do next. How do you join into something as crazy as this? He stood there motionless, almost suspended in time, and was so damn excited if he touched one of the women he'd probably explode all over them. He needed desperately to smoke a joint in order to get control of his emotions. But Indria had frowned at the mention of a joint. What did she have in mind? Indria stared at his crotch. Arthur wanted them to reverse roles and have Elizabeth on him because he knew how good she was. But first he had to get hold of himself. Indria had tilted her head backwards with her eyes closed. The two of them were into each other just as though Arthur wasn't standing in front of them. He leaned down, grabbed his shirt and took out one of the joints.

"Uhhum," he cleared his throat, trying to get their attention.

Elizabeth rolled over on her back and smiled at him. Indria came back up into an upright position.

"Like I asked before, anyone for getting high?" He held the joint in his hand so they could see it. He had to take control of this situation. After all he was the man. Arthur had to control these two freaks just like he controlled Jacqueline.

Indria and Elizabeth shot glances at each other and began to laugh. Elizabeth got up and stood next to Arthur. She took her soft hand and placed it inside his underwear. She began to stroke him.　　　　　Indria spoke up as she watched Elizabeth. "Baby, I'm sorry but we don't smoke no poor folk's drugs."

Arthur found it difficult to concentrate. Elizabeth's soft hand wrapped around the shaft of his penis and, working an up and down stroke, had him panting like a little pet.

"What do you smoke then?" He was ready to do anything that could possibly enhance this wonderful feeling.

Indria grabbed her bag from the side of the bed. She pulled out a small glass pipe and also a cellophane bag with a solid white substance inside. She took a piece of it and placed it on the stemmed end of the pipe.

"Is that crack?" Arthur asked.

Indria smiled. "No, baby. Crack is another cheap ass high. This is pure free-based cocaine. The best high in the world. Make a girl want to act like a freak all night. You game?"

Elizabeth suddenly stopped rubbing on Arthur and sat back down on the bed next to Indria. They both took a turn on the pipe. As soon as they released the cocaine smoke into the air he could tell it took them to another place. He needed to go there with them so he could get all they had to offer. He'd never desired cocaine because of its addictive nature. But if he was to get the full impact of pleasure these two beautiful women had promised him, he couldn't hold back.

Arthur slid his underwear over the top of his feet and kicked them toward the corner. He sat on the bed between Elizabeth and Indria.

Elizabeth slid her head down between his legs. Indria handed him the pipe and lit the end with the cocaine rock. She said, "Inhale, baby, hold it a few seconds, then release it. And then baby go off to paradise."

Chapter 21

Jason felt satisfied with the progress he'd made on his manuscript. Since that night when he'd driven over to the Black Zebra, only to be stood up by Dominique, he'd dedicated his time to writing. He'd talked with Raquel on a couple of occasions, but fought off the temptation to interrupt his writing and spend a night with her. He really did like her a lot, but that certain fire didn't burn deep inside him for her. Dominique had him going and because of that he couldn't allow Raquel all the way in.

And anyway, the first year was almost up and that meant he had to finish writing, do all the editing and find a publisher in just a little over twelve months. That would be a very tall order. If necessary he could talk Big Casey into publishing it himself. Many good Black writers were forced to go the self-publishing route first. His mind wandered back to a conversation with a couple of brothers who had done just that. Now they had publishers for their works. Bottom line is that he had to stick to a discipline for the next four months.

Earlier in the week he'd finished the scene with Hula Jack telling the other slaves the story of Nat Turner. This evening he'd been writing about the last leg of the slaves' journey to their new homes in the deep South. They were in the hole of a Mississippi gambling boat being transported from Memphis to Natchez. He planned a scene down in the hole where the boiler explodes. It doesn't harm any of the white customers up top, but does kill five of the slaves trapped in the fire below.

As usual Jason had procrastinated a good deal of the evening. Somehow his mind kept wandering off to Dominique and would he ever get a chance to take her out. Why she affected him in such a strong manner he didn't know. Hell, he hadn't even kissed her and felt this way. It couldn't be her beauty since Jason had a history of dating the prettiest women at USC and Angela was a strikingly beautiful woman.

Jason yawned and stared at the clock on his desk. It read 1:30 in the morning. He then stared at the phone, hoping it might ring and it would be Dominique asking him for another ride home. But he doubted seriously that she'd ever call. Maybe she expected him to call her and find out what happened. Should he call and insist on an explanation for last week's behavior? She would probably laugh at him so it was best to leave well enough alone and keep his eyes on the prize.

Tomorrow evening, in a special session, the Leimert Park Writers Group would critique his first four chapters and, given his previous confrontation with them, they'd probably be extremely critical of his work. He didn't mind criticism, after all the first lesson he learned about writing was that writers must have a thick skin. If you have other writers critique your manuscript and assume all you will get is praise, then you are in the wrong business. He didn't expect adulation, but only hoped that he would hear constructive criticism and not just bullshit. Judging from his previous meeting with the group, he wasn't sure what to expect.

Again glancing at the clock, he thought about quitting for the night and starting out fresh in the morning. But he really wasn't sleepy and could probably knock off another ten pages. At least try to finish the scene when the overseer discovers Sally has been providing food to her elderly father who had a year ago been turned off the plantation because of his age. Jason would take his time and get this right because this was one of the most touching scenes in the entire novel.

Just as he began to concentrate on his writing the phone rang. Not a good time to break his concentration. The ideas flowed freely and that writer's voice prodded him to ignore the phone and keep writing. But it had to be an emergency. Anyone calling that late didn't call for a friendly discussion. Calls at that time always meant trouble. He tossed his pen on the desk and grabbed the phone.

"Yeah, what's up?" he asked.

"Are you in a nasty mood?" Dominique asked almost in a whisper.

Jason had slouched down in the chair, but now came to a rigid and upright position.

"Who is this?" he asked even though he knew.

"You've forgotten about me already?" Dominique asked. "I'm kind of disappointed. This is Dominique. You remember me?"

Jason couldn't help but smile. "Oh yes, the young lady who called desperately needing a ride, then stood me up."

"You showed up that night? I didn't really think you were coming so when I got the opportunity to get a ride, I jumped on it."

"Yeah, I bet that's not all you jumped on," Jason said sarcastically and waited for a response but there was none. He'd made her angry and didn't want to do that. Maybe she told him the truth and really didn't believe he'd show up. "I'm sorry, that was mean. But I was disappointed coming all the way over there and you just left." Still a silence. "Hello, you still there?"

"Yes, I'm here," Dominique replied. "Since you're irritated maybe we should just hang up."

"No, no, don't do that. Is there something wrong? I mean it's two o'clock in the morning and people usually don't call at this time for small talk."

"There is in a way," Dominique answered. "I'm about to get off and sometimes I call a cab. But this one jerk has been hanging around the club all night long, and I just need to have a man pick me up so he'll think I have a boyfriend or a husband."

"You mean you don't have a boyfriend?"

"No I don't. I don't have time for that kind of nonsense. But in times like this a man's presence really helps. So I was hoping that you would be a real sweetheart and help me out. And this time I won't offer to pay you."

"Don't you guys have a bouncer or someone to protect you

all when you leave the club?"

"Never mind!" she snapped. "I'm sorry I bothered you. I won't do it again."

"Wait, wait!" Jason shouted into the phone with a bit of desperation in his voice. He prepared to hear the click, but it didn't happen. "I can pick you up, but it'll take about an hour."

"That's fine. I'll be in front of the entrance to the club at three o'clock. And please be there."

"I will," Jason assured her. He wanted to add that she should make sure she was there, but he'd almost lost her with his earlier smart remark. So this time he refrained. "I will be on time."

"Thank you," Dominique said and hung up the phone.

Jason glanced at his watch. It read 2:15. He had forty-five minutes to get to the Northeast side of town. He hadn't shaved all day, and had on an old pair of jeans with a USC sweatshirt and tennis shoes. There was no time to shave and change clothes, so she would have to take him just as he was. Why all the excitement when this woman had already stood him up just last week? He'd accept her weak explanation and act like last week never happened.

But if she pulled the same stunt tonight, he'd definitely cross her from his list. Suddenly the phone rang again. His heart sank and he felt a lump in his throat. She was calling to cancel. He looked at the caller ID and a different kind of apprehension grabbed him. Jacqueline's name illuminated on the panel and the only reason she'd be calling this late would have to do with Arthur. If he answered, it would probably hinder his plans to pick up Dominique. But if he didn't, and something happened to his sister, he would never forgive himself. Sometimes being the oldest was a drag and one hell of a burden. He snatched the phone from its cradle.

"Hello, Jacqueline, what's going on?"

Jacqueline sounded hysterical. "It's after two and Arthur's not home."

"Jacqueline, what do you want me to do about it? Hell, I have no idea where he is."

"Don't you know where he hangs out? I know sometimes he goes to those clubs. Can you go check? Or maybe he's hurt or in the hospital."

"Jacqueline, calm down. I haven't the slightest idea what clubs he goes to. And if he's hurt the hospital will notify you and if he's been arrested at least you know he's safe." Jason glanced at his watch. Almost two-thirty. Much as he hated to do it, he had to cut this short.

"Please, Jason, you have to help me find my husband. I'm worried sick."

Jason could hear her crying. He knew she wasn't so much worried as pissed off.

"I tell you what. I have to make a run for about an hour. I'll call you when I get back. If he isn't home by then I'll call the police."

"You promise me, you're going to call me?"

"Yes, Jacqueline, and don't you call Big Casey. If he has any idea that Arthur is mistreating you, he'll fire him. And that'll make your situation worse than what it already is."

"I wouldn't dare call Daddy. But please call me when you get back. If he's not home by then, I'll be worried sick."

"I'll call you, okay?" Jason glanced at his watch. "Now I have to go. You alright?"

"Yes, I'll be alright until I hear from you."

"Good, call you as soon as I get back." He hung up the phone and rushed out the door.

u

Jason turned into a practically empty parking lot at the Black Zebra. It was after three o'clock and the club had emptied out. A few customers mingled around their cars, probably hoping they would be able to catch one of the girls who might need a ride and luck up on a late night date. He studied the men while passing by on his way to the front entrance. He speculated on the creep that might be stalking Dominique and shook his head in disgust as he tired to imagine the fear a woman must experience when attacked by some maniac unable to control his urges. Jason also wondered how Dominique could deal with going to that back room and not knowing if the man she is with is some kind of sick pervert.

Jason pulled up in front of the entrance but did not see Dominique. She probably was still inside, especially with a bunch of men standing outside. He put the car in park and relaxed in his seat. This time he would not try to go inside and find her. One time was enough. He laid his head back on the headrest and looked over towards the door and still no action. Why wasn't she coming out and how long should he wait? He glanced at his watch. Already three-thirty and no movement. He was just too damn nice and too easy. Jason needed to take on Elliott's attitude about women. If he did, he wouldn't be sitting outside a club this late at night waiting for a woman who over the past eight hours had probably helped at least a dozen men climax by dancing practically naked in front of them. It was just too much for him to handle.

Jason started the car and the door to the club swung open. Dominique walked outside with a half dozen other women. She looked gorgeous with her hair pulled back in a bun and makeup perfectly applied. Her sweater and tight jeans with heels accentuated her shapely body. No wonder some nut was trying to get next to her. Jason looked over at the men standing by the cars to see if any of them moved toward the entrance. They didn't, in fact they remained in place. A couple of the girls waved at the men and headed their way. Dominique stopped momentarily right outside the door. Jason opened the passenger side door and waved at her. She spotted him, smiled and headed toward the car.

She slid into the passenger seat, turned and stared into Jason's eyes. A large smile covered her face. "What a beautiful car. I never knew I was dealing with a man of such means."

"Not really," Jason rejoined. "Let's just say I'm very careful how I spend my money."

"I see. I'm still impressed."

"Well, Ms. Impressed, where am I taking you?" Jason pulled away from the curb and headed down the long driveway. He glanced at the men who had been standing by their cars when he pulled up. A couple of them were hugging two of the girls who had hurried down toward them when they broke off from Dominique. The third member of the group stared at Jason as he drove by. Evidently he was the one who had planned on being with her.

Dominique leaned near Jason and waved at her friends. She then relaxed back in the seat. "I'm really hungry," she said. "Feel like getting something to eat or is it too late for you?"

"Not at all. In fact I was just about to invite you to have a snack or coffee or something."

"There is a nice late night restaurant up Wilshire Boulevard not far from my apartment complex. That'd be fine with me."

"You got it, let me entertain you." Jason opened up a middle section compartment and pulled out a number of CDs. "Take your choice."

"You can choose," she said and laid her head back on the headrest.

"What's your preference?" Jason asked.

"Nothing loud. Something soft and relaxing. I usually listen to jazz after I get off work."

Jason dug through the CDs with one hand while also keeping his eyes on the road. He'd just made his way onto the 110 Freeway and the entire Los Angeles area was still all lit up. Looking at the city while going south on the freeway was thrilling. Los Angeles was beautiful and, looking at the symmetry of the buildings and all the creativity that seemed to be all around them, brought on a natural high for Jason. Having Dominique in the car with him made the high even more pleasurable.

He found the perfect music for the moment, inserted the CD in the holder, caught a quick glimpse of Dominique who was resting her head back, and he smiled as the smoothly rapturous sounds of Miles Davis Blue Dolphin Street poured out of the player. All negative thoughts and questions he'd entertained

Chapter 22

A slender young lady escorted Jason and Dominique to a table next to a window with a view of Wilshire Boulevard, still buzzing with traffic at four o'clock in the morning. The restaurant was also crowded with late night partiers grabbing a bite to eat before they retired for the evening and early risers who were grabbing breakfast before going on to work. Jason sat on one side of the booth designed to hold four, and Dominique on the other side. They had been quiet since Jason had put the Miles Davis CD on in the car. In fact he was certain that Dominique had fallen off to sleep. Now they sat across from each other studying the menu.

Finally the waitress approached their table, placed water in front of them and asked, "Are you ready to order?"

"Not yet," Jason answered.

"Take your time," the waitress instructed and walked away.

"Made up your mind on what you want?" Jason asked.

"Yes, a salad."

"You sure that's all you want?"

"I'm sure."

Jason waved the waitress back over to the table. "A salad for the lady and I'll take a hamburger. And two cokes, please."

"Make one a diet coke," Dominique added.

"You got it," the waitress replied and hurried off.

"You must not be very hungry," Jason said. He picked up his glass and took a sip of water.

"Oh, I really am." Dominique also took a sip of water.

"Why didn't you order something that'll stick to your stomach? Like a hamburger."

"Because I'm a strict vegetarian. And besides, I have to keep this shape so good-looking men like you will keep coming to the club to see me."

"You're kidding. You're a vegetarian." Jason chose to ignore the second part of her comment. He didn't want to be reminded of her profession.

"I hardly ever kid. I am very serious about everything I do. I don't have much time for kidding."

Jason slightly frowned. She couldn't be serious. "Why are you serious about everything?"

"Life is very serious and every minute you spend kidding around is a lost opportunity to do something meaningful."

Again the waitress approached the table and placed the drinks and silverware wrapped in napkins in front of them. Without saying a word, she turned and hurried away. Jason hardly noticed her as he concentrated his attention on Dominique. He wondered about a woman who never found time to kid.

"Don't you think people need to loosen up or they'll explode?" he asked.

"Yeah, well I deal with a bunch of human beings that all they do is loosen up."

Jason grabbed the wrapped silverware and removed it from the napkin. He placed the fork on one side and the spoon and knife on the other.

"The fork and knife are supposed to go on the same side and the spoon is alone on the other side," Dominique instructed.

Jason glanced over at her then readjusted the silverware. He smiled. "Is smiling and laughing okay in your world?" he asked.

Dominique smiled back at Jason. "You bet it is." She reached across the table and took his hand between hers. "I guess kidding around is okay, too, at the right time. I just don't have the chance to kid at all, and when I smile it has to be phony for some fool who really thinks I'm smiling because I like him." She squeezed Jason's hand tighter. "But I am smiling now because I want to."

Her touch, the soft words and deep penetrating look into his eyes made Jason nervous. He took his left hand, grabbed the glass and gulped down more water. His feelings were melting all over the table and he was becoming like jelly for this woman. He needed to back it off a little, but didn't know how. She definitely made an impression with him.

"When's the last time you been back to East St. Louis?" he asked.

Dominique abruptly snatched her hand back and sat very rigid in the chair.

"It's been quite awhile. I don't go back there very often."

Jason knew he'd done something wrong. But how could asking about her visit home be wrong?

"Is your family in East St. Louis?"

"My mother's there. I never knew my father."

"I'm sorry to hear that."

"Why? I didn't miss much."

From her tone Jason discerned this not to be a subject she wanted to pursue. It was becoming clear Dominique was a complicated lady. The waitress brought their meals and that saved him having to search for another subject to discuss that probably would end up creating even more questions about her past. Jason took a large bite out of his sandwich while watching Dominique delicately nibble at her salad. He'd been with many beautiful women in his life, but she surpassed all of them. He savored everything about her. How she held her fork, how she sipped from her drink and, most importantly, how she would stare over at him and neither of them needed to speak. Her smooth smile said it all.

"Sometimes it's a good sign when two people can just enjoy each other's company without having to say anything," she said.

"Yeah that's true. But in a way it makes you feel kind of nervous."

"Why?"

"Because when you're not talking you kind of feel like you're not communicating."

Dominique put her fork down and reared back in her seat. Again that beautiful encompassing smile spread across her face.

"Jason, there's more than one way to communicate," she said. "I'm sure you know that. For example people communicate with their eyes. And when you look directly into someone's eyes and keep that contact, you really are communicating with that person's inner self. It's like two souls in communication with each other. Like they're searching for something more meaningful than mere words can provide."

"You're not afraid to get that deep into another person's inner self?" Jason asked as he took another bite from his hamburger. He didn't necessarily buy into this inner self kind of conversation. But he did find her mysterious and never imagined a dancer capable of any kind of reflective thought. He enjoyed it with her.

She took a small bite from the salad and continued. "How can you ever get to know the real individual unless you dig deep beyond the surface?"

"I don't know. I guess I never gave it much thought."

Dominique leaned forward and reached for Jason's hands. He gladly accommodated her.

"I can't believe a brother as decent as you...a brother who'll go into the back room and not get all stupid with his behavior, hasn't explored the deeper parts of who you really are?"

Jason allowed his hands to go limp as she squeezed them. Her palms were soft just as he imagined her entire body would be.

"I guess I do when I'm writing. In fact I know I do."

Dominique's eyes lit up. "Writing? You're a writer?"

"Well, I want to be. I'm working on my first novel right now. In fact that's what I was doing when you called. I'm at a crossroads with the story. And I really believe I was about to make it over those roads this evening."

"I'm sorry. I didn't know. If I had, I certainly wouldn't have called you."

"That's okay. I've imagined this moment with you since the time I first saw you in the club."

"How sweet for you to say that, but next time you have to promise to tell me. I'd never do anything to interrupt your creativity." Dominique finished her drink. "We should go. I need to get some rest and maybe you can still get some writing done."

Jason finished his coke, grabbed the check the waitress had earlier left on the table. "We can go, but first you have to promise that we'll get together. You told me you don't date customers that you've danced for. You've never danced for me, so you can't really consider me a customer."

"Seems as though I heard this line once before." Dominique slid out of the booth and stood up. Jason also stood up.

"Well what's it going to be?" he asked.

"I guess we can arrange that. But first let's get out of here."

"You got it." They headed out of the restaurant.

This time Jason made the choice of music as they continued up Wilshire Boulevard toward Dominique's apartment. He slid the Barry White CD into the player and moments later the smooth sounds of "There's no better music than love making music," filled the car.

"Are you trying to be suggestive?" Dominique asked. She had her head again resting on the headrest with her eyes closed.

"No, not at all," Jason replied without looking in her direction. "Barry White always seems to fit the mood when you're driving at five in the morning through the most romantic part of the city with a beautiful woman. I also love Freddie Jackson for setting a mood."

"Thank you, sir." Dominique leaned over and kissed him on the cheek. "To place me in the same category with Barry White and Freddie Jackson and romance is a compliment."

"Are you a romantic?"

"Aren't all women romantics?"

"I don't know. I can't get inside a woman's head." Jason momentarily took his eyes off the road and quickly looked over at Dominique.

"Don't you have to create romance in your characters?"

"Yes I do. But the best I can do with my female characters is express romance through their actions. I'd never profess to be able to express a female's thought processes. They're just a little too deep for a male writer."

"Maybe I'll have to give you special training in the thought processes of the female species."

"That'll work," Jason said. "Now I have a couple important questions for you."

"Ask away."

"I know Dominique is probably not your real name. So would you like to share it with me and second how about our next date?"

"I guess I can handle both those questions. My name is Natalie."

"How about your last name?"

"Let's just leave it at Natalie. And yes I would love to go out with you. I don't usually work on Wednesdays and Thursdays. So you pick the day."

"Well, Natalie, how about Wednesday?"

"That sounds good. Oh, here's my apartment building." Dominique pointed to a large apartment complex Jason was about to pass.

Jason hit his brakes and made a hard right turn into the apartment complex. They both laughed.

"I'm sorry. I was so absorbed in your conversation I just got carried away," Dominique apologized.

"Apology accepted as long as you were absorbed in me."

"Is there anyone else? My apartment is up here on the right."

Jason was all smiles as he made the right turn and continued down the driveway. Suddenly, his smile dissipated as he noticed the Mercedes parked in one of the stalls he passed. He caught the license plate and knew it was Arthur's specialized plates. That explained why he hadn't gotten home a couple of hours ago when Jacqueline had called.

"You can let me off right up here," Dominique said snapping him back to his own reality. "I do appreciate your picking me up and I would offer to pay you but I know you'd only get upset."

"Yeah, okay, that's right," Jason said. His mind was still on Arthur's Mercedes. He had to probe to find out if Dominique knew anything about his brother-in-law's transgressions. "Do a lot of women live in this complex?" he asked.

A surprised expression crossed Dominique's face. "Yes, as a matter of fact there are. A lot of dancers as a matter of fact. We all share apartments. Usually three of us to an apartment."

"Do you have roommates?"

"I do, but why all of the questions?"

"I was just wondering. This is a pretty nice complex."

"I'd better get on inside." Dominique took her fingers, kissed them on her lips, and then pressed them to Jason's lips. "So we are on for Wednesday?"

"Yes we are," he answered. His mind was still on Arthur's Mercedes parked at the unit he'd passed a few minutes ago.

"What's wrong?" Dominique asked. "Are you all right? You sure you want to go out on Wednesday?"

"I've never been more certain of anything in this life. I'll pick you up about noon."

"So early. What are we going to do?"

"That's a surprise but you will definitely enjoy yourself."

"I'm sure." Dominique got out of the car, turned and smiled one final time, then hurried up the stairs to her apartment.

Jason watched her until she entered the apartment. For a moment he wondered if Arthur was in that same apartment. Then he wondered what to tell Jacqueline. He started out of the complex and back down Wilshire Boulevard. He was not quite prepared to tell his sister that he saw her husband's car parked in front of an apartment complex, probably a dancer's apartment. Chances were that he was engaged in all kinds of wild sexual acts that, if Jacqueline knew about them, would send her to the hospital.

Chapter 23

Between the crack cocaine high and the two women taking turns ravishing his body with every sexual act possible, Arthur knew he was in paradise. He'd long ago lost track of time. The thought of Jacqueline never entered his mind and this shit was so much fun, he didn't give a damn that he had to be at work in just three hours. He could do this all day and as long as he had some cash and a credit card to go get more money, he'd stay right there in paradise.

From the bedroom, he heard Elizabeth and Indria in the kitchen cooking some cocaine into rocks to smoke. He'd never done cocaine before and had to work up enough nerve to smoke a little marijuana every once in a while. A joint had always been sufficient for him. But now Arthur had graduated to a new high, much more euphoric and pleasurable than a joint. He craved more coke to smoke. He'd already experienced three climaxes and chances of him getting another erection for a while were slim.

Stretched out on the bed with no clothes on, he could hear the two women whispering and giggling. So this is the lifestyle dancers lead. No wonder they had to resort to dancing in the nude. No way could they make enough money to afford their habit if they had a regular job. And this shit could definitely put them in the mood and give them the energy to stay up all night and dance all day. He wasn't a bit sleepy and anxious for some more action. Maybe the cocaine would help him get it up for a fourth time. He didn't like it all soft and shriveled up from so much use. But even shriveled, his weapon was much larger than most men's when they were aroused. With a smile, he recalled yesterday when Indria first saw it and almost freaked out.

She was all over it, and when he buried it deep inside her she practically went out of her mind with pleasure. Now as the two women returned to the bedroom he wanted to give her some more.

Elizabeth sat on the side of the bed next to Arthur and began to stroke him. Indria handed him the pipe.

"Come on, baby, hit this rock," she said. "We don't want you to come down 'cause I sure want some more of what you got to offer. Damn, I can't imagine your wife gets all this all the time. She should be one satisfied lady."

"You going to stay with us all day today, baby?" Elizabeth asked. "Tuesday is our day off and all we usually do is get high and have fun. So you going to join us?"

Before Arthur could answer Indria placed the pipe in his mouth and placed the cooked cocaine on the stemmed end. "Of course he's going to stay with us," she said. "What normal all-American man wouldn't?" She took a lighter and placed it close to the rock. It sizzled and Arthur pulled on it, filling the bowl with a white cloud of smoke. He then sucked it in, held it briefly and released it in the air. His entire body relaxed from the pleasure. It made him feel wonderful. Indria took a hit off the pipe as did Elizabeth. They placed another rock on the stem and smoked that one also.

Arthur felt so mellow he didn't want to do a thing. He just wanted to lie there and stare at these two beautiful women willing to make him feel even more satisfied. Elizabeth took in the cocaine smoke and blew it into Indria's mouth. She held it and then released it. The two women then embraced and laid back on the bed.

"Come on, baby, join us," Elizabeth whispered to Arthur.

He slid down to the end of the bed where the women lay next to each other. While Elizabeth worked her magic on him, his weapon rose straight up, ready for more action. He needed another hit of the cocaine. It was exhilarating, but it didn't last very long. He wanted more so he pulled away and sat up in the bed.

"You got any more of that stuff?" he asked.

"Damn, baby, you want another hit already?" Indria asked.

"I do believe he's getting hooked," Elizabeth added.

"If you want some more, you're going to have to pay for it. We can go get it, but it'll take about an hour," Indria said.

"I don't have any cash," Arthur replied. "But I can give you my credit card. You can get the money out of a machine."

Indria and Elizabeth looked at each other and smiled.

"That'll work," Indria said.

Both Indria and Elizabeth got up and hastily put on their clothes. Arthur also got up, walked over to where his pants had been lying on the floor. He grabbed his wallet and pulled out his MasterCard. Elizabeth walked next to him and took the card.

"I'll need your code in order to get the money out of the machine," she said.

"Four, one, one, four." Arthur walked back over to the bed to lay down. "How long will it take you?"

"An hour, probably at the longest a couple of hours," Elizabeth answered.

"Good," he said. "By the time you all get back I'll be rested and then we can finish what you just started."

"You got it, baby," Elizabeth said as she leaned down and kissed him on the lips. "You rest and we'll be back in about an hour." The two women turned and rushed out of the bedroom. Arthur could hear them as they exited the apartment.

Chapter 24

The blinking red light on Jason's phone caught his attention as soon as he entered his bedroom. He glanced over at the clock. It read six-thirty. The call was probably from Jacqueline in a state of panic since Jason knew Arthur hadn't made it home. How should he handle this situation? If he called his sister he'd have to tell her the truth and listen as she retreated deeper into a state of depression. Or should he lie and tell her that he had no idea where Arthur was and that she should relax and not worry? Maybe just leave it alone and not return the call. But that would cause more mental anguish for Jacqueline and he couldn't sit by while his sister suffered through this agony. What the hell was wrong with Arthur? The son of a bitch had it made. A good wife and an excellent job, neither of which Jason believed he deserved. Here he was laid up at some woman's apartment at six thirty in the morning while his wife worried herself right into an anxiety attack.

Jason sat on the side of the bed staring at the blinking red light. Elliott and his constant criticism of Black women because of their treatment of brothers came to mind. Maybe brothers like Arthur had made them that way. There seemed to be so little commitment, trust and love between the brothers and sisters he knew. Jason rubbed his eyes and sighed. What the hell should he do? He could at least check out the message. Maybe Jacqueline had called to tell him that she was okay and knew her husband would be home any minute. Knowing that not to be the case, he finally hit the play button.

"Hi Jason, this is Raquel. I hadn't heard from you in over a week. Thought I'd check in on you and make sure everything was all right. Hope the writing is coming along just fine. Oh, and by the way I think I'm falling in love with you. Anyway if that thought doesn't scare you away, give me a call soon and let's hang out. Talk to you later."

Jason felt relieved that the call came from Raquel until he heard her confession of love. That caused him to sit straight up on the bed. Momentarily he forgot about his sister and her problem. He sure didn't mean for Raquel to fall in love with him. No way could Jason accept Raquel's love. Her love making, yes. Her love, no. Things were spiraling out of control and becoming progressively more complicated at a time when he had no place for complications in his life. He wanted to snatch the phone, call and tell her no. She couldn't fall in love with him because he had no room in his life for an emotion that intense and serious from someone else. He knew damn well he couldn't give her the same kind of love. Maybe Dominique but not Raquel.

He continued to stare at the blinking light on the console indicating that he still had another message to retrieve. Probably more complications for him to deal with. What the hell, he might as well get it out of the way. He hit the play button and waited for his next dilemma to speak to him through the box.

"Hi, Jason, this is Dominique. Just wanted to call and say thanks for picking me up and I look forward to our first official date on Wednesday. I hope it lasts all night long. Good night and sweet dreams."

Now that's the kind of surprise he really enjoyed. What a difference in his emotions between the two calls. No doubt he had to cut back on spending time with anyone other than Dominique. Raquel felt she was falling in love with him but he had to go where his feelings took him, and that was with Dominique. Jason laid down and placed his hands behind his head. He stared up at the ceiling and thought of his plans to finish a novel. He had to be published within the next year. All this emotional involvement must change but did he have the discipline to make those changes? As he felt himself drifting off to sleep he didn't know the answer to that question.

u

It seemed to Jason that he'd just gone to sleep when the repetitious banging on the door awakened him. It had to be Jacqueline. He glanced at the clock. Just a little past nine and her being at his place that time of the morning meant Arthur hadn't made it home. Jason wasn't surprised. In fact, after he failed to call her back last night he figured she'd be calling this morning. He slipped into his pants, threw on a USC sweatshirt and stumbled out of the bedroom to the front door. He swung it open and was right. Jacqueline stood there looking like she would pass out any minute now. With a very disgusted look, Theresa was next to her. Jason yawned and stood to the side while his two sisters rushed through the entrance and grabbed seats on the couch. Jason sat in the love seat.

"I guess he didn't make it home," he said.

"You were supposed to call me back, Jason," Jacqueline said hysterically. "You were supposed to go out and look for him and damnit, you didn't."

"Hey back up a couple of steps," Jason also increased the volume in his voice. "I am not responsible for your husband."

"Jason, show some sensitivity," Theresa scolded.

"What in the world is it you want me to do? Hell, you all act like I don't have a life of my own," Jason shot back.

Suddenly Jacqueline jumped to her feet and started toward the door. "Come on, Theresa. It's obvious we wasted our time coming over here." Theresa remained seated but stared directly at Jason.

"Sit down," Jason ordered. "Just sit the hell down and try to compose yourself." He turned and glared at Theresa. "What is it you want me to do?" He felt tempted to blare out the truth. Just shout as loud as he could that he did know where Arthur was. Laid up in an apartment, in West Hollywood, with a woman doing only God knows what to him. But what good would that do? Just make his sister more of a nut case. Besides, he cared too much for his sister to do that to her. One of the three of them had to calm down and it had to be him. Jacqueline returned to the couch, sat down and covered her face in her open hands.

"Theresa, you're the more reasonable of the two of you, so please come up with some suggestions."

"We want you to cover for Arthur with Big Casey,"

"You want me to do what?"

Jacqueline now raised her head back up and moved to the edge of the couch. "Please, Jason. I know he's not at work and if daddy knows he just didn't show up, he'll fire him."

This all was getting to be a bit hilarious to Jason. He'd laugh, but it unfortunately was also pathetic. He had to ask her. "Why the hell do you care? The man stays out all night on you and just a month ago he hit you. Why do you care what the hell happens to him?"

Jacqueline seemed to gain her composure and said sternly, "Because he's my husband and that's why I care."

"Have you ever thought maybe he shouldn't be your husband?"

"Oh stop, Jason," Theresa scowled. "Just call Big Casey and tell him that you and Arthur hung out all night and he got sick this morning. Tell him he's too sick to come into work."

"You want me to lie for that sorry excuse of a husband?"

"You're not perfect, Jason," Jacqueline shot back. "After all, you did walk out on Angela and Julianne."

"Now you're going to turn around and make this about me?" Jason got up, walked to the kitchen, leaned his elbow on the counter and stared back at his two sisters.

"God, this is frustrating!" Theresa screamed. "Please pick up the phone and call Big Casey. What do you want us to do, beg you?"

"No, I don't want my sisters to ever beg me. But I do want Jacqueline to stop being an absolute fool to a man who's an absolute jerk." Jason grabbed the phone and dialed the business number. He turned away from both Jacqueline and Theresa. "Hi Dorian, this is Jason. Is Big Casey in?" There was a pause and he moved further away from his sisters. He stood in the middle of the kitchen.

"No he isn't, Jason. Is there a message I can give him? He's out at the site by the airport."

"Yes, please tell him that Arthur won't be in this morning. He and I were out late last night. When we got back to my place he was so sick he couldn't drive home. In fact he's passed out in my room right now."

"Yeah, sure, Jason. I bet he's real sick."

"Just give that message to Big Casey."

"You got it. I'll tell him exactly what you said. And by the way tell Jacqueline I said hello and I definitely feel sorry for her."

"Good bye, Dorian," Jason said and hung up.

Jacqueline got up and approached her brother. "Thank you." She kissed him on the side of the face.

Jason reluctantly hugged his sister. He was really upset with Jacqueline, but being the oldest, he felt compelled to temper his anger and change the subject.

"Did you know your brother is back in Los Angeles?" he asked.

Theresa shot a disdainful glare over at Jacqueline. "Yes, unfortunately your sister doesn't appreciate his lifestyle."

"He told you?" Jason looked over at Jacqueline.

She hung her head down and looked away. Theresa stood up and stared at Jacqueline. "He brought his friend to a lunch date we had with him, and before he could even say hello, Jacqueline exploded on him."

"Why?"

"Because that lifestyle is disgusting," Jacqueline answered.

"You have to be kidding," Jason said with sarcasm. "You have the nerve to judge your brother and call his lifestyle disgusting and your husband is probably..." Jason stopped before he exploded and told everything.

"My husband is what?" Jacqueline screamed.

"Nothing," Jason answered.

"Come on, Jason, do you know something about Arthur you're not telling me?"

"No I don't. But I do think you should call Cedric and apologize."

"When he gets rid of that fairy I'll do that."

"Jacqueline, you're the one that's disgusting." Jason said not caring how his sister took his remarks.

"Why don't you two just cool it?" Theresa interjected. "Let's save this for another conversation. I think we've had enough drama for one morning." Theresa took Jacqueline by the arm. "I'm going to take you back to my place and I have to go on into work. I'm going to lose a half day as it is. After all I'm the only one that has a real job."

"Big Casey's sixty-fifth birthday is next week and I think we should all celebrate with him, including Cedric," Jason suggested.

Theresa opened the door and turned to look at Jason. "Yeah, that would be a hell of a sixty-fifth birthday present for him. His youngest son, who he hasn't seen in over a year, shows up with a gay lover. What do you want to do, put Big Casey in the grave early?"

"Like you said, we've had enough drama for one morning," Jason retorted. He took Jacqueline by the arm and said, "I'll see what I can do about finding your husband. He's probably with some of his fraternity brothers."

Jacqueline hugged him. "Thank you, brother, and if you find him call me at Theresa's. I don't think I want to see him at all."

"Yeah sure," Jason said as his two sisters started out the door. "If I find him that doesn't mean I can get him to go home."

"He'll listen to you," Theresa now interjected her comments as she and Jacqueline walked out of the apartment. "Tell him to get his ass home if he knows what's good for him."

Jason watched as his sisters headed to Jacqueline's Lexus, got in and drove away. He checked the time. Already 10:15. Arthur was definitely out of control and his sister was losing her sanity. Jason couldn't have that. He grabbed his keys and dashed out the door. He knew where the bastard was laid up. He only had to find the right apartment and hope it wasn't Dominique's.

Chapter 25

Jason drove his BMW into the apartment complex and headed to the space where he'd seen Arthur's car parked last night. As he swung around the corner and toward the back he suddenly had second thoughts about his actions. He didn't have the slightest idea what apartment would be the right one and might end up getting arrested if he just started knocking on different apartment doors. He could even get shot. Then if he did find the right one how could he possibly make a grown man go home? Jason slowed down as he approached the area where he'd seen the car. His brain worked overtime contemplating all the different scenarios that could occur. What if he ran into Dominique? That would probably freak her out. She was already nervous about men stalking her. She'd undoubtedly believe Jason was doing the same. What could he tell her? That he was trying to find his brother-in-law who was in one of the apartments laid up with a dancer? Dominique would laugh at him and definitely cancel their date for tomorrow. All of this because Jacqueline is so damn weak she won't leave this man. It seemed that everyone suffered because of her insecurities.

Jason slowed down as he came to the space where Arthur's car had been parked. But it was not there. What a stroke of luck, the son of a bitch came to his senses and went home. Now his sister would be content and he could get back to what he should be doing and that is preparing for tonight. But then there was the possibility that Arthur had moved the car to another space. To be on the safe side, Jason decided to drive through the entire complex. He slowly moved forward in the driveway looking on both sides for any sign of Arthur's car. Damn, what if Dominique spotted him out the window. Too late to worry about that now. He needed to leave satisfied that Arthur had also left. Jason made a couple of left turns and no sign of the Mercedes Benz.

Coming to the exit, he spotted the Mercedes pulling into the complex, heading in the direction where he'd originally seen it. What the hell, Arthur wasn't driving. A white woman sat behind the wheel and a sister in the passenger seat. Had Arthur lost his mind or was he just plain stupid? Suddenly a more frightening thought occurred to him. Maybe these women had harmed Arthur. Maybe they'd enticed him into their place and hurt him, even killed him. Jason's fear for his brother-in-law replaced his anger. He stopped at least thirty feet behind them. The two women parked the car, got out laughing and headed to the apartment directly in front of the car. Damn, he'd left his cell phone at his apartment. Something he seldom did. All this drama made him forgetful.

Jason pulled into the space right next to Arthur's car. He needed to think this thing out for a minute. Chances are those women hadn't done a damn thing to Arthur. The idiot was stupid enough to have allowed them to drive his car, either that or was high and drunk. Jason got out of the car, briskly walked up the stairs to the apartment and without any hesitation rang the doorbell.

Jason could hear people scrambling around inside and also heard voices, but what they said was not audible. He could feel someone's presence on the other side of the door. They were probably staring at him through the peephole. He felt exposed standing there knowing someone could check him out and he could do nothing. Only wait and see what they planned to do.

Finally a woman's voice said, "You'd better get away from our door before I call the cops."

That was a bluff. No way they'd call the police. But be polite and they might cooperate. "I'm sorry to bother you but I was looking for a friend of mine and I believe he might be in your place."

"Ain't no friend of yours here so get away from my door."

"That's strange because I swore I saw two women who went in this apartment driving his car." Now it was Jason's turn to play the bluff card. "So I need to see my friend and make sure he's all right because he never lets anyone else drive that car. His wife has reported him missing to the police, so I guess I'll have to call them and give them this address."

"Just a minute," the woman said. "I'll be right back, don't go nowhere."

Jason's nerves were on edge. What if he confronted some crazy situation and got sucked into a predicament he couldn't control? What if they had a gun when they opened the door, and forced him inside? Regardless he couldn't back off now. He'd come this far and found Arthur. He took in a deep breath and anxiously released it. Jason prepared for confrontation.

The door swung open and Arthur stood there with only his pants on. He looked disheveled and with glassy eyes glared at Jason. Finally he smiled and signaled for him to come inside. Jason glared back at him as he cautiously walked past Arthur into the living room. He noticed the bedroom door closed and the women nowhere in sight. Probably just as well because they needed to talk in private. He had to convince him to get dressed and leave with him. Jason took a seat on the couch and watched Arthur finally sit in the recliner next to the couch.

"How the hell did you know I was here?" Arthur asked.

"Doesn't matter how I knew. What matters is that you get dressed and get the hell out of here while you still can," Jason said. "And where is your shirt? What the hell you been doing?"

"Damn, you're full of a lot of questions," Arthur scowled. "Well I ain't quite ready to go yet. I don't appreciate you bringing your ass over here to check on me."

Jason felt his temperature rising. This arrogant son of a bitch didn't realize he was about to lose everything. If Jacqueline knew about this she'd definitely divorce his ass. But then again, maybe she wouldn't. Jacqueline was that very unique breed of Black woman that had a high propensity for taking bullshit from a weak brother like Arthur.

"I'm only trying to help you out. I happened to be on Wilshire Boulevard and I spotted two women driving your car. Now you know damn well Jacqueline has called the entire world looking for you, so I already knew there was a problem. Actually I didn't know if you had been hurt and your car stolen. When I spotted those two ladies driving it, I figured something was wrong. One thing I do know about you and that is you don't usually let other people drive your car. That's what brought me to the door." Jason paused to try and assess Arthur's disposition. Now he had to bluff him. He started to get up. "However, if you're going to get an attitude, then I can leave and definitely let you handle your business."

"No, no," Arthur shouted. "I didn't mean to go off on you. I'm sorry. Do you know if Jacqueline called Big Casey?"

Jason felt somewhat relieved. Maybe this idiot was coming to his senses.

"No she didn't. I did," he answered. "She wanted to protect you so she asked me to cover for you," Jason sat right at the edge of the couch and glanced over at the bedroom door as it suddenly swung open. The woman who had been driving the car walked out into the living room. Jason caught a glimpse of the other woman, who appeared to be lighting a pipe of some kind, sitting naked on the bed. He only got a glimpse as the other woman quickly closed the door behind her. She stood by the door and said. "Arthur, who is this man and what are you going to do?"

"He's my brother-in-law," Arthur answered meekly.

"That's good, we can keep it all in the family. If you want to join us in the bedroom, we're ready for both of you or however you want to work it." She turned, opened the door and disappeared back into the room.

"Who is that?" Jason asked.

"She's a friend and she has another freak back there with her. You up for it?"

"What the hell are they doing back there?"

"Getting high."

"They're back there smoking crack. Get your stuff and let's get out of here." Jason moved a little closer to Arthur. This whole scene had just gotten real crazy and he had to get out of there.

Arthur refused to get up. Instead he stared at Jason and

allowed a slight pleading to enter his voice. "Come on, Jason. We ain't never hung out together. I know damn well you like to have a good time and party. I know that's why you left Angela and moved out on your own. Let's party together for the afternoon and then I promise I'll leave out of here and go on home."

"You have to be crazy, man," Jason scowled and glared at Arthur. "I don't want anything to do with this bullshit. Now you get your stuff together and let's get out of here or I call Jacqueline and Big Casey and let them both know where you're hanging out."

"You'd do some rotten shit like that?"

"You damn right I would. I'm not interested in partying with you, I'm not interested in those ladies and I'm sure as hell not interested in smoking any crack. And if you know what's best for you, you'll get your clothes and follow me to my place." Arthur glared at Jason. No doubt he was angry but that didn't matter. Jason would never tell Jacqueline or Big Casey about this because it would break his sister's heart which would in turn lead to Big Casey breaking Arthur's body into a number of pieces. The two men continued staring at each other and Jason wasn't sure what this idiot would do. "What's it going to be? You going with me or you going to take up your lady friend's offer?"

"All right, brother, you win." Arthur started back toward the bedroom. "Let me get my clothes and keys and we can get out of here."

"Don't get back there and get tempted. I swear I'll leave you right here," Jason warned.

"I said I'll be right back," Arthur shot back at him. He opened the bedroom door and disappeared for a couple of minutes.

Jason started toward the front door. He would wait another minute and if the fool didn't come out of the bedroom he was gone. Just as he reached for the doorknob, the bedroom door swung open and Arthur came out, this time fully dressed. He hurried over to where Jason stood waiting.

"You were getting ready to leave me?" he asked.

"You damn right I was. I can't stand to be in a place like this.

Let's get out of here. I just don't know what you were thinking."

"Sometimes marriage can get to be a bore," Arthur rejoined. "Of course you wouldn't know anything about that. When you get bored you just leave them altogether." They both exited the apartment and headed for their cars.

"You okay to drive?" Jason asked ignoring Arthur's last comment.

"Yeah I'm okay."

"You can follow me over to my apartment," Jason said.

"No thank you. I'm going home."

"Arthur, you don't look in any shape to go home."

"I'm going home."

"Suit yourself. I've done my part." Jason threw his hands in the air, turned and walked to his car. He didn't bother to look back at Arthur. His brother-in-law had a disdainful and arrogant attitude. But he could do no more than what he'd already done. The rest was up to Jacqueline.

Chapter 26

The ocean breeze sprayed a light mist across Theresa's face as she stood on her balcony and looked over the top of the beach combers out into the ocean. Looking back into her apartment at Jacqueline who had crawled up on the couch and gone to sleep, she shook her head, turned and stared back at the ocean. Her dilemma with Jacqueline was that she loved her as a sister but didn't really like her as a person. If they weren't sisters, raised in the same home and as kids, slept in the same bed, she would have nothing to do with her. Jacqueline was a selfish person who made a mistake and married a narcissistic egomaniac. But she wanted everyone to be understanding of her problem and assumed Theresa and Jason were compelled to help her when she went into one of her many panic attacks. She had a tendency to take advantage of the blood relationship that existed among all of them. But when it came to her showing the same compassion for Cedric, it wasn't there. That made Jacqueline a very selfish person, a flaw in her personality that Theresa could not condone or accept.

The sun sat high in the sky which meant it was already after noon. Earlier that morning, Theresa had decided not to go into work. Just a little too much drama that morning. And she also wanted to be there for Jacqueline just in case Jason called with bad news. She watched a half-dozen young boys, with only swimsuits covering their bodies, shoot past her below on skateboards. Young kids like them had no fears, no anxieties, no complications with life. Her sister and brothers used to be like those boys. Big Casey had provided well for his family. But lately she'd begun to wonder if they weren't taking advantage of their father's love for them. That is all of them except Cedric. For some reason he, instead of using his father's wealth to his advantage, had rebelled against it. She wondered if the homosexuality was only a part of her brother's rebellious nature. Cedric knew there was no way Big Casey would accept the fact that one of his children was gay. That, to him, would represent an imperfection. Big Casey was a perfectionist, therefore, would never understand how someone, especially his son, could consciously choose imperfection as a part of his life.

Theresa turned and looked at Jacqueline still asleep on the couch. Big Casey's prejudice was understandable and even acceptable, but Jacqueline's not acceptable at all. How could she possibly sit in judgment of her brother's behavior when she had her own cross to bear? Jacqueline had essentially purchased a stud in Arthur. She wasn't in love with him and she certainly couldn't respect him. Any possibility of respect went away the first time the man put his fist in her face. So it had to be sex. How long would it take for that to wear off? Over the years Theresa had experienced some excellent lovers. The kind that when they go down on you, it'll make your toes curl. She had men who understood how important it was to be tender and sincere when making love. Men seemed to view sex as a performance, and women viewed it as an act of beauty and grace. She had a number of lovers who understood those differences. But she never became addicted to them. Jacqueline's behavior would indicate that she had an addiction to Arthur's lovemaking, but not to Arthur. Maybe her behavior was also a rejection of Big Casey's insistence on perfection.

"Theresa, are you all right?" Jacqueline's question brought Theresa out of her musing.

"Yes, I'm fine, how you doing?" she asked.

"Okay, but did Jason call while I was asleep?"

Theresa went back inside the apartment and sat with her legs straddling the footstool. "No he didn't. In fact no one's called at all this morning. I decided not to go in today."

Jacqueline sat up on the couch, stretched her arm upward and yawned. "I'm glad you did that. I don't think I could've endured this day alone." She straightened out her clothes, got up and walked over to the entrance to the balcony. "I'm so happy that we have the kind of relationship that we will stick by each other in a time of crisis. And that includes Jason too."

Theresa jerked her head in Jacqueline's direction but remained straddling the footstool. "Who have you stood up for during a time of crisis?" she asked. "Or better still how about the way you treated your brother?"

"You trying to compare my relationship with my husband to Cedric's decision to disgrace the family name by sleeping with another man? And a white man at that?"

"Now that is a brand new twist. You're against interracial relationships also."

"I didn't say that," Jacqueline's tone began to rise. "It's just that two men aren't supposed to sleep together. How would you feel if your child went to visit Cedric someday thinking he was going to see his uncle, and not be able to figure out if he was an uncle or an aunt?"

"God, Jacqueline, you make everything sound so damn disgusting."

"It is disgusting and the best that we can do for our brother is to get him some kind of help. You know a good psychiatrist or something?"

"There are some people who would consider all the crap you take off Arthur as disgusting. That man's been out all night and you don't have the slightest idea what he's been doing."

Jacqueline turned around and glared at her sister. "What are you trying to say?"

"I'm not saying anything, Jacqueline, and I don't want to upset you anymore than what you already have been. A courtesy you didn't extend to Cedric the other day."

"Why are you so hung up on me and Cedric? Remember I practically raised him so I think I know him a lot better than you do."

"You practically raised him, but you and Jason never understood him. Neither did Big Casey and Mama."

"Oh, and I guess you did?"

"A lot better than you all. Remember there are only two years between us just like there are two years between you and Jason. Cedric and I were always closer than you and Jason."

"Jason and I were never that close." Jacqueline walked back and sat on the couch. "I guess I really didn't know him that well at all. I have to tell you I was shocked when he walked out on Angela. Just abandoned her and Julianne."

"Damn, Jacqueline, there you go again." Theresa jumped to her feet and sat on the footstool. "Jason didn't abandon them. He realized they weren't compatible and that Angela didn't share his dreams for the future. He's always taken care of Julianne and certainly does everything possible to help Angela. Two people are not compelled to stay together because they have a child."

"He doesn't take care of his daughter. Daddy does. And this idea that he's going to someday be a great writer was just an excuse to escape his responsibility to his family."

"Stop, Jacqueline, or you're going to make me real angry. All that Jason's done for you and your husband and you can still talk about him that way. I'd say that's pretty damn ungrateful."

"You know your problem, Theresa, is that you always want to see things through rose colored glasses. I do appreciate what my brother does to help me in a time of crisis. But that doesn't mean I can't point out those times when I think he's wrong."

"Pursuing your dreams is not wrong. Failing to pursue them is wrong because it'll make you miserable and in turn you'll make everyone around you miserable also."

"Yeah, but sometimes you have to bite the bullet and just deal with the hand that you have or you made for yourself. No one forced Jason to climb between Angela's legs and get her pregnant. You do the crime and you should be able to do the time."

"My God, now you're saying having sex and a baby is a crime and raising the baby is punishment. That's as bad as all these damn sanctimonious anti-abortion so-called Christians telling a young girl if you get pregnant you have to suffer the consequences. You have to have the baby, just like child-bearing is a punishment and not a joy."

"Don't get all philosophical on me. You know what I mean. Sometimes I think all that education and schooling messed up your mind."

"Maybe you could have used a little more to get you out of your backwoods thinking about people and life."

"At least I have a husband. Someone to spend my nights with and, hopefully, someday have kids with."

"Yeah, sure." Theresa had some other choice words she could say. But instead she refrained and chose to change the subject. "Are you hungry? Do you want to go out and get a bite to eat?"

"No, I'm not hungry," Jacqueline shot back at her rather indignantly. "How can I possibly be hungry and I don't know if my husband has been hurt or not?"

"Knowing Arthur, I'm sure he is quite all right."

"That's the problem. None of you really do know him. He has his problems, but really he is a kind and a sweet man."

"Oh spare me," Theresa scowled as she got up and walked over to the kitchen counter to answer the phone. "Hello, this is Theresa," she said still staring at her sister.

"Hello, Theresa, this is Arthur. Is my wife there?"

Momentarily Theresa moved the phone from her ear and stared at it as if she couldn't believe who was on the other end. He'd never before called her looking for Jacqueline. In fact Theresa wasn't sure she'd ever talked with him on the phone. Even the times she'd call to talk with her sister. He really had done something wrong this time.

"Yes she's here, but I don't think she's in the mood to talk to you," Theresa said and then looked at Jacqueline who jumped up from the couch and rushed over to where Theresa stood.

"Let me talk to her and we can make that decision together," Arthur rejoined.

"Yeah just like the two of you made the decision that you could stay out all night and worry her sick." Theresa had to turn her body away from Jacqueline to prevent her from snatching the phone out of her hand.

"That's family business and none of yours, now please put my wife on the phone," Arthur demanded.

"Is that Arthur?" Jacqueline shouted. "Damn it, Theresa, give me the phone."

"What the hell. You're both crazy." Theresa calmly handed her sister the phone then walked back over and stood near the balcony. She listened as her sister once again demeaned herself.

"You know I'm really quite angry with you, Arthur."

Theresa studied her sister's demeanor, her nervous gestures, and her apparently weakening emotions as she listened to Arthur's explanation and probably his copping a plea for Jacqueline to come home.

"I know you're always sorry after it's over, Arthur. But you promised me the last time this wouldn't happen again." Jacqueline glared over at Theresa and then lowered her voice and turned her body away so her sister couldn't hear the conversation.

Theresa could imagine just how much Arthur begged on the other end. It brought back memories of when she got pregnant in college and how Cleveland had begged her forgiveness for his unkind words. It seemed like Black men were always begging for Black women to forgive them for all the wrong they always do. And it seemed to her that Black men were always making excuses. Long ago she concluded that if a man is always making excuses, he surely is a loser. Because the only people in life who always make excuses are people doing something wrong and that alone puts them in the category of losers. How long, she wondered, would it take her sister to reach that conclusion about Arthur? Jacqueline turned around, walked back over to Theresa and handed her the phone with a slight smile on her face. Theresa knew, at this point, she hadn't learned that lesson.

"He's really sorry for last night," Jacqueline said as though seeking Theresa's support. "He was even crying on the phone. Now don't you think that's a real sign of remorse?"

"Sure it is," Theresa agreed.

Jacqueline ran her hands through her hair trying to straighten it out. She grabbed her purse, opened it, took out a compact mirror and looked at herself. "My God, I'm a real mess. Just look at me. That man's going to be the death of me soon."

"Do you want to shower? I have an extra toothbrush you're welcome to use."

"Oh no, no, I have to get home right away. When a man of Arthur's strength starts crying, it means something is really bothering him." Jacqueline tossed everything back in her purse and took her keys out. "I can clean up when I get home." She rushed over to Theresa and hugged her sister. "I know you don't understand because you don't yet understand love. Someday you will."

"I hope so," Theresa followed Jacqueline to the front door and held it open for her. "Call me when you get home."

"I will and thank you for being there for me." Jacqueline hugged Theresa one more time and hurried out of the apartment.

A scowl covered Theresa's face. She watched Jacqueline scoot down the stairs and out of sight. Jacqueline's words, "that man's going to be the death of me soon," resonated with her.

Chapter 27

The Leimert Park Theater was packed when Jason and Elliott arrived at 6:55 in the evening for his critique by the members of the study group. He had provided them with the first four chapters of his novel and looked forward to positive feedback. The key chapter he wanted to discuss was the third one that tells the story of a loyal servant, Hammond, who reads from David Walker's Appeal and is inspired to assist a young slave girl and her son to escape to freedom. Jason felt the scene was powerful because it had the one ingredient necessary for any story to be successful and that is conflict. His concern also centered on how well the reader would accept the historical fact that many slaves sacrificed their own lives in order to assist others to freedom.

This marked the first time he'd ever had other people read a part of his novel. And these folks represented a cross section of his peers. He walked to the front of the table and shook hands with Devon, who whispered, "Good luck." Jason gave him a long hard stare, then turned to Elliott and asked, "What did he mean by that?" Elliott shrugged his shoulders and took a seat to the right of where Jason would stand.

Looking at the members with their four chapters in front of them, he noticed some papers more marked up than others. He smiled at Sister Shia, the sister who had challenged him the last time he was there, when he had criticized Langston Hughes and other Harlem Renaissance writers. She didn't smile back. In fact, she looked away. Jason glanced at her manuscript covered with red ink. He understood what Devon meant when he wished him good luck. As Devon prepared to call the session to order, Jason recalled the advice given to him by one of Los Angeles' prominent publishers and authors, Dr. Rosie Milligan. She told him to make sure he had a thick skin before he journeyed down this road of writing. Writers who wrote solely for adulation from others should find a different profession because they'll get their feelings hurt more often than they'll receive the kind of compliments they're looking for. Sipping on a hot cup of cappuccino Rosie warned that a lot of what he heard during critiques would be just pure nonsense, but some would be legitimate suggestions. A writer's goal was always to separate the two. Hold on to that which was good and toss all the rest. Standing there watching all eyes riveted on him, Jason would put Rosie's advice to use.

"Brothers and sisters," Devon began. "As you know this is our night to critique one of our fellow writers. Tonight we have the opportunity to offer positive, and I stress positive, feedback to Jason Mitchell. Let's give him a hand for being willing to step into the lion's den."

The members sitting around the table clapped in unison. Jason noticed that Sister Shia hardly clapped at all. But suddenly his attention was diverted from the clapping and Sister Shia. Denise, followed by Raquel, entered the room and stood in the back. Raquel smiled and waved at him She gave him a very seductive look that seemed to convey the message I'm not angry at you because you haven't called in two weeks, but happy to see you. Jason smiled back rather sheepishly. He looked down at Elliott who again feigned innocence by shrugging his shoulders in a gesture he had no idea they would be there. Jason knew better. This was another case of Elliott playing cupid. But he couldn't deal with that right now. He was happy to see Raquel and she looked absolutely ravishing.

"I think it appropriate to allow Jason to explain what he was trying to accomplish with the four chapters we read," Devon suggested.

Jason nervously cleared his throat, gathered his thoughts and occupied center stage. A small stage, but significant as a beginning.

"First I think I should explain the overall structure of the novel," he began. "As you know as writers of fiction we must think in terms of—"

"Why did you steal Margaret Walker's title, 'Jubilee'?'" Sister Shia interrupted him abruptly with a question.

Jason shot a glance over at Devon as if seeking direction. Should he answer or just continue? Nothing came from that direction so he now turned and glared at Sister Shia.

"If you are familiar with Margaret Walker's work, which I am sure you are, you know that her title is simply 'Jubilee.' My proposed title is 'Jubilee's A Coming.'" There is a distinction."

"But you have to admit they are very similar and about the same subject matter. Don't you think the reader will assume that you're taking advantage of a well established title in order to promote your work?"

"That's pretty cynical for you to even conjure up such a story," Jason shot back. He could feel his temperature rising. He again recalled Rosie's advice to never let it get personal and that seemed to be happening. At this point, however, he couldn't ignore Sister Shia's charge. He looked back at Raquel who smiled at him, took in a deep breath and released it. Sister Shia continued to stare at him. Evidently, she wouldn't back down.

"If you read the four chapters," Jason continued, "you'd have noticed that just before Hammond parts company with the young girl and her baby, he tells her to have faith because jubilee's a coming, which became a code word of hope for slaves. Some day jubilee would come and they would all be free." He hesitated for a moment quite pleased with his response. "As you know every novel must have a protagonist with a stated goal. Our job as writers is to get our readers to pull for our protagonist. I have three main characters, any of which could be the protagonist. They all have the same goal and that is to escape to freedom, which translates to jubilee. They all believed that jubilee was coming." Jason made a wide circular motion with his arms for emphasis.

"Rather dramatic, aren't you?" Sister Shia said. "We can do without the drama. And I'm sorry for interrupting. You can continue," she added with even more sarcasm.

Jason ignored her last comment. He was just happy to get back to his previous thoughts. He continued, "As I was saying before, structurally a novel must have a beginning, middle and ending. And that structure fits perfectly for a novel on slavery because we can divide the overall institution into three parts. The beginning is the auction of my three main characters and their brutal march by foot and steamboat from Washington, D.C. to the plantation outside Natchez, Mississippi. The middle part is their bondage on the plantation and the ending is their escape to freedom. What you have read for this critique tonight is part of the beginning." Jason paused for a response from his peers. While waiting he again glanced back at Raquel and she gave him a thumbs up sign. Jason knew he sounded good because he definitely knew what he was talking about.

"I like your action in the beginning," a brother sitting to the right of Elliott spoke up. "But a killing of a white man by a Black man right on the White House front lawn is a little strong, isn't it?"

"But it catches your attention, doesn't it?" Jason replied. "That's my hook. And hopefully I can hook the reader in so he'll want to read on."

"You definitely do that," the brother added.

"I think you're on to something with this plot," Devon spoke next. "You seem to know your craft quite well. But your major problem is that I'm not sure you have an audience for this kind of story. And if the publishing houses don't think it'll sell, they won't touch it no matter how well it's written."

"But does that mean I shouldn't write it?" Jason asked trying to show some humility.

"I'm not saying that at all," Devon rejoined. "But if your eating depends on your writing, then you're going to have to adjust to what's selling. I mean your first job will be to find an agent, and let me assure you, brother, they're all about the bottom line. You don't have to be a polished writer because if it sells they're going to publish it."

Jason shifted back and forth as he stood there listening to

Devon. When he first started writing he pledged that he would never give into the temptation to write just for the money. He believed he could rise above the fray and write something he'd be proud for his grandchildren to read someday. For that reason he didn't want the critique session to go in this philosophical direction about the nature of Black literature. Instead, he wanted to stick to the nuts and bolts of writing and especially the nuts and bolts of his first four chapters. But now there was no way he could get around this discussion since Devon had taken it that way. He felt compelled to respond.

"I don't know how you all feel, but I'm going to tell you that my stories are already inside me just waiting to be told. For some reason I've been chosen to be the medium to tell these stories. I can't change that. I have to write the stories that are a part of me and I can't conjure them up in order to try and get rich."

"I feel you, brother," Devon said. "Okay, other questions."

Jason let out a big sigh of relief. He focused his attention on a sister who shot her hand up. Jason recognized her from the previous meeting.

"I like the way you make Hammond a hero, even though he dies within the first fifteen pages of the novel. At first I thought he was going to be your typical Uncle Tom who worked for the master in the kitchen and thought he was better than the field slaves. Do you elaborate on that theme later in the novel?"

"Yes I do," Jason answered. "When they get to the plantation I try to include all levels of the slave hierarchy through my different characters."

"Let's get back to the four chapters we read," Devon interjected. "You introduce three characters at the very beginning of the novel. One being Marcus, the other Levina, and then Isaac. Did you model these three characters after any real life slaves?"

"I'm glad you asked that," Jason said. "Marcus is based on Frederick Douglass, Levina on Harriet Tubman, and Isaac after a free man who was kidnapped and sold into slavery, Solomon Northup."

"Very unique and very good," Devon commented. "But I still

believe you're going to have a difficult time finding a publisher for this genre. Would you ever consider publishing it yourself? A lot of brothers and sisters have gone that route initially."

"I haven't really given it a lot of thought. I think I'm good enough to catch the eye of a major publishing house."

"But isn't that the problem with Black writers?" Elliott asked.

"What do you mean problem?" Sister Shia got back into the discussion.

"We let white folks dictate what good writing is when we allow them to make the final decision as to what is publishable."

"How you going to get around that when they control the money and own all the publishing houses?" A brother wearing long dreadlocks and a dashiki spoke up for the first time.

"Hell, Black folks got money, man," Elliott rejoined. "If a group of brothers would pool their money they could start their own publishing company."

"You ain't going to get two brothers to rub two nickels together," a tall light-skinned sister said. "How you going to get them to invest thousands of dollars together and make it work?"

Jason shot a glance over at Devon to see if the brother would let this conversation, which was off track, continue. He seemed engrossed in what was being said. Jason relaxed and continued to listen.

"Maybe a group of sisters should get together and do it," Elliott suggested. "Let's face it most of the writers and poets are sisters and definitely most of the readers are sisters. They could make it a systemic thing, from the writing, to the publishing, to the reading. There's enough Black female reading clubs to support a whole bunch of authors. The internet book club created by Tee C. Royal, what's it called, RAWSISTAZ could do it themselves."

"Not that many," Sister Shia spoke up again.

"Let's say, then, there's enough to support good writers, maybe we could get rid of these piss poor so-called novelists who can't write worth a damn. Just cause you got a story to tell doesn't mean you can," Elliott said and then relaxed back in his chair.

"Speaking of good writers, let's get back to Brother Jason," Devon finally interrupted the discussion. "Are there any more questions or recommendations for Brother Jason?"

"Yeah, I still say he should change the name so it doesn't look like he's trying to ride on Margaret Walker's success," Sister Shia said.

"Anything else?" Devon asked. "Nothing else, then Brother Jason, good luck and we look forward to reading the next four chapters any time you're ready to step back into the lion's den."

"Thank you all," Jason said. He folded his papers and headed to the back of the room. Elliott got up and followed him.

"You brothers are welcome to stay for the remainder of the meeting." Devon he got up and walked to the head of the table.

"We would stay but we promised these ladies dinner at an early enough time so they can get home at a decent hour. They have to work in the morning," Elliott answered. "But we will be back next week."

"When you're ready for the next four chapters, just let me know," Devon said to Jason. "I think you have a great subject matter and an exciting novel."

"Thanks, brother," Jason said. "We will be back." He smiled at Shia as he followed Denise, Raquel and Elliott out of the theater.

Chapter 28

Sitting across from Elliott and Denise, but tightly snuggled up close to Raquel in the booth at Lucy Florence Coffee Shop in Leimert Park, it dawned on Jason that this was the first time all four of them had been together since New York. Raquel had caught him off guard showing up at the theater with no advance warning. Just like she had caught him off guard when she left the message confessing her love for him the other night. Now that he had come down from his natural high, he wasn't sure he wanted to spend the rest of the evening with her. That would add to his anxiety about her confession of love. And furthermore, in less than twenty-four hours, he would possibly be spending quality time with Dominique. If he made love to Raquel later on that evening, it would lessen the full impact of what could possibly occur tomorrow. What a wonderful dilemma. Raquel took his hand and began to rub the top part of it.

"You were absolutely wonderful in there," Raquel said, then leaned toward Jason and kissed him on the cheek.

"You were rather impressive," Denise added. "You really do know your stuff when it comes to writing. Are all writers as knowledgeable as you?"

"I would like to think so," Jason said humbly.

"Don't be so damn modest," Elliott said. "You know damn well half the Black writers out there don't take the time to study writing. I bet most of them haven't even taken a course on writing or read a book about it."

Denise turned and stared at Elliott. "Well how do they write then?"

"They just pick up a pen, start writing something on paper and when they're finished, they call it a novel," Elliott answered.

"Don't be so hard," Jason said. "There are a lot of brothers and sisters who have studied the art. In fact a lot of them majored in English and literature in college. That's more than I did. I majored in business, so all my knowledge is self-taught."

Raquel positioned her arm inside Jason's and snuggled even closer. "If they don't study the art of writing, then how do they manage to get published?"

"I don't know if I really want to tackle that tonight," Jason responded.

"Hell, I will," Elliott blurted out and leaned forward on the table. "White publishing houses have two different standards, one for Black writers and one for whites. They don't hold Black writers to the same rigorous test they hold white writers. They even establish special imprints for Black books."

"What's an imprint?" Raquel asked.

"It's a special label under which specific kinds of books are published," Elliott answered. "The imprint identifies the book as being Black."

"What? You have to be kidding," Denise shouted. "That's like segregation in the south when you had Black bathrooms and white ones. Do any whites publish under the Black imprint?"

"I don't think so." This time Jason answered. The waitress approached the table and they placed their orders. Jason continued. "I don't know for sure, but I don't think so."

"Well do they only publish Blacks under one label?" Denise continued.

"No they don't," again Jason answered. "They would never place Toni Morrison under a Black label. She is too universally known."

"Then what you're saying is that they market the books under a Black imprint to Black audiences?" Denise asked.

"That's usually who is going to buy them," Elliott said.

"And you're saying these books are not held to the same rigorous standard as are the white publications?" This time Raquel asked the question.

"I'd say that's pretty much the truth," Elliott said.

Raquel continued the questioning, "Well then what does

that say about what white publishing companies think about the Black reader?"

"It's pretty clear isn't it?" Jason said.

Denise adjusted her body in the chair and leaned forward. "How come you're so hard on stories about romance and love?" she asked looking directly at Jason.

"Because you have so many writers telling the same kind of story," Jason replied. "I mean how many times can you read about the same thing; girl meets boy, boy screws girl, boy leaves girl, and girl's heart is broken? And all you women love to read it and relate to it in your lives. You go to bed crying, feeling so sorry for the heroine because she reflects your own lives."

"Damn, brother, I thought I was the cynical one," Elliott added to the conversation. "At least the sisters are making a payday."

"That is rather cynical and I'd say somewhat unfair," Raquel added as she pulled her arm away from Jason. "We happen to be more emotional than men and we aren't afraid to express our feelings."

"Yeah, why you going to come down so hard on sisters when you consider all the shit we have to take from you brothers?" Denise entered the fray. "We're the ones that keep this race together. We take your crap and we keep on ticking, fixing dinners, washing clothes, going to PTA meetings by ourselves, and on top of that working to support our family 'cause usually the trifling daddy is off starting a family somewhere else."

"Whoa, easy," Jason said as he threw his arms in the air. "I surrender. I've already been attacked pretty good tonight. I don't want to struggle through another battle."

"Brother, you just have to learn how to be more sensitive and in tune with the plight of the opposite sex," Elliott said smiling.

"Like you are?" Jason shot back at Elliott.

"He certainly is," Denise interjected.

"Okay, you all stop picking on my baby," Raquel said as she again put her arm through Jason's and moved in closer. "I've decided to take on the task to sensitize my baby to the emotional side of the female."

"Sounds good to me," Elliott said as the waitress brought the food to the table.

u

Jason pulled up in front of Raquel's apartment building, parked the BMW, and walked her to the second floor apartment. He had to handle this situation delicately. They'd just had a conversation about romance novelists and how men leave the women after they've conquered the sex. He didn't plan to spend the night with her, but didn't want to appear to be one of those brothers he described in a romance novel. As they approached the door he decided not to go in and to also let her know that their relationship had been moving much too fast. But he just didn't want to sound like one of those jerks in the novels.

Raquel unlocked the door, cracked it open, then turned and faced Jason.

"Are you coming in?" she asked with doubt in her voice.

"I don't think so, not tonight," Jason said.

"What's wrong, Jason?" she asked leaning against the door. "You haven't called me since New York and to be quite honest, you didn't seem too excited to see me this evening. Am I becoming one of those scorned women you seem to detest in the romance novels?"

"That's not fair. I don't think you're scorned at all. I really have been trying to concentrate on my writing and there for a while I seemed to be doing everything but writing."

"Did the words scare you away?"

"What words?"

"You know the three words you Black men fear more than the plague? Boy, if a woman wants to dump one of you guys, just start talking about love."

Jason placed both hands on Raquel's arms and said, "Please don't get defensive. I've enjoyed the times we've been together. But I'm just on a mission and I can't afford a beautiful distraction like you."

"Jason, do you have someone else? If you do, please tell me

so I won't waste my time on a relationship that is obviously going nowhere. And I will not play second best. I have too much pride and, to be honest, too much to offer to allow myself to be put in that position."

"Raquel, you're taking this all wrong."

"Well then tell me how I should take it."

"Listen, I don't want to fight and argue with you—"

"We're not fighting or arguing, Jason. We're simply both getting a better understanding of what we are doing or what we are going to do from here on."

Jason inched a few steps back from Raquel. He could feel her hurt and anger. Why did it always have to come down to this with him? He was tempted to reach out, take her in his arms and make love all night. But that wouldn't be fair to her because his mind would be on tomorrow and Dominique.

"I'm tired, I've been through an ordeal today," he said. "And last night I had to go out and find my brother-in-law for my sister. That took half the night, so can we just put this on hold until tomorrow?"

"You're going to call me tomorrow?" Raquel asked.

"I promise," Jason said relieved that she was letting him off the hook.

Raquel moved forward to kiss him. He took her in his arms and they kissed, not passionately, but in a cautious manner.

"You go home and write and write tomorrow too," Raquel said, now smiling.

"I will," Jason replied. "All day tomorrow."

"I lo...I'll talk to you tomorrow." Raquel turned and went into the apartment, closing the door behind her.

Jason felt guilty as he made his way down the stairs and to his car. He had lied twice just to get out of that situation. He wouldn't write all day tomorrow, and he probably wouldn't call her. No wonder sisters loved to read relationship novels. They needed to be reassured that the very man they made love to, gave their heart to, wasn't the only jerk in the world.

Chapter 29

When Dominique opened the apartment door and smiled at Jason he felt his knees weaken. She looked ravishingly beautiful. They momentarily embraced and headed for the BMW. Jason had the top down and the sun was shining with just a slight breeze. He placed an old classic CD, Errol Gardner's Concert by the Sea, in the player, and headed south on Highway 111. He had noticed when Dominique came out of the apartment she had an overnight bag. He didn't ask any questions but just smiled.

With music softly playing, Dominique finally asked, "Where are we going? I probably should have asked that earlier. But then I guess I trust you."

"Good," Jason replied. "Just lie back and relax for the next two hours. Let me be the driver."

"Two hours," she said still relaxed. "Maybe I should begin to worry. I thought we were going to a late lunch, not Vegas."

"Would you be disappointed if we were going to Vegas?"

"No, not really. I worked Vegas for a few months before I finally ended up in Los Angeles. A girl can make a lot of money there."

"I don't want to hear about that today," Jason said. "Let's just act like you don't do what you really do. Is that okay?"

Dominique raised her head and sat up. "Jason, I do what I have to and I am that same person you visit in the club just in a different setting, so please don't try to make me someone else. I am not a school teacher or a banker or a lawyer going on a trip with you. I am a dancer and that's what I do for a living." She took her left hand and gently rubbed it along the side of his face. "Leave all that alone and let's just enjoy ourselves." She smiled. "Can you do that for me please?"

Jason also smiled. This woman had a very unique ability to make him feel like putty and what surprised him most is that he enjoyed it. "You have a deal. But I can tell you we're not going to Vegas."

"Where then?" Dominique sounded like a little child. "Please tell me. I'll make it worth your while if you do."

"And if I don't?"

"I'll still make it worth your while." Dominique laid her head back against the headrest. "Oh I don't care where we're going. This just feels so great, the sun and the breeze. That'll make anyone happy regardless of where we're going."

"Okay since you look so beautiful and innocent, I'll tell you. We have a condominium in Palm Springs. So I thought we'd have an early dinner and then hang out for a while. You ever been to Palm Springs?"

"I love it down there." Dominique again sat upright. "I've been down there one time. And it wasn't to dance and it was with a bunch of girls. So I'm like a virgin."

Jason took his eyes off the road long enough to stare over at her. "You really are an amazing person, you know that?"

"Now that you told me I know it. But what makes you think I'm amazing? After all you just met me a few weeks ago."

"I guess intuition. Sometimes you just get a feeling about someone. And I had that feeling the first time I saw you at the club. You must come from good people."

"Maybe I'm this way because I don't come from good people." Dominique's words suddenly sounded cold.

"I've noticed whenever I mention anything about family you seem to change. Is there a reason for that?"

"Are you looking for something, Jason?"

"No, I was just curious."

"Let's just say some things are better left alone. But since you raised the issue of family, what's yours like?"

Jason hit the eject button and removed the CD that had just ended. He picked up the next one, already lined up, and stuck it in the player. Oscar Peterson Plays Duke Ellington filled the airspace.

"We're a typical Black family," he said. "I have a brother who just moved down here from San Francisco with his gay lover. He doesn't dare visit his father who would probably kill him because he's gay."

"Sounds like a pretty understanding father."

"He's a good man, but a typical old-fashioned Black man."

"How about the rest of your family? You have any sisters?"

"Yeah, I have two. They are as opposite as two people can be. One is in a screwed up marriage with a husband who doesn't know his head from his ass."

"I meet a lot of them in the club."

"You might have met him because he loves to visit the clubs and spend money."

"I'd say he's just typical of hundreds of very lonely men or frustrated ones, not happy with their job or their marriage."

"I have another sister who I think you would really like a lot. She is one independent woman, a lawyer who lives in Venice. She refuses to go into private practice and make a lot of money. Instead she works for legal aid."

Dominique again laid her head back on the headrest. "Is making a lot of money a high priority for you?" she asked.

"Isn't it for everyone? How you going to make it in the most materialistic country in the world without money?"

"By getting in touch with your inner self."

"Yeah, how do you do that?"

"It takes a clear understanding that you know you are not from here and all this is temporary and for the most part unpleasant."

"That's a pessimistic view of life."

"Of this life, yes. Of our real existence it's not pessimistic at all."

Once again Jason took his eyes off the road and looked over at Dominique. She was sending him mixed signals and made it difficult for him to read her. A dancer who obviously danced because she wants to make a lot of money, talking about the inner self and an existence beyond this one that she seemed to believe was superior. He straightened his head back around as he drove up behind a large truck.

"Would I be out of place if I ask you why in the world do

you dance when you have such deep thoughts about life and existence? I always thought dancers were in it only for the money and a good time right here and now."

"We are in it for the money because we need it to survive just like other people in this world. And every once in a while we like to have nice things, take trips, and most of all have some kind of security."

"There are some dancers who get off on doing drugs and don't have the kind of attitude you do."

"Jason, don't be silly," Dominique came back at him. "There are Wall Street brokers heavily into heroin, but that doesn't mean all brokers do drugs."

"Good point. I'll give you one there."

"I don't know if I want it," Dominique said teasingly. "It depends on what you're giving."

"It'll all be good."

"We'll see." Again Dominique rested her head back on the headrest and closed her eyes.

Jason looked at her and smiled. This was turning out to be much nicer than he'd imagined.

u

A little after two o'clock they turned on North Indian Canyon Boulevard and headed toward Jason's favorite restaurant. He made his way to South Palm Canyon Drive, where Johnny Costa's Ristorante, was hidden away from the restaurants on the row, creating a romantic setting. Dominique still slept and he didn't want to wake her. Momentarily, he thought of Raquel and the times they had been together. He didn't get the same kind of feeling being with her that he got with Dominique. It was a feeling of fulfillment, just like doing something extraordinarily good for another human being. Jason felt he provided her with a certain amount of security and in return felt secure within himself. Even though he anticipated the sexual part of their relationship there was more than just that, and that also made him exuberant with joy. He finally turned into the parking lot at the restaurant and nudged her.

"Come on, sleeping beauty, it's time to eat."

"Oh my God, I can't believe I slept all the way here." Dominique stretched and rubbed her eyes. "You must be upset with me. I've been terrible company."

"As a matter of fact I enjoyed the solitude. It gave me the opportunity to figure out a couple of scenes in my story." He opened his door, hurried to the other side and opened the door for her.

She smiled as she started out of the car. "Someday you're going to have to tell me how you come up with stories to write. I think that's so exciting."

"You got it." Jason closed the door and they headed inside.

The maitre'd greeted Jason and Dominique at the door. "Good day, Mr. Mitchell. How was your drive down from Los Angeles?"

"Fine, Louis, We had good sunshine and a nice breeze." Jason took Dominique by the arm and added, "And of course beautiful company certainly helped."

"And who is this beautiful lady?" Louis asked.

"Dominique, this is Louis, the maitre'd, and also an old friend of the family."

With a surprised and sheepish expression all over her face, Dominique extended her hand to Louis. He held it and said, "You are in excellent company, young lady. I know the entire Mitchell family and they are all class people."

Dominique said nothing, but continued to display a sheepish and satisfied expression. Jason looked at her and smiled. He'd scored a big victory with this display of importance. Louis led them to a table next to a large picture window that gave them a perfect view of the mountains contrasted against the blue sky, the sun slightly dipped behind the peaks. The early afternoon hour meant the restaurant was practically empty, like they had the entire place to themselves. After the waiter took Dominique's order for champagne and Jason's for cranberry juice and soda, they both settled back in the chairs and relaxed.

"I have to admit I'm thoroughly impressed. You do have a

touch of class, Mr. Mitchell," Dominique said.

"Just a touch?" Jason asked smiling.

"I don't want you to get the big head."

"Pleas believe me, I am quite capable of putting this all in perspective. This is not me. This is Big Casey. We all benefit from his many years of labor."

"Big Casey?"

"Yeah, that's what we call our father. It's kind of a term of endearment that puts him in a very special category. It's symbolic, meaning his magnificence is greater than just a father. We had to create a special category for him and we express it by calling him Big Casey."

"Do all of you feel that way about him?"

"Pretty much so with probably the exception of Cedric."

"He must be quite a man." Dominique smiled as the waiter placed the two drinks in front of them.

"Are you ready to order, Mr. Mitchell?" he asked.

Jason looked over at Dominique and she shook her head no. "Give us a little more time, please," Jason answered.

"Yes sir, just signal when you're ready to order or if you want another round of drinks," the waiter said, turned and strolled away.

"It's amazing the kind of respect money can buy," Dominique said.

"I'd like to think it's more than just the money." Jason took a sip from his drink. "Respect is more than money, it's also behavior."

"You going to tell me these folks treat you the way they do for any other reason than they know at the end of the day you're going to leave a big tip?"

Suddenly Jason's radar warnings kicked in. Dominique had assumed the defensive posture he'd detected before. The day had been so wonderful he didn't want to spoil it now. He still had to make his point, but gently.

"I've been very fortunate, Dominique, and I'm very much aware of that. Why I was given the breaks in life that I have, I don't know. But I never take it for granted. I always want to remain humble and always very thankful."

His words seemed to relax Dominique. "Why do you think things happen the way they do?" she asked.

"I'm not sure I know what you mean."

"You know, why were some people born into so many good things and then others must confront a very ugly reality?"

"Are you questioning why God does things the way He does?"

Dominique now shifted her position in the chair and sipped from her drink. "If there's a God, He's not very fair in how He treats us. But then maybe we chose our own plight here in this existence. When you think about it, that's the only answer if God is all loving and fair and equal in His treatment."

Jason took another sip from his drink. He then leaned forward. "That's reincarnation. Is that what you believe?"

"I don't know, but I do believe there has to be a better reason for all the inequities in life than what you get from the church."

"I guess, then, you don't belong to a church?"

"No I don't. The church let me down a long time ago."

"What happened?"

"It's not important right now." Dominique was abrupt with her answer. "I think I'm ready to order."

Again Jason could detect the warning signs. He signaled to the waiter who quickly hurried over to the table. He looked at Dominique.

"When it does become important I hope I'll be around so you can share it with me."

After dinner they walked up the Boulevard and took in the warmth of the air outside. Jason took her hand and tucked it neatly inside his and she came close to let him, and he knew it was all good. They passed a jazz theater featuring a young singer who sounded much like Nina Simone and sung a medley of the late artist's hit songs. Dominique insisted that they catch the late afternoon show since Nina was her favorite artist, and of course Jason complied.

u

Night had fallen when they exited the theater, but the Boulevard bustled with people just like it was a Sunday afternoon. As they strolled toward the car Dominique threw her arms up and took in a deep breath of air. She swung Jason around and hugged him right there in the middle of the sidewalk. He blushed as all the passer-bys smiled at them. Just before they reached the car, Jason stopped and bought a bottle of Dom Perignon for later in the evening. When they finally got to the car and he opened the door for Dominique it occurred to him that throughout the entire evening he hadn't thought of their love making. There was a different dynamic at work, one that seemed to take them, as a couple, beyond the physical to another plane. He never felt this way about any other woman he dated. He slid in the driver's seat and started toward the condominium, knowing his fulfillment came from just being in Dominique's company and bringing a certain joy to her.

Jason unlocked the front door, swung it open and motioned for Dominique to enter. She glided through the door and when she had a full view of the inside, she let out a loud sigh.

"Enter, my queen," he said as she rushed by him and headed over to the large picture window. He followed her over and placed his arms around her waist. She pulled his arms tighter around her leaving her hands on top of his. They both looked out at a very full moon that seemed to be so close they could see all the peaks and valleys on its surface. Close by, one extremely bright star stood out and it was surrounded by what looked like millions of smaller twinkling stars. It was a perfect evening for the introduction of love between two new lovers.

"This is absolutely beautiful," Dominique whispered. "I'm so awestruck I can hardly talk."

"You don't have to," Jason also whispered. "Just be here right this minute with me and take it all in." He let his head relax, buried in Dominique's long hair. She felt so soft he thought maybe she might melt right into him. He could feel her warmth and her joy and that excited him. No need to hold back. He felt his blood flowing in the right places and his erection was snugly placed against her and she did not move. It couldn't get much better than this.

"Just think most people will never experience anything close to this," Dominique finally broke the silence.

"But we are," Jason said. He didn't want to spoil this moment by going off into another conversation about the haves and the have nots. "And let's just cherish it all and be grateful that we have the chance to do just that."

"You're right." Dominique broke from his embrace, turned and faced him. "You've been so good to me, now it's time for me to be good to you." She looked around the living room. "Do you have a CD player down here?"

"Yes, it's over there on the stand."

"Good. Now I want you to come over here and sit down." Dominique directed him to a large oversize chair.

"What are you doing?" he asked laughingly.

"You'll see, now just sit down." She forced Jason down in the chair and then opened her overnight bag. She removed a CD, walked over to the player and pushed it in. "I know you like Freddie Jackson quite a bit, so that's the CD I brought for the occasion. Now you have to tell me, what's your favorite song?"

Jason had a pretty good idea what she planned to do.

"I guess I'd pick I Could Use A Little Love Right Now."

"Good choice. Perfect." Dominique forwarded the CD to song number 4. She hurried back over to where Jason sat. "Now I also recall that you paid for two table dances and I never performed."

"Dominique, you don't have to—"

"Hush. I know what I don't have to do and that's what makes this so much more enjoyable and especially meaningful. Now lean back and let me entertain you." Dominique slipped out of her flats and moved in closer to Jason. "Just so you'll know, I've never done this outside the club with anyone else. So I guess you could say you're becoming very special to me."

Jason was frozen in place, almost like he was suspended in another stratosphere. He started to respond but just as he did Freddie Jackson's smooth voice filled the room.

Dominique smothered Jason with her closeness. She slid her body down the front of his, all the time keeping rhythm with Freddie Jackson. Jason pulled her blouse out of her jeans and put his hands underneath so he could rub her back. Her skin felt soft and smooth. He was so excited he didn't know if he could control himself. Dominique kissed him on the neck, on the side of his face, and finally on his lips. All the time Freddie Jackson influenced the atmosphere. Without breaking her rhythm, Dominique removed her blouse, slid off her pants and backed up a couple inches. She slowly danced in place. Jason got up and moved in closely to embrace her. They stayed close, slowly moving only the lower portion of their bodies.

"I can feel your heart beating," Jason whispered.

"I know and it scares me," Dominique also whispered. Her voice seemed to crack.

Jason moved her back a little and looked into her eyes. They were filled with tears.

"What's wrong?" he asked

"Nothing, I just..."

"You just what?" Jason knew something was wrong. He pulled her in close. "Tell me what's wrong? Isn't this perfect?"

"Yes it is and that's why I'm frightened."

"Don't be."

"Jason, could you be happy just holding me tonight?"

Her request hit Jason unexpectedly. But for some reason he didn't get upset. He knew he could hold her and still feel satisfied. Almost anything she wanted would be all right with him, as long as they were close and together.

"I tell you what," he whispered. "Why don't we go upstairs, take a shower and then we can hold each other? Would that make you happy?"

"Very much so. But, Jason, if you insist, we can make love. I can make you feel good."

"Only if you're ready. But being with you is okay with me. Just holding you is satisfaction."

"Thank you."

Chapter 30

"What?" Elliott screamed into the phone. "You're telling me you took that woman to Palm Springs, gave her the A-team treatment and you didn't do anything but hold her?"

"That's right and don't you dare say anything offensive about her." Jason had arrived back at his apartment and couldn't wait to tell Elliott about his first date with Dominique.

"Brother, I'm not going to say anything offensive about her. But you, you're another story. How to hell you going to take that freak all the way to Palm Springs and do nothing but hold her?"

"You're disgusting. And don't call her a freak."

"I know what you're capable of. Remember those Raquel moans a while back."

"You know sometimes I wonder why I even bother with you."

"Because I keep it real. Something you need in your life."

"You definitely keep it foul."

"When you going to see this heartthrob of yours again?"

"Tonight. We're having dinner."

"If you don't tap it tonight you'll give us brothers a bad reputation. You're obligated to the brotherhood."

"You know what you can do with your brotherhood."

"Well at least I know Raquel tightened you up the other night. You're not walking around here about to explode from an overdose of cum."

"You know it really is a mystery to me how a brother with so much poetic talent, such great use of metaphors, can have such a foul mouth the rest of the time."

"That's my Dr. Jekyll and Mr. Hyde personality. But back on a serious note, when you going to get back to work? I know damn well you haven't done anything since the other night when you were critiqued. You probably won't do anything tonight. So what's up? You're on a time schedule and it's quickly running out. You'll soon be out on your ass if you don't get busy. And then we'll see how much your new love cares for you."

"There you go again. So you're saying that it's the money that's got her interested."

"I'm not even sure she's interested since she didn't give up anything last night. Now Raquel's interested and she showed you as much the first time you went out with her, and in New York. And also the other night."

"She didn't show me anything the other night because we didn't do anything."

"You left that girl hanging that way? What the hell's happening to you? Man, you'd better leave that Dominique alone. I see nothing but problems with her and you sure don't need any more problems right now."

"I have to be truthful to Raquel and to myself. I'm just not feeling her all the way. You know what I mean?'

"Hell no I don't know what you mean. Raquel blows your brains out of your head with number one loving. Dominique leaves you with a hard on just like she does with every one of those suckers at the club, and you telling me you feel her."

"I know it's hard for you to understand 'cause you one of these cut and dry brothers. It's one way or no way and that one way is your way."

"Better my way than theirs. Here you spent time and resources on that woman and got nothing in return."

"How do you know I didn't get anything?"

"Well let me re-word it. You got nothing measurable."

"Look here man, I'm going to let you go 'cause you definitely talking too crazy for me."

"That's cool. I guess you need to rest after all that activity you engaged in last night," Elliott laughed.

"As a matter of fact, it was an active evening. But not the kind you'd ever understand."

"When we going to get together and hang out, maybe go to the club and check out some new ladies?"

"Very funny. I'll give you a call sometime tomorrow."

"You got it. I'm out."

Jason placed the phone back on the bed stand, turned on his computer and went to the chapter he'd been working on a few days ago. Actually he'd done nothing on the manuscript since his confrontation with Sister Shia and the other members at the theater. He was working on the chapter that leads to a betrayal of friendship between Isaac and Marcus. He'd feel good about the day if he could finish that scene.

Jason closed his eyes and tried to get into his characters, something necessary for him to write. But instead of visualizing the characters, his vision was on Dominique. Maybe Elliott was right. She manipulated men. Some fools would spend hundreds of dollars, and the most she would have to do to collect is dance close to them. That's all she did with him last night and he'd definitely spent a lot of money.

Isaac's betrayal of Marcus and the beating is where his mind needed to be. The plantation in 1836, not Palm Springs in 2014 is where he needed to concentrate his efforts. Maybe he shouldn't have been so damn understanding last night. He should have forced the issue and insisted they have sex. Actually she owed him more than just a hug and a kiss.

This whole dating scene was nothing but a game, men trying to get over and women trying to not give it up. If that's true, she won last night and all the tears and drama was staged. Jason slapped the front of his forehead in a gesture of frustration. Hell, he sounded like Elliott. What he experienced last evening was beautiful. She had told him she'd never danced in that manner for anyone else, and the tears were real. And when he dropped her off this morning she insisted they have dinner tonight. No doubt she planned to make up for last evening. She just didn't want to make love the first night out on a date and suggested they get together tonight so she could make up for it.

Jason got up, went into the kitchen and poured himself a glass of ice water. He did that more out of nervous energy than thirst. He just couldn't get it together. Instead of returning to the computer, he sauntered over to the CD player and placed a Nina Simone CD inside. He hit the play button and then sprawled out on the love seat staring up at the ceiling as Nina Simone sang Just Like A Woman.

Jason lay there for over a half hour listening to Nina. He allowed his thoughts to travel freely between last night with Dominique and the betrayal scene he needed to finish in his novel. Momentarily Dominique was in control. Visions of her perfectly structured caramel brown body flashed before him. And then there was the unexplained moment in the evening when she moved back from him and invited him to dance with her. Then the tears so suddenly and the plea that they only hold each other. Was it genuine or some kind of game? The mystery was too much to hold inside. That evening he would question her regarding that rather unstable behavior. Tonight he would clear it up. In the meantime, back to the plantation. Abruptly he clicked off the CD, went back into the bedroom and returned to the manuscript, determined to finish the scene on betrayal.

Chapter 31

The Los Angeles County Poverty Law Project was housed on the second floor of what had once been a movie theater in south central Los Angeles. Theresa shared an office with a paralegal. Her furniture consisted of a desk, an executive swivel chair, two chairs that sat in front of her desk, a five-drawer file cabinet and a Dell computer. On Thursday afternoons she usually stayed in the office and got caught up on paperwork. She had scheduled a couple appointments for the afternoon, one with an ex-drug addict who had gone through treatment and wanted to get her two children back from foster care, the other with two lesbians who claimed they'd been fired from their jobs from a local grocery chain because of their sexual preference. While drinking a cup of hot tea she busied herself going over the particulars of the first case. Of the two, she'd enjoy working on the first one the most. Not that she didn't think the two lesbians had a real complaint, but she would much more enjoy helping a mother get her children back than assisting two pissed-off women get even with their employer because he wouldn't condone their lifestyle.

Theresa needed to concentrate on the work in front of her, but for some reason she was stuck on her sister. She just couldn't understand how Jacqueline could be such a fool, and then on the other hand be such a bigot when it came to their own brother. She paused in her reading to sip from the tea. Big Casey's sixty-fifth birthday was in a couple of weeks. It would be a great gift if all his children were there to celebrate it with him. He definitely would be surprised to see Cedric. But it would have to be without his other half. She wondered if Cedric would be open to such a suggestion and knew what she must do if there was going to be any possibility of getting all four siblings to Big

Casey's house for his birthday. First she had to patch up the rift between Cedric and Jacqueline. She didn't have much time. Theresa tossed her pencil down on the desk and sighed. Why did she take on these burdens all the time? While Jason, Jacqueline and Cedric were busy attending to their personal lives, she had none at all. Again, she sighed, picked up the phone to call the number to the motel in Hollywood assuming her brother was still there. She could only hope that he had registered under his own name.

"Extended Stay Suites," the operator answered the phone.

"Could you ring Cedric Mitchell's room, please?" Theresa asked and held her breath. After about fifteen seconds the phone rang, so she relaxed.

"Yes," the voice on the other end said.

"Hello, I'm looking for Cedric Mitchell. Is this the right room?"

"Yes it is. Who's calling?"

"His sister, Theresa."

"Just one moment." There was a pause and she heard the same person in the background. "Cedric, it's for you and don't be long. I'm expecting a call from an agent."

What a nice person, Theresa thought.

"Hello, this is Cedric."

"Hey baby, this is Theresa. How you doing?"

"I'm fine, but I was just thinking about you. Really I was."

"Why? What's up?" she asked. Momentarily Theresa forgot that she'd called him. She detected something wrong.

"I'd rather talk to you face to face."

"Fine, that's why I was calling. How about dinner this evening? My dime."

"Sounds good to me, where and what time?"

"How about eight and I'll pick you up? And do you think we could do this alone?"

There was a long pause and for a moment she thought she'd lost him. Finally he responded.

"Yes we can do that, but how about a little earlier than eight?"

"We'll make it an early dinner. Does seven sound better?"

"Ring me from the lobby."

"See you then," she said and hung up.

One down and one to go she thought just as a loud commotion broke out in the lobby. Harriett, the paralegal, jumped up and headed toward the door. Theresa followed closely behind her.

When they swung the door open, a young Black girl, no more than eighteen, broke loose from the grip the receptionist had on her and rushed toward Theresa.

"Are you the lawyer who's supposed to help poor people?' she asked getting right up in Theresa's face.

Initially Theresa froze. She didn't know if she should slug this young juvenile or embrace her.

The young girl continued to confront Theresa again asking, "Are you the lawyer that helps poor people?"

Theresa finally responded. "Yes I am. How can I help you?"

The girl looked back at the receptionist, then at Harriett and said, "Can I talk to you alone? This is a real private matter."

Again Theresa hesitated and studied the girl for a moment. She didn't look dangerous, just desperate. She held the door open and waved her in, then looked at Harriett and the receptionist. "It's all right. Give us a few minutes."

"You sure?" Harriett asked.

"Yes I'm sure." Theresa followed the young girl into the office and closed the door. She signaled for her to take one of the chairs in front of the desk. She walked around the desk and sat in her chair.

"Why were you making a scene out there?" Theresa asked the girl. "And what is your name?"

"My name's Tosha and I just got mad cause the lady out there said there wasn't no way I could see you on such short notice."

"Those are usually the rules. You should've called and made an appointment."

"I'm sorry but what's happened to me couldn't wait until next week or next month when they probably would've told me I could see you. By then I might be dead."

"Dead?" Theresa came to an upright position and leaned

across the desk. "Is someone trying to kill you? If they are you should go to the police."

"Well the son of a bitch done already killed me and I just want to get even before I die."

"Please, watch your language," Theresa admonished. "Nothing's so bad that you have to use that kind of vulgarity."

"Yes it is," the girl shot back. "The bastard done gave me HIV and didn't even tell me." Suddenly the girl began crying. "I don't know what to do. I ain't got no insurance and I got a little baby girl. I don't know what's going to happen to us."

Theresa snatched up a handful of tissues out of the box on her desk, got up and sat in the chair next to Tosha. She placed her arm around the girl and handed her a couple of the tissues. The young girl took them and blew her nose. Theresa kept her arm around her. She wanted to cry with her, but couldn't afford to get emotional. She had to find answers and that meant keeping emotions out of it. Holding back her own tears, she asked. "Do you have family here in Los Angeles?"

"Not really. My daddy's locked up and my momma's strung out. I ain't seen her in a couple of months and when I do all she ever wants is money." The girl started crying loudly. "I can't leave my baby with her. I got two uncles, but ain't either one of them no good."

"What about grandparents?"

"They in Jackson, Mississippi, but they won't talk to us because of momma's problems and because daddy's locked up."

"What do you mean, they won't talk to you?" Theresa moved in just a bit closer to the young girl who began to shake.

"They're real religious and they claim the devil got hold of both momma and daddy and unless they change their ways they can't come to their home."

"How about you, have you talked with them?"

Tosha jerked back from Theresa's grip. "You going to help me or not?" she shouted.

"I'm going to try to help you, but first I need to find out all the information I can about you."

"You sound just like them damn social workers who want to get all in your life instead of doing anything to help you." Tosha continued to shout.

"Now calm down." Theresa's voice rose slightly. "Where are you living right now?"

Theresa's stern tone seemed to work with Tosha as the young girl relaxed back in her chair.

"I'm staying at a friend's house off 135th Street. But he told me I can't keep staying with him unless I can pay some rent. And I ain't got no money until I turn tricks and since I got this shit in my system I ain't about to turn no tricks." Tosha again started crying and the shaking increased.

Theresa glanced at her watch. It was nearly five o'clock. She needed to get out of there and head toward Cedric's in the next half hour. But she felt for the young girl and didn't want to leave without helping her out. She also needed a few more answers.

"Where's the baby's father?" she asked.

"He lives in the same house that I do."

"Wait a minute. I thought you stayed with a friend?"

"That's right."

"What about your boyfriend?"

"He ain't my boyfriend. He just lives there in another room."

Theresa was getting a better understanding of exactly what was going on.

"Are you strung out?" she asked.

"No, I swear I been clean ever since my baby was born."

"How old is your baby?"

"She's five months old."

"Oh my God." Theresa jerked away from the girl. "Has the baby been tested for HIV?"

"No she hasn't 'cause I think I just got it."

"How do you know when you contracted it?"

"I really don't know, but even if I had it a friend of mine told me that babies are protected against any kind of diseases the mother might have."

"Where is your baby right now?"

"She's next door at my girlfriend's house. She said she could watch her for a couple of hours."

"Give me your address where I can contact you later this evening."

Tosha sprang from her chair and moved away toward the door. "No, you think I'm crazy. I ain't dumb. I know you gonna give my address to social services so they can come and take my baby away from me. I'm getting out of here." Tosha grabbed the door handle and started to open the door.

Theresa jumped from her chair and ran toward the door. She grabbed Tosha just as she was about to exit. "No, you can't run. You have to let me help you," Theresa said as she allowed a bit of pleading in her voice. She held Tosha tightly and being the bigger of the two, she had no problem restraining her. "You just can't run. You need help and I'm going to do everything I can to help you."

Finally she felt Tosha's entire body go limp. Again tears filled her eyes. "Sit back down and give me your address. Later on tonight I'm going to come and get you and your daughter."

Tosha relaxed her head on Theresa's shoulder and continued to sob.

"Tosha, your address," Theresa said, firmly this time.

"I don't know the address. Honest I don't know it. But I know the house."

Theresa reached over on her desk and picked up a pen and paper. She scribbled her cell phone number on the paper and handed it to Tosha. "This is my cell number. Do you have access to a phone?"

"Yes, there's a pay phone at the corner where I live."

Theresa got up, walked around the desk and opened her purse. She took out a ten dollar bill and also some change. She handed it all to Tosha. "Here is some money for you and the baby. And I do mean the baby. Do not buy any drugs with this money."

"I won't, I promise," Tosha said. She took the money and stuffed it in her pocket.

"You'd better not or I'll hunt you down," Theresa said with a smile. She noticed that Tosha allowed a slight smile on her face. "When you get where you're staying, get the address and call me. I'll be by at ten o'clock to get you. Now it's important that you and your baby come out at ten and be prepared to leave. Don't tell anyone where you're going. Whatever clothes you have leave them there. We'll get you some clothes tomorrow. Whatever clothes, toys or anything you have for the baby, leave them there also. We'll get her everything new tomorrow. Do you understand?"

"Yes, but why are you doing all this for me?"

"Don't ask any questions right now. Just go back to that place, call me with the address and be ready to leave at ten o'clock. Can you do that for me?"

"Yes I can. I can be strong when I have to."

Theresa led her over to the door and opened it. "Well this is the time for you to be strong. If you want to get back at that boy for what he's done to you, first you have to be strong."

"I will, ma'am, I will." Tosha hesitated as she stood there staring at Theresa.

Theresa grabbed her and they hugged. Tosha turned and Theresa watched as the young girl left the office. She wasn't quite sure what she had done. Whatever it was she knew it was necessary. Whatever it took she had to save this young girl and had to get that five month old baby out of the pit of hell.

Chapter 32

Cedric walked out of the motel toward Theresa's car. It appeared to Theresa that he'd lost quite a bit of weight. He looked older and somewhat haggard. After her late afternoon with Tosha the first thought that flashed in Theresa's mind regarding Cedric's appearance was HIV. Could her brother possibly be a victim of that dreaded disease? And if so did he contract it from Aaron? It would be a burden she just wasn't sure she could handle. That might be what he wanted to talk with her about. She momentarily closed her eyes and whispered, "Please God not that." Cedric waved at her and she waved back.

"Hey sis, what's happening?" he asked and climbed in the front seat of the car.

"Just living," Theresa said, leaned over and kissed Cedric on the cheek. "You hungry?"

"You'd better believe it."

"The way you look I'd say you stay hungry a great deal of the time." Theresa pulled out into the heavy Hollywood traffic and headed toward the restaurant.

"So you noticed I've lost weight." Cedric turned and smiled.

"I guess you have. Have you been trying?"

"Yes because Aaron has to keep his weight down for his acting. You know Hollywood likes them thin and pretty."

Theresa pulled up to a red light and came to a stop. She glanced over at her brother, then smiled. His weight loss was deliberate and not because of AIDS. She felt relieved, but also compelled to further comment.

"What's wrong with you? Why you want to lose all that weight and look like you're sick? You'd better start eating."

"I'm okay sis. I like to support my partner as best I can and I can do that by watching what I eat just like he has to watch what he eats."

The light turned green and Theresa floored the accelerator. "Well you're not supporting him tonight, so you're going to eat and I mean that."

Cedric turned and again smiled at his sister again.

u

The early dinner crowd was just arriving at Lowrey's Steak House Restaurant in Beverly Hills. The ambiance was quaint and rich. The tables were covered with white tablecloths and the waiters wore tuxedoes. Theresa and Cedric managed to get a booth in one of the quieter parts of the restaurant. It was already seven-thirty and she would have to take him back home then get over to the other side of town to pick up Tosha. It dawned on her that she hadn't checked her messages to see if the young girl had left the address.

When Cedric got up to call Aaron, she pulled out her cell phone and checked for messages. There were none. Theresa shouldn't have let the girl out of her sight, especially after what she told her about the house where she lived. As she watched Cedric head back to the table she could only hope the girl would call.

"How's everything with your friend?" she asked. She dropped the phone back in her purse, leaving it turned on just in case Tosha called.

"He's a little upset, but he'll be alright."

"Why's he upset?"

"Oh be serious, Theresa," Cedric snapped. "You made it quite clear that you didn't want him to join us for dinner."

"I didn't say he couldn't join us, but Cedric, we have some serious problems we need to deal with. And I just thought it would be best if we talked alone."

"That makes three strikes with my family against the person I plan to marry."

"Marry? You two plan to get married?" Theresa blurted it out before thinking.

"Yes we plan to marry. Isn't that what people who love each other do?"

Theresa leaned across the table so that she could be closer to her brother. Somehow she had to let him know that her concern had nothing to do with his sexual preference, but only with the difficulty he would confront. "Cedric, I want you to know that I'll always love you regardless. But do you all realize how difficult life is going to be for the two of you?"

"We had no problems in San Francisco. And so far we've had no problems here in Los Angeles. So I don't know what you're talking about."

"Those are only two cities out of a country with thousands of cities where the people will make your life hell if you wind up living in one of them."

"We'll just have to make sure we don't."

"Is that what you wanted to see me about? You and Aaron getting married?"

It was Cedric's turn to lean halfway across the table. "Yes and one other thing."

"What's the other thing?" Theresa asked almost nervous to find out. Before Cedric could answer the waitress came up and took their orders for dinner. After she walked away Cedric answered.

"The other thing has to do with our need for money. A couple of weeks ago, Jason loaned us some money to get a place and get settled in. I thought I'd have a job by now, but it just hasn't worked out yet."

"How much money do you need?"

"I guess a couple thousand dollars would do. That way I could pay our rent, get some groceries and toiletries. And Aaron could give this agent he found an initial retainer."

"You want me to give you money to pay for his agent?" Theresa asked rhetorically with great emphasis.

"Why is that such a strange request? It costs money to break into the movies."

"I'm very much aware of that," Theresa shot back at him.

"Maybe that's why he should find a job."

"Theresa, please don't try to tell us how we should run our affairs."

"Hell man, if I'm going to loan you two thousand dollars I'm definitely going to have my say."

"Then let's just forget about it. Take me back to the motel." Cedric started to get up.

"Sit back down, damn it," Theresa said. "You know that's all you ever do is get up and run when things don't go as you plan or you hear something that's not pleasing to you. I'm not Big Casey and I'm not Jacqueline, now sit back down."

Evidently the sternness in Theresa's voice worked. Cedric sat back down and looked away.

"Do you really think that you and Aaron are getting off to a very good start? You're down here in one of the most expensive cities in the country and neither one of you has a job. And to make it even worse, your friend is trying to break into the most difficult industry in the country. Cedric, you just don't come to Hollywood one day and the next day land a starring role in even a B movie, not to mention A."

"Why is it no one in this family wants to accept me?" Cedric asked.

Theresa could see tears in his eyes. He hadn't changed since their childhood when it had always been so easy to hurt his feelings and cause him to cry. She recalled a time when he was seven and she eight and he had hidden in a closet. She went in there with him, put her arms around him and promised that she would make everything all right. Now, almost twenty years later, she had to do the same thing again.

"Okay, I'll get the money for you," she said. "But there is something you have to do for me."

"What?"

"Big Casey's birthday is in two weeks and I want all his children there for the occasion. It's his sixty-fifth and there is something special about a man's sixty-fifth. It's like a turning point in their lives."

"What's so important about sixty-five? He still has a lot of years in front of him."

"Let's hope so, but I still want to make this very special for him."

"I guess you want me to leave Aaron behind?"

"Yes, just this one time," Theresa said softy. "I know how hard that must be for you, but we need time to work on Big Casey."

"I don't know, Theresa. That's like I'm accepting something's wrong with my love for Aaron. And I'm not willing to do that."

Theresa had to conjure up all her persuasive skills to convince Cedric. These were lawyer skills at their highest plateau. "It's not that at all. It's simply accommodating a man who is from a different time and generation than you. It's giving him the dues he deserves. And it's also doing something to make your mother happy. She'd love to have us all there to celebrate with Big Casey."

"It's going to cause a rift in my relationship."

"He'll get over it, especially when you bring in another two thousand dollars to keep a roof over his head, food in his stomach, and money for his agent."

"You make it sound like he's some kind of gigolo."

"Oh stop it, Cedric," Theresa again snapped at him. "You have to stop being so sensitive. Listen to me and listen good. I'm about to give you two thousand dollars of money I really don't have to give. I'm doing it because I love you and I can't see you down here with no means to survive. But it doesn't mean I have to like what you're doing to yourself. It's your life and you have that right. I also have the right to express my opinion, especially when I feel my baby brother is doing things not in his best interest."

Cedric sat straight up and looked directly at Theresa. "I'll be there," he said.

"Good. Now let me give you this check." She pulled out her checkbook, wrote out two thousand dollars and handed it to Cedric. "Don't worry about paying me back. My payment will be your showing up for Big Casey's birthday. Do you need me to pick you up?"

"No, I have transportation," Cedric said dryly. He took the

check and stuffed it in his pocket.

Suddenly the cell phone rang in Theresa's purse and she snatched it out. "Hello, Tosha?"

"Yes ma'am, but I got to hurry up and get out of here. This man knows I been to see somebody about my condition, and he's in here getting drunk. I think he's going to hurt me."

"Tosha, give me an hour. Go out in the front. Don't take anything but the baby. I'll be there in less than an hour. Do you hear me?"

"Yes ma'am, I hope I can last that long. He's getting awfully mad."

"If he tries anything you tell him you have an attorney who's on her way over there. And if he harms you I'll have him thrown in jail."

"Yes ma'am."

"Now give me the address."

"7530 135th Street."

"I'll be there. You be outside." Theresa finished and closed the phone.

"What's going on?" Cedric asked.

"Come on we don't have time to eat."

"What's up?"

"Just ride with me, Cedric. We have to go save a young girl's life." Theresa took out twenty dollars and left it on the table. They both jumped up and headed to the car.

Theresa shot out into the traffic. She made it to the 110 Freeway and headed toward the 110.

"Damn, Theresa, you'd better slow down!" Cedric shouted at his sister.

"You relax and don't bother me," she replied. She reached the 110 South and headed toward 135th Street. Theresa checked her watch, it read 8:30. She had a good twenty minutes to get there. "Damn it, I should have never let her out of my sight," she muttered. "If something happens to that girl I'll never forgive myself."

"Who is she anyway?" Cedric asked.

"She's a young girl with more problems than she deserves."

"How do you know she doesn't deserve them?"

"No one deserves to be HIV positive with a five month old baby and an insane man threatening her life."

"Damn, that is rough. How old is she?"

"I don't know for sure. But she can't be any more than eighteen. And her life is pretty much over before it really got started."

"She can get treatment," Cedric suggested. "There is so much new medication now that a person can get, they can live a long and normal life."

"Be serious, Cedric. She's Black and poor. She has no one to help her. This isn't Magic Johnson with the ability to get a million dollars' worth of treatment."

"What do you think you can do for her?"

"I don't know, but I have to do something." Theresa exited the freeway and turned right on 135th Street. "Look for 7530."

She slowed down and they strained to check out addresses. Half the houses didn't have visible addresses. Theresa's work often took her out into the rougher neighborhoods like this one but never this late at night. It was a different picture she saw now than what she observed during the daylight hours. The street was void of activity. It made her a bit nervous. She had done the right thing when she insisted Cedric accompany her. He was a big man like his father and even though he was gay and probably wouldn't fight, his presence could possibly serve as an intimidating factor.

Theresa finally spotted the house with no Tosha standing out front. That meant she'd have to conjure up enough nerve to go inside and get her. She pulled the car up to the curb and parked it. She studied the old rundown house for a few minutes, then handed Cedric her cell phone.

"Here take this. If I'm not back in five minutes call the police and then come in there and get me."

"What are you gonna do?"

"I'm going in there and get her."

"Damn, Theresa, that's a crack house. Ain't no telling what they'll try to do to you."

"That's why I want you to call the police after five minutes. And by all means come in there and get me."

"I'll do better than that. I'm going in with you."

"No I'll be all right. But just in case, you stay here so you can call for help if necessary."

"Okay, but only five minutes. After that I'm coming in there." Cedric took the cell phone from Theresa.

She sighed one time and got out of the car. After she made it to the porch, she turned and looked back at Cedric. Again she took a deep breath, released it and knocked on the door.

It seemed an extremely long time before someone finally shouted from inside. "Yeah, what you want?"

"I'm looking for Tosha. I was expecting her to be waiting outside when I pulled up."

"Who the fuck is you?"

"I'm her lawyer, and you'd better get her out here in the next minute or there's going to be trouble. And I'm pretty sure you don't want trouble to mess up your evening."

"Just a minute."

Theresa turned and looked back at Cedric who had his eyes on her and that comforted her. She turned back toward the door in anticipation of the person inside opening it. Instead she heard Tosha.

"Ma'am, I've changed my mind. I don't want to go with you. Please leave us alone."

Those were the last words Theresa wanted to hear. Didn't that young girl realize the danger she was in and that she needed to get to a doctor and have her baby checked for the virus? She had to talk some sense into her head.

"Tosha, you have to come with me, honey. You're sick and your baby might be sick. I know you want to save your baby, don't you?"

"No, ma'am, just go away."

Theresa again turned and looked back at Cedric as though she needed assurance that her back-up was still there. He smiled at her and she then turned and faced the door. She had to get tough, something Theresa was well equipped to do.

"If this door doesn't open in the next minute then I'm going to signal for my assistant to call the police. Look out the window at my car and you'll see he's just waiting for my signal. If you cooperate, we'll be out of here in the next minute and you can get back to whatever it is you were doing."

She could hear some scrambling around and then suddenly the door swung open. The stench from inside practically knocked her over. It was dark, but she recognized Tosha standing off to her left holding the infant. Theresa slowly stepped inside the house. As she did, a man started to close the door. She caught it before it closed.

"I'm not staying long so no need to close the door," she said. "Furthermore my associate sees the door closed, the police are here in less than ten minutes. Not enough time for you to clean up this place and flush all that junk away."

"What the fuck you want, lady?" the man asked.

"I want Tosha."

The man grabbed Tosha by the arms and flung her, with the baby, in Theresa's direction. "Okay you got her. Now get the fuck out my house."

Theresa finally got a full view of Tosha and she practically choked when she saw the girl's face. Her eyes were swollen and blood trickled from her nose. She clung tightly to her baby. Theresa was tempted to say something to the man, but her better judgment decided against it. She just needed to get Tosha out of there and deal with these bastards later.

"Come on, Tosha." She placed her arms around the young girl and led her out the door and onto the porch. They needed to get to the car and out of there before this man did something crazy.

"You stupid ass bitch, don't come back here looking for nothun 'cause your ass got nothun comin'!" the man shouted as he followed them out on the porch.

Theresa picked up the pace hurrying down the steps and to the car.

Chapter 33

Jason pulled into the packed Black Zebra parking lot at one o'clock in the morning, feeling ambivalent about what had happened earlier in the evening. Until the call came he had been productive, having completed the middle section and moved on to the ending of his novel. He felt inspired by Dominique, knowing that he'd be taking her to dinner early in the evening. They would have the entire night to continue pursuing what he perceived as a growing and meaningful relationship. And he was anxious to consummate their relationship with some love making at some point in the evening. Jason had done the understanding bit and the just hold me close act. Now it was time for some serious love making. Some toe-curling sex like Eddie Murphy and Robin Givens had in Boomerang. The thought of being with her had inspired him and provided the energy to dive right into his writing. And then the phone rang.

"Jason, I'm going to have to cancel on dinner this evening."

"Not even a hello or how are you doing?" Jason asked.

"I'm as disappointed as you are," Dominique said defensively. "But three girls called in sick and when that happens we're expected to fill in. You know we don't have a union."

"If you have to cancel, I guess you don't have a choice."

"I know, but I do have a choice over who picks me up. Would you be willing to do that?"

"Yeah, I guess. What time?"

"Jason, if it's going to be a burden for you I can find other transportation. I was just hoping that we could salvage some of the evening."

A smirk covered Jason's face. He thought of telling her no, but knew that wasn't possible. "Salvage some of the evening," he repeated. "The evening will be over by—"

"Jason, we don't have to go through these changes. I'll find other transportation."

"Wait, don't hang up. What time?"

"I'll be ready to go at three. Is that too late for you?"

"No, I'll be there."

"Thank you, sweetheart, you won't be sorry."

Jason pulled into an empty parking spot, turned off the engine and headed into the club. After Dominique's call he could no longer concentrate on his writing. He couldn't get away from Elliott's cynical reaction earlier in the day when Jason told him what had happened in Palm Springs. That Dominique might be using him dominated his thoughts. Maybe he shouldn't have let her off the hook, and insisted they have sex. For that reason he decided to get to the club a couple hours early so that he could study her behavior with other customers. It would be tough if he watched her disappear into one of the private rooms with someone else, but if he planned a relationship with her he'd better get used to the lifestyle.

Jason paid the cover charge, went inside and found an empty table back in the corner away from the three stages. He glanced at all three dancers, and Dominique was not one of them. He then stared in the direction of the private rooms fearful that she might be back there. Suddenly the thought occurred to him that he was really spying on her. What an absolutely insane thing to do. If she felt he was checking on her, she would probably tell him to kiss off. But he was already inside and had to let the chips fall where they may. The waitress approached him.

"You looking for Dominique?" she asked.

"Not really, but in a way, yes."

"Sounds kind of confusing." She smiled at him. "She's in the dressing room. You just missed her on stage. I'll tell her that you're here."

"No don't. I want to surprise her."

The smile left the waitress's face and she stared for a moment at Jason. "Better to let her know you're here," she said. "She's been pretty busy this evening."

"That's fine, but I don't want to interfere in her work."

"A little advice, my friend. I know Dominique, and she don't like games. Now can I take your order?"

Jason's expression hardened. He never considered what he was doing a game. "Yeah, you can bring me a cranberry juice and soda."

The waitress wrote the order on a pad and without saying any more, turned and walked away.

After forty-five minutes, four dancers who approached him for table dances, and his second cranberry juice and soda, Dominique finally appeared on center stage. She wore all black and had her hair flowing loosely over her shoulders. Her movement was perfectly synchronized to the music. As soon as she appeared on stage a half dozen men jumped from their chairs and rushed forward. With her soft and easy motion, Dominique made her way to each man, kneeled in front of him and accepted his dollar bills. She knelt in front of one man dressed in a business suit and carried on a conversation. Jason could tell that he was probably one of her regulars. She kept smiling and talking and at one point ran her hand across the side of his face. He felt a tinge of jealous emotion. She got up and made her way over to another man with money in his hand. She still hadn't seen Jason and he thought for a moment that maybe he should sneak out and go home. It would be rather embarrassing if he was there and she planned to leave with someone else.

Finally the music ended and Dominique started off the center stage and toward the side one. Just as she reached the second stage she looked in Jason's direction and her face seemed to light up. She waved and smiled at him. At that moment his emotions were mixed. He felt both good and bad at the same time. The fact that she created an excitement in him that he'd never experienced before made him feel good. He looked at his watch. A little after two, so she obviously was dancing her last set. With less than an hour to go, it would probably be best if he waited for her outside in the car. Dominique stared directly at him when she began to dance. He couldn't hold the smile any longer. She waved at him and also smiled. This was the perfect time for Jason to make his exit. He signaled to her that he'd be outside. She acknowledged his signal. Jason watched for a few more minutes while the man with the business suit followed Dominique to the second stage. She knelt in front of him to take his money, but at the same time looked in Jason's direction. As he watched her work her magic he got up and headed out of the club.

Jason had waited about an hour when he finally spotted Dominique exiting the club with a number of other dancers. To his dismay he saw a man jump from his car which was parked closer to the door than Jason's and hurry toward Dominique. Damn, she planned to leave with him. Jason watched carefully as Dominique froze in place and the other girls stopped with her. It didn't look as though she'd planned this at all. She looked around as if she were looking for him. The son of a bitch was scaring her. Jason jumped from his car and hurried in her direction. She smiled when he approached.

"Come on, Dominique, let me take you out for a late snack," the man said. He stood right in front of her.

"I don't think so," Dominique replied. "In fact my ride just arrived."

Jason approached her, brushing right by the man and ready for a fight if necessary. "Are you ready to get out of here?" he asked Dominique while glaring at the man.

"Wait a minute, baby, I guarantee you I can pay more money than this guy," the man said. He moved closer to Dominique.

"Mister, I suggest you back off." Jason turned and faced the man.

"Hey fella, mind your own business. I done spent a hell of a lot of money on this woman and I expect a payoff."

Jason went into his pocket and pulled out 2 twenty-dollar bills and tossed them to the man. "Consider this a refund, now get the hell out of our way."

"I don't want your damn money. I can buy and sell both of you!" the man shouted as he moved in closer to Jason.

"Come on, Jason, let's go." Dominique grabbed Jason by the arm and started to pass by the man.

"Not that easy," the man said and grabbed Dominique. Jason had to act. He moved in, broke the man's grip on Dominique then stood between them. He could smell the strong stench of alcohol on the man's breath.

"I suggest you'd better go and sleep it off, my friend," Jason said sternly.

"If I do it's going to be with her." The man tried to reach around Jason and grab Dominique.

Before Jason could grab the man, the bouncer who had informed Jason that Dominique had left him that first night, shot out of the door and in seconds had the man in a choke-hold. He pulled him away from Dominique and Jason.

"You all go ahead," the bouncer said as he continued to hold the choking man by the neck. "I guarantee you, he won't bother you anymore."

Dominique stared at the man and there for a moment Jason felt that she wanted to rush to his defense.

"Come on let's get out of here," he said as he took her by the arm and led her away. She took one final glance at the man and then left with Jason.

They had driven for about five minutes before Jason finally asked, "You all right?"

Dominique who had rested her head on the headrest, sighed and closed her eyes.For another minute she said nothing and he glanced over at her. He would wait until she was ready. It seemed as though he was always being patient with her. Finally she said, "Why do men have to be so immature?"

"I don't think it's the man so much as the alcohol. Those guys stay in there for hours just hoping to get close to you ladies and, in the meantime, they get pretty drunk."

"So what you're saying is that it's our fault?" she asked without looking over at him.

Elliott's comment about the hustle shot through his mind and he was tempted to say yes. But that would definitely cause further turmoil and they had endured enough for the evening.

"No, I'm not saying that at all."

"What are you saying, Jason? I want to know." Dominique turned and faced him.

Jason looked over at the Staple Center and then at the many buildings all lit up behind it. He then moved into his right lane and took the exit to the I10 Freeway all the while wondering why he was reluctant to speak his mind with her. Was he that desperate to get her in the bed? Had he lost that kind of control of his emotions? The answer had to be no. He would take her home without causing a commotion and then turn away from her. This entire situation was getting too complicated and it hadn't even gotten started. He finally looked at Dominique who still stared at him, obviously waiting for an answer.

"I'm saying, Dominique, that I think I'm going to leave this alone."

"Why?" she asked now in a softer tone.

"I don't know. Maybe because my emotions are rushing out of control to a place I don't think I'm going to like," he said. "Maybe because of what you do and I'm not sure I can adjust to it. Just a whole bunch of reasons."

"If you think you're taking me home, I don't want to go."

"What do you mean?" Jason turned and looked at her. She smiled and he weakened.

"Why can't I go to your place? I bet you have someone else there and that's why you had to take me out of town for our first date."

"Wrong on all accounts," Jason rejoined. He approached Crenshaw exit, the one he'd take to his place. He had to make a quick decision. Five minutes ago he was determined to take her home and be finished with it, but now the smile had changed all that. "I very much live alone and I took you to Palm Springs because I felt you deserved the very best."

"You don't feel that way anymore?" Dominique reached over and placed her hand on his arm and gently rubbed it.

Jason suddenly shot over two lanes, almost hitting another

car, and took the Crenshaw exit. If this was a game as Elliott had suggested then she had won again. He made the left turn on Crenshaw and headed to his apartment.

U

Dominique flopped down on the love seat, tossed off her shoes and relaxed her body. Jason headed for the CD player and was searching through his collection when she said, "Please, something very soft and relaxing."

He smiled, grabbed an old jazz CD by Dave Brubeck and placed it in the player. The room came alive with the smooth sounds of Paul Desmond on the alto saxophone and Brubeck on the piano playing Stardust. Jason then sauntered into the kitchen and opened the refrigerator. There were a couple cans of Sprite inside.

"I'm sorry I don't have any food to offer, but I do have a Sprite if you'd like one."

"All I want is you over here next to me. I hope that's not too tall a request." She looked in his direction.

Jason closed the refrigerator and made his way back into the living room. He sat down next to Dominique and put his arm around her. She leaned her head over on his shoulder and kissed him on the neck. Jason closed his eyes and took it all in. This was just the way he imagined it would be. He began to rub her bare arm and her skin was smooth and soft. She moved in even closer and began to rub his leg. Within moments of her touching him, his erection was complete. It suddenly dawned on him that they really hadn't kissed a lot in Palm Springs. After they went to bed and held each other, they both drifted off to sleep. What he did remember about their kiss was the softness of her lips. He took her chin and turned it in his direction. He then kissed her and felt her body go limp. Again Dominique's lips were soft, wet and full.

The wonderful melodic sounds of Brubeck on the piano and Desmond on the saxophone added a certain spice to the atmosphere. He began to rub her leg through her pants and unbuttoned the front of her blouse. He then slid her pants down. When he touched her bare leg, the skin was just as he'd imagined, also soft and smooth. She finally unzipped his pants and placed her hands inside, feeling and rubbing his erection. Jason was so excited he could lose it right there, and that would be a disaster. Finally Dominique pulled her hand out and pulled away from him.

"Let's take a shower. I want to be absolutely clean and fresh for you," she said.

Jason pulled up, all the time kissing her. He finally released her and said, "That sounds like a wonderful idea. But no just holding tonight. Is that a deal?"

She smiled, stood up and said, "That's a deal. I love your music, I love jazz. Could you put some more on?"

"No problem," Jason said. He got up and walked over to the player. This time he picked John Coltrane For Lovers Only to play next. Brubeck had just gone into his rendition of How High the Moon. Jason wasn't sure just how high the moon sat in the sky, but he was sure of just how high he felt at that moment. He followed Dominique into the bedroom. When he entered the room he noticed the red light on the phone flashing. No way would he retrieve the message. He hurried over and unplugged it from the wall socket. No matter what the emergency he wouldn't be disturbed.

Dominique sat on the side of the bed and took off all her clothes. Jason stood on the other side of the bed near the phone and also undressed. He couldn't take his eyes off her. Everything about Dominique was perfect. Full breasts, small waist, round full backside and beautiful long shapely legs. Jason was determined to enjoy every inch of her body.

He walked over to where she had laid on the bed, took her hand and they went into the bathroom. He turned on the shower and they got under the hot titillating water sprouting from the nozzle. Dominique lay back in Jason's arms and he felt the entire softness of her body. He gently rubbed her down with the suds. He slid his hand over her full breasts and down over her soft stomach. But just as he neared her pleasure palace, she stopped him. He frowned slightly but continued his motion with his hands, making sure not to touch her beyond that point. He could only hope this wouldn't be a problem. Dominique turned around, and with soap covering her front side hugged him tightly. Again they kissed. She sudsed her hands and applied soap to his back from the top to down below his buttocks. They both stood embracing under the flow of the hot water and allowed the soap to run off their bodies.

After a couple of minutes standing there embracing tightly and kissing, they finally broke loose and stepped out of the shower. Jason had reached the point of sensitivity so that if he were touched he would probably explode. He had to make the first time long and lasting. He tried thinking about other things, his writing, his dumb brother-in-law and even Elliott in order to calm down. But nothing worked. Damn if he lost it when he first entered her, he could only hope that she'd understand that it wouldn't always be like that.

Dominique sat on the side of the bed while Jason dried her body. When finished, she took the towel and began to dry Jason, slowly working her way down the front of his body, then his legs, Finally when Dominique finished she loosely wrapped the towel around her body, pulled back the bedspread and lay on the sheet. Jason watched her every move with anticipation. He slid in the bed next to her and began to kiss the front of her body, slowly making his way down between her legs. Before he could get to where he planned to spend some time, she grabbed his head and stopped him.

"I don't want you to do that," she whispered.

"Why?" he asked as he slid back up next to her.

"Maybe someday when we really get close I'll tell you. But not right now, please, Jason, just make love to me."

Jason felt a little disappointed. He knew not to push the issue of oral sex with her. But he wondered how could they possibly have a good sex life without some oral foreplay? Maybe as time went by she'd change. He'd known other women who refused to jump right into the oral sex thing. Not all women were free and open like Raquel. Jason pulled his body up next to Dominique, reached over into his dresser drawer and grabbed a condom.

"I'm sure you want me to use this."

"Right now, yes. But after we get to know each other much better and completely trust each other, no, I don't want you to use that."

"Fair enough," he said as he slid the condom up and around his erection. He then straddled Dominique. She closed her eyes and seemed to relax.

Jason softly kissed her lips and then lowered his body on top of her. She wrapped both arms around him and quietly moaned to his movement. Even with the rubber she felt wonderful. In the background he faintly heard John Coltrane's melodic and smooth sounds playing Like Someone in Love. But the sounds of music slowly faded away. All he could hear were her wonderful moans and her grip tightened as he reached that point of ecstasy. She seemed to arrive there with him and they both experienced the pleasure of a climax at the very same moment.

Chapter 34

The clock on the night stand read six o'clock in the morning and Dominique was not lying next to him. Jason had just awakened and reached over for her. He shot straight up. No way would she leave without waking him? He jumped out of the bed and rushed into the living room. Dominique sat on the couch with legs tucked under her and arms folded. She had her eyes closed and seemed to be meditating. Jason didn't know if he should disturb her but he had to make sure she was all right. On second thought, he decided to stand there for a few minutes and just observe. She had wrapped the towel around her body, but it couldn't hide the beauty she possessed. He felt a surge of joy shoot through him as he recalled their love-making. They hadn't done all the other things he usually did in order to achieve total satisfaction, but there had been a certain beauty between the two of them that made it much better than all other times.

He really cared for this woman in a very special way. Just standing there looking at her excited him. He wanted to rush over there and take her in his arms again. For some reason he felt an overwhelming desire to protect this woman. After last night, he would have a very difficult time going back into the Black Zebra and watching her dance in front of a bunch of abusive men. Having now lain with her, kissed her, talked with her and made love to her, he knew there was a great deal more to her than being a dancer. But would she ever open up and share that something with him?

She remained completely still just as though she didn't know he was in the room. Suddenly his mind shifted to Big Casey and Hazel. If this relationship became serious what would they think of her? The most judgmental would probably be Jacqueline.

Theresa and Cedric would accept her regardless of her profession. The only unpredictable one would be Big Casey. But why was he tripping? Chances were they probably would never become that serious. Too many obstacles stood in their way. His writing and her career would preclude them from anything more than a casual relationship. "A fun fuck" as Elliott would often say. The bottom line was that he wouldn't care what anyone else thought. He knew she had the potential to completely take all his emotions and at this point he wanted that to happen. Finally she began to stir a little, turned and smiled at him.

"How long you been there?" she asked.

"A couple of minutes of just admiring you."

"You're so sweet," Dominique whispered. "Have you always been this sweet? They just don't make many as nice as you." She brought her legs back down and stretched out on the couch. "Please come and sit next to me. Last night was absolutely wonderful."

Jason sat on the love seat next to her. She laid her head on his shoulder and again the feeling of protecting her overwhelmed him.

"May I ask what you were doing?"

"Meditating, silly."

"That's what I thought. Are you into some Buddhist stuff?"

"I would say more of transcendentalism," she answered and kissed him on the cheek.

"I guess you're not much into traditional Black church, you know the Baptist and Methodist?"

"Not really. They're much too restrictive."

Jason began to stroke her long black hair through his hands. "How do they restrict you?" he asked.

Dominique wrapped both her arms around Jason and snuggled in closer to him. "They tell you that you only have one opportunity to get your soul right for eternity. If you don't make the first time, regardless of the obstacles you might confront, then you go to hell and burn for eternity."

"You saying you don't believe in Heaven and hell?"

"I definitely believe in Heaven, but I have my doubts about hell. Why would a God who loves us all equally send some of us to hell and allow the others into paradise? That doesn't seem very fair to me."

Jason felt a little nervous with such a heavy conversation about religion. He wanted to turn to a much lighter discussion. "I guess you're right," he said. "Are you happy right now, right at this minute?"

"Very much so," Dominique answered. She again reached up and kissed him on the lips. "Oh my God, I haven't even brushed my teeth and I'm kissing you."

"That's what love is all about," he said. "Sharing the funky moments as well as the more pleasurable ones."

"Love? How did that word creep into our conversation?"

"Don't take it too seriously. I guess you can say I was using it rather loosely."

Dominique instantly pulled up and sat in an upright position next to Jason, but not cuddling quite as close. "That's an emotion you shouldn't use loosely, and you definitely shouldn't make a joke of it."

Jason also assumed a more rigid position. It seemed he constantly had to be cognizant of what he said and how he said it with Dominique. He recalled the waitress warning him that Dominique was not the joking kind of woman. That her demeanor always assumed a more serious posture.

"Are you always so uptight about everything?" he asked.

"No, I'm not uptight right now. In fact I feel quite relaxed in your company and that is rather unusual for me."

"Why?"

"I don't think it's something I want to discuss right now." Dominique got up and headed back to the bedroom. "At some point we will have that discussion. But right now I think I'm ready for round two." She leaned back against the bedroom door and allowed the towel to fall to the floor. "How do you feel about that? You ready?"

Jason sprang off the couch and hurried over to her. He placed both arms around her naked body and together they entered the bedroom.

"I've been ready from the moment I woke up and reached over for you," he said.

"Well, you got me now."

They both laid back down on the bed close to each other.

"I hope for a very long time," he said.

"Funkiness and all?"

"You got it." He pulled her into his arms and they kissed all over again.

Chapter 35

Arthur relaxed in one of the lounge chairs on the balcony watching the sea gulls circle the water, waiting to swoop on their prey. The sun was just beginning to disappear behind the ocean and it gave off a radiant red sunset. Jacqueline was gone when he got home from work. She left a note telling him that she was at Hazel's helping plan Big Casey's sixty-fifth birthday bash. Why it took so much time and energy to plan a fucking birthday party he just didn't understand. And the way they all pampered that big son of a bitch was disgusting. You'd think he had a brass ass or something.

He smiled and took a sip of the martini prepared when he first got home. The real reason they all kissed Big Casey's ass, from Jason to Theresa, was because he provided them with a lifestyle fit for only the rich. The one that didn't seem to be bothered with all of them was Cedric. Arthur didn't know Cedric all that well since he carried his spoiled ass off to San Francisco. The one that really pissed him off was Theresa. She acted so fucking arrogant and independent, making on like she didn't need a man in her life. She reminded him of that arrogant bitch Dominique. The uppity bitch wasn't nothing but a dancer and she had the nerve to go moralistic on him. He'd get even with her someday, just as he would get even with Theresa for always sticking her nose in his business. They both acted like they were dykes. Shit he could do both of them at the same time just like Indria and Elizabeth. That bitch Indria got off when she first saw his size. She tried to swallow it, but it was definitely too much for her to handle. So it would also be too much for Theresa and Dominique.

Arthur took a much larger sip of the martini. He hadn't been back over to see Elizabeth since the last time he did the crack cocaine and had an orgy with those two freaks. Damn, they were good! Some of the best sex he'd ever had, nothing like here at home with Jacqueline. He'd promised her that morning she got back from Theresa's that he'd change his ways. Not stay out late at night and definitely not stay out all night. It took a lot of promises, cajoling and love making to convince Jacqueline not to leave him. No way could he let her decide when their marriage would end. That would be done at his discretion and only after he had all his ducks in order financially. In the meantime he'd just keep screwing her ass into oblivion and leaving her dick whipped.

But he was getting bored coming home from work early every evening and spending all his time with one person. Still, there wasn't much he could do since his job and considerable income depended on keeping her happy. He chuckled as he considered staying there from now on and only having sex with his wife. Just live the life of a gigolo because that's pretty much what he was doing now. It seemed only fair that if Jason could stay home, write and still get paid, why couldn't he stay with Jacqueline, have sex and get a payday also? Hell the work he did at headquarters didn't amount to much. He still hadn't sat down with Big Casey and talked about his position with the company. He'd see him in the mornings, they'd say hello, and then Arthur wouldn't see him again until the end of the day. Based on Big Casey's behavior, Arthur wasn't really sure the man even liked him. He probably tolerated him because of his daughter.

Arthur glanced at his watch and it read a little past seven. The martini just didn't do it for him and he didn't have anymore marijuana. He needed to call his source, run back into town and stock up on another stash. But he really didn't crave the weed. He wanted those two freaks sucking over his body while he sucked on the pipe. No telling how long Jacqueline would be over to her mother's house. He probably could make it over to Elizabeth's, hit on the pipe a couple of times, get some oral pleasure and make it back home before Jacqueline got back. Hopefully, that freak Indria would be over there and he could really take a trip into paradise again. He took a final sip of the martini, picked up his cell phone and dialed the number.

"I was wondering how long it was going to take you to call," Elizabeth said on the other end.

"I had to lay low for a while. The old lady was really bent out of shape when I stayed out all night," Arthur explained.

"Arthur, you know I need some money."

"I figured that. That's one of the reasons I called."

"And what was the other reason?"

"I was wondering if you had any of that stuff?"

"The cocaine?"

"Don't say that over the phone."

"Grow up, Arthur. No one is interested in our conversation. But yes, I do have some. That's why I need some money."

"How about your friend, is she there?"

"What friend is that, Arthur?"

"You know, Indria."

"So you like her, huh?"

"She's all right. Not as good as you. But the two of you together are dynamite."

"She'll be here by the time you get here."

"I'm on my way."

"Don't forget the money."

"How could I possibly do that?" Arthur hit the off button on the cell phone. He rushed inside closing the balcony door behind him. He had to hurry and make it all the way to Hollywood, then smoke on the pipe and get sexual pleasure all before midnight. Jacqueline would not get home before then. He couldn't mess up again. He had too much to lose, but on the other hand, he had to see the two freaks before he went out of his mind from boredom. Somehow he had to balance the two needs so that neither one would be jeopardized.

Chapter 36

Jason could feel Dominique's eyes on him as he sat with his back to her at the computer trying to finish off another chapter. He turned around and sure enough she lay there stretched out across the bed, head propped in her hands and arms in an upright position. She smiled at him and he smiled back, then turned to continue his work. Suddenly he felt arms around his neck, soft breasts against his back, and moist lips teasing along his neck line. Jason turned around in his chair and pulled her down into his lap.

"I can see now that I'm going to have trouble getting any work done with you around," he said and then kissed her.

After a few moments she pulled away from his kiss. "Is that all bad?" she asked.

"No way, not in this world." Jason ran his hand along her arm. "You can interrupt me anytime, anywhere."

Dominique jumped from his lap and sat back on the bed with legs tucked under her body. "No, I don't want to be a nuisance to you," she said. "You go back to work. I'll just sit and admire you."

"What do you mean admire?" Jason asked.

"Anyone who can create a story with characters that make people happy or sometimes sad is to be admired. That's a talent straight from God."

"Thank you." Jason got up and bowed in her direction. "Now all I have to do is finish it, find a publisher, and let the entire world marvel at my genius."

"And to think you're going to let me be a part of all this."

"Right now, right this minute, you are my driving force. I get my inspiration from you."

"All in one week."

"Why is that so hard to believe?"

"Because things just don't happen that fast."

Jason walked over and sat next to Dominique. "Are you telling me that you don't want them to happen that fast?" he asked.

"No, I'm not saying that at all."

"Just how fast do you want this to happen?"

"Jason, you can't manipulate a relationship to fit some kind of time frame. I believe when you begin to measure the extent and degree of human emotions you do begin to manipulate. And I don't want that to happen with us."

'That's fair enough. So we just take it from day to day."

"Will that work for you?"

"I guess it will have to," he said, got up and walked back over to the computer. "Are you hungry?"

"Not really. I just want to sit here and watch you work."

Jason sat back down and turned to face the computer. He could feel her presence all over the room. It wasn't like she just sat on the bed. Dominique was everywhere and under this extreme scrutiny he couldn't write. He rubbed his forehead and stared at the monitor. His biggest problem was trying to put a handle on her. She didn't fit his perception of a dancer and yet that's exactly what she did for a living.

For the past five nights he'd picked her up at the club, a fact that made her lifestyle a reality. But once they were alone she was different. And the worst part is that she continued to hold back on sharing her experiences with him, making it that much more difficult to understand why such a beautiful, deep thinking woman would be involved in such an ugly profession. At some point he knew she would have to share her secrets with him in order for their relationship to grow. Until that happened it was imperative that he hold back his emotions and keep control of this situation. But with each passing day, being in her company, he wasn't sure he'd be able to control his feelings.

"Your mind is wandering," Dominique said softly.

"I know and that's not good. I really do need to concentrate more on this particular chapter."

Dominique got off the bed and again strolled over next to

him. This time she did not hug him, but instead stood off to his left and stared at the monitor.

"What are you trying to accomplish?" she asked.

Jason continued to stare at the monitor. For the first time since they'd been together he felt a slight irritation. He wasn't comfortable with this intrusion. He didn't know what he'd gain by answering her question. So he chose to ignore it.

"Jason, I asked you a question." Dominique now had some irritation in her voice.

He abruptly turned and faced her. "I'm sorry but it's really difficult to concentrate with you staring over my shoulder."

"My, aren't we touchy," Dominique shot back at him and then moved away.

He swung his chair in her direction and held his arms open. "I'm sorry, come back over here."

"No, I won't come there. What do you think, I'm some kind of puppy that responds to your up and down behavior?"

"Come on, Dominique, isn't that a little drastic?"

"Jason, don't ever treat me like a child."

"I'm sorry, that wasn't my intention." Jason hurried over to Dominique, wrapped his arms around her and felt her weaken in his embrace. "You're not a child and I am very much aware of that." He kissed her on the cheek and held her even closer. "Are you hungry yet?"

"A little."

"Good, I'll take a break and get us some breakfast." Jason sat on the side of the bed and began to put on his shoes.

Dominique jumped back in the bed and pulled the covers over her. "And while you're gone I'm going to watch something absolutely stupid on television."

"Yeah, what is that?"

"It's ten o'clock. I think the Jerry Springer show is on. That's pretty darn stupid."

"Finally we agree on something." Jason finished lacing his shoes and stood up.

"We agree on a lot of things," Dominique said.

"You're right, we do." He was not about to get into another spat with her. "What is it you'd like to eat?"

"I don't know. Surprise me."

"You might not approve of my choice."

"I will even if I don't."

"There you go getting confusing on me again." Jason started for the door.

"Anyone who can write a novel can easily figure out what I mean," she said just as the phone rang. Dominique snatched it from its cradle and Jason froze in place.

"Hello, Jason Mitchell's residence," Dominique said.

There was a pause and for that moment Jason's instincts told him that the person on the other end was someone he wouldn't want to know about Dominique.

"Yes, he's here. One moment, please." Dominique did not smile when she handed him the phone. He let out a long sigh as he dreaded hearing the voice on the other end.

"Yeah, this is Jason."

"Who is that who answered your phone?" Angela shouted. "You now let your women answer your phone. She must be someone awfully special."

"Slow down, Angela," Jason said as he turned his back to Dominique. "She's a friend and what do you want?"

"I thought maybe you might want to spend a little time with your daughter since you haven't seen her in over a month. But I guess I was mistaken since I now know your time is taken by other interests."

"Don't be ridiculous and of course I want to see my daughter." Jason kept his back turned to Dominique.

"I just finished talking with Jacqueline and she invited me and your daughter to Big Casey's birthday party, something you didn't do. Maybe you'll get a chance to say hello to your daughter. Are you bringing your friend?"

"That's none of your business."

"If you do I hope she's someone decent since your daughter will more than likely meet her."

"Is that the only reason you called?"

"No, as a matter of fact I wanted to let you know that I didn't get my increase on the child support like you promised."

"I'll check on it with my lawyer."

"Jason, how am I ever going to allow your daughter to spend the night with you when you have strange women staying there? My daughter will be exposed to, God forbid, who knows what."

"Angela, I have to go." Jason finished and hung up.

He stood there momentarily, took in a deep breath, then turned and faced Dominique. She wasn't smiling, even though she had no reason to be upset. Jason then placed the phone back in the cradle and sat on the side of the bed. Dominique had gotten dressed.

"That was my daughter's mother," he said.

"I never even knew you had a daughter."

"I don't know why I hadn't mentioned her. It wasn't like I was trying to keep her from you."

"Jason, why did you tell her that I was just a friend?"

"Aren't we friends?"

"Don't get cute. You know we are friends, but aren't we also lovers?"

"You know we are, but I don't see why I have to advertise that fact to the world."

"I wouldn't consider your ex-lover and the mother of your child the entire world."

"What difference does this make?" Jason got up and started toward Dominique.

She pushed him away and moved toward the bedroom door. "No, not this time. I think I want to go home. I didn't know I was with a man who was ashamed to let others know that we are lovers." Dominique stopped right at the door and turned to face him. "You really are ashamed of what I do for a living. Well just remember where you met me. If you're ashamed of what I do, what does that say about you?"

"Dominique, I am not ashamed of you and I want us to stop this fighting." Jason again tried to approach her, but she opened the door and started out.

"Maybe I mis-read you," she said as she again paused to look at him. "I usually don't get a wrong feeling about the men that come into the club, but I sure did it with you."

"You're really blowing this out of proportion. There is nothing between Angela and me. We happen to share the same child and because of that I have to talk to her."

"You bastard, you really think I believe that."

"Dominique, what's wrong with you? I've never heard you curse before." He again tried to reach out for her and she moved away.

"Let's just say that men like you bring out the worst in me. My entire life from a small child on, I've had to deal with men like you."

"Please don't stereotype me." Jason felt his temperature rising. Maybe it was best to just have it out with her and let her leave. He didn't need all this complication.

"I'm sorry, Mr. Mitchell, but if the stereotype fits, wear it." Dominique opened the door, walked out and slammed it shut.

Jason couldn't believe she had walked out that way. He hurried over to the door and started to open it, but his instincts stopped him. As much as he wanted to go after her, he decided to leave it alone. His need to protect her had to be subdued. She had blown this whole incident far beyond where it should have gone, and he couldn't continue caving into her moods. Elliott had it right all along. This entire sex thing was a game and there could only be one winner. It was vicious and ugly, but all the time camouflaged in pleasure and sexual gratification. No one was better prepared to play this vicious game than a woman who made her living getting over on men.

Jason sat on the couch, took in a deep breath and released it. In the end this relationship had to fail. Better now than later when he would have invested all his emotions in her. He got up and headed back to the bedroom and the computer. Best way to get over her was to dive back into his work. He sat down and started typing the chapter on the great escape and the use of the Underground Railroad.

Chapter 37

The day seemed to be dragging slowly by at the Poverty Law Office. For some reason Theresa couldn't concentrate on the many briefs on her desk that begged for attention. Instead her thoughts kept fluctuating between work and two new residents at home. After weeks of playing big sister and aunt to Tosha and her daughter, Theresa had become used to having them at the apartment. It was cramped and her two guests had to sleep on the couch. Often, however, she would take the baby into her room and let the child sleep in the bed. She hadn't yet told anyone in the family of the two new additions in her house. She figured she'd wait and tell them at Big Casey's birthday celebration in a couple of days. She would show up with Tosha and the baby and deal with anything negative because the two who might criticize her decision would be Jacqueline and Hazel. How ironic, the females in her life who should be most understanding would not be at all. Many times she'd thought about calling Jason and telling him. She needed a supporting hand from him. Theresa shifted through a pile of papers Harriet placed on her desk. She would call Jason that evening, invite him over, and introduce him to her new family.

Theresa glanced at her watch. Already one-thirty and she wasn't into her work. Tosha offered a real challenge. In fact, it was probably the biggest challenge she'd confronted since she had to make the decision to have an abortion. Theresa paused in her work as she recalled that time in life and the tremendous impact it had on her. In many ways that act defined and directed her life to this time when she decided to bring another young girl, much like herself, only from a different circumstance, into her home. Often she would stare at Tosha playing with the baby and see visions of her own child, imagining how that little one would have made a difference in her life. It bothered her that she took away that potential life. But now she could make up for her mistake by being a good friend to Tosha and possibly a good role model for the young girl and the baby.

They still needed to get the baby checked for HIV. Whenever she mentioned going to the clinic Tosha objected. She would argue what one of the other girls living in the house had told her that the child while in the womb was protected from any kind of viruses or infections the mother may have. Tosha suffered from denial. She refused to accept the reality that she may have infected her daughter with a life-threatening disease. What a burden for anyone to carry, no matter how short their life might be. Tosha had been extremely irresponsible with her reckless behavior, but that didn't mean she didn't love and care for her child. That love prevented her from doing what needed to be done and that is get the baby checked for the infection. Theresa would wait another week and then if Tosha still refused she would force her to do the right thing.

Theresa got up, sauntered over to the window and stared out on Central Avenue. Across the street stood a series of low rent apartments. Kids played in the fenced-in dirt yard with no grass or trees for shade. Many of the swings were broken and the slide leaned to one side so they couldn't use it. Every time she looked across the street at the apartment complex depression set in. It was like a jungle over there and Theresa always thought that the children growing up in that environment had been dealt a loaded deck full of bad cards. How could they ever compete starting out at such a disadvantage? That's probably what happened to Tosha and ultimately would happen to her daughter if she didn't die of AIDS first. Theresa had to make this work for Tosha and her baby no matter what it took.

As she turned and started back to her desk, the door swung open and Jacqueline, along with Hazel, came rushing through. She froze in place, shocked to see the two of them in her office. Something must have happened to Arthur or possibly Big Casey. Theresa didn't know if she should greet them with a smile or just stand there and wait for something to happen. What that something would be is what momentarily frightened her.

Hazel spoke first. "My God in Heaven, child, this is where you work?"

"What in the world brings you all down here?" Theresa finally asked as she hugged her mother. "I'm surprised that you even knew how to get over here."

"We were putting the finishing touches on the birthday party for Daddy and we thought you might want to join us," Jacqueline said.

"I don't know, I do have a couple of cases I need to work on this afternoon."

"It sure didn't look like you were doing too much work when we came in," Jacqueline countered.

"Come on, Theresa," Hazel said. "We girls don't ever do anything together anymore. When you both were young we used to always hang out, going shopping and having lunch together. Indulge your mother and join us."

Theresa glanced over at Harriet who had stopped working to listen in. She smiled at Theresa.

"Okay, let's go," Theresa blurted out. "You're right, we need to do a girl thing. What's the plan?"

"Good!" Hazel again hugged her baby daughter. "We're going to Beverly Hills to find Big Casey's final birthday present, and then we'll have lunch."

"Or an early supper, just depending on how long it takes," Jacqueline offered as the three of them started out of the building.

Theresa followed closed behind and sighed, hoping that this would not be a repeat of her last lunch with Jacqueline.

u

It was after four o'clock when the three women walked into Ruth's Chris Steakhouse on Rodeo Drive, to have a late lunch. The maitre de escorted them to a booth, with Hazel sitting between her two daughters. Jacqueline and Hazel both ordered martinis and Theresa an Evian water. Hazel stretched her arms across the table and gestured for her daughters to take her hands. Theresa and Jacqueline complied.

"I'm so proud of the two of you," Hazel smiled. "You two are as different as day and night but it makes me feel good to know that no matter how different you are, you're still awfully close to each other." Hazel squeezed Theresa's hand tightly. She then released both their hands and relaxed back in her chair. "You know, Theresa, that your sister has really gotten her marriage back together. And she told me that you helped her work through her hard times."

Theresa turned and stared at Jacqueline. She'd gotten her marriage back together? That was news to her.

"Now all we have to do is find you a good man," Hazel continued and stared directly at Theresa. "You can't go through life as a single woman. And you definitely can't go through life without having any kids. There is no higher honor for a woman than to give birth to a child."

"Mama, you don't have to be married to have children," Theresa blurted out without really thinking. So far they'd had an enjoyable afternoon. She didn't need to spoil it by challenging Hazel.

"Oh goodness, child, don't talk silly. You can't bring illegitimate children into this world."

"Mama, shame on you," Theresa shot back. "How can you say that when you have a grandchild who I'm sure you don't consider illegitimate? Jason and Angela weren't married."

"That's different," Hazel retorted.

"How's that—"

"Please, Theresa, can't we have an enjoyable afternoon without you challenging everything?" Jacqueline interrupted her.

Theresa deliberately shifted her body in the chair and took in a deep breath before she said something to Jacqueline she would regret. "Mama I can always adopt."

"Oh no, honey, you must have your own children. When you adopt you just don't know what you'll be getting. All these young girls getting pregnant and all strung out on drugs. My God, you might get stuck with a crack baby or something. No, have your own and you'll know what you're getting."

Fortunately the waiter brought the drinks and placed them on the table. It gave Theresa a moment to consider how she should respond to her mother. She sipped from the glass of water and relaxed. It was probably best that she leave this conversation alone. She briefly thought of Tosha and her young daughter. With people like Hazel thinking the way she did, what chance did those two poor souls have? It just tightened Theresa's resolve to help them. But at that particular moment, as she stared across the table at her sister, smug and hypocritical, and mother arrogant and snobbish, she knew better than to continue this line of conversation.

"How is Big Casey adjusting to reaching that magical age of sixty-five?" she asked Hazel.

"I think he's looking forward to it," Hazel answered. "He's been feeling kind of tired lately. He needs to think about retiring."

Theresa took another sip from the Evian. "He doesn't have anyone to take over since Jason decided to do his artistic thing. Has he mentioned anyone he might trust to run the business?"

"No, I don't think he wants to deal with the reality that he's going to have to retire someday," Hazel said. She took a sip from her martini.

Suddenly Jacqueline seemed to come back to life as she leaned forward. "I think Arthur is perfect for the position," she said proudly. "Does daddy ever mention the possibility of him taking over someday?"

"Honey, your father doesn't talk about anyone taking over. He thinks he's superman and will be there forever." Again Hazel drank from her martini.

"Well, Mama, I think you should raise the issue with him," Jacqueline said. "After all we know his health hasn't been the best and Arthur is at headquarters learning the business. It's obvious that Jason doesn't want to take over. And Heaven only knows what Cedric's doing up there in San Francisco. Only one he has to depend on is Arthur."

Theresa wanted to reach across the table and slap her sister. What a selfish way to think! Everything was always all about Jacqueline. Instantly she had a rather hateful thought. Maybe her sister was getting exactly what she deserved from her deceitful and trifling husband.

"By the way, has anyone heard from Cedric?" Hazel abruptly asked. "Wouldn't it be wonderful if he would be down here for Big Casey's big day?"

Theresa glared over at her sister as she figured Jacqueline shared similar thoughts about what Hazel just said. They both seemed to be silently communicating should they tell Hazel the truth about Cedric. Did she have a right to know that her youngest son was not only living in Los Angeles, but was also gay? Theresa could only hope that Jacqueline shared the sentiment to spare their mother since she seemed to be having a great afternoon with her daughters. The truth would eventually come out, but it was not necessary for it to surface right now.

"Well, have any of you heard from Cedric?" Hazel insisted on pursuing the issue. "Actually I should direct that question to Theresa. You two were always close and if he did communicate with anyone it would be you."

"No, I haven't, but I wouldn't be surprised if he just showed up at Big Casey's party," Theresa said.

"I wish I knew how to contact him," Hazel continued. "I'd send him an airline ticket and make sure he'd be here. That would make your father very happy."

A slight smirk appeared on Jacqueline's face as she sipped the last few drops of her martini. Theresa tensed up fearing what mischief her sister was up to.

"Mama, have you ever wondered about Cedric living up in San Francisco, never coming home to visit or never calling?'

"What do you mean wondered about him?" Hazel asked.

"You know he and his father were always at each other. Why he couldn't get along with his father I just don't know. All the rest of you have a wonderful relationship with Big Casey. So I'm not surprised he hasn't called."

"He could have called you," Jacqueline retorted.

"I expect you girls to call me, which you always have done, except that one period when Theresa went off to college. I expect the boys to call their father and Jason is quite good at that. What are you driving at anyway?"

"Oh, I don't know. San Francisco is kind of different than anywhere else in the country, with the exception maybe of New York," Jacqueline continued with her subtle insinuations.

Theresa caught her eye and gave Jacqueline a hard stare as if to say leave this alone.

"If you're trying to insinuate that my son may be gay, just stop that nonsense." Hazel surprised Theresa with that outburst. She never thought her mother would catch the subtle hints. But where to go from here now that Jacqueline had pursued this game with their mother?

"Those things do happen in San Francisco," Jacqueline continued.

"Those things happen everywhere, but not to a Mitchell," Hazel shot back emphatically. "And especially not to one of Big Casey's sons. My God, if that happened we might as well dig his grave."

"But what about you, Mama, how would you handle it?" Theresa now asked. She'd planned to leave the subject alone, but since it was out there, she figured they might as well know what they would have to deal with soon.

"I'd be more concerned about your father. You know he has that heart condition and I don't know if he could stand that kind of shock." Hazel hesitated and gave a very stern glance at her daughters. "Why are you asking me these kinds of questions about Cedric? Do you know something you're not sharing with me?"

"No, Mama, not at all," Theresa quickly answered. "We just

know the life styles in San Francisco and have to at least consider that possibility."

"Let's just remember there are more heterosexuals than the others," Hazel said. "It's just those gays always make a lot more noise and get more attention. I'm certain that Cedric is just like his brother and you both know how much Jason loves women."

"You're right, Mama." Theresa stared at Jacqueline as if to question why she even raised this issue. Jacqueline looked away as the waiter approached the table to take their order. Theresa decided to say no more on the subject. But as she began to examine the menu she was very much aware of just how interesting Big Casey's birthday party really would be.

Chapter 38

Damn, this freaky shit excited Arthur! He leaned back on Elizabeth's headboard and watched while Indria and Elizabeth lay between each other's legs. It was Friday and he'd been over at the apartment since three o'clock in the afternoon. He'd left work early and as usual no one questioned him. Arthur felt like an invisible man just existing at headquarters. At first that really did bother him, but now, as it worked to his advantage for escaping into an afternoon of pleasure, he didn't mind.

The three of them had already smoked up a couple hundred dollars of cocaine. He had to admit the two freaks wore his ass out. So at that point all he wanted to do was smoke some cocaine and enjoy watching them do each other and in doing so, would eventually get an erection. But he'd have to refrain from any further sex with them. For the past two months since that all night encounter he'd maintained some control. He had to get home by at least nine o'clock, about the same time he figured Jacqueline would get back from her afternoon outing with Hazel. Arthur grabbed a small rock, placed it in the pipe, lit it and pulled on the other end. It was a damn good hit and he felt it throughout his entire body. The cocaine energized him, made him sensitive and he wanted to join the women at the other end of the bed.

As good as he felt, and as good as they would also make him feel, he still had to refrain. At times like this he hated the idea of being married. This was living off the hook and he could do this all the time. Best part about it, he did it so well and these freaks loved his weapon.

A second hit of the cocaine took him even higher. Suddenly his mind wandered away from the freaky shit happening right in front of him. He closed his eyes and images of Dominique danced before him. He could visualize her naked body dancing all over his body, feel her smooth, soft skin sliding down the front of him and imagined her at the bottom of the bed with Elizabeth and Indria engaging in all the freaky shit they were doing. Then again, he wouldn't want to share her with anyone else, not even the women. Arthur was certain that at some point in the future their paths would cross again and this time he wouldn't blow the opportunity to lay all his twelve plus inches of pure pleasure on her.

Elizabeth interrupted his fantasy as he felt her wet soft lips all over his body. Damn, he'd been determined not to go another round with these two freaks. He needed to rest his body just in case Jacqueline would be frisky when he got home. But nothing she could do compared to what pleasure he felt right at that moment. Arthur lacked the will power to stop them for fear they might get upset and never do it again. That he wouldn't be able to handle. As the two women took him to an even higher plateau of pleasure, he relaxed, forgot about Jacqueline and her needs and let it happen.

u

Arthur had come down from his cocaine high by the time he pulled into the driveway at his townhouse. A state of depression had set in, something not uncommon when he lost his high. When it happened before, he mentioned it to Elizabeth and she told him to just get high all over again. He could only do that when he was at her apartment. Arthur was also tired and after three climaxes within the past four hours, knew he wouldn't be able to perform anymore that evening. When he hit the garage opener and the door lifted he hoped that Jacqueline's Mercedes wouldn't be there. But he had no such luck, which meant he'd have to face her in this condition. It was only eight- thirty and she'd be up waiting for him. Jacqueline had just come off her period and usually was horny as hell at that time. He parked his car next to hers, got out and headed inside. If she was in the mood he probably could get it up for a fourth time, but she'd have to give him a hell of a lot of help, something she didn't always like to do.

Arthur swung the door open hoping that Jacqueline had decided to go to bed early. Again, no such luck. He made it through the kitchen and caught the smell of fried chicken.

He glanced into the dining room and saw the dinner table set up for two. Jacqueline turned to face him and then ran and threw her arms around his neck.

"Guess what, Arthur honey?" she practically screamed in his ear. "I think Big Casey's going to retire soon and Mama practically assured me that he plans to name you as his replacement."

"What?" Arthur replied in complete shock. He found a heavy dose of energy. "You have to be kidding? She really said that?"

Jacqueline kissed him on the cheek and broke loose from him. "She didn't exactly say that." She backed off her earlier words. "But we talked about Jason not wanting to do it. And God only knows what Cedric's going to do, so honey that leaves only you." She smiled and this time kissed him on the lips.

Arthur's enthusiasm waned as he stared at his wife. She had to be either the most naïve or the dumbest woman in the world. Big Casey hardly recognized that Arthur existed in the office. He'd probably make that white boy head of the company before he'd give it to him. And then there was the possibility that he'd give it to Theresa. She was Big Casey's favorite. Hell she looked just like him, had a law degree and definitely was smart enough to run the company. Arthur's body sagged and he felt the effects of his earlier activities. He didn't want to continue this conversation because it would really piss him off. How dumb could Jacqueline really be?

"What's wrong, Arthur?" Jacqueline interrupted his musing. "You feel all right?"

"I don't know what it is," Arthur replied. "I appreciate what you're saying, but the fact that I don't really know where I stand with Big Casey and does he really plan to elevate me in the company has been weighing on me lately."

"Come on, you sit on down." Jacqueline led him over to a

chair at the table. "I'll fix you a plate and then give you a rub down."

"Jacqueline, I—"

"Just hush and let your woman take care of her man. And later on I can give you dessert better than you can imagine." She smiled as she turned and headed into the kitchen.

Arthur stared at Jacqueline rambling around in the kitchen. Dessert, hell, if she only knew the kind of dessert he'd just enjoyed she'd leave him alone knowing there was no way she could measure up. Of all the nights, why did Jacqueline want to lay all this special treatment on him tonight? Arthur knew damn well she'd expect something in return, and he wasn't sure he could deliver. After the two freaks it would take some time for him to build up for his wife. And he didn't have the cocaine to stimulate his senses.

Maybe if he just let Jacqueline go down on him, it would get him an erection. But hell, after what he'd just experienced a few hours ago there's no way Jacqueline could match that. If he didn't get an erection she'd damn well know something was wrong. In all their time together he'd always been able to perform. She'd probably freak out; in fact, he'd freak out himself. Arthur took great pride in his exceptional sexual prowess. Suddenly his thoughts flashed back to earlier in the evening in Elizabeth's bedroom. He looked over at Jacqueline as she loaded a plate with fried chicken, mashed potatoes, and green beans. Probably at that moment Elizabeth and that sexual lunatic Indria had someone else up in that room devouring them with sexual ecstasy. And here he sat with his plain old wife who struggled to keep him happy.

"You thinking about me and the lovemaking we're going to lay on each other tonight?" Jacqueline asked as she placed the plate filled with food in front of Arthur. She sat on his lap and tightly folded both arms around him. "We really have something to celebrate tonight," she said and kissed him on the neck.

Arthur forced his arm around Jacqueline's waist. "And just what is it we're going to celebrate, my slow demise at the company?"

"Don't talk like that, sweetheart. Mama didn't come right out and say it, but I'm sure that Daddy's going to retire within the next six months and he's going to make you top man in the company. Now eat up so we both can eat up a little later." Jacqueline got up and sat in the chair across from Arthur. "Doesn't that sound like fun?"

Arthur lay across the bed still fully dressed. He listened to the water in the shower. The sounds of Teddy Pendergrast filled the room, creating an atmosphere for lovemaking. Jacqueline started the CD before she undressed and got in the shower. She'd asked Arthur to join her, but he'd refused. He'd told her he was going to smoke a joint while she showered. But he didnt do that. Damn, if he only had a hit of the cocaine he'd be all right. Without it he wasn't sure he could pull this off. And if he didn't he'd have a hell of a lot of explaining to do. He finally heard Jacqueline getting out of the shower. A few minutes passed and Teddy Pendergrast was into "Turn off the Lights, Light a Candle."

Arthur closed his eyes and willed himself to get an erection. Hard as he tried, he still remained limp. Jacqueline came out of the bathroom with a towel loosely wrapped around her body. Arthur could never recall feeling guilty. It was an emotion he didn't need and refused to acknowledge. But for some reason, at this moment as Jacqueline turned off the light and slid in the bed moving very close to him, he felt a slight tinge of guilt, in a way, dirty. Less than three hours ago he lay naked with two other women, now he was in the bed with his wife who definitely wanted him naked again.

"Arthur Hannon, I love you so much that it's scary." She placed her body so that they were touching. She began to rub him on his stomach, slowly working her hand down to his pubic hairs.

Arthur could sense his body getting aroused. Maybe he could pull this off after all. He turned his body toward Jacqueline. Teddy's deep and romantic voice filled the room. He pulled Jacqueline in closer and kissed her on the lips. The longer the kiss lasted the more he could feel her excitement. She finally wrapped her warm soft hand around the shaft of his penis. Damn it was working, he was getting an erection.

"Damn, Arthur, I can feel you growing right in my hand. It's so fucking big. I want you to put it in me, baby. Make me want to holler," she whispered while still stroking his aroused penis, she slid down in the bed.

Arthur pulled her back up next to him. He couldn't let her do that after what he'd done earlier in the evening. He knew how badly she wanted to because of the size. But there would be no way she could perform at a level he'd experienced earlier and that might spoil the evening.

"No, baby," he whispered. "I just want to make love to you. Let me satisfy you." She lay on her back. "Let me do my job, baby." He rolled over on top and slid his erection inside her. The further he went inside the more Jacqueline relaxed and moaned.

Arthur began to move his body in an up and down motion. He relaxed and allowed himself to enjoy the penetration. Just as he felt her climax, he smiled and thought what a hell of a stud he really was.

Chapter 39

Sitting at the computer, trying to put the finishing touches on the escape scene and effectively bring his novel to an end, seemed impossible for Jason. The problem was Dominique. It had been five days since she walked out. He figured that after she cooled off, she'd call him. But that hadn't happened and the struggle was unbearable. How, after such a brief relationship, could he possibly be so deep into her? A couple of times he started to call her, but he had promised himself when she left to let it go. It was just too complicated as she was complicated. Yesterday he started to call Raquel, get with her and allow himself to forget Dominique. But he couldn't do that. His feelings for Dominique were much too strong to be put aside through a relationship with someone else. But what could he do? Could he handle it if he went to the club to see her and she refused to talk with him? Elliott had warned him about women who used sex as a method of making their money. She didn't sell her body, but she sold the tease.

Jason slammed his hands down on the keyboard, then spun his chair around and rubbed his forehead. He didn't like this torture. He walked out of the bedroom, stood placidly in the living room recalling the morning he'd stared at Dominique while she meditated. Wonderful memories of that morning teased him unmercifully. Was it lost forever? Would he ever experience that feeling with her again? It wasn't about lovemaking. It was about love. Two distinctly different feelings. Something that men like Elliott never understood.

Jason shook his head from side to side. What the hell was wrong with him? The woman danced practically naked, exposing her body to any man who had the money and was willing to give it up. To put it more bluntly she was a low life, one step above being a prostitute. And then again, maybe she had sold her body. After all, he really didn't know her that well and she was awfully secretive about her past. Hell, she probably had someone in the back room at the Black Zebra right then turning them on for money. Given his standing in life, how could he possibly have genuine feelings for her?

Jason strolled over to the CD player and studied a stack of them all lined up on the rack. It made no sense trying to write at that particular moment. His thoughts were deeply entrenched in Dominique and he must work this out. He pulled out a CD by his favorite female artist. From a young age Jason had always loved Gladys Knight, especially when she sang with the Pips. Her love songs might be torture at that moment as he struggled with his feelings for Dominique. He placed the CD in the player and hit the start button. Jason strolled back over to the love seat, fell down in it, and allowed his legs to hang over the end. Maybe one of Gladys' ballads would put this all in perspective. Gladys' soft and hypnotic sounds flowed through the room with Where Peaceful Waters Flow.

Jason closed his eyes and a vision of Dominique gliding on the stage came to him. He could see her full breasts, slim waist, and long shapely legs. Then the vision changed and she was in his arms, squeezing and holding on to him. The feeling of protecting her overcame him again. Jason had never in his life lost control of his emotions but he could feel it happening now. Why he felt this overwhelming urge to protect her he didn't know. After all, she made it in a world he barely understood and she seemed to do quite well. Why would she need him? Maybe it was just the opposite and he needed her more so than the other way around. That thought frightened him, being dependent on a dancer for his emotional security. But did it really mater what she did for a living as long as they cared for each other? If everyone in his universe rejected her, did he feel that he could still love her?

The timing of his musing and Gladys' sounds were perfect as she began her rendition of Love Finds Its Own Way. Jason had to concentrate all his emotions on the words. He listened intently as Gladys sent them hurtling through the room in perfect harmony with piano, horns and drums. The lyrics resonated with his thinking and were those that spoke of true love being synonymous with patience and understanding. In that setting, love will find its own way between two people who really do love each other.

Jason suddenly perked up. It came clear to him through the music. He and Dominique only needed each other for, as Gladys sang, love needs no guiding light, it only needs two people and they can find their way through the darkest night. It was the darkest time they had yet encountered in their young relationship. If they were going to make it work, nothing could matter but the two of them. Jason had to tell her that right at that moment. He'd go to the club and let her know that he felt love and he wanted to pursue that feeling with her no matter what anyone else might think, because with her the feeling was all good.

Jason jumped from the couch, slipped into his shoes and headed out the door. This time no fear or doubts would stand in his way. He would crash the party going on at the Black Zebra and let Dominique know that whatever he felt was real and growing and that is all that mattered to him. He must make that perfectly clear with her.

The parking lot at the Black Zebra was full. Maybe that was an omen, a sign that he shouldn't pursue this woman. She'd probably snub him when he went in or better still ask the bouncer to remove him from the premises. Jason slowly drove through the parking lot looking for an open space and hoping to spot any car that might be exiting the lot. Despite his silly thought about an omen or whatever other ridiculous thoughts he might conjure up he must go inside. Finally he spotted two men exiting the club and heading in his direction. He pulled up next to them and rolled down his window.

"Hey, are you leaving?" he asked.

"Yeah, we're out of here," one of the men answered. "We're

back the other way. Go to the front and turn around. We'll hold the place until you get there."

"Thanks." Jason hurried to the front of the driveway where he had some room to maneuver. He turned around and returned to the space where the two men waited for him.

Once parked, Jason hurried his step to the club entrance. The same bouncer who had come to Dominique's rescue the night he picked her up stood in the doorway, smiled at Jason, and swung the door open after he paid the ten dollars. As soon as he got inside he looked at all three stages. Dominique was not on any of them. He then did a cursory search of the club and didn't see her sitting at any of the tables or in the back corner giving some man a table dance. He went cold as he imagined her in the back room all over some sick bastard, having to rub against his erection and possibly get him off. That picture depressed him.

He wanted to turn around and get the hell out of there. But at that point, running was not an option. Jason looked around the room at all the lecherous bastards, groping and pulling on the dancers working their way around to the tables. He would have to offer her some kind of security so that she would feel comfortable giving up this life. After finding a table in the far corner of the club away from the three stages, the waitress approached him before he had settled in.

"I know who you're here to see," she said with a wide grin.

Jason smiled at her. "You do," he replied. "Since you know that do you know where she is?"

"What if I told you she's in the back room with some tall, handsome, and rich white man? How'd that make you feel?"

Jason's heart practically sank down to his feet. "I guess there's nothing I can say."

"I'm just joking with you. She's around here somewhere. She finished her set about ten minutes ago. But she hasn't been back out to socialize. You know what I mean." The waitress again smiled at Jason. "She's been acting kind of funny lately. Just like she don't want to be bothered with nobody. She acting like these girls act when they find themselves a sugar daddy and don't have to be bothered hustling these dollars all night long."

"I'll have a cranberry juice and soda," Jason said, obviously in an attempt to ignore what the waitress said.

"You want me to tell her you're here?" she asked while also writing down Jason's order on a napkin.

"No, I think I want to surprise her."

"Might not be a good idea. Once you men start dating these girls, worst thing you can do is start hanging around in here and surprising them. It's you the one that ends up being surprised." The waitress turned and started to walk away.

"What makes you think I'm dating Dominique?" he asked.
 She stopped dead in her tracks and turned around. "The only people we ladies in this club trust is each other," she said. "These ladies have to share their feelings with someone. They sure can't do it with these drunk-ass losers who come in here with a selfish attitude that all they want to get is their own pleasure. Know what I mean?" She turned and walked away.

Jason reared back in the chair and allowed his eyes to wander from stage to stage. All three stages were lined with men flashing dollar bills to give to their favorite dancer. In return they would get a little attention, maybe a smile or a kiss on the cheek. If they were willing to part with some large bills they could get a trip to the back room where the attention became a little more intimate.

The dancer on center stage had attracted a large contingent of men, almost as large a number as that which seemed to follow Dominique from stage to stage. It amazed him how some of these men could stay in the club for hours and dole out their entire paycheck. That would never happen to him with Dominique. If they left the club later on in the evening together, he was going to demand some changes be made so that he wouldn't be made to look like the many desperate men running from stage to stage throwing money at the prospective dancer they pursued, but would not leave with when the club closed.

The waitress placed Jason's drink on the table and smiled when he gave her a ten dollar bill and told her to keep the change. Jason took a sip from his drink and a young girl strolled up to him.

"Hey, honey, can I join you?" she asked.

"No, thanks," he said with a smile.

"Well, can you at least give me a tip?" The young girl lifted her leg and let her foot rest right on the tip of the chair where Jason sat.

He went in his pocket, pulled out 3 one-dollar bills and carefully tucked them inside the garter on the girl's bare thigh.

"Thanks, honey," she said and moved on.

Jason reared back in his chair and got comfortable again when he spotted Dominique coming out of the dressing room. As usual she looked stunningly beautiful. Was it his imagination or could he actually feel his heart beating at a very rapid rate? As she glided around the front of the club, stopping to talk to patrons, she didn't see him. He hoped she wouldn't, at least not right then. It made him feel both warm and nervous to know that she'd actually laid in his arms, smiled and cried with him and made love to him. Their relationship had to get back to that point.

He noticed that she never stuck her leg out begging for a tip. She wasn't on the hustle like the other girls in there. He watched as she smiled at a very nice looking man. The man got up and gave her a hug. She didn't reciprocate and quickly moved on to another table. Why didn't she look in Jason's direction? She probably knew he was back there, but didn't want to acknowledge him yet. All part of her game. But the waitress had warned him the last time he was there that Dominique did not play games. He had to put an end to this game thing he was playing with himself and needed to let her know that he had come to get her.

He got up to confront her but right at that moment Dominique looked in his direction. He froze in place. The next few seconds would be critical. Would she smile at him or turn and continue what she was doing? He sighed in relief when she did smile. She excused herself from the man she'd just begun a conversation with and hurried toward him.

Jason wanted to break out in a great big smile, but forced himself to withhold it until he knew how this would all work out. Dominique did not hold back at all. With a smile all over her face, she strolled right into Jason's arms and rested her head in his chest. For a moment neither one of them said anything and Jason could feel all eyes in the club on them. He pulled her in tightly and kissed her on the cheek.

"I think everyone is watching us," he said.

"Do you care?" she asked without moving her body from its resting place.

"No, not really. But won't the management get mad with you showing this kind of affection for one customer?"

"Do you care?" she asked for a second time.

He finally got the hint. "All I care about is you and I want to get you out of here."

She finally broke from his embrace. "Right now?" she asked.

"Whenever you're ready."

"Can you wait until closing time?"

"I guess so, as long as I don't have to sit here and watch you go to the back room with someone."

"I think I can handle that," she promised and then changed her tone. "Oh God, I've missed you this past week." She sat down at the table and he did also.

"Why did you take off like that?" he asked even though he knew the answer.

"I thought you were ashamed of me and didn't want to let anyone know about me."

"That's crazy. I want the whole world to know about you."

"Even your daughter and her mother?"

"Most of all my daughter and I don't care about her mother, other than giving her the respect she deserves because she's my daughter's mother. Can you live with that?"

"I guess I can and can you live with the fact that I must get back to work?"

"No I can't, but I will." He smiled at her.

Dominique got up, leaned over and kissed Jason on the cheek. "Thanks for thinking about me," she said. "I'll see you at two-thirty." She backed up from him still holding his hand until both their arms were fully extended. She gave him one last smile. "I'll be looking over here for you and I want you to know all my thoughts will be with you for the rest of the evening." She finally turned and walked away.

u

"Do you believe love is on our side?" Dominique asked Jason as she lay in his arms on the love seat in his apartment.

In the background the sounds of Gladys Knight's The Way We Were filled the room. Jason couldn't respond because it was all so perfect. He kept his eyes closed and listened to Gladys. His thoughts concentrated on how he could keep Dominique happy so that all his moments would be just like this and not how they'd been for the past week without her. If this was love it definitely had two dimensions. The first being an all encompassing feeling of joy and the other a frightful feeling of despair. He felt his emotions moving to a place beyond his control. If that was how love worked, it could be good or it could also be deplorable depending on how the relationship progressed.

"Jason, did you hear what I asked you?" Dominique again asked. She lightly tapped him on the leg.

"I heard you, but I'm just a little shocked to hear you use that word."

Dominique placed her right hand on the side of Jason's face, then reached up and kissed him softly on the lips.

"Would it bother you terribly if I told you I've never felt this way about anyone and it scares me that it has happened overnight?"

"No, not at all," Jason said in a very subdued and mellow tone.

Dominique adjusted her body so that she sat upright next to Jason with her legs over the top of his. She looked directly into his eyes and smiled. "There is a song they love for me to dance to at the club. Every time they play it and I dance to it, well it attracts a crowd and—"

"Dominique, I don't care to hear about this," Jason cut her off.

She took two fingers and placed them on his lips. "Be quiet please and let me finish," she whispered and smiled. Dominique continued to plead her case. "Let me make my point. The club and the dancing mean nothing. What matters is what I feel I must confess to you about you." She stopped and stared into his eyes.

"You got it," Jason said. His body somewhat stiffened. He feared what was coming, but he had to give her this room. And also her penetrating eyes were so strong that he felt she communicated from a deeper source, tucked somewhere in his mind.

"It's one of the most beautiful love songs, but for a long while it had no meaning to me. The song is, You Know How to Make Me Feel so Good. Have you heard it?"

"Definitely," Jason answered. He jumped from the love seat and hurried over to the CD player.

"Wait," Dominique called out to him. She got up and followed him over to the player. "Before you play it I want you to know that it's a song I have danced to many times with no feeling at all. But the other night when they played it I felt it deeply. I've never had anyone make me feel good in my entire life so I couldn't relate to the words. Now I can." She took Jason's hands and moved in very close. "Now play it and I want to feel good only with you."

Jason took the CD and slipped it in the player. He forwarded it to the seventh track and then pulled Dominique close in his arms. At that moment he had to be strong for her, even though he felt so weak he could just drop to the floor. Suddenly the room filled with the sounds of Teddy Pendergrast and Sharon Page as they sang about love, something new to Jason but at this point very comfortable to him. Jason wrapped his arms tightly around Dominique's body and she reciprocated by hugging him around the neck and resting her head on his chest. They both moved slowly to the music just as they had done in Palm Springs. Jason could feel Dominique move in even closer as Sharon sang about the importance of two people in love sharing a closeness that nothing, to include certain circumstances in life, could ever

Chapter 40

Theresa sat on the balcony of her apartment and studied the low-level clouds slowly breaking up over the ocean. It was early morning and Tosha and the baby were asleep on the couch. Tomorrow was the big birthday bash for Big Casey. Theresa still hadn't mentioned anything to the family about the two new additions to her household. She also hadn't talked to Cedric since their dinner when he promised to show up at the party without his lover. She recognized those two explosive situations could possibly erupt on Sunday, especially the Cedric situation. Theresa didn't know what she would do if her younger brother broke his promise and brought his gay lover like he did two weeks ago at the restaurant. But he had promised her that he wouldn't do that and she had to take him for his word. Still it made her nervous and she considered that maybe she should call him just to be reassured that Cedric wouldn't do anything that stupid.

She turned and glanced back into the apartment. Tosha began to stir around on the couch. The baby still slept so this was a perfect time for Theresa to talk with the young girl about getting the baby checked out. She'd get some resistance from her because since she'd moved in with Theresa she seemed to be in denial about her condition as well as the baby's. She felt nothing but empathy for Tosha having to possibly live with knowing she gave her child such a dreaded disease. But Theresa also recognized that her behavior would also be irresponsible if she didn't get that child in for a check-up. Today it would be discussed. She got up from the chair and strolled back into the living room. First she would try to convince Tosha that getting the examination was the best thing to do. If that didn't work she would force on her the reality that they didn't have any other choice.

Tosha sat on the couch rubbing her eyes when Theresa sat next to her. "How you feel this morning?" she asked.

"I feel kind of good, but I'm still scared."

Theresa took the young girl's hand. "Why are you afraid?" she asked. "You no longer have to be worried about the baby's father. I plan to send the DEA over there and bust that whole bunch of crack heads."

Tosha suddenly jerked her hand away from Theresa. "No ma'am, you can't do that. You don't know them like I do. I swear they'll find us and hurt all us, including the baby."

"Calm down. I won't do that, but I don't want you feeling afraid all the time." Theresa moved Tosha back away but still had her hands on the young girl's arms. "You carry so much fear in you. You don't have to be afraid because no one can find you here."

"But you got to promise me you won't put the police on Oscar."

"I promise I won't," Theresa said. That was the first time Tosha had mentioned the father's name. "But we do have another very important matter we must discuss."

Tosha jumped to her feet and hurried over to the balcony entrance. "Boy it sure is pretty out here," she said. Theresa knew the young girl had moved and changed the subject because she knew what was coming. "How do people get to live out here and others don't?" she asked.

"It just depends on how much money you make and if you can afford it," Theresa explained.

"I ain't ever going to have a chance to live somewhere like this 'cause I ain't going to have that kind of money. I come from poor people and I guess me and my baby gonna be poor forever." Tosha hesitated to turn and look back at Theresa who still sat on the couch. "You believe in a God, Miss Theresa?" she asked.

That question caught Theresa totally off guard. It was the last thing she thought she would hear from Tosha. But the question had been put out there and she couldn't ignore it.

"Yes, certainly I believe in a God," she answered.

"Well I guess you would because you living such a good life," Tosha shot back.

"I don't think my believing in God has anything to do with my lifestyle," Theresa retorted somewhat defensively. She had to remain cool even though Tosha's question irritated her somewhat.

"I don't mean to sound rude, Miss Theresa, but why do people in my condition need to believe in God? He ain't done nothing but make my life miserable."

"God didn't make your life miserable. The conditions under which you were born and the irresponsible behavior of your parents has made your life miserable."

"But I didn't ask to have them kind of parents. God gave them to me. So can't you say He's responsible for my misery? Just like I'm responsible if my baby is sick, but she didn't ask to be born sick. God could've spared her, but He didn't."

Theresa stared into Tosha's eyes and to her surprise the young girl did not flinch or look away. This was not the kind of conversation an eighteen year old girl should be having about life. Instead she should be out enjoying her youth and having fun with her friends. But chances were good that Tosha never was young. She had been forced to age too fast and now possessed an older woman's mind in a young girl's body.

Theresa envisioned the apartment complex across the street from where she worked and the young girls she had seen the other day playing on the grounds. They seemed so carefree and unconcerned, but at what point would all that change? At what point had it all changed for Tosha so now she questioned God? Tosha asked questions for which no one had answers. Why all the inequities in life? And if God was real and fair why would He continue to allow these things to happen?

Theresa took Tosha's hands and squeezed them tightly. Even though she didn't have any answers and worst of all, no one seemed to have answers, she had to try.

"I don't know how to give you an answer or explanation that will satisfy you," Theresa ruefully admitted. "But I know you can't give up because I'm not going to let you."

"Miss Theresa, I'm gonna die," Tosha sounded contrite. "But I don't want my baby to die and if we can save her life, please promise me you'll keep her. Please, Miss Theresa, don't send her back into that world that had me all hung up and strung out."

For the second time since they had been together, Theresa saw tears in Tosha's eyes. She grabbed the young girl and held her close. Theresa didn't want to let her go. If she could just protect her in her arms, then she would do that.

"Yes," she finally answered Tosha. "But that's not going to happen. We're going to get you the best treatment that money can buy in this country."

Tosha broke from her grip and leaned back on the couch. "You got that much money?" she asked.

"I don't, but I know someone who might," Theresa answered forcing a smile on her face.

Tosha reached over at the end of the couch and took her baby in her arms. She had just awakened and began to cry. Tosha bounced her up and down in her lap. She then hugged her.

"Guess what? Miss Theresa going to make us both well. We're going to be all right."

Theresa could feel the tears welling up in her eyes. "Why didn't you give your baby a name?" she finally asked.

Tosha again pulled her daughter in close. "I didn't want to give her a name I guess because I knew she was gonna die. It just seemed to make it so much easier if she remained nameless."

Theresa suddenly jumped up and took the baby from Tosha. She had to do something. If she sat there listening to the young girl she would burst out crying.

"What we need to do is get over to the clinic and start the process to save you and your baby's life. We need to get her examined to see if she has the virus. And we need to get you tested again."

"I don't know, Miss Theresa. I'm really scared." Tosha remained seated.

"I give you my word," Theresa scowled, not out of anger with Tosha but more from frustration. "Neither you nor this baby is going to die anytime soon. Now get up and let's go do what we must to help both of you get better."

Tosha slowly got up from the couch and reached out for the child. Theresa pulled the baby in closer to her chest.

"I'll carry the baby. You need all your strength to do what we have to this morning. Now go wash up and get dressed."

Tosha hesitated for a moment, but when the scowl on Theresa's face seemed to grow more intense she finally turned and started toward the bathroom.

"When this crisis is over, we're going to give this baby a name," Theresa continued. "Do you hear me?"

Tosha stopped, turned around and smiled at Theresa. "Yes ma'am. I would like that," she said then turned and disappeared into the bathroom.

Once Tosha had closed the door to the bathroom and Theresa heard the shower running, she sat back down on the couch, pulled the baby in close and cried.

Chapter 41

Arthur lay in the bed still naked from last night when he had miraculously made love to Jacqueline twice in less than two hours. Counting the three times he had been able to get it up over Elizabeth's, he had performed five times in one night. Damn he was a hell of a stud. He probably should be in that kind of business. At one point he'd considered being a male stripper, something he'd make a fortune doing, even more than that uppity stripper Dominique.

He rolled over on his side and stroked his penis. Good job, he whispered as he heard Jacqueline out on the balcony. She was talking to Hazel about the big day tomorrow. He pulled the covers over his shoulders as he tried to deal with this family bullshit. There was always some kind of family affair with the Mitchells. They'd only gone to his mother's house one time for any kind of celebration. It was always over to Altadena and the Mitchells.

That's one of the reasons he treated Jacqueline the way he did. He could never be sure if her loyalties were with him or with the rest of her family. Other women made him feel more like a man than his own wife. She treated him more like a piece of ass. Just one big stud with something for her to enjoy. He was more than that. He was a man with a great deal of class, even if the entire Mitchell family never acknowledged it.

Tomorrow he would go over there and be ignored while everyone fawned over that big son of a bitch, Casey. Well he sure wasn't going to make a fuss over him. After all, the bastard hadn't said more than ten words to him since he'd moved to the headquarters over a month ago. And he sure the hell had nothing to say to Jason after he embarrassed him by coming up on him at Elizabeth's apartment. That self-righteous bastard felt he was too good to party with Arthur and the ladies that morning.

He chuckled as he imagined Jason with Elizabeth and Indria. He probably would freak out once they started freaking all over his body. Jason really was kind of nerdish. Not the kind to hang out at strip joints. He probably wouldn't even know how to talk to one of those freaks that dance at the Black Zebra. Dominique would definitely blow him away if she ever danced close to him, letting him get a feel of that fine ass body. It was time for him to go back there and pick up where he left off with that freak. His approach would be different. She wanted to be pampered, made to think that she was different from the rest of those sluts that danced for money. Well for a piece of that ass, he'd accommodate her and once he got over, kick her out of the bed.

Tomorrow he'd also have to act decent with Theresa and she with him even though they both couldn't stand each other. Whenever Jacqueline spent any time around her sister she came home all demanding. That was a result of Theresa poisoning Jacqueline's mind with all that independent feminist bullshit. Theresa had a problem; the woman was frustrated and horny because she wasn't getting any steady sex. That's one thing Jacqueline didn't have to worry about. She definitely got her share of the best loving in town. That's why she'd never leave him. No way could she survive without what he had to give her. Hell, he could call her in the room right then and have her hollering from sheer pleasure in less than ten minutes. Arthur smiled and thought what a hell of a talent he had.

"Arthur, could you get up and get dressed?" Jacqueline startled him out of his musing. "I want you to ride with me to the market. There's a few things I need to get for tomorrow. And you still haven't bought Daddy a gift."

Arthur turned over on his back to look at Jacqueline standing at the entrance to the bedroom. "Hell, Jacqueline, this is my day to relax. I don't feel like fighting that crowd at Central Market on a Saturday morning. And who said I was going to buy Big Casey a gift?"

"What are you talking about?" Jacqueline chided him. "You can't go to someone's birthday party and not take a gift."

"I know that you got him something. Why can't that be from both of us?"

"God, Arthur, that's so tacky and ghetto. Sometimes I think you feel you're still living in south central Los Angeles."

Arthur shot straight up in the bed. "What the hell is that supposed to mean?" he snapped.

She stared at him for a good half minute. "Listen, I'm sorry. Just get ready so we can go. If you don't feel like buying a gift that's your business." Jacqueline walked over and stood next to the bed. "We don't ever do anything together anymore. It's like you go your way and I just sit at home and wait for you."

Arthur threw the covers on the floor, leaving his body totally exposed. "Yeah, bullshit!" he shouted. "I work my ass off all the time and all you ever do is run over to your mother's house."

"All right, Arthur, I don't want to fight with you. But would you please get ready and go with me? I would love to spend a Saturday afternoon with my husband."

Arthur slid out of the bed and headed for the shower. As he passed by Jacqueline, she teasingly popped him on his backside. "Baby you sure were good last night. I don't know what got into you, but whatever it was I'd like to see a whole lot more of it."

"I'm sure you would and I'm sure you will," he said with a smile. He turned on the shower and climbed inside, all the time smiling over his five-time performance last night.

u

After two hours of going in and out of practically every gift shop in Beverly Hills, Arthur felt like his legs would fall off. He was short of breath and downright tired. Last night left him totally exhausted. He wanted to get in bed, pull the covers over his head and sleep until next week sometime. But his better judgment told him to follow Jacqueline's instructions and buy Big Casey a gift. He did work for the man and kissing his ass was sometimes required if a person wanted to reach their goal in the business world. Even though he didn't believe Jacqueline last night when she told him that he'd been chosen to head the company next year when Big Casey retired, it was better to play it safe and buy him the damn gift. He spotted a cigar shop, a perfect place to get a gift. Big Casey loved to suck on those cancer sticks. He'd buy him a dozen expensive cigars, maybe they would speed up his time to die.

He grabbed Jacqueline by the arm and dragged her into the cigar store.

"Arthur, why are we going in here?" She didn't wait for an answer. "I know you're not going to buy Daddy some nasty cigars when you know darn well he needs to quit."

"Come on, woman," Arthur shot back at her. "This is my gift and I'll buy what I want." Arthur practically pulled her into the store. "And anyway I'm not going to buy any cheap cancer-causing cigars. I'm going to get the best. The ones that are cancer- proof."

"Be serious," Jacqueline replied. "All cigars are cancerous. I don't care if they are home grown or straight from Dominican Republic."

Arthur smirked as they approached the counter. His concern was not about Big Casey's life. He looked inside the glass counter at the various brands on display. Jacqueline broke loose from his grip and moved back away from him. Arthur figured that was her way to register displeasure. The salesman approached Arthur from the other side of the counter.

"Yes sir, may I help you pick out a good brand or do you already know what kind you want?"

Arthur ignored the salesman as he continued to peruse the different boxes. Finally he spotted a box that read "From Dominican Republic."

"That one right over there," he said to the salesman while pointing to the box. "Are those the very best?" he asked. "I need the very best because they're for a very special man who be-lieves in nothing but the best."

"Yes, these are superb cigars. One of our very top sellers," the salesman answered.

"How much for a box?" Arthur asked.

The salesman glared at Arthur as though he had said something wrong. He immediately recognized his mistake. They were in one of the most exclusive business areas of Beverly Hills and a person didn't ask about the price.

"They're a hundred and twenty five-dollars for a box," the salesman finally answered.

"Good, I'll take two boxes," Arthur said.

The salesman pulled two boxes out from the display case. "Would you like them wrapped?"

"No, that's not necessary."

"Arthur, please," Jacqueline said as she walked up and stood next to him. "Don't be so ghetto. Yes, he would like the two boxes wrapped together. And please make sure the wrapping paper is appropriate for an older man's birthday."

The salesman gave both of them a disdainful look, took the two boxes and headed to the back of the store.

After the salesman disappeared, Arthur's first instinct was to slap Jacqueline. Her habit of equating him with the ghetto was getting a little tired and she'd done it twice today. Instead he walked toward the far end of the counter studying the various kinds of cigars inside. He had to get away from her before he did something he'd regret. Even though she needed to get her arrogant ass whipped, this was not the right time or place.

A few minutes later the salesman returned to the front with the two packages wrapped in a collage of colors. Arthur had been patient with Jacqueline, but he had to get some kind of dig in on her. He had to let her know he didn't appreciate the ghetto reference. He picked up the two packages and practically thrust them in her face.

"Is this sufficient for you?" he asked.

"Yes, Arthur," Jacqueline answered in a much more subdued tone. "They look very pretty."

"How will you be paying for this, cash or credit card?"

Arthur pulled out his wallet and removed the same credit

card he'd given to Elizabeth. He handed it across the counter to the salesman.

"Put it on this one," Arthur instructed him.

Again the man gave Arthur a disdainful look and then proceeded to scan the card through the machine. He stared at the machine waiting for an approval. The longer he waited the more he stared.

Why the delay? The card should automatically clear. Arthur had over five thousand dollars in that account. He'd given the man a debit card so it shouldn't take that long to be approved. Jacqueline moved in closer to Arthur and gave him a hard stare.

"Don't you have money in that account?" she asked dryly.

"Hell yes," Arthur shot back at her all the time keeping his eyes on the salesman. "I should have over five thousand."

"Obviously something's wrong," Jacqueline chided.

Finally the salesman handed Arthur the card back. "I'm sorry, sir, but this card was rejected."

"What! For what reason?" Arthur snapped at the salesman.

"It never tells us why, sir," the salesman replied. "Do you have another card you'd like to try?"

Arthur's eyebrows furrowed and his steely eyes pierced the man before him. "That's impossible!" he shouted. "I know I have the money in that account. Try it again."

"Sir, there is no need to try the same card," the salesman said with some irritation in his tone. "Do you want to try another card or pay with cash?"

"I want you to try the damn card again," Arthur demanded. "Something must have been wrong with the connection the first time you tried. I got over five thousand dollars in that account."

"Sir, there is no need—"

"Here, use this card." Jacqueline interrupted the salesman and thrust her credit card across the counter.

The salesman snatched the card and slid it across the receiver. It immediately printed a sales slip. He handed it to Jacqueline who signed it and gave it back to him.

"Thank you," the salesman said with an obviously forced smile.

Chapter 42

Exhilaration consumed Jason's mind and body as he sat at the computer putting the final touches on his initial work of fiction. Dominique had gone into the living room to read and listen to Miles Davis' jazz rendition of George Gershwin's Porgy and Bess. Jason could hear the sounds of, Bess you is my woman now. His thoughts wandered momentarily as he related to Davis' sweet trumpet. He would often pause in the middle of his writing and just listen to one of the many jazz masters that served as inspiration for his creativity. A broad smile fell across his face knowing that his woman sat in the next room and not on the stage dancing on this particular night. He had talked her out of going to the club, despite the fact that Saturday night was the busiest and the most productive of all nights. With tomorrow the big day for Big Casey's birthday bash, he wanted her to rest and be ready to meet his family, something she had told him she didn't look forward to doing. He imagined all the disappointed men who would show up hoping to see Dominique. If Jason had his way, that would soon become a permanent disappointment for them. Soon he would take her out of that business forever.

Jason glanced over at the clock on the nightstand. It read a little past nine o'clock. Miles Davis had just begun his rendition of Summertime. There was something very special about that song because it captured the beauty as well as the tragedy of Black folks' existence in the South when the living was very difficult, but somehow they managed to make it easy. Jason was convinced that Gershwin must have had a Black composer as a ghostwriter. Only someone Black could create the special quality of the lyrics in that song. His mind wandered further away from his writing and more toward the living room. Why fight it. He got up, stood in the doorway and smiled as he looked at Dominique curled up in the love seat reading Tony Morrison's Zula. The same feelings he felt that morning when he walked into the living room and admired her while she meditated, came over him again. That feeling of protecting her from whatever problems or tragedies she may have suffered in the past. He didn't want to disturb her, but couldn't resist. He strolled to the back of the love seat, leaned down and wrapped both arms around her neck. She immediately put the book down and relaxed in his embrace. Jason closed his eyes, held her close and listened to Davis play There's a Boat Leaving Soon for New York. Miles Davis with his orchestra backing him up was so overwhelming they could only hold each other and listen.

Dominique finally broke the silence. "I'm a little nervous about tomorrow," she whispered.

"Do you like Toni Morrison?"

"Yes I do, but sometimes she's awfully hard to follow."

"I know. I believe that's her trademark."

"Do you think she does it on purpose?" Dominique asked.

"She has to. You have to work at it deliberately in order to make literature like reading philosophy."

"Well, I just don't believe she writes for Black people, but you're trying to change the subject."

Jason slid over the top of the love seat and snuggled close to Dominique. "What do you mean, I changed the subject?" He kissed her on the forehead.

"That was a very sweet gesture," she said with a smile. "But that's not going to work. I'm really nervous about tomorrow and I just don't know if I can do this."

"I'm surrprised! Of all people you shouldn't worry about meeting strangers."

Dominique jerked back away from him. "And what is that supposed to mean?" she asked, but before giving him a chance to answer she continued. "I have asked you before to please separate what I do for a living from me as a person."

Jason pulled her back into his arms. This time he was determined to take control. "I meant that you as a person and not a dancer are a charismatic, well informed individual who reads Toni Morrison and listens to Miles Davis. An individual that has some very deep thoughts about life, who meditates and can easily converse with anyone at any level of society. That is what I mean, so now you can apologize."

Dominique smiled and again wrapped both arms around Jason's neck and whispered, "Thank you. That was very kind and I do apologize."

"Apology accepted." Jason pulled her closer. They had just relaxed into a deep and passionate kiss when the doorbell rang.

"I can ignore it and they'll have to go away," he said.

"That wouldn't be very polite," Dominique whispered. "But if you think it might be one of your ex-lovers then just ignore it," she added smiling.

Jason thought of Raquel. Would she dare come by without calling? And exactly how would he handle that situation? He now seriously considered ignoring the doorbell as it rang for a third time. Finally, he kissed Dominique on the forehead, jumped up and headed for the door. He owed no one and he sure wasn't going to be apprehensive about answering his door.

A frown covered Jason's face as he grabbed the doorknob and swung the door open. He was relieved to see Elliott.

Elliott smiled at him and said, "You going to let me come in or you got a couple freaks back there in the bedroom you trying to keep all to yourself?"

Jason stepped to one side and pulled the door half closed. "Be cool, man, I have company," he warned. He then opened the door, moved aside and allowed Elliott to enter. His friend walked past him and gave Jason a perplexed look. He then saw Dominique sitting on the love seat.

"Oh, I see what you mean," Elliott said as he continued into the living room and took a seat.

Jason followed closely behind and sat back down next to Dominique. "I don't know if you all met at the club," he said. "But let me make a formal introduction. Dominique, this is my main friend Elliott." He paused to let it register and then continued.

"Elliott, this is the love of my life, Dominique." A momentary silence followed and Jason felt nervous, not sure what might explode from Elliott's nasty mouth.

"Yeah, I've seen you at the club," Elliott finally muttered. "You're the lady that draws all the attention. You draw men to you like bees to honey."

Dominique smiled and then grabbed Jason's hand and squeezed it tightly. She looked directly at Elliott. "And you're the man responsible for making it possible for me to meet Jason. I want to thank you for that."

"It always makes me feel good when I can bring two lovers together," Elliott said. He also smiled and looked at Jason. "Sometimes it works out and then at other times it can be quite disappointing."

"And why is that?" Dominique shot back at him.

"No telling why," Elliott replied. "You just never know how things are going to work out."

"I don't have anything to drink," Jason interrupted, not liking the direction or tone of the conversation. "I do have some Sprite."

"No that's okay," Elliott answered. "I'm not going to stay long. I just thought maybe you'd like to go to the club for a few minutes. But it looks like you brought the club to you."

"And what is that supposed to mean?" Dominique blurted out before Jason could intervene. He rolled his eyes and let out a sigh.

"Don't you dance at the club?" Elliott asked.

"Come on, man, lighten up," Jason intervened.

Dominique adjusted her body so that she turned in Elliott's direction. Jason tried to hold her hand, but she pulled away.

"This is not about the club," she said dryly. "Whatever you may think it's all about, you have it wrong," she continued.

"I know what it's all about," Elliott shot back. "It's always about the money."

"Stop it!" Jason scowled at Elliott.

"Stop what, Jason?" Dominique asked pulling even further away. "Is this some kind of game you boys play?"

Jason sensed Dominique's defense mechanisms at work. "No, this is no game at all," he said. "Elliott has a very negative outlook on male and female relationships."

"That's really too bad." Dominique looked directly at Elliott. "But you shouldn't try to poison other relationships just because you had a bad experience or two."

Jason stared hard at Elliott as he rustled around in his chair. Elliott could be explosively offensive but he had to let this play out.

"My relationships have been up and down. Most of them have been positive. But that's because I usually don't allow them to be dictated by emotions and not reason."

"That's good to hear," Dominique said. "Too many times relationships are about feeling good and nothing else."

"You have something against feeling good?" Elliott asked as he moved to the edge of his chair. "If you do, you sure are in the wrong business."

"Elliott's getting ready to leave on a poetry slam tour," Jason blurted in an attempt to cut off this cat and mouse game.

"That's wonderful," Dominique replied. "So we're sitting here with a future celebrity."

"I kind of owe it to Jason and a couple of friends that went with me to New York a few weeks ago. The good company and the deep conversations were my stimulus."

Dominique moved even further away from Jason. She snuggled against the arm rest. "Then I guess I should congratulate Jason also," she said and then got up. "Listen, I don't want to interrupt you men having a night out," she said.

Elliott also jumped up. "No, no, not at all. I didn't mean to break up anything. I just wanted to holler at my brothah before I leave on Monday."

Jason finally got to his feet and took Dominique by the arm and pulled her close. "I didn't know you left this Monday. Maybe we can get together a few minutes tomorrow evening. We'll be over to Big Casey's birthday party most of the day but I can give you a call when we get back on this side of town."

Elliott was at the door. "No, that won't work. Tomorrow I'll be with my baby all day since I won't see her for a month." He opened the door halfway. "Dominique, it was a pleasure meeting you. I hope I'll see you soon and take care of my boy. He sometimes does stupid things, but I still got to hang with him. And he definitely has skills." Elliott smiled as he grabbed Jason's hand and gave him a vigorous shake.

"I'm going to work real hard to make sure I'm still here when you get back," Dominique said. "And maybe soon I'll get a chance to meet that special lady of yours."

"That would be interesting, and I believe we can make that happen." He turned and walked toward his car.

Jason watched as Elliott opened the door to his Buick and climbed in the driver's seat. When the light in the car came on, Jason almost fell over as he saw Denise sitting in the front seat and Raquel in the back.

Chapter 43

Jason heard the water running in the shower when he woke at a little past seven in the morning. He turned his head in the direction of the bathroom and smiled. Last night had turned out to be a perfect evening. The first meeting between Elliott and Dominique got tense there for a minute, but it worked out well. Dominique had finally met someone very close to him and today she would meet all the others who would be a part of their life in the future. This would be her first encounter with the Mitchell gang and if last night was any indication of things to come, then he felt confident that Dominique would win their hearts. Not that it really mattered, but a relationship always went smoother when the families got along. Jason reached on the other side of the bed, grabbed Dominique's pillow and pulled it close to him in a hug. He held it that way for a minute, then put it down and sprang out of the bed.

He crept into the bathroom, threw back the shower curtain and got in. Jason pulled Dominique close to him, kissed her on the neck and then placed his hands on her breasts.

"Jason, stop," she scolded. "Didn't you get enough last night?" She turned and kissed him. They kissed as the water cascaded over their two naked bodies embraced as one. Jason slowly moved his hands down her back, over the top of her buttocks, and down the back of her thighs. He pulled her even closer to his body.

"My God, you're ready for more sex," she whispered as she kissed him on his ear lobe.

"I can't help it." He also kept his voice at a low whisper. "It's what you do to me."

With the hot water steadily pouring down over them, Jason kissed her on each breast and down the front of her stomach.

Before he went too far, she pulled him back up.

"Let me do this," she said.

Jason lifted her up and Dominique gently took his penis and slid it slowly inside of her.

"Without protection," he said.

"I trust you because I love you," she whispered.

Finally inside her, Jason pushed as though he was going to go all the way through her. With each push, she moaned. It felt so good he couldn't hold it even though he would try. She seemed to sense that.

"Don't, sweetheart," she said. "Let it go and I want to feel all of you deep inside me. Let it go, darling, let it go."

Right at that moment he pulled her close and beyond. He closed his eyes and just as he felt that extreme pleasure only two lovers can experience, he released and they both screamed together.

Dominique held her arms straight up in the air and spread her fingers to allow the wind to blow between them. Jason had taken the top off when they got in the car so the sun could shine brightly on them while it wasn't yet too hot in the city. The car sped down the 110 East heading for Altadena and Big Casey's birthday party. After making love under the shower they said very little. Words weren't necessary. Their love making had expressed all that was needed. Now on the freeway they remained reticent. The jazz sounds of Freddie Hubbard broke the silence. For a moment Jason's thoughts drifted back to last night. What would have happened if Denise and Raquel had come to the door with Elliott? And a bigger question was why they hadn't? Probably a woman's intuition. Raquel instinctively knew there had to be someone else. No man just walks away from a woman as beautiful and intelligent as she for no reason. And that reason was usually going to be another woman. Would he ever be able to apologize or in some way make it up to her? Or better still would he ever see her again? He really didn't like the messy ending, but after the first evening with Dominique there was nothing else he could do. Now the two of them were so deeply into each other no way he could do anything else but stay away from Raquel.

"Thinking about your ex-lovers?" Dominique asked.

Her question snapped him out of his musing. "No," he answered sheepishly.

"Well I don't care if you are as long as you know they are your ex-lovers," she smiled.

"It's like no one exists but you. I'm so into you there is no way I could have any room anywhere in me for someone else."

"You're telling me I have you all to myself?"

"That's exactly what I'm telling you."

"Good because I don't ever want to share you, not even your thoughts, with anyone else."

Jason glanced over at her, and then returned his attention to the road. "After this morning you definitely don't ever have to worry."

"You like that kind of action," she smiled.

"And I want a lot more of it."

"I'll see if I can accommodate you from now on."

"Just me?"

"Just you."

Jason pulled up to the front of the house and parked the car. He started to get out when Dominique grabbed him by the arm and started to squeeze.

"This is your parents' home?" she asked.

"This is it." Jason started to open the door, but she squeezed even tighter.

"I can't do this. This is a mansion. I've never been in a house this big and beautiful." She hesitated and stared straight ahead at the house. "No I can't do this. Please take me back to Los Angeles."

"Don't be silly," Jason scolded. "You'll love my parents as well as my sisters and my brother if he shows up."

"Jason, I talk a good game and I show confidence in the club because that's my terrain. This is way out of my league. No I can't do this."

"Okay, if you can't do it, then neither can I."

"What do you mean? It's your father's sixty-fifth birthday. This is an important day for your entire family. You have to do it."

"But I need you with me. Come on let's do this before my nosey mother, who I know is looking out the window at us, figures we're having some kind of fight."

"Oh my God, that makes it even worse. Take me back to Los Angeles right now."

"We're not going back to Los Angeles because this is a very special day for me and I want to celebrate it with my friend and lover," Jason said with a firm voice he'd never used before with Dominique. "Now please you'll be great in there and I promise you everyone will love you. And remember no one knows you so everyone starts at the same place in time." He took her hand and held it. They both stared at each other. "Please do this for me, and I'll be eternally grateful to you."

Dominique broke from his grip and turned to open the door. "You better believe you will be," she said.

"No, you let me open the door for my queen," he said as he quickly got out of the car and rushed over to the passenger's door. He opened it and Dominique gracefully got out.

"Here it goes," she whispered.

"You're right," Jason replied. "Here goes the best looking couple in all Los Angeles County." He took her by the arm and they strolled to the house.

Jason swung the front door open and Hazel stood in the foyer just as though she knew he and Dominique were about to enter the house. She looked inquisitive and Jason knew why. Dominique was the first woman he'd brought around Hazel since he broke off with Angela.

Once inside the house they both froze for a moment. He could feel Dominique's grip tighten around his hand. He attempted to move forward but she stayed in place. Jason gently jerked on her hand and she slowly approached Hazel.

"Mother, I have a very special person I'd like for you to meet,"

Jason said as he broke loose from his grip on Dominique's hand, hugged his mother and kissed her on the cheek. Hazel stood her ground all the time staring at Dominique. "This is my friend Dominique." Jason turned and faced Dominique. "This is my mother, Hazel Mitchell."

"Mrs. Mitchell, it is my pleasure," Dominique said as she reached out to shake Hazel's hand.

Hazel reciprocated and firmly gripped Dominique's hand. "Well my son certainly is full of surprises," she said. "Jason, you never told me you were bringing a friend."

"I wanted to surprise you and Big Casey," Jason explained.

"You certainly did that," Hazel said and then gave Dominique a polite hug. "Welcome to our home," she continued. "Your father is out on the patio firing up the coals for some ribs and chicken."

"Sounds great," Jason said. "We'll go out and help him." He again took Dominique by the arm.

Hazel interrupted him. "You go back there and help your father," she said. "Me and this young lady are going to do other things." She smiled at Dominique.

A frown crept across Jason's face as he thought to himself that the third degree was about to begin.

"Come along, dear," Hazel said. "My two daughters should be here any minute. By the way, Jason with his bad manners never told me your last name. And where are you from?" Hazel led Dominique toward the kitchen. A reluctant Dominique followed, but did manage to turn her head and look at Jason with a perplexed expression as she finally disappeared behind the kitchen door.

Jason shook his head and started toward the patio. He swung the door open and headed toward Big Casey who looked up.

"If it isn't the young genius novelist," Big Casey said with a wide grin. "Give me a hug from my oldest child on my sixty-fifth birthday."

Jason hugged his father and patted him on the back. "At least you could have waited until I had a chance to say happy birthday, old man."

Big Casey kissed his oldest child on the cheek and released him from his grip. "You move too slow and who you think you're calling old?" Big Casey retorted. "I may be sixty-five today, but ain't nothing I can't beat you doing. Well maybe with the exception of finding the prettiest girls in all of Los Angeles. I saw that young lady you came in with. She is gorgeous. I'm proud of you, son." Big Casey paused to stir the coals that had cooled to embers. "Where in the world did you meet her? What is she an actress or something? Being a writer has its benefits, doesn't it?"

"She's a wonderful person that I met a month ago. And I'm telling you she is top notch," Jason said.

"Now remember our agreement. No serious entanglement until that first novel is published. You haven't forgotten, have you?"

"No, I haven't," Jason answered rather meekly. "But I am pleased to report that I have finally completed the first draft." He wanted to shift the subject because he did remember his agreement with Big Casey, but wasn't sure he could live up to that promise now that Dominique had invaded his space.

"Congratulations, that's great. When do you go to press? We really have a lot to celebrate today." Big Casey grabbed a slab of ribs and placed them on the grill. The smoke created from the heat and the juice from the ribs filled the air and presented a delicious aroma throughout the yard.

"That smells awfully good," Jason remarked. "In a few minutes you're going to have all the neighbors wandering over this way."

"Let 'em come. The more the merrier. This is a day for celebration. I'm sixty-five and in great health, you're about to be published and hanging out with absolutely gorgeous women."

"Woman," Jason corrected his father. "Not women, just one."

"Sounds kind of serious to me. Looks like you might be back working for the company real soon."

"Don't bet on it, old man. I still have my eyes set on my prize."

"Looks to me that you might have your eyes set on a different kind of prize."

"Not until I reach my goal."

"Just be prepared to pay up," Big Casey chided. They both looked toward the house as they heard the chimes from the front door sound off.

"I'll be right back." Jason turned to walk back into the house.

"The coals look just fine and the meat is cooking on time, so I'll go in with you." Big Casey followed closely behind Jason. "And anyway, I need to meet this young lady who's going to make you lose your bet."

Just as Jason made his way next to Dominique and placed his arm around her waist Hazel opened the door. Angela, with Julianne, stood outside. When Jason saw who it was he dropped his arm. Dominique turned and shot him a menacing glare. He quickly placed his arm back around her waist. Jason got the message loud and clear. He wasn't about to make the same mistake all over again. With his arm tightly around Dominique's waist they moved closer to the entrance. Hazel swung the screen door open and Julianne ran straight into her arms.

"Hi, grandma," she said.

"Hi, baby." Hazel kissed her granddaughter on the cheek. "Come on in," she said to Angela, who stood firmly outside the door and stared directly at Jason.

"No thank you, Mrs. Mitchell," she said still with her eyes riveted on Jason. "I have other plans for today. However I wanted to make sure Julianne got a chance to spend Big Casey's birthday with you all."

"Thank you, sweetheart," Big Casey said. He moved to the door and then hugged Angela.

"Someone had to make sure your granddaughter spent some time with you all," Angela continued. "I'll be back to get her at six."

"You sure you can't stay until the girls get here?" Hazel asked.

"No ma'am, but thank you for asking"

"Daddy," Julianne called out. She broke from Hazel and rushed over to Jason. He removed his arm from around Dominique's waist and picked up his daughter.

"Hi, baby," he said. "How's my little angel?"

"I'm fine," Julianne shouted and then turned and stared at Dominique. "Is this your new girlfriend mommy said I'd meet today?"

"Yes, this is daddy's friend and her name is Dominique."

"Pleased to meet you," Dominique said as she extended her hand for Julianne to shake.

Before Julianne could take Dominique's hand, Angela rushed inside the house and snatched the little girl from Jason. "Mommy has to say goodbye, baby," she said to her daughter. "You be good, mind your grandparents, and I'll see you at six." Instead of giving her back to Jason, Angela carried Julianne back to the front door and put her down there. "You love Mommy?"

"Yes, Mommy, I love you."

"Good, I'll see you this evening. Happy birthday, Mr. Mitchell and thank you, Mrs. Mitchell, for inviting your granddaughter." Angela turned and walked away.

Jason tried to place his arm back around Dominique's waist but she moved away. He turned to look at her, but she stared straight ahead. Jason could feel the tension building and he had to do something to defuse it before he lost her again. Angela had acted just like an ass on purpose. He turned to say something to Dominique but was cut off.

"Here comes Theresa," Hazel shouted as she pointed to the driveway. "And she has someone with her."

Jason figured it had to be Cedric. She'd probably gone and picked him up to make sure he came. But he watched as Theresa got out of the car, went to the passenger side back door and took a baby out of the seat. He then watched in silence with everyone else as Tosha got out and the three of them started toward the house.

Big Casey picked up Julianne, and with Hazel stood at the door as Theresa and Tosha approached the house.

"Happy birthday, Daddy," Theresa shouted. She hurried up to him and hugged him with Julianne squeezed in between.

"Hey there baby girl. How's my wheeling and dealing lawyer daughter?" Big Casey asked.

"I'm doing just fine," she answered, turned and looked at Jason, then Dominique. "Brother, how are you and more important who is this lovely lady standing next to you?" she asked.

"I'm hanging in there and this is my most special friend Dominique," he said with emphasis. He had to spruce it up to pacify Dominique.

"You hanging around this guy who thinks he's going to be some kind of famous writer?" she said to Dominique. "My hat's off to you, girlfriend."

Dominique finally smiled and that made Jason feel much relieved.

"Theresa, who are these two young people with you?" Hazel finally asked.

"I'm sorry, this is Tosha and her baby," Theresa answered her mother. She moved back and stood next to Tosha. "They're staying with me right now."

"They're staying with you?" Hazel continued to prod.

"Yes, Mama, they are staying with me."

"What's the baby's name?" Big Casey asked.

"Well, Daddy," Theresa hesitated for a moment. "She doesn't have a name. Not yet."

"The baby doesn't have a name?" Hazel said. "How can the baby not have a name?"

"Mamma, that's a long story. I'll explain it all to you later."

"Well how about explaining it right now?" Hazel's voice rose slightly.

"Not today, Hazel," Big Casey intervened. "Today is my day and we'll have none of that."

"I was only asking—"

"I know what you were asking and what you were doing. But not today." Big Casey interrupted his wife. "Now let's all go out on the patio and I'm going to check on those ribs."

"Can I play with the baby, Aunt Theresa?" Julianne asked as she grabbed her aunt's hand and followed her and Tosha behind Big Casey who turned and headed for the patio.

"She's just adorable," Dominique whispered to Jason as they also headed for the patio.

"Who?" Jason asked both surprised and pleased that Dominique was talking to him.

"Your daughter, silly."

"Yeah, she's a little doll."

"You going to let me spend some time with her today?"

A big smile crossed Jason's face. "You better believe I am. She needs to know you because you're going to be in her life for a long time."

"Thank you." Dominique pulled Jason close and kissed him on the cheek.

"Where are you going, Mother?" Jason asked Hazel as she headed in a different direction from everyone else.

"I'm going to call your sister. She told me she'd be here real early. I want to find out what's holding her up." Hazel disappeared behind the double doors leading into the family room.

Chapter 44

"**A**rthur, this in no way is over yet!" Jacqueline shouted as they took the off ramp from the freeway and headed up Orange Grove Boulevard on their way to the birthday party. "I told Mama I'd be there early to help her get ready. But no, you had to run off this morning to take care of some kind of business." Jacqueline turned sideways in the Mercedes and glared at her husband.

Arthur kept his eyes riveted straight ahead on the road. He tried to tune her out. Since they'd left Malibu close to an hour ago it had been a constant badgering and picking at him. And why? Because they were late getting to her parents' house to kiss up to Big Casey. Late last night he'd finally figured out what happened with his debit card. That first night over Elizabeth's with that other freak he'd given them the card to go get more drugs. Like a damn fool he'd given them the code also. That's all they needed to drain him. He was so damn mad he had to confront them right then. That's why he'd gotten up and took off before Jacqueline knew what happened. And then when he got over there, that white ass bitch refused to answer the fucking door. He could have killed her. And that other Black bitch too. He would have beaten both their asses real good. They probably knew he'd figured out what happened and refused to open the door. But he'd get to them tomorrow or maybe even later that evening after he finished playing husband in front of this silly ass Mitchell family.

"You hear me talking to you, Arthur? I want to know where you had to run off to this morning."

"Damn, woman, you don't have to shout at me," Arthur finally answered her. "I told you I'd explain it all to you later."

"You're damn right you're going to explain this bullshit." Jacqueline straightened her body and crossed her legs. Without looking in his direction she continued, "And I also want to know why your debit card didn't clear yesterday. The way I figure it you must've had over five thousand dollars in that account. Do you know how embarrassed I would have been if for some reason I used that card and got rejected? What a fucking idiot you can be at times."

Damn, Jacqueline was pushing her luck. Arthur squeezed the steering wheel tightly. He had to make sure his hands were locked in place or else he'd be tempted to smack Jacqueline right in the mouth. He didn't need to be taken through all these changes. The money was gone and the bitch had stolen from him. Knowing that alone was enough punishment and he could do without this bullshit.

"I guess the missing money must have something to do with all those late nights you stay out. I can't believe I've been such a big fool." Jacqueline turned and stared out the window.

Arthur glanced over at her. One more word and I'm going to knock her ass right out the door. Hell, putting up with her nagging wasn't worth it. Now he realized why he stayed out all night and ran to the clubs. Jacqueline didn't look good enough and the money he made working for her father just wasn't worth having to take this kind of bullshit. Soon he'd have everything in order and he'd be in a position to dump her, then Arthur could pursue those women he believed would be much more satisfying like Dominique at the club. As they approached the entrance to the Mitchell home, Arthur felt confident that his relationship with Dominique would be considerably different the very next time they met.

U

Jason watched his sister exit the house and head toward the barbeque pit where he sat keeping Big Casey company. She had been in the family room with Hazel, Dominique and the kids. So far everything seemed to be going well. Jacqueline and Arthur would be there any minute and hopefully Cedric was on his way. It looked like it would be a successful sixty-fifth birthday celebration for Big Casey and for that Jason felt grateful. Not even Arthur, with his silly ways, could mess up this day.

Theresa suddenly stopped walking toward him and said, "Jason, I need to talk to you in Daddy's study, please."

Jason shot Big Casey an expression of curiosity. His father shrugged his shoulders and continued to turn the meat on the grill.

"Go ahead, I'll be okay," Big Casey said.

Jason followed Theresa inside the house and into Big Casey's study. They both sat in the two chairs in front of the desk.

"How's Dominique doing with our mother in there?" he asked before Theresa could say anything.

"She's doing well," Theresa answered. "Mama seems to like her and that's different for a woman who never liked any of your girlfriends until after you broke up with them."

"That's not true. She always seemed to get along with Angela."

"Getting along and liking someone are two different things when it comes to women, and especially to mothers with their sons," Theresa offered as a retort. She then smiled and continued, "Why are you so concerned if she and Dominique are getting along? You have plans you want to share with me first?"

"You never know." Jason adjusted his body in the chair. "Why'd you want to see me?" he asked.

"Not so fast," Theresa shot back at him. "You didn't answer my question."

"What question was that?"

"Boy, don't play coy with me."

"I did answer you. I said you never know."

"What does she do? Is she a writer also?"

"No I wouldn't say that. But why did you want to see me?" Jason wanted to change the subject and that bothered him. Thankfully Theresa was the first to ask him about Dominique's profession. It bothered him that he couldn't tell her that Dominique danced for a living. And if he couldn't tell Theresa, the most understanding of the women in the family, how was he possibly going to tell Hazel? Jason found some comfort knowing he wouldn't have to deal with that problem right away.

Theresa snapped her finger. "Hello, Jason, are you still with me?"

"Yeah I'm here. What's up? Why'd you want to see me alone?"

"It's about Tosha and her daughter."

"Okay, what about them?"

Now it was Theresa's turn to readjust her body in the chair. She moved right up to the edge and said, "Tosha came in to see me a couple of weeks ago. She wanted to find out if our program would represent her in court?"

"Represent her for what?"

"To sue her boyfriend for infecting her with the HIV virus."

"What?" Jason blurted out loudly.

"Ssh, not so loud. I don't want Mama coming in here."

"I guess you don't."

Theresa looked back at the door. "I'm thinking about taking both of them in permanently."

"What?" Jason blurted out a second time. "You're planning on taking on the responsibility of a young girl who's infected with AIDs?"

"It's not AIDs. It's only HIV. And I'm not even sure she has the virus. She believes she does because the young guy who got her pregnant has tested positive."

"How about the baby?" Jason asked.

"We don't know yet. They were tested yesterday. We'll know in a week."

"Where are her parents?"

"It's a long story. Let's just say they are of no help."

"Damn, Theresa, I know you like to fight for the underdog and I've always admired you for that. I mean I admire the way you try to deal with Jacqueline and that asshole she's married to. But to take on this kind of responsibility, I just don't know."

"I can't help it, Jason. It's in my blood."

"If it's in your blood you sure didn't inherit it from your mother. She's going to have a fit when you tell her."

"I know and I have to figure out how best to tell her."

"Just knowing you brought someone into her house that

might be HIV positive is going to send her through the roof. But when you tell her they may become a part of the family, I just don't know how she'll respond. Please don't tell her today. We don't want anything to happen that'll spoil this day for the big man."

"I agree. That's exactly why I asked you to come in here. But understand I had to tell someone. The only other person who knows is Cedric."

"Cedric? How'd he know?"

"He was with me when I picked her up."

"I'm sure he had no problem with it. He's got his own problem he has to deal with."

"You're right. Big time. I just hope he doesn't do anything stupid and bring his friend over here today."

"Cedric is bold but not crazy."

"Let's hope so. You seem to be the only one without drama," Theresa said just as the two of them heard the front door open.

"I plan to keep it that way." Jason smiled at his sister. He could hear Jacqueline greeting Hazel. "I guess we should go greet our crisis in the making," he said. They both got up and headed to the foyer.

Jason detected a shocked expression all over Dominique's face when he entered the foyer and walked over to be by her side. She was staring at Arthur, so Jason also glanced at his brother-in-law. He appeared to be the usual bland Arthur so why the frown from Dominique? Just as he approached her, Hazel grabbed her by the hand.

"Jacqueline, have you met Jason's friend Dominique?" she asked.

"No, I haven't," Jacqueline replied as she approached Dominique and took her hand. "You're so beautiful. Are you in the movies?"

Dominique failed to respond. She still seemed to be concentrating on Arthur and that bothered Jason. He pulled her in tighter to him.

"Dominique is someone I met at my writing group. You know

the one I told you all about over in Leimert Park." Jason now noticed a smirk on Arthur's face.

"Aren't you going to introduce me to your friend?" Arthur asked as he moved a little in front of Jacqueline and closer to Dominique. He held his outstretched hand toward her.

"Dominique, this is my brother-in-law, Arthur Hannon, and of course my sister Jacqueline."

Arthur grabbed Dominique's hand and Jason could feel her body go rigid. She seemed to reluctantly return Arthur's handshake.

"I could almost swear I've seen you somewhere," Arthur said. He finally released her hand.

"Oh really, Arthur," Jacqueline said. "Where do you think you've seen her?"

"I don't know, but it'll come to me."

"Hi, Aunt Jacqueline," Julianne shouted as she came running from the other room and jumped into Jacqueline's arms.

"Hi, baby girl," Jacqueline replied. She gave Julianne a kiss and then put her back down. "Where's Daddy?" she asked.

"Out at the grill," Hazel answered. "I guess we should all join him."

"Yeah, let's go wish the old man a happy one," Arthur added.

They started toward the patio. As Jason turned to follow them Dominique grabbed him by the arm and pulled him back.

"What's wrong?" he asked.

"I need to talk with you alone."

"Right now?"

"Yes, right now."

Arthur stopped at the door, turned and looked back at them. "Aren't you all going to join us?" he asked. "I might remember where I met you," he continued to stare directly at Dominique.

"We'll be there in a minute," Jason said. "We can go into Big Casey's study."

He took Dominique by the arm and they headed into the study. "What in the world is wrong with you?" Jason asked.

"I'm sorry, Jason, but I need for you to take me home."

"What's come over you? You know I can't take you home right now. How would that look?" Jason sat down in one of the chairs in front of the desk and looked up at Dominique.

She hurried over and sat in the chair next to him. "I'm sorry, Jason, but I don't think this is going to work out. This just isn't a good idea. I'm not good at meeting families. In fact this is the first time I've ever done anything like this."

"Like what?"

"Meet the family of someone I'm dating."

Again Jason found himself confronting one of Dominique's petulant mood swings. This one was much more intimidating to him. Most important, however, he worried about her. What had happened in the last half hour to cause this kind of change in her behavior? Or better still, what was it about Arthur that affected her? Suddenly it hit him. Arthur always frequented places like the Black Zebra. He remembered Arthur telling him that's where he met the two freaks. Damn, he'd probably seen Dominique at the club and knowing Arthur he was all over her. He could expose her to the family and that explained Dominique's sudden change in attitude. If that were the case would he be able to handle the situation? He wasn't sure. But he also recognized his absolute weakness and submission to her. He couldn't allow his pride to trap him. Jason had to get beyond an obsession with her profession if he wanted to escape an emotional collapse like the one he felt the last time they argued.

"Jason, are you listening to me?" Dominique asked as she took his hand into hers and gently began to rub it. "I love you, baby, but I don't think I can handle this. There is just so much you don't know about me and I was foolish to think we could get beyond that fact."

"Yes, we can," he finally said." Just bear with me today and I promise you I'll do whatever you want to make this work."

"I can't—"

"Yes, we can." He cut her off. "It doesn't matter what it is."

Dominique placed two of her fingers to his mouth. "Being here could become very uncomfortable for me and I'd probably make it uncomfortable for you."

"Don't do this, please. Don't make me choose between you and Big Casey's sixty-fifth birthday. Let's just make it through the day and whatever it is we'll deal with it later." Jason held her hands tightly in an effort to keep her there. He could see the sadness in her beautiful soft brown eyes. He saw the anguish in her face and it made him sad but also more determined. She finally dropped her head and stared at the floor.

Suddenly the door swung open and Julianne came bouncing into the room. She ran directly to Dominique, broke Jason's grip on her hand and took it into hers.

"Daddy, your girlfriend's very pretty," she said.

"Well thank you very much," Dominique said and finally a slight smile covered her face.

"My Mommy's very pretty too," Julianne said.

"She really is," Dominique concurred. "You're really lucky to have such a beautiful mother. And you're pretty too."

"My Daddy was lucky to have her, but they couldn't get along. That's why they got a divorce."

"Sometimes that happens, sweetheart," Dominique said softly.

"I hope if you marry my Daddy you guys will stay married. Are you going to marry my Daddy?"

Jason's eyes met Dominique's straight on. He'd really not thought of marriage and he could only wonder if Dominique had ever given that any consideration. Jason felt his feelings were strong enough and he couldn't imagine anyone meaning more to him than she did at that moment, but marriage took it all to another level.

They both stared at each other, momentarily ignoring Julianne who continued squeezing Dominique's hand. He'd never thought of Dominique as a mother. Her profession precluded him from placing her in that category. But now that his daughter had raised the issue of marriage, children were the logical extension. If he could just climb in Dominique's head and eaves- drop on her thoughts. This all was beginning to feel surreal, out of the zone of reality. He did have a daughter, someone who would forever be in his life, and any woman he married would have to deal with that also. Was Dominique the kind of woman that could handle that important fact? He just didn't know.

"Daddy, are you going to get married?" Julianne asked.

"At this point, sweetheart, Dominique and I are just very close friends," he said all the time looking at Dominique. Her expression seemed to change. "But you never know what might happen in the future." Jason picked Julianne up and kissed her on the cheek. "Now why don't you go back and talk with your grandmother? You don't get to see her all that much and you need to take advantage of every chance you get to spend with her."

Jason put Julianne down and she backed away from him. "Daddy, I don't get to see you that much either." She turned and ran out of the room.

"I think she's a little angry with you," Dominique said.

"She'll be all right. She's my angel."

Dominique moved in close to him. She took both Jason's hands and smiled. "I really do think you should take me home," she whispered.

"Let's not start that all over again." Jason pulled her close and placed both arms around her.

She pulled away. "Jason, don't, your daughter might come back in here."

"We're only hugging."

"I know but there are so many different things happening I just don't think it's a good idea. Now I really do want you to take me home."

"Dominique! What is wrong with you?" Jason moved back away from her. "What do I tell Big Casey? You didn't want to hang around and help celebrate his birthday?"

"Jason, I saw the expression on your face when your daughter asked if we were going to get married."

"And exactly what did you see?"

"It's a look I see all the time at the club when I ask a customer if he's married. It's like I have invaded a place where I'm not allowed to go. It's okay to have fun with me, but don't take it any further than that."

"That's not what I was thinking. You're all wrong. In fact I was wondering if you'd ever thought about marriage and a family."

Dominique kissed him on the cheek and took his hand again. "Well then I'm sorry, but I still want you to take me home."

Jason let out a deep sigh as a sign of surrender. "Okay, let's go excuse ourselves."

"I don't mean to be rude. Just tell your father I don't feel well and you can always come back. That way you can spend some time with your daughter." She tightened the grip around his hand. "You know that's important too."

"You're right," he said and smiled.

They made their way back to the patio where everyone appeared quite relaxed in lounge chairs around the pool. Big Casey still busied himself at the grill. Jason noticed a broad smile on Arthur's face as they stopped at the front end of the pool. Again he could feel Dominique's body stiffen. She seemed to be staring directly at Arthur. From the frown on Jacqueline's face, she obviously noticed also. Julianne was busy playing with the baby in Tosha's lap. Before Jason could say anything Theresa jumped from her chair and hurried over next to them.

"Where have you two been hiding?" she asked.

"Dominique wasn't feeling well," Jason explained. "We were in the study."

"Oh, honey, I hope you're feeling better," Hazel said from her lounge chair.

"You okay?" Theresa asked placing her hand on Dominique's arm.

"I feel somewhat better," Dominique replied. "But I do think I need to go home."

"Don't do that," Arthur said as he reared up in the lounge chair. "We've not seen Jason with such a beautiful woman in a very long time."

Jacqueline leaned up in her chair and smacked Arthur on his arm. "You just stop. I'm sure we'll get a chance to see Dominique again."

"Why don't you go inside and lie down for a while?" Theresa suggested.

"I appreciate that, but I also have a long day tomorrow and I need a good night's rest. I'm going to go home, take some pain medicine and call it a day."

"Where do you work?" Arthur shouted.

Jason shot a scowl at Arthur. Dominique remained silent.

"Didn't you hear Jason say she's a writer just like him?' Jacqueline answered for Dominique.

"Good, good, what kind of books do you write?" Arthur continued.

Everyone seemed to be waiting for an answer as they glanced over at Dominique. Jason knew that made Dominique even more anxious to get out of there. Without replying he took her by the arm and walked over next to Big Casey who had stopped his work at the grill long enough to look toward Dominique and Jason.

"Mr. Mitchell, I'm sorry," Dominique spoke first. "I didn't mean to leave this early on your celebration, but I really am feeling under the weather."

Big Casey laid the barbecue brush along the side of the grill and hugged Dominique. "That's okay. You just get better and make sure Jason brings you back to visit with us soon." He kissed her on the cheek and turned to his son. "You coming back?" he asked.

"Wouldn't miss this opportunity to celebrate you getting another year older," Jason answered.

"I'll walk with you all to the door," Theresa said.

Jason and Dominique waved to the others and the three of them started toward the door. Jason swung the door open and they stepped outside. He was about to say good-bye to his sister when he spotted a car coming up the driveway. It had to be Cedric because he was the only other person who would have the combination to open the front gate. But there were two people in the car. As they came closer Jason spotted Cedric in the passenger seat and Aaron driving the car. He glanced at Theresa who also looked at the two passengers with a shocked look on her face.

"I don't believe this!" Jason shouted and headed toward the car. Theresa was close behind him. Dominique stayed back on the porch.

Jason stepped right in front of the car and held his hand in the air signaling for Aaron to stop. He then rushed to the passenger side, snatched the door open and glared menacingly at his brother.

"What do you think you're doing?" he shouted at Cedric.

Aaron leaned halfway across Cedric and spoke first. "Why are you shouting at him?" He glared right back at Jason. Cedric seemed to shrivel up in the seat.

"I'm not talking to you," Jason shouted at Aaron. "This is a family matter and I'm going to ask you to stay out of it." He turned back to his brother. "Why do you want to spoil your father's birthday this way?"

Suddenly Cedric seemed to get a burst of energy and courage. He launched forward in the seat. "I'm doing no such thing," he said in a shrill voice. "I told Theresa, in fact I promised her, that I would show up today. And I'm keeping my promise."

"But I specifically asked that you not bring him with you. And you promised me that you wouldn't."

"Cedric, how could you?" Aaron shouted from the driver's seat.

"Aaron is a part of my life and hopefully will always be a part of my life," Cedric said ignoring Aaron's comment. "My family needs to know that."

"Oh God, I think I'm going to be sick," Jacqueline said.

Jason looked back at Jacqueline who stood next to Theresa. He noticed that Arthur remained back on the porch next to Dominique who stared straight ahead. She seemed oblivious to all that was happening or else she was ignoring Arthur. The front door remained open and Jason feared that any minute Big Casey would walk outside. Hopefully, he was still busy at the grill. Jason could handle Hazel walking out on this fiasco, but not his father. He needed to go somewhere that wouldn't attract any attention. He reached inside the car and grabbed Cedric by the arm.

"Let's get out of here before your father comes out." Cedric got out and they headed toward the guest house. Jason noticed that Dominique walked off the porch and headed toward his car. Theresa, Jacqueline and Arthur followed them to the guest house. Aaron jumped out of the car and walked close behind.

"Cedric, we don't care what kind of lifestyle you've decided for yourself," Jason said with a slight pleading in his voice once everyone was inside. "But your sisters and I do care what impact your choice of lifestyle has on the man inside and your mother."

"Are you telling me that I can't go in there and see my mother?" Cedric asked defiantly.

"Not with him, you can't," Jason answered decisively.

"Well, we'll see about that." Cedric grabbed Aaron by the arm and moved to the left of Jason. "Come on, it's about time you meet the tyrant in person," he said to Aaron.

Jason quickly moved to block his exit from the guest house. "I'm sorry, brother, but I can't let you do this."

The room became quiet and still. It was like they all were waiting for Cedric's next move. Jason and Cedric stared defiantly at each other. They had only fought once in their lives. Jason was much older than Cedric and when they were growing up it wouldn't have been a fair fight. But now Cedric was grown and could probably challenge his brother, but Jason would not allow that to influence his determination to stop him.

Finally Theresa moved forward and elbowed her way between the two brothers.

"Cedric, why don't you go in first and talk with them?" she pleaded. "If necessary tell them about your decision in life. If they are all right with it, then you can take Aaron in. If not you'll want to leave anyway, so you just excuse yourself and no one will be harmed."

Cedric ignored Theresa. He grabbed Aaron's hand and started to go around Jason, who again blocked his path.

"I'm sorry, little brother, but I can't let you do this. Now go in the house and you can talk to Big Casey and Hazel. I'm sure they'll be happy to see you. But you are not going to do it your way."

"Oh quit playing with him and put him off the property," Jacqueline said tersely.

"Nobody's putting me off my mother's property." Cedric turned and glared over at Jacqueline.

Jason noticed Arthur with a major smile across his face. He obviously enjoyed the action.

"You're right," Theresa said. "You have just as much right to be here as any of us. But you don't have a right to spoil this day. Now please make up your mind. Are you going in there alone or are you going to leave? Hazel's going to be out here any minute now to find out where we all are. So what's it going to be?"

Again, a long silence.

"All right, we'll leave," Cedric finally said. "But I will be back at another time. And I will be back with Aaron and the three of you might as well get used to seeing him around."

Jason let out a deep sigh and everyone in the room, with the exception of Arthur, seemed to do the same. Jason stepped aside in order to let them out.

"Cedric, we don't want to stop you from seeing the folks. But with what you want to do, we just ask that you do it gently," Theresa moved in close to Cedric and hugged him. "We love you and we want you in the family."

"Speak for yourself," Jacqueline spoke up. "I don't want a thing to do with him as long as he lives that dirty lifestyle."

"Shaddup, Jacqueline," Jason said harshly.

"Don't talk to my wife that way!" Arthur shouted at Jason.

They all looked over at him with shock on their faces including Jacqueline.

"Brother-in-law, you don't have room to talk with the kind of woman you brought to your parents' house," Arthur continued.

"What are you talking about?" Jacqueline asked as she and everyone else turned their attention away from Cedric.

"Ask him what his new girlfriend does for a living," Arthur continued. "I can guarantee you it isn't what he said inside. She's a cheap stripper at a men's club."

"What my girlfriend does for a living isn't any of your business, you sick bastard!" Jason shouted.

"Jason, how dare you," Jacqueline also shouted. "You don't have to call my husband names."

"Husband, my ass," Jason retorted. "You don't call what you have a marriage. I'd call it a sickness."

"Come on, Arthur, we don't have to listen to this. We'll see you all back in the house." Arthur followed Jacqueline out of the guest house.

"Let's get out of here," Jason said.

"You all right?" Theresa asked Jason.

"I'm fine, but I'm not sure this family is," he said as they all left the house.

He and Theresa stood outside the guest house as Cedric and Aaron walked hand in hand back to their car. Jason glanced at the front door fearful that either Hazel or Big Casey would walk outside before his brother made it to the car. Once they were in the car and driving off, Jason turned to Theresa.

"I'm not sure I'll be back as long as Jacqueline and Arthur are here. I'll call Big Casey later."

"You want to tell me about it?" she asked as they both walked to the BMW.

"I will but not right now."

"I understand, brother. We're both carrying some heavy baggage, but not half as heavy as Cedric and Jacqueline. I just hope we can get through all this drama and back to living normal lives."

"Maybe drama is our normal life. I guess I should write my next novel about my own family. After all, that's what a novel is, all drama." He kissed her on the cheek, got in the car and drove off.

Chapter 45

With a firm grip on the steering wheel and his foot pressed heavily on the gas pedal, Jason shot onto the 110 Freeway heading back to Los Angeles. He didn't bother to take the top off and played no music. It was a much different atmosphere than his ride that morning over to Altadena with Dominique. She sat snugly hugging the passenger door and stared straight ahead. The two had said nothing since leaving Big Casey's birthday party. Jason had no reason to be upset, but he just couldn't handle the possibility that she'd entertained Arthur at the club. It was silly to concern himself with that possibility. That's what she did for a living. He knew it going into the relationship, but his brother-in-law had pushed him to the limits. Worse still it gave that lowlife Arthur something to flaunt over him.

Jason drove up behind a truck in the middle lane. He shot around it in the passing lane. For the first time since they'd left, Dominique turned and stared at him. He didn't look her way. Instead he increased his speed as he shot around one of the many sharp curves on the freeway.

"Please slow down! You're making me nervous."

Jason ignored her and in fact increased the speed. He'd been caving in to her concerns from the first time they'd met. It was a case of him always bowing down to her wishes, but not this time. Not after what he'd heard spewing from Arthur's foul mouth.

"Jason! Please slow down or pull off the freeway and let me out."

"And if I do that, what are you going to do, hustle the first man along for a ride?"

"What?" Dominique shrieked. "How dare you. What's come over you?" She turned and squarely faced him. "Why are you acting like this?"

"I guess I just don't like the fact that my lady may have entertained my lowlife brother-in-law in a gentleman's club."

Dominique straightened her body and stared straight out the window for a second. She then looked at Jason. "So that's what this is all about?" she shot back at him. "Jason, you have to know that you are acting awfully immature."

"Is it true? Did you ever entertain him?" He ignored her attempt to embarrass him out of pursuing the issue.

"Frankly I don't think it's any of your business who I have entertained." Dominique held her arms in the air and brought them down so that her hands smacked against her thighs. "I have to admit I really did over-estimate you and that really is disappointing."

Jason glared over at her and then looked back at the cars in front of him. This time he moved back into the center lane and shot past a Chevrolet only going the speed limit in the passing lane. After he passed the Chevrolet he quickly moved again into the fast lane. He continued with his eyes straight ahead. He wanted to leave it alone but couldn't.

"I thought maybe you'd use a bit more discretion in who you danced for," he said sarcastically.

"I guess I don't use much discretion," Dominique shot back. "After all I danced for you."

Jason felt an empty sensation throughout his body. What in the world was he doing? Dominique was right, he was acting like a child. But again he couldn't get beyond that ugly fact.

"Are you placing me in the same category as that sorry bastard?"

"No, I'm really not. But why are you acting like this? You knew what I did and I assumed you were able to deal with it. Or at least try to."

"I thought I could too, but I never imagined it could get so complicated."

Dominique released a deep sigh and ran fingers through her hair. "All my life I've been hoping to meet a man that I could consider a decent human being. Not even a gentleman, but at least decent. When we went into the private room the first time you came in the club I—"

"The second time," Jason corrected her.

"All right the second time," she continued. "I thought you were going to be that different person when you weren't trying to grope all over me."

"Is that what Arthur did, grope all over you?"

"Please stop," Dominique shouted. "I am not going to allow you to attack me this way."

"You practically danced nude in front of my brother-in-law. How did you think I would respond?"

"First of all I didn't even know you at that time, so his being your brother-in-law is quite irrelevant. But what is relevant is your attitude."

Jason almost missed his turn-off for the 110 Freeway. He had been driving in the left lane and had to quickly cut in front of a couple of cars in order to get over to the ramp. He noticed Dominique holding on tight to the armrest.

"Sorry," he whispered.

"Jason, I hope you are planning to take me home."

"Is that what you want?"

"I don't think it really matters what I want. I think it's necessary."

"Why do you always want to run off when things aren't going your way?"

"It's not that at all. Jason, I don't think you're ready for this kind of relationship."

"And what kind of relationship is that?"

"Oh please, don't try to be coy with me. It doesn't fit your personality."

"I am simply a man with weaknesses."

"It appears that one of your weaknesses is that you can't handle a relationship with a woman who dances for money."

Her terseness made Jason's stomach tighten. Had he backed himself into a corner and couldn't get out? He didn't want her to go home, but then wasn't sure he could handle a relationship with a dancer and especially one who had danced for his brother-in-law.

"Damn it, Dominique, why couldn't you have been a school teacher, a nurse, or anything other than a dancer?" Before he could turn to face her, he felt the smack on the side of his face.

"Jason Mitchell, you make me sick," Dominique shouted. "You don't know anything about me. You have no idea what I've been through, you son of a bitch."

Jason took his right hand and rubbed the spot where he'd been struck. She'd actually cursed him. He was getting even more entrenched in that corner because deep inside he didn't want to lose her and didn't want her to go home. He'd been through that one time before and it made him miserable.

"Okay calm down," he said in a much subdued tone. "I guess I am acting rather childish. It's still early so why don't we stop somewhere and get something to eat? We'll both feel much better afterwards."

"I don't want to stop anywhere with you. In fact I don't even care to be around you. Please take me home."

"Come on, Dominique," he pleaded. "You have to understand it took me by surprise back there."

"And next week if you find out that I danced in front of someone else you know, am I going to have to suffer through another of these episodes?"

"No I don't think—"

"I know I won't have to because I won't continue with this mistake and I'll never make it again. Just take me home."

Jason turned and looked at Dominique who did not look his way. He made his exit off the Freeway on his way to Wilshire Boulevard and her apartment. He finally turned on the radio to KJLH. A sardonic smile crossed his face as the song playing at that moment was Harold Melvin and the Blue Notes, The Love I Lost.

u

Instead of going home as he had planned on doing, Jason went back to the birthday party. He'd told Theresa that he wouldn't return, but after his fight with Dominique he needed to be close to family, even if it meant Jacqueline and Arthur. He really hadn't celebrated with Big Casey because of all the disturbances throughout the day. So many incidents happened very little time had been dedicated to the person to whom all of them owed so much. Jason felt bad about that, and after he'd been disappointed in his inability to deal with Dominique, he needed to do something to feel good about himself. What better way than to spend an evening with the man who meant so much to him? He parked the car, let himself in and headed to the patio.

Big Casey sat at the picnic table with a cigar in one hand and a shot of Scotch in front of him. The birthday cake had been cut and Julianne, along with Tosha and the baby, sat in a couple of lounge chairs near the pool. Hazel sat next to Big Casey with Theresa, Jacqueline and Arthur. When he entered the patio area they all looked at him. He noticed a very smug smile on Arthur's face. Jacqueline quickly looked away. Theresa and Hazel smiled at him as did Big Casey. His father took in a deep drag on the cigar and blew it out.

"I'm glad you made it back," Big Casey said. "We just cut the cake and there are still some ribs and chicken over there next to the grill. Grab you a plate and dig in."

Before Jason could respond Hazel spoke up. "Why did your friend have to leave so early?"

"She really wasn't feeling well," Jason said as he took a seat at the picnic table next to Hazel and directly across from Arthur. He glared over at him. "I'm surprised to see you're still here," he said.

"We were getting comfortable," Arthur replied. "I'd just given Big Casey his present, a box of real good cigars. In fact I bought them in Beverly Hills yesterday so you know they are the best."

"We all gave Daddy his presents," Jacqueline spoke up. "Where is yours?"

"I don't really think that's any of your business," Jason shot back. He then turned and looked past Hazel to Big Casey who seemed to be in a daze, not paying any attention at all. "I got so tied up that I didn't get your gift," Jason said to his father who didn't turn and look his way. "Dad, you hear me?" he asked.

Big Casey jerked his head as if he was just coming back to reality. "That's okay, son. I got all I need with my family right here with me."

"It's not quite complete," Jacqueline added.

"I know," Big Casey said. "I wish Cedric was here. I worry about that boy all the time. But I figure he's doing fine since he hasn't contacted anyone in over a year. You kids only contact your family when something's going wrong."

Suddenly Theresa became engaged in the conversation. First she looked at Jason and then said, "That's kind of cynical isn't it?"

"Truth is what it is," Big Casey said, slightly slurring his words.

"Daddy, are you all right?" Jacqueline asked.

"Just a little tired, but other than that, I'm fine. After all you got to remember I'm now sixty-five." Big Caey rubbed his forehead. Beads of sweat covered his face.

"You're still a young man, with plenty left," Hazel said with a smile.

"Daddy, do you ever wonder about Cedric being in of all cities San Francisco?" Theresa asked.

"What do you mean?" he replied. "San Francisco's a great city. Me and your mother used to drive up there all the time and spend a weekend. We couldn't do that anymore after you all started coming."

"I know it's a great city," Theresa continued despite Jason's hard stare at her. "You do know there is a lot of homosexuality up there."

"Girl, hush your mouth," Big Casey said. "Ain't no way one of my sons could be funny. Ain't that right, Jason? You know your brother pretty well and I'm sure he'd tell you if he was like that." He paused and smiled. "And I know darn well you're not gay. Not after that beautiful woman you had with you today."

Both Theresa and Jacqueline stared at Jason. He didn't look at Jacqueline, but at Theresa. He noticed that she moved her head up and down as if to say yes, you have to tell him. He'd already had his own draining situation with Dominique and wasn't up for another one. Cedric probably would return with his lover and without any advance notice. That wouldn't be the best situation. No doubt it could have an adverse effect on their father.

All of a sudden Big Casey's expression changed. "Well, son, have you heard from Cedric?"

Hazel joined in the conversation. "Jason, you heard your father. Have you talked with Cedric and is he all right?"

"We've all heard from Cedric," Jacqueline jumped to her feet and shrieked. "He lives with a—"

"Jacqueline, shaddup!" Jason shouted.

"Don't tell me what to do," Jacqueline shot back at him. "Daddy, Cedric lives in Los Angeles. And he lives with another man. They moved down here about three months ago. The man he's living with is trying to become an actor and Cedric is supporting both of them. Now it's out and everyone can feel better." Jacqueline finished and sat back down.

Without looking in Jason's direction Big Casey asked, "Is that true, Jason? Is what your sister's telling me the truth? Has the entire family been holding this from me?"

"Yes it is," Jason answered. "But he really wants to see you and try to explain."

Big Casey brought his glass up to his mouth and swallowed the Scotch. He then put the cigar out and got up. "What's there to explain? All of you misled me." He dropped his cigar on the ground and started toward the house.

Theresa jumped up as did Hazel and they both moved toward Big Casey.

"Daddy, we just didn't want to hurt you. We didn't know how to tell you."

Big Casey didn't look around at his daughter who was right behind him. Instead he stumbled toward the door.

"Dad, you okay?" Jason asked as he jumped to his feet to help him.

Before he could get to him, Big Casey stumbled one more step and then crashed to the ground.

Chapter 46

Fear shot through Jason's body, his eyes were riveted to the ambulance, as it screamed down the driveway and onto the street with Big Casey's motionless body inside. There was no way this could be happening. Not to Big Casey, a giant of a man who Jason could never remember being sick. He couldn't fathom the thought of his father's mortality. Other people, both young and old, had heart attacks and strokes, but not Big Casey. He couldn't die because that was not an acceptable option. He and his father still had a lot of things to accomplish together. Getting published really would lose much of its meaning to Jason if he couldn't share it with the man who'd made it all possible for him. And more important, Big Casey didn't die; he just smoked his cigars, drank his Scotch and loved his family. He still had a lot more of all three of those things to do.

"Come on, Jason, we have to get to the hospital," Theresa shrieked.

He turned and faced Hazel. She was frantically hugging Jacqueline. Tosha, with Julianne and the baby, stood back near the door. They all were silent. Suddenly Julianne began to scream.

"Is grandpa dead? Is grandpa dead?" She ran to Jason and jumped in his arms.

Theresa hurried over to them and took her from Jason.

"No, baby, your grandfather is not dead." She stared at Jason and then at Jacqueline. Julianne had been the first one to use the dreadful word that they all had been thinking.

"Julianne, you stay here with your grandmother and Aunt Jacqueline," Jason said. "Your Aunt Theresa and I have to go see about your grandfather."

"You going to bring him home so we can finish the party?"

she asked her father.

Jason glanced over at his mother who still had her head buried between both hands, leaning against Jacqueline. Arthur stood next to both of them saying nothing.

"Yes, we're going to bring him home," Jason finally answered. "Now you be a big girl and help take care of your grandmother."

Julianne ran over to Hazel and hugged her legs. "Okay, Daddy."

"Mother, we'll call you just as soon as we hear something," Jason said.

"No, we're all going down there." Hazel finally spoke up.

"Mama, stay here please," Jacqueline said with tears rushing down her face.

"Come on, Theresa, let's go," Jason shouted. "We'll call you as soon as we hear something." Theresa followed him to the BMW. They both jumped in the car and took off.

u

Jason sped into the visitors' parking area at the Huntington Hospital. They rushed out of the car and hurried through the emergency entrance.

"Where did they take the patient that just arrived?" Jason shouted at the lady behind the counter.

"Which patient?" she shot back. "We just had a patient in an automobile accident and then one who suffered a stroke."

"The stroke patient."

"They've taken him to ICU, but you can't go in there. Go through those double doors and follow the red line until you reach the waiting room. I'll notify the staff that you're here and they'll send someone to talk with you just as soon as they know something."

Jason and Theresa shot down the hall, through the double doors, and into the waiting room. There were a number of other people already inside. Two older women were rubbing their eyes with handkerchiefs and a man was pacing the floor muttering something.

Jason and Theresa found two empty chairs next to each other and sat down. Jason stretched his legs, extending them out, and rested his back. He closed his eyes and let out a deep sigh.

"This can't be happening," he whispered. Before Theresa could respond he continued, "I know it is, but I just can't accept it as real."

"We've been fortunate as a family or maybe I should say we've been blessed," Theresa replied. "Tragedy is something we haven't dealt with at all."

"Why now?" Jason questioned. "He's only sixty-five with plenty of good years left."

"He's not gone yet, Jason," Theresa said with irritation in her voice. "Big Casey's real strong so he might be up and around in no time."

Jason pulled his cell phone from his pocket and started dialing a number. "We'd better let mother know what's happening."

"Yes, Jason," a frantic Jacqueline answered on the other end. "How's Mother?"

"She's about as fine as she can be given the circumstances. Now how is Daddy? We've been waiting here on pins and needles. What took you so long to call anyway?"

"Calm down, and don't start attacking me. Now put Mother on the phone?"

"No, you tell me what's happening and I'll tell her."

Jason felt his temperature rising. Why Jacqueline would insist on this silly behavior he didn't understand. He wasn't, however, going to get sucked into any kind of confrontation with her. For now she could have her way.

"He's in intensive care right now. We don't know the extent of damage done to his heart."

"Why aren't you in there with him?" she screamed into the phone.

"Jacqueline, the doctors won't allow family in the room while they're trying to stabilize his pressure. You need to calm down."

"Don't start telling me what to do and don't try playing big brother," Jacqueline shot back. "I haven't forgotten how you talked to my husband and that's not over yet."

"What the hell's wrong with you?"

The other people sitting in the room looked over at Jason and he turned his back to them. He lowered his voice, "Our father just had a stroke. He's in intensive care and you're talking about how I talked to that fool husband of yours. I'll call you when we hear something." He finished and slammed the phone shut.

"That really went well," Theresa said.

"I don't understand her relationship with that loser of a husband," Jason replied and then sat down next to Theresa. "What the hell is she trying to prove staying with that fool?"

"Don't be so harsh," Theresa advised and patted Jason on the shoulder. "You know they say love is blind."

"If that's love they have going on, please spare me the burden." Jason stared straight ahead at the wall on the other side of the room. He could feel Theresa's eyes all over him.

"Do you want to tell me what Arthur was talking about back at the house?" she asked.

"What do you mean?"

"Come on, brother," Theresa prodded gently. " You can share your secrets with me. Remember I'm here for you. I didn't hesitate to share mine with you. We need each other in order to keep all the others together."

Jason stared and smiled at his sister. Their age difference always prevented them from sharing intimate secrets. Now that they both were grown, age no longer mattered.

"I did meet Dominique at a dance club," he said.

"By dance club, do you mean strip joint?"

"Yes, but that sounds so crass."

"It is what it is, brother." She paused for a moment and then continued, "I'll tell you one thing for sure, the Mitchell boys are full of surprises."

"What do you meant by that?" he asked rather defensively.

"Your choices for partners in life really don't reflect your background," she said with a smile. "One son dating another man and the other son a woman of the night."

"She's not a woman of the night."

"Don't be so touchy. You know what I mean."

"It doesn't matter. She broke it off with me this evening."

"Don't tell me why because I think I know."

"And why then, Ms. Know It All?"

"You probably showed your immaturity when you found out that Arthur had seen her in the club. Am I right?"

"Yeah, I guess somewhat you are."

"What am I missing?" Theresa reached over and took Jason by the hand. "How silly you're being."

"I know, but I don't know if I can fix it."

"The better question is do you want to fix it?"

"What do you mean by that?"

"Are you fooling yourself, because she's a beautiful woman, into believing that you can handle a serious relationship with a woman who makes her living by making other men happy?"

"She doesn't exactly make other men happy."

"See what I mean? You can't even face up to what she does. The lady makes men feel good by placing her very beautiful and well structured body in front of them and allowing them to fantasize. I can imagine that's probably what happened with Arthur and now you're all uptight. If you can't handle it, she was right in breaking it off."

"Whose side are you on?" Jason asked with irritation.

"I'm always on your side, brother. But that doesn't mean I'm not going to give you the truth the way I see it."

"That's you for sure," Jason said as the doctor entered the room and headed toward where they sat. They both stood to greet him. "How is he, doctor?" Jason asked.

"He had a pretty serious stroke," the doctor said. "But I think he's going to make it."

"Oh thank God," Jason replied as he hugged Theresa.

"But his damage is severe and it'll be a while before we know how much damage has been done to his nervous system. Right now he's lost use of his body on the left side. He, by no means, is out of danger yet."

"When will he be?" Theresa asked.

"We won't know that for a while," the doctor answered.

"Can we see him?" Jason asked.

"I'm afraid not. He's still in intensive care. He'll be there all tonight. We'll see how he's doing in the morning and then family members can visit him according to his improvement."

"Has he regained consciousness?" Jason continued to ask the questions as Theresa stood next to him tightly gripping his hand.

"He recovered consciousness for a moment or two and then was out again. You all are welcome to stay here at the hospital, but my advice is to go home and get some rest. You have a very hectic week in front of you."

"There's no way we can just see him for a minute? Please, doctor, we don't have to get close." Jason pleaded with the doctor.

The doctor hesitated for a moment, looking first at Jason and then at Theresa.

"Okay, but from outside the room. You can look through the window and only for a minute. Sometimes patients can detect a loved one is near and that can cause them anxiety." The doctor led Jason and Theresa out of the waiting room and down a long corridor. "Prepare yourself for what you are about to see. This is your father, but you're about to see him in a different light. Just keep in mind that he is a very sick man and without all those tubes he might not make it. Don't panic because the tubes are not permanent. Only until he gets past the critical stage and is stabilized."

Following the doctor down the hall, Jason glanced into some of the rooms they passed. He stared at patients in the condition the doctor had just mentioned. His thoughts returned to Theresa's comments back in the room about them being fortunate as a family that they hadn't faced tragedy. They stopped and stared through the window at Big Casey. Jason had to hold Theresa as her body went limp. They had put a white robe on Big Casey and there appeared to be over a half dozen tubes inserted into his body pumping different kinds of fluids into him. A nurse sat in a chair at the foot of the bed with a chart and a pen. She appeared to be monitoring a couple of the different machines that sent vital signals from Big Casey's body. The nurse would look at the machines and then make notations on the chart.

Jason stared at his father. He felt choked and tears filled his eyes. He squeezed Theresa's hand. She had dropped her head and he could hear her sobbing. After standing there for a few minutes the doctor finally signaled for them to leave. He led the way back down the hall and they followed.

Once away from the room Theresa burst out crying. Jason held his sister and tried to console her. The doctor, who seemed immune to this kind of behavior, spoke first.

"We hope we can move him out of intensive care soon. I'll allow only one visitor at a time while he's still there." He pulled a card out and handed it to Jason. "If your father has a doctor you can have him call me tomorrow."

"My father's been diabetic for a few years now."

"Do you know if he was taking care of his diabetes?"

Jason reflected back on the many times he'd asked Big Casey to stop drinking and smoking cigars. "He was a social drinker and loved a good cigar every now and then. In fact, he'd put out a cigar just before he passed out."

"That's not good," the doctor said. "Please have his doctor contact me tomorrow."

Theresa broke from Jason's grip and moved closer to the doctor. "Is he going to be all right?" she asked.

"At this point I can't really answer that question. As soon as he's stabilized I imagine his doctor will get all the specialists needed to determine the extent of his damage. But our most critical concern right now is to get him conscious so he doesn't slip into a coma."

"Oh God no," Theresa shouted.

Again Jason grabbed her and held her close to him.

"Why don't you all go home and get some rest?" the doctor advised. "There's not much you can do here. If his condition changes we'll call you."

"Thank you, doctor," Jason said. He lead Theresa down the hall but she broke from his grip.

"No we can't leave him," she shouted. "I know if we leave him we won't ever see him alive again. When you leave loved ones in a hospital they die."

"Stop that," Jason scolded. "Big Casey's too strong and stubborn and he loves life too much to die. He has a lot of living to do." Jason took a tight grip on his sister's arms and forced her down the hall and out of the hospital.

u

It was after midnight when Jason and Theresa arrived back at the house. Jacqueline and Hazel sat close on the couch in the living room. Tosha and the baby were sleeping in one of the large recliners. Arthur sat in one of the other recliners. When Jason and Theresa walked into the room they all perked up.

"What happened? How is he?" Hazel asked. "Why haven't you called before now? I've been waiting all evening. How is he?"

Jason shot a glance at Jacqueline, but quickly decided not to make an issue out of the obvious fact that she had failed to tell Hazel that he had called.

"Jason, Theresa, how is your father?" Hazel asked again.

"He's still unconscious, Mother," Jason answered. "We'll know better in the morning just how much damage was done."

"Damage, what kind of damage? Why didn't you stay there with him? He's got no one there." Hazel jumped from the couch and headed toward the open door. "I need to get down there right now so he'll know he's not alone. Our Lord in Heaven, what if he wakes up and there is no one there."

Jason caught his mother before she made it to the doorway.

"Mother, he's in intensive care and you can't be in there with him. Now the doctor told us that they'd call if there's any change in his condition." Jason led his mother back over to the couch and sat down next to her. When he sat down Jacqueline hunched closer to the end. Jason noticed but refused to respond.

"We had a chance to look at him, and it looked like he was

doing fine," Theresa said as she took a seat in the only unoccupied chair in the room. She looked for a moment at Tosha who was waking up.

"Fine!" Jacqueline exclaimed. "How can he possibly be doing fine and he's unconscious and in intensive care?"

"He's alive and the doctor believes he's going to recover," Theresa shot back at Jacqueline.

"Well what do we do, just sit around here and wait for something to happen?" Hazel asked now in a more subdued tone.

"At this point there's not much else we can do," Jason answered. He placed his arm around his mother's shoulder. "Big Casey's going to be all right. He's not ready to leave here yet."

Jason's words of encouragement and his touch seemed to relax his mother. She leaned back on the couch and closed her eyes.

Arthur, who'd remained silent all this time, finally spoke up. "I hate to be the one to bring up business at this time. But what are we going to do about the company?"

Jason shot a menacing look at him. He noticed that Theresa did the same.

"We don't really need to deal with that right now," Jason answered. "I think Howard's quite capable of handling the business until we get through the initial stages of this crisis."

Arthur seemed to melt back into the chair with disappointment all over his face. Jacqueline moved forward on the couch. "Why Howard?" she asked. "Arthur's been at the headquarters long enough to know the day to day operations and after all he is family."

"What are you suggesting?" Jason asked dryly.

"I'm suggesting that my husband should have the opportunity to run the business until Daddy recovers," Jacqueline blurted out.

"You want your husband to have the opportunity to take advantage of your father's sickness?" Jason shot back at her.

"How dare you say something like that," Jacqueline shouted.

"Jason Mitchell, I think you're way out of line. And this is not a decision that only you can make. This is a family decision."

"At this point there is no decision to be made," Jason said. "We are only talking about someone to temporarily fill in for Big Casey. This is not open for a great deal of discussion."

Jacqueline jumped to her feet. "What do you mean it's not open for discussion? You're not the only one who has something to say about this."

Hazel brought her body forward on the couch. "Jacqueline, sit down. You all cut out this nonsense in Big Casey's home while he is in intensive care. At this point your only concern should be your father's health and not who is going to do what at that business."

Jacqueline sat back down and put her arm around Hazel. "Mama, I'm sorry, but we can't let a stranger to the family run that business while we're worrying about our father."

Hazel jerked away from Jacqueline's arm. "Your husband's not much better," she said in a shrill voice.

"Mama, please." Jacqueline covered her mouth as if in shock, then continued, "You can't mean that."

"Jacqueline, don't be so stupid," Hazel shot a response to her daughter. "The man beats on you and stays out all times of the night and you want him to run your daddy's business."

Jason and Theresa both looked over at Arthur. He had melted further down into the chair with his head so bent his chin touched his chest. Hazel also glared over at him. "You been mistreating my daughter for a long time and I'm sorry if she wants to stay with you and take that abuse that's her business. But I'll be damned if I'm going to allow you to run this company because your behavior tells me that you're not up to the job."

"Mama, I'm not going to let you talk about my husband that way," Jacqueline's voice rose.

"What are you going to do, run on back up to Malibu and let him abuse you some more?" Hazel asked her daughter.

"Mama, calm down," Theresa finally said something. "You don't need to get excited and none of you all need to be talking about the business." She turned and looked at Jason. "I think you need to put your writing on hold for a while and run the business. We don't know how long Big Casey's going to be incapacitated, so you're the oldest and you're trained with a business background. In fact you know more about the business than anyone else. So, Mama, I think Jason should do it until Big Casey is back on his feet."

"No, not him," Jacqueline cried.

"Jacqueline, please keep quiet," Theresa's voice now rose.

"Don't you dare tell me to keep quiet in my father's home. In fact, I think it's time for us to leave."

"Jacqueline, what is wrong with you?" Hazel asked. "Your father is in intensive care and you're acting selfish?"

"Mama, you're being terribly unfair to my husband and to me. You let Theresa bring these strangers into your home from God knows where and Jason shows up with some woman right out of the ghetto and Cedric shows up with his freakish lover and you're jumping on me."

"What do you mean Cedric was here?" Hazel asked.

"I can't believe you," Jason stared directly at Jacqueline. "Why don't you go on home and cool off? Evidently you're really upset about Big Casey because you're talking crazy."

"Jason, what does she mean Cedric was here?" Hazel again asked.

Jason gave Jacqueline one more very hard look and then turned to Hazel. "He was here, Mother, but he brought his lover with him."

"What do you mean he brought his lover?" Hazel shrieked. 'What in God's name is happening to this family? Oh Lord you all are going to be the death of your father and me."

"Mama, please settle down," Jacqueline said as she moved closer to Hazel.

Hazel pushed her daughter away. "Just go home, Jacqueline. Take your husband and go. I am not going to let him run your father's business. All you have done is pressure your father to push him into positions that he doesn't deserve."

Finally Arthur jumped to his feet. "Why are you all attacking me?" he asked.

"Stay out of this," Theresa said, glaring at Arthur. "This is strictly family business."

"My husband is part of this family," Jacqueline shouted at Theresa.

"You know what, you're ridiculous," Theresa turned and said to her sister.

"All right, all this bickering has to end," Jason again jumped into the fiasco. "Everyone go home."

"No," Hazel interjected. "I want Theresa to say here with me. I don't want to be alone. Not tonight. This is the first time in years that your father won't be here. I don't want to deal with that alone. Jason, you go find your brother and tell him I want him over here tomorrow. I don't care about no damn lover and any of that mess."

Jacqueline again put her arm around Hazel. "Mama, you sure you don't want me and Arthur to stay here with you? After all Theresa's got that girl and her baby."

"No, you go home," Hazel said but this time she did not push Jacqueline away. "Tomorrow, Jason, I want you to go to the office and whoever you decide should run the business until your father is well, will be fine with me."

"Come on, Jacqueline, it seems like we are not welcome here," Arthur said. He headed for the door without looking at anyone.

Jacqueline followed her husband. "Mama, you need to think about this. I'll call you tomorrow." She refused to look at Jason or Theresa. "If you hear anything about Daddy, please call me," she said and disappeared out the door with Arthur.

Hazel returned to the couch and sat down. Theresa hurried over next to Tosha who had watched the entire ordeal with a shocked look on her face. The baby did not wake up. Theresa picked up the little girl and cuddled her close to her breast.

"Jason, I want you to go and find your brother tonight and let him know what has happened to his father. He needs to be with his family throughout this ordeal." Hazel had turned and looked directly at Jason.

"What if he insists on bringing his friend with him?"

"I don't care. We need our family to stay together."

"What about Jacqueline?" Theresa asked. "She's pretty upset."

"Jacqueline will be all right. She loves her Daddy and she'll be here. But she also loves that sorry excuse for a man that she married. We have to be patient with her."

"Mama, you weren't very patient with her this evening," Theresa said.

"Believe me, I was very patient. I didn't tell half the truth. Big Casey has wanted to fire Arthur for a while. The reason he hasn't is because he knew how it would affect Jacqueline. That man sure loves his children. If he knew how badly Arthur had treated Jacqueline he would've torn him apart." Hazel again began to cry. "Oh God I can't believe this is happening."

"Mother, go to bed and rest," Jason instructed his mother. "This has been a long day and a lot has happened. You need to rest. I'll go see Cedric and make sure he's over here tomorrow. And I'll take care of everything at the business."

"Yes, I'm going to do that," Hazel said, her voice weak. "Theresa, you put those babies in the guest room and you take your old bedroom."

Jason headed toward the door and Hazel followed close behind.

"Find my baby boy and make sure he's over here tomorrow," she said to Jason.

"I will, mother, and you go rest." Jason opened the front door.

"And you remember your father's going to need you after this. You make sure you're here for him. I don't care about no book or no woman. Do you understand?"

Jason kissed his mother on the cheek and gave her a tight hug.

"I'll be here, Mother. That's a promise." He closed the door and headed to the car.

Chapter 47

Arthur reared back in a lounge chair on the balcony of the townhouse and stared out into the darkness surrounding the ocean. He could hear the roar of the waves crashing on the shore. The ride from Big Casey's had been in total silence. Jacqueline tried to strike up a conversation with him, but he wasn't in the mood. He wanted nothing to do with her or anyone with the name Mitchell. It was quite clear how that family felt about him and they weren't ever going to let him run that company. He now knew why Big Casey never spoke to him. They really did believe he was mistreating Jacqueline. All along she had been calling them and reporting about his behavior.

They treated him like some kind of kid when the real fuck up was Jason who lived like he was totally irresponsible. Talk about somebody being a lowlife, it was him. The son of a bitch had no more class than to be dating a lowlife dancer and even lied to his family about her profession. And they all had the nerve to be upset with him.

"Arthur, aren't you coming to bed?" Jacqueline shouted from inside the townhouse. "You have to work tomorrow and it's already after one o'clock."

He chose not to answer. He didn't want to say anything for fear he'd really go off on her. The other night she'd assured him that he was in line to take over the business after Big Casey retired. She misled him and somehow he had to make her pay for that lie. Arthur picked up the cigar box, opened it and took out a joint. Maybe if he got high he could tolerate being in the same apartment with her. Jacqueline was sickening and he knew soon he'd make his move to leave. He lit the joint, inhaled the smoke and the euphoric feeling took over.

He needed to escape from his reality because he disliked it so much. Why did he have to be born poor? And why did his mother have to get pregnant by someone Black? He was better than Black, a common nigger. That was his legacy and he hated that also. He took another strong hit off the joint and blew the smoke out into the sea breeze.

Arthur leaned further back in the lounge chair and propped his feet up on the top of the railing. There was no worse fate in life than to be born with parents that were Black and white. The best and the worst and he was forced to live a life that accentuated the worst. He felt himself getting high and it helped him to relax. He was one half of what the best life had to offer, but had to accept less than that because of that sorry son of a bitch his mother had married. And then he had to be subservient to that big Black son of a bitch Casey Mitchell and his son.

For a while he'd believed that Hazel liked him, but now he knew that wasn't the case at all. After another hit from the joint Arthur's body relaxed and he could now tolerate Jacqueline. All he needed was some music to help him forget today's fiasco.

He threw the small portion of the joint over the top of the railing, got up and sauntered over to the CD player. He flipped through the CD collection until he found the right one, placed it in the player, and turned it up. Arthur hastily returned to the patio, sat back in the lounge chair and reared his head back while waiting for the sounds.

After a brief delay the quiet of the apartment was broken by blaring horns. He always enjoyed his music when the volume was up and especially enjoyed it when he was high. Just as he escaped deep into the sounds blasting away throughout his head, the music abruptly stopped. He jerked around and Jacqueline stood in the doorway.

"What the hell you think you're doing?" he shouted at her.

"I turned that down and I want you to come to bed," she answered not moving from her position.

"You'd better turn my music back up." Arthur jumped out of the chair and turned to face her.

"No, Arthur. You'll wake up the entire complex and the next thing we'll have the police here."

"I don't give a fuck about that. Turn my music back on or you'll definitely be sorry."

"What you going to do, Arthur? Hit me again?" she asked defiantly. "You're pretty good at doing that."

"Jacqueline, I got no fight with you, but please get out of my way. Right now I want to hear my music and I want it loud so it'll wipe out all this other bullshit I have to deal with."

"What bullshit is that, Arthur? You've got a pretty damn good life. So where is all this bullshit you have to deal with? I haven't done anything to you but try to love you."

"You Mitchells don't know how to love anyone but your fucking egotistical selves. Now get out of my way. I want to listen to my music not argue with you." Arthur knocked Jacqueline to the side and went back into the apartment.

Jacqueline was right behind him. She grabbed his arm and he jerked away from her.

"What the hell is wrong with you?" he scowled.

Tears exploded from Jacqueline's eyes. "Why are you acting like this? You know what we just went through and you're acting all crazy."

"There you go again. Shit, everything is always all about your family and that fucking father of yours."

"Arthur, don't talk like that. Not after what happened earlier. How can you be so insensitive?"

"Insensitive to what, that big fucker?"

"How dare you," Jacqueline cried. She lunged toward Arthur and started beating him with her fist.

Arthur pushed her toward the couch. She fell down and spread out on the cushions. Arthur started toward her with his fist balled up. He suddenly stopped and glared down at her motionless body.

"I should beat your ass real good, but not this time. I won't give your asshole family that pleasure." He turned and headed for the bedroom. Arthur grabbed his suitcase out of the closet and began to toss his clothes inside. Just as he was about to close the suitcase, Jacqueline walked up behind him and grabbed his arm. Her demeanor had changed.

"What are you doing?" she asked. "Where are you going?"

"I'm getting the fuck out of here," he said as he snatched the suitcase off the bed and headed toward the doorway.

"Wait, Arthur, please, we can work this out," Jacqueline pleaded. "You don't have to leave. Everything's going to be all right. I'm going to talk with Mama tomorrow and make her understand that she should let you run the company. She's just upset right now because of Big Casey. She didn't mean any of the things she said." Jacqueline tried to hug Arthur but he pushed her away.

"Your mother and your entire family made it quite clear what they think of me. And how they feel about me is exactly how I feel about them. That includes your sorry whiny ass as well. Now get away from me before I hurt you."

"Please, baby, don't do this," Jacqueline begged. "I don't want to do this without you." She again tried to grab his arms. Arthur's impulse overwhelmed him and he hit Jacqueline in the face. With the first blow the rest came naturally. He began beating her with hard blows to the head and on her shoulders and then in the stomach. All the abuse Arthur felt he had taken from the Mitchell family, he now gave back to her. He beat her until she finally did not move, then stared at her bloody body and laughed. It was now all even. He could leave and feel vindicated and finally free from his bondage.

Arthur stopped at a Bank of America ATM before getting on the highway. It was Jacqueline's account, but he had access to it. He withdrew three hundred dollars and would take the remaining ten thousand out in the morning. He got back on the highway and headed toward Hollywood. He knew Elizabeth would be happy to see him, especially since he had some money. He would stay with her for a couple of days, get high, have fun and then find himself a place to live. He had enough money to last a couple of months until he could find another job. He knew that once those bastards saw what he did to Jacqueline this time, there was no way he would have a job and good riddance.

Arthur could handle that because his plans had gone wrong and there was no need for him to hang around. Jacqueline would definitely be angry because of the beating and especially when she checked the account and found no money in there. But he had just as much right to that money as she did. And she would have done the same thing to him. He just beat her to the punch. He'd always been one step ahead of her and that's how it should end, with him on top.

Chapter 48

Despite Hazel's pleading with Jason to find his brother and tell him about Big Casey, after he left his mother's house he just didn't have the energy and wasn't up to the task. The day, to say the least, had been disastrous. Jason wanted only to go home. So when he reached the Crenshaw exit he took it and drove straight to his apartment. Everything that could possibly go wrong had managed to do so. Not only was his relationship with Dominique over, but his best friend lay in a coma in a hospital. Somehow he knew he'd make it through the emotional loss of Dominique, but he didn't know how he could handle it if Big Casey died. That possibility hadn't really worked on him until he got home and was alone in the apartment. Now he had to confront it and it made him so nervous he felt ill.

Jason plopped down on the bed fully dressed with only the night stand light on low. He wanted to listen to some music but couldn't think of any appropriate for the mood that consumed him with sorrow. He placed his hands behind the back of his head and stared up at the ceiling. His thoughts fluctuated, one moment thinking of Big Casey stumbling to the ground and the next of Dominique turning to him and telling him that it was over. It seemed as though his problems had just started.

Most disturbing was that he had disappointed the woman he loved with his behavior. She trusted him to be mature enough to handle all nuances that went into a relationship with her. Evidently he never fully understood the overwhelming magnitude of those nuances. When put to the test he had failed miserably. A writer should be someone who has a sense of fairness and not necessarily propriety. The latter was for those who felt they had a right to judge other people's behavior. In one day and on two different occasions, he had failed to live up to the kind of person he thought he was; he failed the test with Cedric and Dominique. He should have been shoulder to shoulder with his brother in the confrontation with Jacqueline over his chosen lifestyle and he shouldn't have reacted the way he did in the car with Dominique. Jason recognized that he still had a lot to work out in his own personal growth as a man and as a writer.

He got up, sat on the side of the bed and noticed the blinking red light on the answering machine. His spirits lit up slightly as his first thought was of Dominique. She'd called to tell him she'd changed her mind and would like for their relationship to continue. He reached over and hit the play button.

"Hey, my brothah, this is the life I was born to live," Elliott said. "I wish you guys were here with me. You know, Raquel and Denise. That was a beautiful weekend we had in New York. Life should always be that wonderful. Anyway, our first performance was in Washington, D.C. It was great. Tonight we leave the nation's capital and tomorrow we're in Baltimore. I'll call you from Philadelphia in a couple of days. I should be back in town in a couple of weeks. I'll see you then. By the way Raquel misses you and still cares despite the rotten way you treated her. If you're not totally lost in Dominique give her a call. I'm out, brothah. Talk with you in a couple of days."

Jason hit the off button and lay back down on the bed. Had he really made a mistake? Should he have stayed with Raquel and given their relationship more time? The woman was as close to perfect as one could expect. But he was obsessed with Dominique. He could never go back now despite Elliott's encouraging words. He loved Dominique and that was an emotion that could only be determined through passion. And passion was by its very nature irrational. That's how he felt right then, very irrational, and he wasn't sure if he liked that feeling. Dominique made it quite clear that she didn't believe he could handle a relationship with her and his past behavior confirmed that he couldn't. If somehow they did get back together he would always be trying to prove her wrong. She would be in total control and that wouldn't be love.

Again Jason sat on the side of the bed. He really needed to work this all out and soon. Tomorrow his entire world would change when he was forced to return to the business world. He'd have to deal with the reality that his father might be ill for a very long time. Big Casey would want no one else in charge of the business but him. Any further writing would be put on hold. There was no way he could abandon that man who meant so much to him. In the final equation it worked out that he couldn't have the woman he loved or the profession he'd come to love.

Having settled on that reality he picked up the phone and dialed Raquel's number. The phone rang five times and Jason was prepared to hang up when finally it was picked up on the other end. During the silence he felt silly. Why was he doing this? What did he possibly expect to accomplish? Most important how would she respond?

"Hello, Jason, and why are you calling me this late?" Raquel asked.

"I'm sorry but I really don't have an answer to that question. I just needed to talk to someone."

"You mean a bright man like you can't come up with something more original than that? I'm disappointed in you."

"Okay, be disappointed, but please talk."

"Why should I? Give me one good reason why I shouldn't just hang up this phone and go back to sleep."

"You can easily hang up the phone but you probably wouldn't go back to sleep."

"That's awfully presumptuous of you and I must say awfully arrogant. And that's something I never thought you were, Jason. You never came across as someone who was self-involved. That, as a matter of fact, is why I was so willing to open up to you. That was a real mistake."

"It really has nothing to do with me. It has more to do with your own curiosity. You'd never know why I chose to call you at one o'clock in the morning after not communicating with you for over a month." There was silence on the other end. He found the silence comforting. The fact that she did not hang up meant he just might be hitting at the truth. He continued, "I wanted to say something very different and unique to you but the words aren't there."

"Jason, nothing you can say, no matter how different and unique, can serve as an excuse for how you treated me. So why don't you first start with an apology and then tell me what's happened that you finally called me?"

"That's fair."

"No, it's not about being fair, but it's a start. I have no obligation to be fair with you."

"I'll be quite honest." Jason felt her coldness but he was reaching for something and had to find out what it was. "I'm not sure why I picked up the phone this late and called. I certainly had no right to and I apologize for any hurt I caused you. Today was probably the worst single day in my life. I may have lost two important parts of my life and when that happens to anyone, it's always nice to have someone to talk with."

"So now I'm part of your therapy?"

"Yes, that's a pretty decent way to explain the call."

"Would you like to come over and talk? And I do mean just talk."

"I'd love to."

"I'll see you within the next hour."

"Thanks."

u

Jason made it to Raquel's apartment in Burbank in a little over a half hour. As he pulled into a parking space he realized that his mind had been somewhere out in space during the entire drive. His thoughts had meandered around so many different issues all bottled up inside him. He had drifted from Big Casey lying in the Huntington Hospital with an assortment of needles sticking in his arms, to Dominique and his inability to move beyond her profession. Then there was his writing that, because of Big Casey's condition, might have to be put on hold. Jason got out of the car and headed to Raquel's apartment. When he got to the door it swung open and she stepped outside. That caught him by surprise.

"I thought it would be better if we went somewhere for coffee," she said.

"Isn't it kind of late for coffee?" Jason asked.

"It's kind of late for talking, but if I'm willing to sacrifice my sleep to talk with you, at least you can do it my way."

"You got it," Jason conceded. He wanted to kiss her only on the cheek, but felt her resistance and backed off.

"There's an all night diner a couple miles away. You want to drive or do you want me to?"

"No, I can drive." Without another word spoken, they got in the car and headed to the diner.

Jason and Raquel sat across from each other in a booth. The waitress took their order for two coffees and they both relaxed.

"I could make this very difficult and uncomfortable for both of us by asking you a bunch of questions about why you treated me so badly," Raquel said dryly. "But that's not my style. I'm not the kind of woman who loves control of a negative situation. And at this point that's exactly what this is."

"Thanks. I don't know if I can handle that."

"But it is a conversation that we might have to deal with some day. All depends on where we go from here. But more important you said you needed to talk to someone and I have to admit it made me feel good that you chose me as that person."

The waitress placed the two cups of coffee on the table with a number of small containers of cream. "Can I get you all anything else?" she asked.

"No, thank you," Jason answered without looking up at her. He stirred cream and sugar in his coffee. "Earlier this evening my father suffered a stroke. He's in a coma right now."

"Oh, Jason, I'm so sorry, you poor man. I know how much your father means to you. Is he going to be all right?"

"Right now we don't know. They'll know a lot more in the morning."

"I'll pray for him." Raquel held out her hands to him. He locked them with his.

"Funny, that's something no one in my family really articulated as an option. No one, not even my mother, thought about praying."

"You don't know that for sure. Your mother didn't pray in front of you, but if she's a Black woman probably at some point after you left she got on her knees and prayed. Some people can't express that emotion as openly as others."

"Thanks, that makes me feel better."

"Have you prayed for your father?"

"No, I haven't. That's something I never felt Big Casey needed."

"Everyone needs prayer at some point in their life. And this might be that point for him and for you."

"That's fine, but not from me."

"Shame on you and don't say that. It makes you sound like some kind of barbarian."

"You never struck me as being a religious kind of person."

"You never gave me a chance to get that close to you, remember?" Raquel took a sip from her cup.

Jason scooted around in the booth trying to find a comfort level. He didn't want to talk about religion and praying. He wanted to discuss Dominique, but wasn't sure how that would go over with her. Would she feel insulted if he asked her advice on how to handle his inadequacies?

"Something else is on your mind, Jason. What is it?"

"Nothing really," he lied.

"Jason, you're too mature and too smart to play these kinds of games. Are you having problems in your other relationship?"

"How do you know I have someone else?"

"Again, don't be silly."

"I saw you sitting in the back seat of the car when Elliott came by the other day."

"How did that make you feel?"

"Not too good about myself."

"Who is she and what happened?"

"Elliott didn't tell you anything?"

"No, he's a real friend to you."

Jason again shuffled his position in the seat, picked up the coffee cup and drank. "I don't think this is something we should talk about."

"Okay, then do you want to talk about us?"

"That's interesting that you would refer to us as in a pair."

"How else can I discuss the two of us?"

"I don't know but I just found it interesting."

"What is she like? What is it that she had that made you move so quickly to her?"

"I don't know. It's strange because I can't really get a good grip on it."

"Let me help you and then maybe you'll be able to handle it better than what you seem to be doing right now."

"I know and I'm much too old not to be able to."

"Do you love her?"

"That might be too heavy an emotion for me to describe what I feel for her."

"You men are cowards." Raquel now shuffled her position and drank from her cup. "Are you running away from your emotions for her just like you ran away from my emotions for you?"

"I thought we weren't going to talk about us?"

"We must because somehow I think it's all tied together."

"Maybe in some kind of convoluted way it is."

"It's not convoluted, Jason. Its life, emotions and the way you deal with them." Raquel paused for a moment, obviously to allow the effect of what she said to sink in. Suddenly she switched on him. "How has all this affected your writing? As I recall the reason you gave for backing off us was because you needed to concentrate more on your writing. How's that working out?"

Jason ran his index finger along the edge of the cup as a delaying tactic. He really wanted to push his conversation about Dominique a bit further, but he wasn't positioned to do that.

Raquel was in charge at that moment and he had to let her exercise that control.

"I finished the first draft," he finally said.

"Congratulations, that's wonderful. Are you pleased with it?"

"Yeah I think I am. But I have a lot of work to do. The fun part is the creative writing. The work is the revising and editing."

"If there is anything I can do to help, let me know. I really mean that."

"Thanks, I'll definitely keep that in mind."

"I have to be at the school early in the morning. We're preparing for the new semester and I really do need to get some rest."

"You got it," Jason said nervously. He pulled four dollars out and placed them on the table. "Thanks for letting me bend your ear."

"Jason Mitchell, you are a fool, but I like you a whole lot. I don't want to see you hurt. I don't know what this other lady's intentions are, but mine are always meant to help you."

"I know you'll find this very hard to swallow, but I care for you also and if you don't mind I'll call you again."

"Please do and we'll take it from there. Keep in mind I don't have much confidence in you."

"I understand because quite frankly I don't have much confidence in myself. And starting in the morning I have to fill in at the business which means I can't write."

"Simply one more obstacle for Mr. Jason Mitchell to overcome. You can do it. I have confidence in your ability to handle that kind of challenge."

The two of them got up and started toward the exit.

"Thanks for the vote of confidence," Jason said. "Now all I have to do is find that same kind of confidence once again in myself."

"You will," Raquel said and kissed him on the cheek. They walked out into the cool summer California air and headed to the car.

Chapter 49

The ten employees sat in the conference room stunned into silence. They listened to Jason explain that Big Casey had suffered a stroke last night. He sat at the front of the conference table where his father would usually sit and conduct his weekly Monday morning meeting. He waited until nine-thirty to make sure everyone was there and then gave them the news. Arthur's absence was quite conspicuous. Jason wasn't about to call Jacqueline and ask about him. He could imagine him laid up at the dancer's apartment stoned out of his mind and his excuse would be that he couldn't handle the rejection. Determined not to tolerate Arthur's childish ways, Jason would fire him if he didn't show up in the morning in spite of Jacqueline's protests.

"Can we all go to the hospital and see Mr. Mitchell?" Big Casey's administrative assistant asked.

Jason managed a smile. "That's a nice gesture, Charlotte, but I called this morning and he is still in intensive care. I'll be heading over there this morning and I'll call you all as soon as I hear something."

"At least we can send some flowers and help brighten up the room," another female employee suggested.

"Be patient," Jason advised. "Let's just get him out of intensive care and then we can begin to pour all our love on him. Right now, however, you all had better get back to work. I know it's going to be difficult, but we have to treat this just like another work day."

"It's good to have you back with us," one of the bookkeepers said as they all got up to leave the room. "I wish it was under different circumstances, but it is good to see you again."

"Thank you." Jason's words were terse because he really

wasn't in the mood to talk and he definitely wasn't looking for compliments. He really didn't want to be there. "Howard, could you please hang around?" he asked.

"Definitely," Howard sat back down at the conference table.

Jason waited until everyone had left and then closed the door before he sat back down next to Howard. "I can't do this without your help," he said and placed his hand on Howard's shoulder.

"Don't worry, I'll be here for you. I know this may be difficult for you to understand, but Mr. Mitchell's like a father to me. I spend so much time with him I feel like he is my father sometimes."

"I know you do and I appreciate that. I know he would want you to play a key role in running the business while he recovers."

"I can fill you in on all the projects we're working on and what we've recently bid on," Howard suggested.

"In time. Right now there is no way I could concentrate. As a matter of fact I need to get over to the hospital. I told my mother I'd be there by ten and it's already after ten."

"You want me to send Arthur over there when he shows up?"

"I'd prefer to send him home permanently, but no, I imagine he'll be with Jacqueline at the hospital."

Howard scooted up to the edge of his chair and leaned in Jason's direction. "Between you and me, I believe Mr. Mitchell was going to let him go real soon," he whispered.

"I know but right now we're not going to deal with that. Let's just keep him doing whatever he's been doing all along."

"That's nothing."

"I get your drift but we need to get through this crisis." Jason got up. "And I need to get up to the hospital."

Howard also got up and pushed his chair back under the table. "Please send our prayers to Mrs. Mitchell. And let her know she doesn't have to worry about this place. Everybody will put a hundred and fifty percent for her and the boss."

Jason moved in close to Howard and the two men hugged. "Thanks," Jason said as his voice cracked a little. He'd controlled his emotions well until now. He had to get out of there before he broke down and cried. He turned and hurried to the door.

u

Jason merged into the traffic on the freeway heading toward Pasadena. He scooted over into the left lane and picked up speed. He was in a hurry to get to the hospital where he would spend the rest of the afternoon. He sped past the turn off to the highway that would take him to the Black Zebra. Most of the morning his mind had been occupied with his father's condition and what needed to be done at the company. He had very little time to think of Dominique. Now as he sped pass the turn off he'd taken so many times to pick her up, a sadness came over him. He really did care for her and didn't want their relationship to end.

The time he'd spent last night with Raquel had been comforting. However, it wasn't the woman whom he'd come to love. What madness a relationship could be. He really wanted to be able to handle the fact that she danced for a living, but every time control of his emotions were tested he failed. If he suddenly turned his car in the opposite direction, rushed to her apartment and pledged his love for her, and promised never to let her past bother him again, would she believe him? And whenever they were in Arthur's company, would he see images of her all over him, dancing for the sole purpose of getting him sexually excited?

Now his thoughts meandered back to that first night in Palm Springs. Her tears had been genuine and signaled her cry for security, someone to love her, care for her, and understand her. He'd passed that first test, but since then he'd struck out badly.

Jason moved over to the right lane and took the Orange Grove exit. He turned left at the stop sign and headed toward the hospital. His thoughts again turned to Dominique. He clearly recognized that she made him acknowledge he'd never loved before. Despite all the relationships he'd experienced over the years, including the one with Angela, he never knew what it was to love another person until Dominique. Love had to do with that uncontrollable drive he felt to always protect her. He wanted to make her feel secure and safe. That kind of feeling, with its absolute power over him, could only be explained as love. Now he had to let all that go because, ultimately, he was unable to protect her the way he perceived she wanted to be. Maybe some day he'd have the opportunity again and that frightened him because he couldn't assure himself that he wouldn't fail a second time.

Jason finally made his turn off Orange Grove Boulevard to the hospital. He found a spot in the visitors' parking lot and rushed to the emergency entrance. He went right by the nurse station where they had stopped for directions last night. He made it to the same waiting room they'd occupied, swung the door open and looked toward Hazel who sat in a chair across the room. As he headed to his mother, he smiled at Theresa. Tosha and the baby sat in a chair next to Theresa. Jacqueline and Arthur were not there.

"Where's Cedric? Where is your brother?" Hazel asked.

"I don't know, mother, I didn't get a—"

"You didn't go by his apartment last night and tell him about his father?"

"No, mother, I didn't. But when I leave the hospital today I'll go and find him. How is the big man doing?" he asked. He took a seat between Hazel and Theresa.

"His condition hasn't changed much," Theresa answered.

"How are you holding up, mother?" Jason asked.

"I was doing fine until you came in here and informed me that you haven't told Cedric that his father might be dying."

"I'm sorry, but I really was exhausted last night."

Hazel glanced at her watch and looked away from Jason. "Where in the world is Jacqueline? I just knew she'd be here when I got here. Have you talked with her, Jason?" Hazel again looked directly at Jason.

"No, I haven't talked with Jacqueline. She was a little bit upset with me yesterday and I'm not so sure she wants to be bothered with me." Jason paused for a second and waited for the next attack. It didn't come so he continued. "I went by the office early this morning and informed the staff what happened. Arthur was not there and we're going to have to do something about that."

"Never mind Arthur," Hazel snapped. "You just make sure you're there everyday watching over your father's business until he gets back on his feet. I don't care nothing about a novel or any of that nonsense. You have to protect your father's investment for him. You're the oldest and it's your responsibility."

Jason felt a bit irritated with his mother, but checked his feelings. She had to lash out at someone because she definitely was emotionally drained. Over the years she'd dealt with a lot of issues when it came to Big Casey but nothing like this. Then again Hazel was being a bit selfish herself. She lashed out with no consideration that all of them were caught in an emotional trap. What they should be doing is reinforcing each other's strength so they could endure the worst if it happened. Jason started to tell her just that but the door swung open and the nurse came in. They stood there frozen in place, fearful of what she would say.

"Any news?" Jason asked.

"Mr. Mitchell opened his eyes briefly and then drifted back to sleep," the nurse said. "His vital signs are improving, but he's a long way from being removed from intensive care."

"Can we see him?" Hazel asked.

"Only one of you can go in right now," the nurse answered. "I assume that will be you, Mrs. Mitchell. So you want to come with me?"

Without speaking to either Jason or Theresa, Hazel followed closely behind the nurse and out of the room. Jason glanced over at his sister.

"How are you holding up?" he asked.

Theresa looked up at him and smiled. "I'll make it, but I'm not so sure about Mama. Before you got here she went off on Jacqueline and Cedric for not being here. For some reason I'm being spared her wrath which is very unusual. And that's why I'm worried about her."

"She always challenged you but she has more confidence in you than she does in Jacqueline. She understands Jacqueline's vulnerabilities and her weakness for that fool she married."

"Amazing how complicated life can be," Theresa said.

"I don't know if life is complicated. Maybe it's the people who have to play out this life that are complicated."

"You have a point. Think we better call Jacqueline and make sure everything is okay?"

"That's not a bad idea, but you'd better make that call," Jason said. "She's probably still mad at me."

"I guess if I was married and you talked about my husband the way you did about Arthur, I'd be a little bent out of shape also."

"Not if he was like Arthur." Jason watched as Tosha switched her position in the chair while holding the baby. "When are you going to tell her about them?"

"Not for a while. We don't need any more drama." Theresa paused and glanced over at Tosha. "Aren't you surprised how easily Hazel accepted them into her home?"

"That's probably due to a mother's instinct."

"What do you mean?"

"She knew she wanted you to be there with her last night for support. And she instinctively knew the only way that would happen is if she accepted them also."

"How's your situation?" Theresa asked conveniently changing the conversation.

"What do you mean?"

"Come on, when you left last night I knew darn well you weren't going to find Cedric. You had to go and work things out with your friend."

"I didn't and I can't."

"You can't because you really don't want to?"

"Oh hell, Theresa, I don't know." Jason got up, walked over to the counter and poured some coffee into a cup. He turned and stood there. "She's a very complicated person and even if I did love her I'm not sure I can handle all those complications."

"What do you really know about her other than she's a dancer?"

"That's just it, I don't know a thing and she wouldn't share anything with me." Jason hesitated for a moment as he flashed on their time in Palm Springs. "She's a very emotional person and I believe she's hiding a lot of hurt. I just don't know if it's because of a bad past relationship or if it goes much deeper than that."

"You being insecure about what she does for a living sure won't help her find a comfort level with you."

"Thanks for that."

"We have to deal with the truth even if we don't like it. I discovered that by working with people who have no hope in life, and truth is such a disaster they stay as far away from it as they possibly can."

"Let's deal with another truth," Jason said. "What if our father doesn't make it? What if we lose him?"

Theresa got up and walked over to stand next to her brother. She turned and faced him squarely. "I don't know about that truth," she said and then hugged him. Theresa poured herself some coffee and returned to her chair. She placed the coffee cup on the table next to her and then got her cell phone out of her purse. She didn't say anything nor did she look at Jason. Instead she dialed a number and relaxed back in the chair. After a full minute she finally turned off the phone. "Jacqueline is not home so I can only assume that she's on her way over here."

"Her distinguished husband didn't show up for work this morning. Howard said that Big Casey was planning to let him go."

"In what lifetime?" Theresa asked. Jason jerked his head and a frown covered his face. "Well maybe that's an inappropriate expression right now," she said. "But you know there's no way he would do that to Jacqueline."

"You're probably right," Jason added, the frown disappearing. "To be quite honest I don't think he's going to hang around now that he knows he's not fooling anyone but Jacqueline."

"I take it you don't think he loves your sister?"

"Be serious. Men like Arthur don't know how to love anyone but themselves."

Theresa stared at Tosha and the baby as she again adjusted her body. "You're right, but if it wasn't Arthur it would have been someone similar to him. Jacqueline was always a sucker for a pretty boy."

"Probably because she's always been so insecure."

"That's interesting, Jacqueline and Cedric are both insecure and the two of them can't get along for a minute." Theresa again got up and hurried over to Tosha and took the baby. Tosha was sound asleep and the baby was close to falling out of her arms. Theresa returned to her seat and began rocking back and forth.

"You do that quite well," Jason said jokingly. "When are you going to get married and start your own family?"

"Be serious. No way with all these jerks out here now. The Black men are so dumb and irresponsible when it comes to sex it makes you want to be celibate. Look what this poor young girl has to endure because of some knucklehead."

"You don't date at all?" Jason asked. He realized that he knew very little about his younger sister's personal life because they were always busy dealing with Jacqueline's.

"I go out after work for drinks with some of the people at the office. And I have a friend that I'll every once and a while go to a movie or play with. But nothing you might call steady."

"You mean you're not getting any?" Jason said smiling.

"Jason, you're not supposed to ask your baby sister anything like that. But no, I'm not and I'm quite content."

"You're not going the way Cedric went?" Again Jason smiled as he continued to tease his sister.

"No, my brother, I have no desire to hold and sleep with someone softer than me." Theresa shifted the baby from one shoulder to the other. "But let's get back to you. Look at the mess you're in from getting some as you put it. Seriously what are you going to do? You going to let Dominique just walk out of your life?"

"I don't want to, but I don't know."

"If you can't handle it, then your best bet is to leave it alone. Find someone who is safer. You know someone who fits your lifestyle."

"I was dating someone like that before I got involved with Dominique."

"You sure been a busy boy," Theresa said. Now it was her turn to smile. "What happened?"

"Dominique happened."

"When you leave here and after you see Cedric, you need to go find Dominique and apologize. And just pray that she still cares enough to have you back."

"Damn, Theresa, you don't make this easy."

"Here is your test. If the next time you're out with someone else, but all your thoughts are with Dominique, then you'll know that whatever you have to do, you have to get her back."

A scowl covered Jason's face as he realized that's exactly what happened last night when he was with Raquel. Before he could respond to his sister the door swung open and Hazel came crying back into the room. The nurse had an arm wrapped around her. Theresa jumped from her chair, forced the baby into Jason's arms and then rushed to her mother. She placed both arms around Hazel who could barely stand and led her to a chair.

"How is he?" she asked the nurse.

"The same, but his vitals continue to slowly improve. There is no need for you all to stay here. He'll be monitored closely and when there is a change in his condition we'll call you."

"No, I'm going to say right here," Hazel blurted out. "Theresa, you take those children home and, Jason, you go do what you should've done last night. I'll be all right."

Jason stared at his sister and their thoughts seemed to merge. "Someone needs to be here with you, Mother," Jason said.

"The only one left is Jacqueline and she's not here obviously. And if she was I'd probably have to hold her up. So you all go on and do what needs to be done. I'll be here when you get back this evening. There's a cafeteria in the basement so I can get something

Chapter 50

Jason had to get his bearings on the uncontrollable events taking control over him all at the same time. Heading back toward North Hollywood sent mixed feelings through his body. The last time he made this ride was to take Dominique home. Now he had to deal with that emotion all over again. He would also have to deal with a bitter and angry Cedric, who again might insist that he bring Aaron along with him as acknowledgement of his own victory over everyone in a time of crisis. Hopefully when Jason got to his brother's apartment Aaron would be gone. Without the influence of his lover, Jason might be able to convince him that it's in everyone's best interest that he go to the hospital alone.

Driving up Wilshire Boulevard, he passed the late night restaurant where he and Dominique had first talked outside the club. His thoughts rushed back to his conversation with Theresa about truth. He was now forced to deal with his own truths. Because of the breaks in life he'd been able to pursue his individual dreams, something most Black folks never experienced. What was he really doing with that opportunity? Jason wanted to be a chronicler of the Black experience, but he might have to sacrifice his dream in order to fulfill his responsibility if Big Casey didn't make it. He also wanted Dominique to be a part of his life. She occupied every aspect of his life. But he was now handcuffed, unable to pursue her again and make it right between them. He couldn't cheat Hazel and for that matter Big Casey by deviating his attention, emotions, and time away from them. The Mitchell family crisis demanded his energy. At that particular moment it meant finding Cedric and forcing him to understand what he must do.

Jason pulled into the parking lot at the Guest Suite Motel,

found a parking place, and slowly walked up to the suite Cedric had rented. He took in a deep breath, released it and then knocked on the door. He could hear someone moving around inside. Finally the door swung open and Aaron stood there in front of him with a defiant gaze.

"I need to talk with Cedric," Jason said.

"He isn't here," Aaron replied.

"When will he be back? It's important that I talk to him."

"Why, so you can make him feel like shit all over again?"

Jason adjusted his footing and glared right into Aaron's gaze. "I don't have time for this nonsense. Please tell me when my brother will be back?"

Aaron also adjusted his body in the doorway but looked away from Jason. "I don't think he'll be coming back."

"What do you mean, he won't be coming back?"

"Just what I said," Aaron shot back defiantly. "When we got back last night, he was real angry and depressed. He told me he couldn't handle this life. It was fine when we were in San Francisco, but not down here. He didn't take anything with him and he left the car for me. He might be back because he didn't take his clothes, but I don't know how he plans to get around unless he finds someone else."

"Aaron, it's absolutely necessary that I find him," Jason said with a slight pleading in his voice. "His father suffered a stroke last night and he needs to know that. Do you have any idea where he might have gone?"

"The only place I can think of is the shelter off Hollywood Boulevard. I don't think he knew anyone, so he couldn't have gone to anyone's house. So the only place would be the shelter."

"Thank you," Jason said. "If he comes back, tell him to call his mother. Let him know everything is all right. We just want him with the family right now." He turned away and rushed to his car.

Jason drove slowly up Hollywood Boulevard as he looked on both sides of the street for his brother. The traffic was extremely heavy and it appeared to Jason that everyone else was also looking for someone. He stopped at the traffic light and watched as a young shabbily-dressed boy walked up to the driver's side of the car in front of him. He exchanged words with the driver, then hurried to the other side of the car and got in. Suddenly it dawned on Jason that many of the drivers were looking for young boys, but for other reasons than his. He had to be careful; the last thing he needed was to be picked up for solicitation. But how could he find the exact location of the shelter unless he asked someone? He had to find Cedric so he'd just have to take that chance.

He spotted a young Black man in tight jeans and a cut-off shirt. Jason pulled over to the curb and signaled for him to come to the car. Jason had to let the young man know he wasn't hustling him and only wanted information. He needed to do it quickly before the police saw him. He hit the button and the window rolled down. The young boy leaned down and stuck his head inside.

"Can you tell me exactly where the shelter is located in this area?" Jason asked beating the young man to the punch.

A perplexed expression spread across the young man's face. "The shelter?" he asked.

"Yes, the shelter," Jason stressed to him.

"Why would you need the shelter? Wouldn't you rather have a date?" the young man asked, smiling.

"I'm afraid not." Jason reached in his pocket and pulled out a twenty dollar bill. He handed it to the young man who did not hesitate to take it. "I need to find my brother."

"Oh, another one of those good guys to the rescue. You want to save your brother from who he really is. Hell no, I don't know where the shelter is." He moved back away from the car and did not give the twenty dollars back.

It would be futile to protest, so Jason signaled for another young man who had just turned the corner and hurried in his direction. He looked in front and in back of him to make sure the police were not watching. The second young man hurried to the passenger's side and extended his body inside the car.

"Man, this is a beautiful car you got here," the young man

said. "Do you want to take me for a ride? I can give you a real treat while we cruise the boulevard."

His suggestion disgusted Jason. He feared that Cedric might be forced to do the same. "I just want to know where the shelter is located," Jason said quite harshly.

"My, my, don't we have an attitude," the young man said.

"I'm sorry, I just have to get to the shelter."

"Are you vice?" the young man asked.

"No, I'm not vice and I'm not homosexual. I just need to find someone. I have information he needs to know."

"What's his name? I might know him."

"It's Cedric. Cedric Mitchell."

"No, I don't know him. Sorry and good luck." The young man removed his head from inside the car and walked away.

Somewhat dejected, Jason worked his way further down the boulevard where he might find someone willing to help him. He saw a large contingent of teenagers standing near the corner. He again waved one of the boys over to his car. He had left the window rolled down so the man leaned inside and smiled.

"This isn't what you think it is." Jason was on the defensive.

"What is it then?" the young man asked.

"I'm simply trying to find the shelter in this area."

"That's easy," the young man replied. "It's two blocks up, turn right and you can't miss it. Why are you looking for the shelter?"

"I have a friend I need to find."

"Good luck," the young man said.

"Why do you say that?"

"Because if a person don't want to be found, chances are good they won't be. The people who run the shelter protect the people from intruders like you." The young boy removed his body and walked away.

Jason watched the young boy as he mingled with his friends, then straightened up and continued up the street. The traffic seemed to be heavier and he was forced to creep up Hollywood Boulevard. Armed with the information he needed he no longer looked at the young men who lined the streets. He didn't understand how anyone could find pleasure in this kind of lifestyle. Try as he may he couldn't help seeing two young men standing in an embrace right in the middle of the sidewalk. While kissing, one of the men had his hand busy rubbing the other's buttocks. It turned Jason's stomach and it bothered him that Cedric had gotten caught up in this madness. He had to do something to shock him back to his senses. Maybe breaking up with Aaron would be the act that would straighten him out. When he found his brother, Jason would insist that he stay with him until he overcame this silly obsession with being different. Wasn't being Black in America different enough for him?

Jason stopped right in front of the shelter, but could not park because a large "NO PARKING" sign glared at him. A couple of the men who'd been standing in front of the shelter started toward the car. Maybe if he gave them some money they'd go inside for him. He rolled down the window and the more aggressive man leaned inside the car and smiled at Jason. He'd already experienced the smiling act and now it pissed him off. But he needed the man's help, so he forced a slight smile.

"Can you help me out?" Jason asked as he showed the man a twenty dollar bill.

"Yeah what is it you want?" the man asked. "Your kid inside the shelter and you come to rescue him?"

"Maybe it's his lover," the other man outside the car said.

"It's neither one," Jason replied dryly. "But someone is in there that I'd like to talk with. And I'm willing to pay you if you'll go inside and check to see if someone named Cedric Mitchell is in there?"

"Let me have the money and I'll go and check it out," the man said.

"Don't bullshit me," Jason said and handed the man the twenty dollar bill. It was a long shot, but at this point he could do nothing else. "I really need to talk to him."

"We have some honor," the man turned and shouted back at Jason as he hurried inside the building.

"I hope so," Jason whispered while looking out the rearview

mirror for the police. He saw none so maybe he could find Cedric and get out of there before the police showed up and made him move his car.

Fifteen minutes had passed and the two men were still inside the shelter. Convinced that he had once again been ripped off, Jason started to pull away when the two men came back followed by Cedric. Jason stared incredulously at his brother who appeared disheveled and disoriented. He shook his head and frowned.

Cedric spotted Jason and quickly turned back toward the entrance to the shelter. Jason had to act fast. He had to get him before he made it back inside. The words of the man who'd given him the directions echoed in his ears. If someone didn't want to be found they wouldn't be. He turned the car off, jumped out and ran toward Cedric. The two men who'd gone inside to find him stopped dead in their tracks as Jason shot by them. He caught Cedric before he got back inside and wrapped both arms around him.

Cedric fought back as he tried to break Jason's grip. "Leave me the fuck alone," he shouted.

The two men did not intervene, but continued to stare as the brothers struggled.

"Cedric, stop!" Jason yelled. "I have to talk to you. It's about Big Casey, He had a stroke last night and your mother wants you with the family. She knows all about Aaron and she doesn't care. Stop fighting me." Cedric's body went limp as he gave into Jason's demands. "Man, I'm sorry I stopped you back at the house yesterday, but I just didn't think Big Casey and Hazel could handle it."

"Is he going to be all right?" Cedric asked without looking at Jason.

"We don't know yet. But you know Big Casey. He's going to hang in there as long as he can." Jason directed Cedric toward the car. "We need to get back over there. We need to let Mama know we're there for her."

"Is Jacqueline there?" Cedric asked with defiance creeping

back into his voice.

"Not yet, but she will be sometime during the day. I'm telling you brother you have to leave that alone for Mama's sake."

Cedric got into the car and Jason hurried over to the driver's side and got in.

He turned and stared at his brother. "Are you all right?" he asked.

"Physically yes but emotionally no."

"I talked with Aaron and he told me what happened."

"It's too traumatic for me to discuss and now this with Big Casey. I don't know if I can handle all this," Cedric whispered and then covered his eyes.

"Let's go get something to eat. You'll feel better. A little food always helps to put things in a proper perspective. It'll give us a chance to talk and catch up on a whole lot of time. We really haven't talked since you've been back." Jason glanced over at his brother who rested his head back on the headrest. Jason pulled out into traffic and headed for a quieter part of town.

Cedric ate like he hadn't eaten in weeks. He was eating so much and so fast, Jason was afraid he might get sick. Jason stared at his younger brother. He still found it difficult to believe that Cedric had chosen such an alternative lifestyle. He wondered had he done that just to defy his father. Or did he do it to hurt him? If he could get Cedric to open up and discuss the past year maybe then it would all make more sense. His dilemma was how to approach the subject with him.

"You know eventually I was going to ask you whatever made you decide on that kind of lifestyle." Jason kept a very calm demeanor. Not defiant or challenging, just real calm. "There is so much I don't know about you and they always say it takes a crisis to bring families closer together. Maybe this is our crisis."

"I thought it was usually funerals." Cedric stopped eating long enough to respond.

"We don't want to be that extreme. None of us are ready for that much crisis."

Cedric again stopped eating and stared across the table at

his brother. "He can't die," he said in a cracked voice. "Me and him didn't ever get along, but I've always loved him and admired him for what he accomplished."

"He's not going to die because you still have to tell him those things."

Cedric put his fork down and a contemplative expression covered his face.

"Following behind you wasn't easy," he said.

"What do you mean?"

"I mean I could never get my bearings on my own life. I was always trying to stay caught up with you and it always seemed that Big Casey would let me know I wasn't doing too good of a job."

"What are you talking about, Cedric? Big Casey always believed in you, but he got frustrated because you'd never buy off on his realities. Yours were always different."

"But isn't that the way it's supposed to be? Each new generation's realities change?"

"I guess so, but he didn't recognize that." Jason reached across the table and took a large pickle Cedric had left on the plate. He took a big crunchy bite and continued. "None of this explains why you made the decision to go gay. Do you really understand why?"

"No I can't, but I know it felt good in many ways and it was safe."

"Safe from what?"

"All those things expected of me. If I was gay I knew there would be no expectations."

"So it was deliberate?"

"No, it's not that easy. It wasn't deliberate because I fought it for a while."

"I guess the big question is whether or not you're going to get back with Aaron and if not will you continue that lifestyle?"

Cedric suddenly banged his hand on the table, rattling all the dishes and drawing the attention of the other customers. "Damn it Jason, this is not a decision you just sit back and make.

This is not about rational decisions, it's strictly about emotions."

"Okay, don't get upset," Jason said in a hushed tone.

"You act like my behavior is some kind of freak show that I can duck in and out of when I get ready." Cedric threw the napkin on top of his empty plate. "Let's go see Mama."

"Okay, but don't you think you should go and get what few clothes you have from the motel?"

"I'd rather not."

"What are you going to do?"

"I was hoping maybe you could loan me some money to get a few things."

Jason shot his hand across the table for Cedric to take. Cedric grabbed his brother's hand and vigorously shook it.

"I guess we can do that," Jason said.

"Thanks, brother, but aren't you afraid you'll get AIDs holding my hand?"

"I didn't think about that because I never entertained the possibility that you are infected."

"You know it's a disease of gays."

"And sickle cell anemia is a disease of Black folks."

The two brothers finally got up and hugged. Jason patted his brother on the back and then broke the hug.

"Now it's time to go give your mother the kind of support she needs from her youngest son."

"As long as I have some support from her oldest son."

"You do."

"Let's roll."

Chapter 51

Theresa held the baby close to her chest and rocked back and forth in one of the lounge chairs in the waiting room at the hospital. Hazel had dozed off as had Tosha. It was a little past two in the afternoon and try as she may Hazel had been unsuccessful in getting her daughter to leave the hospital. Theresa stared at both her mother and Tosha. Her emotional attachment to the young girl and her baby grew stronger with each day and now she was certain that her love for her mother was also growing stronger. Their relationship had not been the best but she was satisfied that Hazel also loved her, and all the fighting between them was due to her mother's determination that she always have the best. As she watched Hazel switch positions in the chair she wondered would her mother make a fuss when told that Tosha and the baby would be a part of Theresa's family and by extension a part of the Mitchell clan. She was surprised and pleased at how well her mother handled the fact that Cedric was gay. Her love for her son and concern that Cedric be with the family during a time of extreme crisis outweighed all other considerations. That was a good sign. Hopefully she would handle the possibility that Tosha and the baby were HIV positive just as well.

It had been a very long time since the two of them shared a private time. They needed to do just that so they could heal the wounds that had been festering between them for years. Theresa had a strong urge to wake her right then and confide in her the many crises she had endured by herself over the years. Both Big Casey and Hazel had always viewed her as being strong, impenetrable, devoid of personal weaknesses. They viewed Jacqueline as the one most vulnerable. What they never recognized was that she also had weaknesses for which she had also needed help. All these years she'd carried the weight of an abortion on her shoulders alone. She never told Jacqueline or Jason for fear they might slip up and reveal her secret. She never wanted to do that again. That's why she'd grabbed Jason at the house yesterday and told him about Tosha and the baby, only to find out that same day Jason was also carrying baggage. She smiled as she thought how deceptive appearances could be. The perfect upper-middle-class family that had achieved the pinnacle of success, the American dream, suffered the same frailties and insecurities as any other family. The difference being that they could struggle with their problems knowing they had financial security.

Theresa adjusted the baby as she began to wake up. She worried about Jacqueline because her sister loved a very unstable man. They hadn't been able to reach her all morning and she hadn't called. She appeared to be pretty upset when Hazel rejected her suggestion that Arthur run the company while Big Casey recovered. Theresa looked over at Hazel who still slept. She then got up, strolled over to Tosha and nudged her.

"Is something wrong, has something happened?" Tosha asked while rubbing her eyes.

"No, nothing's changed," Theresa whispered to her and then handed her the baby. "I need to go outside and call my sister. She hasn't called and I'm kind of worried about her." She leaned down and kissed Tosha on the forehead. "I'll be right back." She headed out the door into the hallway.

The phone rang five times and Theresa was about to hang up when finally Jacqueline answered on the other end.

"Theresa," she said.

"Yes." Theresa was struck by Jacqueline's weak voice. It sounded like she'd been crying. "Are you all right?" she asked.

"I guess so."

"What do you mean you guess so? Where is Arthur and why didn't he go to work this morning?"

"He wasn't feeling good," Jacqueline said. "I think yesterday was too much for him."

Theresa instinctively knew that Jacqueline was lying. But why pressure her on the subject. Getting her down to the hospital was much more important.

"We need you down here with us," she said.

"Are you all at the hospital? How is Daddy?"

"Yes we are and you should be down here yourself to see about your father."

"Is Mama down there?"

"You know she is," Theresa shot back. She felt irritated with Jacqueline's questions that circumvented the issue at hand.

"Where's Jason?"

"He went to get Cedric. I assume they're on their way here also." There was complete silence on the other end. "What's wrong, Jacqueline? Didn't you hear what I said? Your mother wants you down here."

"I don't know," Jacqueline mumbled into the phone. "I just don't want to be around Jason after the way he talked to me last night. I certainly don't want to be around Cedric."

Theresa moved the cell phone away from her ear and stared at it as though she couldn't believe what she'd just heard.

"I can't believe you, Jacqueline. Your father is in intensive care and you're worried about a silly disagreement you had with your brothers."

"You just don't understand," Jacqueline mumbled again. "I'm going through some real serious problems."

"Jacqueline, did you hear me?" Theresa said firmly.

"Yes I heard you, but I need to be here with my husband. I'm sure you all will be enough company for Mama."

"Jacqueline, I'm going to hang up now before I say something that later on I'll regret. I can't believe your incredible selfishness."

"I'm telling you that you just—"

Theresa snapped the cell phone closed and tightly squeezed it between her hands. She tilted her head up in the air and closed her eyes. She hesitated for a minute and then went back into the waiting room. Hazel began to stir around in her chair. Without saying anything Theresa sat down in the empty chair next to her mother, hoping that she would not mention Jacqueline.

"Did you call your sister?" Hazel asked.

"I thought you were asleep."

"I was until I heard you leave the room. Did you call your sister?"

"Yes, I did."

"Is she on her way?"

"Yes, she is," Theresa lied.

"Good. Now where are your brothers?"

"Mama, why is it absolutely necessary to have everyone here at the hospital?" Theresa snapped at her mother. She was sorry before she'd finished, but it irritated her knowing that Hazel believed they were all so close when in fact they weren't.

"What do you mean why is it necessary? That's your father lying in there fighting for his life and you ask me a question like that? My God, girl, I thought you'd matured."

"Okay, Mama, please don't do this," Theresa pleaded. "I'm sorry. All your children will be here soon." Theresa buried her head in her hands. She just wanted to get out of there and retreat to her cove on the beach. But there was no way that would happen. All she could do was grit her teeth, take in a few deep breaths and endure.

u

Jason pulled into the parking lot at the Huntington Hospital and found a parking spot. He turned off the engine and started to get out. Just as he reached to open the door Cedric grabbed his arm. Jason turned to look at his brother.

"Are you ready?" he asked but from the look on Cedric's face Jason already knew the answer. He straightened back in the seat and placed both hands on the steering wheel. "You're having problems with this?"

"Yeah, I am," Cedric replied. "The other way would have been much easier."

"The anger and defiance?"

"Yeah. As long as I thought they'd be upset with me it was easier to handle that way. I could put all the blame on them and I wouldn't have to care what they thought."

"That's why you insisted on bringing Aaron on Sunday, isn't

it?"

"You always were pretty smart."

Jason placed his right hand on Cedric's shoulder. "I don't think your lifestyle is going to be the center of attention," he said. "I just think your mother wants you in there with her. She can't handle this alone and she wants all her children as support." Jason patted his brother's shoulder a couple of times. "Don't get me wrong. I would be surprised if Hazel was supportive of your lifestyle. But she won't make that an issue until after she gets through this crisis."

"Would you be surprised if I told you I'm not sure I like that lifestyle either?"

"No, I wouldn't be," Jason replied. "Maybe it was something you had to do at that time."

"Shouldn't the decisions we make in life improve the condition of our life?" Cedric asked.

"In the ideal world, yes they should. But we don't live in that kind of world."

"Hey, brother, I'm not saying I'm going to change, but I'm not sure I'm going to continue to live like that."

"Why?"

"Because you spend too much time being angry at all the people who look at you as being different."

"Please don't get too profound on me. I'm carrying my own baggage right now." Jason turned and opened the door. "Are you ready for this?"

"As ready as I'm going to be."

"Good, then let's go see your mother. God knows she wants to see you."

Jason swung the door open and the two of them stepped inside. Theresa was the first one to look up. Hazel, Tosha and the baby still slept. Finally, Hazel began to stir. She rubbed her eyes and then spotted Jason and Cedric. A smile spread across her face. She jumped out of the chair and rushed to Cedric, pulled him close in her arms, and hugged him tight. Jason stared over at Theresa and could see the tears in her eyes. He felt choked up also as Hazel continued to squeeze her baby boy. They finally broke from their embrace and Hazel spoke first.

"Your father needs you, Cedric. He's very sick and he needs his entire family here with him."

"I'm here, Mama." Cedric's words were jerky and uneven. He also began to cry. "I'm here for you, Mama. I'm here for you."

They hugged again and then Hazel moved back a step but continued to hold his hand. "How could you just walk out of our lives the way you did?"

"Mama, I didn't have much of a choice. Big Casey made it quite clear what he thought of me back then."

"Boy, you're so silly. Your daddy loves you just like he loves your brother and your sisters."

"How's he doing?" Cedric asked and Jason breathed a sigh of relief. They didn't need to reflect on the past; they had to deal with the present.

"Last time they were out here they said his vital signs had stabilized which is good," Theresa finally spoke up. "They should give us a progress report real soon."

Cedric hurried over to Theresa and gave her a hug. He looked over at Tosha and the baby. "I see that you still have your new family with you. How's she doing?"

"They're both doing fine," Theresa answered as she looked over at Tosha.

"Did you get her tested?"

Theresa instantly smacked Cedric on the arm.

"What's wrong?" Cedric asked. Theresa's eyebrows furrowed and she pursed her lips. "Oh I get it," Cedric said.

"You never told me the children were sick," Hazel said. "What's wrong with them? She's such a cute baby. I hope nothing serious."

"No, Mama, just a general checkup. I just want to make sure they are both healthy."

"Good, once we get your father home and all set up I'll go with you to the doctor. Cedric can go with us."

"We'll see, Mama. Let's take one thing at a time," Theresa said. She glanced over at Tosha, now wide awake. "You hungry?" she asked her.

"Yes ma'am, and I need to feed the baby."

Theresa got up from her chair. "We're going to the cafeteria. Anyone hungry?"

"I am," Cedric said.

Jason shot a quick glance at him. How could he possibly be hungry after all he'd just eaten? He started to ask him that but then decided to leave it alone. He'd always followed behind Theresa and adulthood hadn't changed his behavior.

"I'll stay here with Mother," Jason said.

"Let's go," Theresa instructed and they all followed her out the door.

Jason flopped down in the chair where Theresa had sat. He held his head back and closed his eyes. He was exhausted and it wouldn't take much for him to drift off to sleep.

"I'm worried about your sister," Hazel blurted out just as Jason had willed his body to relax.

He started to ask her which sister, but he knew who she was referring to. "You haven't talked to her?"

"No, I haven't, but Theresa talked to her earlier."

"Well there you have it. She's all right."

"She's not all right, Jason," Hazel snapped.

Jason rose in his chair and stared incredulously at his mother. She wouldn't dare!

"I understand Arthur didn't show up to work."

"You're right, he didn't."

"I know something is wrong," Hazel continued. "There is no way Jacqueline wouldn't be here unless something is very wrong out there."

"I'm sure she'd call us if something was wrong."

"Not this time. I hurt her feelings when I told her Arthur couldn't run the company. And no telling what he did when they got home."

"He's not crazy. And he'll be in tomorrow." Jason hoped this line of thought would soften his mother's concern for Jacqueline.

"Jason, you have to go out there and get your sister," Hazel demanded.

"Wait a minute, Mother, I just can't go out there and demand that she come into Los Angeles with me."

"Why not? She's family and we have to stick together. You're the oldest and it's no more than what your father would insist you do."

"No, you can't ask me to do that. She's really angry with me."

"I don't care about her anger. I told both you and Theresa that the entire family should be here. And I know Jacqueline understands that. So there has to be a reason why she's not here."

"You want me to go and get Angela and Julianne also?"

"Don't get smart. Angela is not family and Julianne is too young. Now if you don't want to do it, I'll do it myself."

"Okay, Mother, when do you want me to do this?"

Before Hazel could answer the door opened and the doctor walked in, "Mrs. Mitchell, your husband is conscious now and would like to see you."

"Praise the Lord," Hazel screamed and covered her face with both hands for a moment. She then turned to Jason and hugged him. "Your daddy is going to be all right."

"Mrs. Mitchell, he's awake right now, but I have to tell you that he's suffered serious nerve damage and his pressure is very high. It will be days before we know whether he has suffered permanent nerve damage."

"What do you mean?" Hazel put her hand to her throat.

"It means, Mother, that Big Casey might be paralyzed," Jason said.

"Oh no, not him," Hazel closed her eyes. "There is no way Casey Mitchell can survive, paralyzed."

"It's a troubling thought, but there often is no acceptable alternative," the doctor added.

"Can we go see him?" Hazel asked having calmed down slightly.

"I'd prefer that only one person go in. He is quite weak and we don't want to excite him."

Hazel turned and stared at Jason.

"You go," Jason said. "I'll wait and let the others know what has

Chapter 52

A low fog covered the highway and a slight drizzle was falling, enough to force Jason to use the windshield wipers. As he sped up the highway to Jacqueline's he could hardly see the ocean due to the fog cover. Instead of looking beautiful and inviting, the ocean had a rather ominous appearance. Jason didn't want to make this trip but after Hazel returned from the Intensive Care Unit she insisted that he find Jacqueline and make sure she understood how important it was for her to be there when Big Casey totally regained consciousness. He conceded and told her that after he stopped by the office he would make that ride up the coast to check on his sister, even though he thought it ridiculous. Instead he felt he should be checking on Dominique, but did understand his Mother's insistence that all four of Big Casey's children be at the hospital. The point being there was absolutely nothing he wouldn't do for his children, therefore Hazel figured his recovery would be enhanced if he saw the five people that meant the most to him right there when he regained consciousness.

Jason again glanced to his left at the clouds rising up from the ocean. Shaking his head, he thought of the many times Arthur had driven this dangerous stretch of the highway totally blasted out of his mind. For some strange reason Jason didn't believe that Arthur would be at the apartment when he got there. In fact his missing work that morning was no coincidence. He could visualize Arthur at the woman's apartment in North Hollywood getting high or drunk and justifying his behavior on the grounds he would never be the head of Mitchell Construction. If he ran off and left Jacqueline alone to struggle with her insecurities, Jason pledged he would not go on another mission to find him. And he would also give Howard the authority to fire him tomorrow if he again failed to call in or show up for work. Big Casey may have tolerated that kind of behavior from him, but he wouldn't. It would create a problem with Jacqueline who felt the best way she could hold on to Arthur was through his job protection. Somehow she had to get weaned off her dependence on a man who really couldn't take care of himself and certainly not her also.

He finally reached the complex, pulled into the driveway and found a parking place. Jason exited the car, wondering how long he would have to continue to assume the responsibility to keep the family intact. Earlier it was Cedric and now it was Jacqueline. The first time his mission had been successful. This time he wasn't sure he would succeed.

Jason rang the bell and braced for the confrontation. As he waited his mind shifted momentarily to Dominique. Instead of being out here ringing his sister's doorbell he should be at Dominique's place pleading with her to forgive his childish behavior. He needed to be taking care of his own affairs not other people's problems. Still there was no answer. So he rang again. This time he leaned hard on the ringer for emphasis. That wouldn't bring her to the door any faster, but it felt good.

This evening he would stop by the club and feel out Dominique's mood. Maybe she'd thought it through and realized his behavior really was not that unreasonable. Just maybe she'd miss him so much that his behavior yesterday wouldn't even matter. There was still no answer so instinctively Jason tried the door handle. To his dismay and surprise it opened. He stood there for a moment contemplating whether he should go inside. Even though it was his sister's home there was something eerie about invading someone's private space. But he had to find out what was going on, so he stepped inside and closed the door.

"Jacqueline," he shouted from downstairs. No answer so he checked out the downstairs bedroom. It was empty. He hurried over to the steps, stopped and again called out. "Jacqueline, Arthur. Anyone home?" Still no answer. Jason slowly made his way up the stairs. At the top he looked toward the patio because the door was wide open with wind and rain freely blowing inside. He saw the top of Jacqueline's head, hurried over to the doorway and stepped out on the balcony.

"Jacqueline, are you all right?" Jason stepped in front of the lounge chair and stopped in shock when he looked at his sister. He hardly recognized her. She had a swollen and deeply discolored eye. Her lip was busted and swollen. Jason's thoughts flashed back to 1994 and the pictures shown all over the world of Nicole Simpson after O.J. had beaten her. Both Jacqueline and Nicole were pretty women, but you couldn't see the beauty in Nicole a dozen years ago, and you definitely couldn't see it in Jacqueline as she sat there with her head down and body slouched in the chair.

"What has he done to you?" Jason shouted as he moved in closer to her. "What happened? What did that son of a bitch do, Jacqueline? What did he do?" He shouted even louder.

"I tried to stop him from leaving," Jacqueline whispered. She could hardly talk because of the cuts and the swelling. "I didn't want him to leave."

"What do you mean you didn't want him to leave? Have you looked at yourself in the mirror? I know you have to be really hurting."

"The pain's not so bad right now. I called my doctor and he had some pain medicine sent over. It makes me dizzy and puts me to sleep. I like that because then I don't have to face what's happened."

"I have to get you out of here." Jason leaned down and took her by the arm.

"No! I can't leave because he might come back to apologize. And I have to be here for him." She pushed Jason's hand away. "You all broke his heart when Mama told him how she felt about him, and he'll need me."

"Are you crazy? He just beat the living crap out of you. He doesn't need you, he needs a good ass whipping."

"Jason, you can't do anything like that, please."

"Jacqueline, at least let me take you to emergency. You need to be treated. Your entire face is swollen. You need some medical treatment." Jason pleaded with his sister, hoping he could talk some sense into her.

"I'll go to the hospital if you'll help me first," Jacqueline said still in a low tone.

"What are you talking about? I want to help you by taking you to the hospital."

"Go find him for me. Please, Jason, you did it before. You know where he might hang out. That girl you brought to Mama's, he might be where she dances."

"Jacqueline, are you crazy?" Jason's voice shrieked. "I am not going out of here and look for your husband, because if I found him I'd probably try to kill him."

"Jason, I just need to know that he's all right. Once I know that then I promise you I'll leave him. I'll pack my things and move back to Mama's and file for divorce. But just let me know that he's all right? I can't throw away my years of marriage and not know where he is or what has happened to him. I do love him, Jason. I can't help myself."

"No, I can't do that, Jacqueline. How long are you going to chase after him?"

"How long would you chase after someone you desperately loved?"

Jason turned and stared out to the cloud-covered ocean. The drizzle had now turned to rain and they both were drenched. Momentarily the thought shot through him that the reason he didn't want to look for Arthur at the Black Zebra was because he just might see him there with Dominique. No wonder she ended their relationship. He couldn't seem to conquer this childish behavior.

"I asked you, brother, how long would you chase after someone you really loved?"

Jason turned and faced his sister. "I don't know, Jacqueline. I really don't know, but I do know we need to get you some help."

"I'll be all right until you find him, then I'll go to the hospital.

These pills are really strong and they'll keep me content until I hear from you."

"Take it easy on those pills." Jason picked up the pill box and read the instructions. "It says to take only one every twelve hours. Be careful. These things could kill you."

"That might not be so bad either."

"Don't talk like that, Jacqueline," Jason shot back at her. She scared him and he had to find Arthur before she did something irrational. But he had to at least know the extent of her desperation. "Do you realize how desperately sick this is?"

"You never realize that when you're in love. You wouldn't know because you've never been this much in love."

"And I hope I never am." Jason felt disgusted with himself because he had served as an enabler to her weakness.

"Brother, please help me," Jacqueline pleaded with him. "I'm so sick I can hardly breathe. I feel my chest is caving in on me. Please help me."

"I'll go," Jason said with both anger and defiance. "But if I can't find him you have to stop feeling sorry for yourself and go to the hospital."

Jacqueline forced herself up, but Jason grabbed her before she fell back into the chair. Jacqueline tried to hug him, but he pushed her away.

"I don't want a hug and I don't want to hear that bullshit about how much you appreciate this or how much you love Arthur. This is the very last time for me, do you understand?"

"Yes I do," Jacqueline whispered as she relaxed back in the chair.

Jason reached down and grabbed her arm. "Let me help you back into the house. My God, you're drenched. You need to dry off and get some sleep. And watch those pills." He led her back inside the townhouse and locked the balcony door. Jason helped her into the bedroom and watched as she laid back down on the bed. "I'll call you later and let you know what happened. I have my cell phone on, so if you feel sick call me. Do you understand?"

"Yes I do," Jacqueline answered. She grabbed a towel near the bed and wiped her body. She then lay down in the bed and pulled the covers up over half her body. "I do want to rest. I just want to sleep."

"Good, you do that." Jason turned and headed out of the townhouse, his disgust with his sister apparent

U

Stretched out across bed with no clothes on Arthur again experienced the euphoric feeling that the cocaine and the loving brought him. This time it was only Elizabeth. When he arrived the other night she told him that Indria had gotten into some kind of trouble and had to leave town for a while. He was disappointed because she was the real freak, but Elizabeth had made up for whatever he missed. When he gave her five hundred dollars and told her to get the best cocaine in town she was elated. The fact that she had stolen from him was now insignificant since he would need her for sex and lodging for a while. They free-based and had sex all night, but were running low. Lying there on the bed he listened as she cooked up the last batch to last them through the rest of the day. Later that night he knew they'd have to go and get more. He didn't mind because he still had plenty of money.

Arthur loved being high because he didn't have to face the reality of his life. He closed his eyes and thought back on what had happened over the past twenty-four hours. The truth had finally surfaced and the burden of Jacquline and her family was off his back He escaped relatively unscathed and wanted nothing to do with any of them, especially Jason. If he saw that bastard again he'd beat the shit out of him. That probably wouldn't happen, because he sure wouldn't come looking for him again like before. It would serve no purpose because there were no longer any pretensions between that family and him. It was all over and now he could get on with his new life.

He leaned up in the bed and looked into the kitchen. Arthur

enjoyed being with Elizabeth much more than Jacqueline. And it even got better with Indria. Maybe he could just stay there with her for a while. The apartment couldn't be compared to the Malibu townhouse, but the damn good loving would compensate. He'd been paying her rent for over a year, and coupled with the money she'd stolen, entitled him to some squatter's privileges.

The question to be answered was how she would respond if he made the suggestion to spend some time with her. He knew very little about her life and always made it a point not to question what she did all the time he wasn't there. She often took part time dancing jobs to earn money for her cocaine. She may even have someone giving her money on a regular basis like he did. That could cause a problem because there was no way he would share her.

"How you doing in there, baby?" Elizabeth shouted from the kitchen.

"Missing you," he shouted back.

"You're not missing me, sweetheart, you're missing the cocaine."

"That too."

"It'll be ready in a few more minutes, so just chill and relax. I'm going to take real good care of you. What time do you have to get out of here?"

"I might not have to leave at all." Arthur was anxious for her reply, but she said nothing. He waited another minute and then repeated himself. "Did you hear what I said? I might not have to leave at all."

Elizabeth walked into the bedroom with a large rock of cocaine on a mirror. She stopped right next to the bed and sat on the side close to Arthur. She had a rather solemn look.

"What are you talking about? Don't you have to get home? Remember what happened the last time you stayed here for a couple days? You've been here most of last night and all of today. What gives?"

"Nothing. I just might want to spend a little more time with you."

Elizabeth placed the mirror on the night stand next to the bed. "Wait a minute, Arthur. I'm not looking for a roommate."

Arthur scooted up in the bed and reared back on his elbows. "What the hell is that suppose to mean?"

"Are we going to have a problem here?" she asked.

"No problem, just tell me what you mean?"

"It means that I have a life outside of you just like you have one outside of me. This arrangement has worked quite well and I'm not looking to change it any time soon."

"Are you telling me that you wouldn't want me to stay here with you?"

"No, baby, I wouldn't want you to stay here with me anymore than what you now do. What's happened between you and your wife?" Elizabeth took the pipe and handed it to Arthur. She then broke off a small piece of the rock and placed it on the stemmed end. She lit it and Arthur inhaled the smoke, held it and then blew it out. Elizabeth then did the same. This particular batch tasted even better than the one before and he could feel it throughout his entire body. He lay back against the bed and closed his eyes.

"You still haven't answered me," Elizabeth said. "Has something happened at home?"

Arthur slid back down in the bed and stared up at the ceiling. Damn, it felt good. He didn't want to waste his high talking about Jacqueline, instead wanted Elizabeth to go down on him and intensify the satisfaction he felt at that moment. He reached his arms out for her, but she pulled away. Arthur turned on his side and stared at her.

"What's wrong, baby?"

"Nothing, Arthur, I just want you to answer my question. You've been here a day and a half and not once have you talked about going home."

"Is something wrong with me being here all of a sudden? Am I in your way and are you expecting someone else?"

"No, Arthur, I'm not expecting anyone else and yes you are in my way as long as you don't tell me what's going on."

"Okay, me and Jacqueline did have a fight and I figured it was time to move on."

Elizabeth grabbed another piece of the rock cocaine, placed it on the pipe and let Arthur smoke it. She then smoked it and laid the pipe back down on the table.

"Baby, what do you plan to do?" she asked.

"I figure I'd stay here for a few days and then find me a place, maybe in Santa Monica. I want to be close to the ocean."

"Are you still going to work for her father?"

"Fuck, no," Arthur shot back. "I'm tired of that damn bunch and don't want nothing to do with them. If I ever see that fucking Jason I might kill his fucking ass."

"Arthur, I don't mind you being here. After all you pay the rent. But you have to know that I have a certain lifestyle and I don't want to change. You think you can handle that?"

"If it's anything like Indria and you together, you better believe I can."

"It's much like that. Somewhat different on occasions. All according to my mood." Elizabeth placed the palm of her soft hand on Arthur's chest and began to rub his hairs. "If you're not working how do you expect us to live?"

Arthur removed her hand, leaned over the side of the bed and grabbed his pants. He reached in his pockets and pulled out a roll of bills he'd gotten from the bank earilier in the day. He waved them in Elizabeth's face.

"I think this will take care of us for a while."

She smiled and said. "I think it will."

"Now can we do what I want before I lose this high?"

Elizabeth placed her head between his legs, wrapped soft hand around his private part and said, "I think I can take care of that request."

Chapter 53

Jason spent fifteen minutes knocking on Elizabeth's door and ringing the bell when he finally gave up and decided to go home. He knew Arthur was there because he saw the Mercedes parked in one of the stalls. He called Jacqueline and told her that he hadn't found him but would look again in the morning. Given her condition he hated lying to his sister, but knew it would be worse if told the truth. She sounded better and assured him that she would go to the hospital in the morning. And once the swelling in her face went down, she'd go and see Big Casey. In the meantime she also assured him that she'd call Hazel to let her know everything was all right. Jason wasn't convinced Jacqueline told the truth, but he would give it a day and if she didn't come around, he'd go back out there.

Finally, at home he could give some much needed attention to his writing. He'd prepared a query letter and the first three chapters for a New York agent who Devon had told him might be interested. He needed to put the material in the overnight mail in the morning on his way into the office. Jason sat at his desk putting all the material together. He felt uncomfortable about Jacqueline. She seemed too resolved to accept the negative outcome of her crisis. She sounded distant when he talked with her, just like she really didn't hear what he told her. For a moment he considered going back out there and not let her spend the night alone. But then again Jason had his own problems he needed to address. His plate was awfully full with the business and his writing.

But lingering like old smoke in the back of his mind was Dominique. How effective could he be helping others if he didn't resolve the problems with the woman he loved? Even though he'd broken down the other night and called Raquel, it didn't feel right. He wanted no substitutes for Dominique, but wasn't sure he could handle the intensity of their love, or if she would even give him that opportunity. He had to find out or nothing else would work for him, not the writing or the business.

Jason sat in the love seat in the living room and recalled the early morning he'd watched Dominique meditating on the couch. He thought of how she ran over to him and they embraced. She teased him and then they went back into the bedroom and made love. Dominique always seemed so protective of her body and somewhat afraid to totally open up to his love making. He remembered how surprised he was that she could be so rigid in the bed and so very loose on the stage. He'd always assumed that anyone who could get in front of a roomful of men and dance naked would be automatically wild in the bed. How wrong he had been about her. Would he ever have the opportunity to tell her that?

The rules of decorum dictated that Jason not fall in love with a woman like Dominique. He was the son of a successful businessman, graduated from the prestigious University of Southern California and now had just finished his first novel. According to the rules of society there was no way he should be harboring a love for a night club dancer. Women like Dominique are there for a man's pleasure and not to be loved. Elliott had it right all along. It's a game of getting over on the other person before they did it on you. But from the start that was never a part of their relationship. They had stripped away all the pretensions and the rules and reached inside each other to find that raw and unencumbered love. How often did a person have the opportunity to reach that kind of bliss with another person? It was a feeling he'd never experienced with Angela or Raquel, or all the other women he'd known intimately over the years. And more frightening, it may be a feeling he would never experience again in life.

Jason's problem was in order to capture that kind of ecstasy again, he would have to capture Dominique's heart a second time. What had this woman done to make him love her so thoroughly in such a short period of time? It was not so much what she'd done, but the feelings she exuded. How could such a beautiful woman harbor the fears and apprehensions that would make any man want to take her in his arms and protect her? She loved Nina Simone's music and now he knew why. It was both beautiful and sad. While in Palm Springs, Dominique had asked the young singer performing Nina's greatest hits to perform Just Like a Woman. He had to hear it even though it would cause him pain.

He got up and sauntered over to the CD player, found the Nina Simone CD with that particular song, put it on and moved the player forward to that piece. Nina broke the silence with her soft, warm, but penetrating voice: "She takes just like a woman. And she makes love just like a woman. And she aches just like a woman. But she breaks just like a little girl." The words had so much meaning to Dominique and when the young singer sang them, she cried. It was the little girl who cried and he never had the opportunity to find out why. There were two Dominiques. The woman quite capable of performing on stage in front of a club full of men, and that included men like Arthur, then there was the other person who broke down and cried because of the serenity and beauty surrounding the two of them at the townhouse in Palm Springs. And that was the little girl reaching out for love. That was the person Jason knew he loved. In reality however, it could only work if he were able to accept the entire Dominique, which included the one who had probably danced for Arthur in one of the private rooms at the club.

Nina's words resonated with Jason as she brought the song to a close. Jason's eyes were moist, his heart quite heavy and his resolve firm. How many times could he go in the club and hope that she would forgive him the way she did the last time they had fought. He didn't know the answer, but that evening would find out.

u

This time Jason parked in an additional parking lot next

to the Black Zebra. The entire place was packed so that meant there would be very few tables inside and the ladies would be busy entertaining gullible men who would give up the money for a compliment. Had he become one of those gullible men and was this whole thing simply foolish? But love could not be foolish, only how one handles it can be considered that way. He'd handled it badly. As he walked into the entrance and paid his ten dollars he prepared himself for possible rejection. He spotted an empty chair at the bar and hurried over to it. He looked at the stage where the dancers made their first performance and there she was. He could feel the anxiety building up within him. The stage was surrounded by men throwing dollar bills at her. She would smile, pick up the money and move on. The music finally ended and many of the men returned to their tables. She stood looking like a bronze goddess to Jason. She smiled at the men making it to her stage, replacing those who had left. She never looked his way.

"Yeah, what can I get you?" the bartender asked.

Jason turned and faced him. "Let me have a Remy Martin on the rocks." He then spun the bar stool back around and stared at Dominique. She knelt down in front of a well- dressed man and engaged him in conversation.

"That'll be six dollars," the bartender said.

Jason didn't turn back to face the man. He pulled a ten dollar bill from his pocket, placed it on the counter while still staring at Dominique. She worked the stage with smooth, effortless motion. The men lined up in front rewarding her performance with dollar bill after dollar bill. She'd told Jason that she never wasted her money on foolishness. She had only so many good years and it was imperative that she save and invest for later years when her beautiful body would no longer attract the patrons. It seemed so long ago when they had that conversation. He had built her hopes up so that she practically dreamed of the day when she no longer would have to do this, but then he had let her down. Words to Nina Simone's song shot through him. "She breaks just like a little girl."

Jason finally took the drink from the counter. He sipped on it while continuing to concentrate on Dominique. There was a secret hidden somewhere deep inside her and even though she hid it well, nonetheless Jason knew it had a tremendous impact on her. Maybe that's the reason she had chosen this profession. The music stopped and Dominique started off the stage without any further conversation with the men who apparently tried to coax her to their table or the back room. He couldn't let her get away and escape to the back. Jason swallowed the last bit of his drink, jumped from the bar stool and rushed to catch up with her. She still hadn't seen him. But the waitress, who had waited on him the last time he was there, stood close to Dominique and tapped her on the shoulder. She stopped and the waitress whispered in her ear.

Dominique abruptly turned around and Jason's eyes met hers. His heart stopped for a moment for fear that she would turn and rush to the back room. But she didn't. She stood there staring at him as he approached her. Jason wanted to take her in his arms so badly he could scream. But the look on her face told him that was not the reason she stood there.

"Hey, Dominique, how about a table dance?" a customer sitting closer to where she stood shouted.

She ignored the man and continued to stare at Jason. "What are you doing here, Jason?" she asked coolly.

"I don't know," he said as he stopped right in front of her. "I just needed to see you."

"In this environment?"

"It's the only way I could see or reach you."

"I'm working and I really don't have time to socialize." She turned and started to walk away.

"How about one of the rooms?" he asked. "Can't we go back there?"

"You have the money?"

"You know I do."

"Two songs and that's it," she said and headed toward one of the private rooms. Jason followed close behind.

Jason settled down on the couch and Dominique stood over him. This wasn't turning out quite the way he'd expected. He felt no warmth or feeling from her. It was all business with no emotions.

"You know the amount and this time I will dance for you," she said.

Jason gave her the fifty dollar bill. Somehow he had to break through her emotionless behavior and reach the Dominique who cried in his arms in Palm Springs. The person he could love and protect. But she wouldn't even look at him as she stood there waiting for the music to begin. The silence was devastating. Finally, of all the songs, the disc jockey played Teddy Pendergrass' "The whole town's laughing at me." Dominique moved in close and worked her body slowly down Jason. He desperately wanted to touch and hold her, but that was against the rules. This was not Palm Springs, or his apartment, but the club and that really defined what he could and couldn't do. She moved to her side and danced all around him making him even more uncomfortable.

Jason wanted to push her away, get up and run out of there. This was not the way he wanted to enjoy the pleasure of the woman he loved. Teddy wasn't helping the situation at all as he sang about the love lost. He could feel the difference between tonight and the many wonderful nights they had spent together at his apartment. This was all mechanical, like acting out a role and once it was over it would have meant nothing to her. Jason strained to stop from screaming that this couldn't be. Their love was much more important and genuine than this act of emptiness. Once the music stopped he'd get up and leave. He didn't care about a second dance because it would be more emptiness. He could take that from someone else, but not her. Finally the music stopped and he felt relieved. Dominique backed away from him and looked off to the left.

"Can't we at least talk?" Jason asked.

"I'm not here to talk," she said dryly. "I'm here to entertain you, make you feel good."

"Stop it, Dominique. You know damn well that's not why I'm here."

"But that's exactly why I'm here."

"There's no way we can get beyond this wall?"

"You're not enjoying yourself?"

"Quite frankly, no, I'm not."

Dominique threw the fifty dollars back at Jason. "Well I'm here to please and if I failed at that, please take your money back." She stood there and stared down at him.

"Dominique, please." He reached out to hold her and she moved back further away from him.

"If you're not satisfied with me, then I suggest you take your money and find someone other than me. One of the other young ladies out there could possibly make you feel better than I can." She turned and started toward the door.

"Dominique, I love you!"

She hesitated at the door, turned to look at him. She started to say something, but didn't and hurried out the door.

Chapter 54

An upbeat mood filled the Mitchell household that morning. Hazel received a call from the hospital informing her that Big Casey made such good progress over the night they would move him from intensive care. Once situated in a private room, the entire family would be able to visit with him. The nurse suggested that they wait until the hospital called before the family came out there. That would be early in the afternoon.

Theresa sat on a bar stool in the kitchen drinking a cup of coffee. After telling Theresa the good news Hazel, who hadn't slept much since the evening of the stroke, decided to sleep a couple extra hours so she would be well rested and alert when she visited her husband. Tosha and the baby, as well as Cedric, were still asleep upstairs. Theresa couldn't help but notice how Tosha had perked up since Cedric came around. And he seemed to pay a lot of attention to the baby. Theresa didn't know what Cedric planned to do with his life, but she felt that he still had a man's desire for a woman. That was a good sign because he could be good for the young girl and vice versa. What he needed was for someone to feel they could depend on him and make him experience being needed and important.

She believed that Cedric would stick by Tosha regardless of the outcome of the HIV test. Now that she had someone who she related to on all levels, maybe he could help her with the results. She needed to talk with both of them that morning before Hazel got up. She also needed to call Jacqueline and tell her about Big Casey. Theresa glanced at the clock on the wall. It was only seven-thirty. She would wait another hour to call her sister and would also call Jason who probably would be at the office about that time.

Theresa felt that she had taken control of the crisis situation for her mother. That's exactly why Hazel had insisted that she stay there at the house with her and not Jacqueline.

Theresa now recognized how much she had underestimated her mother all these years. Hazel, though showing signs of stress, had really handled this entire situation quite well. Theresa was especially proud of the manner in which she dealt with Cedric. Her mother's priorities were her family and, no matter what, she seemed determined to keep them all together. She now felt confident in telling Hazel of her plans to make Tosha and the baby a part of her family regardless of the results of the HIV test. Theresa finished her coffee and started upstairs to wake Tosha and Cedric.

After considerable effort Theresa finally got Cedric and Tosha up and into her bedroom. The baby still slept but they had brought her to Theresa's bed and laid her there. Both Cedric and Tosha sat on the side of the bed while Theresa stood.

"Big Casey's going to be moved this afternoon to a private room. He's making great progress," Theresa began the conversation.

"That's wonderful, Miss Theresa," Tosha said nervously.

"Yeah that's great, but you didn't wake us for just that," Cedric added.

"No I didn't," Theresa turned and looked directly at Tosha. "Cedric knows of your possible condition and he wants to help," she said. "So after we leave the hospital this afternoon we're going to go directly to the clinic to get the results."

"No, Miss Theresa, I don't want to do that just yet," Tosha demurred.

"Honey, you have to," Theresa shot back. "You can't continue to go on without knowing the truth. We'll be with you, however it turns out."

"It's all going to go wrong. I know it will and I don't want to lose my baby. I don't want to die." Tosha covered her face with both hands and began to cry.

"Tosha, you might have the virus," Cedric now joined in. "But then again maybe neither one of you are infected. Heck, you don't even know for sure that your boyfriend was infected."

"He ain't my boyfriend," she quickly replied.

Theresa smiled, knowing that response was meant to send a message to Cedric. "We have to do it, Tosha. We both will be with you, isn't that right, Cedric?"

"Yes definitely," Cedric said. He grabbed Tosha's hand and squeezed it between his. "I'll be there with you so don't worry."

Again Theresa smiled and felt warm inside. She had never heard Cedric exude strength and confidence as he did at that very moment. She saw the possibility of two lost young souls being saved through their shared strengths for each other. Theresa didn't want to get her hopes up too high, but the signs were all there.

"You going to go with me for sure, Cedric?" Tosha turned and looked at Cedric.

"You bet I am," he said proudly.

"Okay, Miss Theresa, I'm ready to do it."

Theresa kissed Tosha on the forehead and patted Cedric on the shoulder. Without saying another word she turned and walked out of the bedroom. She leaned against the wall and bit her lip to keep from crying she felt so good.

u

Jason sat in Big Casey's office with his back to the door, staring out the window. The view was awesome from that high up. He had a clear view of the San Gabriel Mountains that rose high above the city of Pasadena. The smog hadn't settled in and the sun was shining brightly. It was what one would consider a perfect morning in Los Angeles. But not for Jason. His plan last night to confront Dominique and win her back had failed miserably. She wouldn't even consider an apology. Evidently her love hadn't been deep enough to overlook his flaws. As he stared at the magnificent structure of mountains he thought about giving up on her. Just let it go and move on. But it wasn't that easy. All the positive memories flooded his thoughts and affected him. He had never before had to deal with the agonizing and painful question of how do you let someone go whom you deeply love?

He glanced at his watch. It read a little past eleven. He'd received the call from Theresa at ten o'clock about Big Casey being moved into a private room. That joy balanced the emptiness and depression he'd felt all morning long. And then there was the problem of Arthur. Again a no show and he hadn't called. Jason didn't bother to contact Jacqueline because he knew she would not be helpful. Despite her protestations, Jason had instructed Howard to prepare Arthur's termination papers, cut him a final check and he would give it to Jacqueline. Frankly, Jason didn't want to ever see the man again in life. Hopefully, Jacqueline would wake up and realize what a loser he is and divorce him. At least that's what he gathered from their last conversation.

Jason thought of Dominique having to dance in front of egomaniacs like Arthur all the time and his disappointment in himself grew even stronger. Surely no one could enjoy that, so why did he act like such an idiot and give the impression that he assumed she did? Somehow he had to make her understand. He had to break down that wall she'd constructed between them. But first he would give her some time. He would concentrate on the business at hand, which was to keep the company running smoothly until Big Casey could return, and to follow up on that agent in New York he'd sent his manuscript to. Once he accomplished all he needed to at the business, he would go and get the woman he loved and take her out of that lifestyle. Jason spun the chair back around in order to answer the telephone.

"Jason Mitchell," he said.

"Jason, this is your mother and I need you to go and get Jacqueline," Hazel said.

"Mother, please don't start with that nonsense again."

"What's wrong with you?" she shot back at him. "We haven't heard from your sister and we don't know if she's all right and you're not willing to check on her?"

"I was just out there and she was fine." He lied and felt bad, but he was tired of the Jacqueline and Arthur episode.

"Jason, your father's going to notice her not being there at the hospital and he's going to worry. And you do know that could be harmful to him. Do you want that on your conscience?"

Jason took in a deep breath and slowly released it. Over the years he'd often thought that Hazel should have gone into acting. She was quite dramatic when it fit her purpose.

"What is it you want me to do, mother, run this business or baby sit Jacqueline and Arthur?"

"Quite frankly both, if they're in need of your help and they are. That is, the business and your sister. I don't care what happens to Arthur." Hazel paused for a moment and Jason could hear her breathing heavily. "Now if you're too busy to check on your sister, I'll drive out there myself."

He knew it was coming and she delivered the challenge knowing darn well he didn't dare call her on it. "You win, I concede. I'll head out there in the next half hour and one way or another I'll have your daughter for you to see this afternoon." He didn't tell her about the beating. Hopefully some of the swelling would be gone and the shock wouldn't be that traumatic.

"Your sister also," Hazel rejoined. "She is a part of you so don't try to disassociate by referring to her as my daughter."

"I'll see you this afternoon with my sister and your daughter."

"Thank you, Jason. We all love you."

u

Jason's drive up the coast was solemn and disquieting. Low clouds had made their way onto the shore and blanketed the highway. The dreary day at the ocean and the bad weather seemed appropriate. He didn't bother to put the music on in the car, something he always did. It all seemed to be getting so bizarre and strange, with Jacqueline and Arthur leading the pack of strange events. The manner in which he'd beaten Jacqueline clearly indicated he wouldn't return; however, with the two of them anything was possible. She had an unhealthy affinity for forgiveness when it came to her husband. Because of her problems with Arthur, Jacqueline had abandoned the family in time of crisis. She usually ran toward Hazel and Theresa when things got rough, not away from them. Even though he felt irritated having to go back out to Malibu after going out there yesterday, he knew it was best. He smiled as he thought of all the drama that now captured his family and drove them on an hourly basis. He could probably write a novel about his family. After all novels are stories of everyday life with all the boring stuff left out. Lately there hadn't been much on the boring side in the Mitchell family.

The rain began to fall making the visibility even worse. It caused Jason to squint as he slowed down to concentrate on the road. He did a slow burn thinking about more important issues he needed to be dealing with instead of babysitting his sister. Over the past month he felt that much of his time had been taken up dealing with his sister's impetuous behavior. Her only problem was that she had been spoiled more than any of the others by Hazel. Jacqueline knew how to take and really never gave back to others. Jason planned to tell her just that. As he shot around one of the many curves leading to the townhouse, he thought of Arthur. Maybe he would be home now and would put up that weak façade he did the other day. He acted like he was so concerned about how Jason talked to Jacqueline and then went home and beat her into oblivion. He then went to a couple prostitutes and laid up with them while his wife was suffering. What a real lowlife bastard.

Jason sped down the last stretch of the highway before he reached her townhouse and for some reason began to get nervous. The other day when he stopped to see her she was obviously in pain, both physical and mental. When he called and told her he hadn't found Arthur she sounded distant. Putting all these pieces together he understood why Hazel insisted that he check on her. A mother's instinct was always a powerful indicator of things to come. Jason drove into the complex and noticed Jacqueline's car still parked in the same spot from the other day. He didn't see Arthur's Mercedes.

Anxiety began to build in his body and a nervous uneasiness overtook him. He found a parking space and jumped out of the car. The fact that Jacqueline cared so deeply for Arthur was obvious to everyone, but they never thought she might do something crazy if their marriage ever ended. He ran toward the townhouse with that thought dominating his actions.

Overcome with dread and trepidation Jason rang the doorbell while at the same time banging on the door. "Just calm down," he whispered, "you're acting silly, she's probably just fine." Jason rang the bell a second time with more force than the first time. He again banged on the door.

"Jacqueline!" he shouted. "Jacqueline, come to the door. sis, do you hear me?" Still no answer so he grabbed the doorknob and yanked on it. The door was locked. "Damn, damn," he shouted "Jacqueline, are you in there? Please come to the door." He placed his finger on the doorbell and left it there while banging on the door with his fist. Finally, Jason leaned his head against the door and tears filled his eyes as he prayed that Jacqueline would any minute open the door. She could be her usually selfish and arrogant self. She could tell him off for acting nasty with Arthur. Jacqueline could do any damn thing she wanted, just please open the door.

"Sir, is there a problem?" The security officer for the complex stood right behind Jason.

Jason turned and faced the man. "My sister may be in there and may have done damage to herself. Open the door!"

"I'm sorry, sir, I have no reason to go into this couple's town house. The management called me to check on a stranger pounding on the door. No one could recognize you so I'm going to ask you to move away from this building and leave the premises."

"Officer, you don't understand. I believe my sister and husband broke up and no one has been able to communicate with her. I came out here to check on her."

"How do I know you're related to her?"

"Mister, we may be losing valuable time. If she's in there hurt and if we don't get to her, it'll be your fault."

"I don't know," the security guard said.

"What do you have to lose?"

The guard looked away, then turned and knocked on the door. "Hello, is anyone in there?" he shouted.

What an idiot. Jason had already spent ten minutes knocking on the door and no one answered. "She's not going to answer the door because she probably can't. Now will you open the door so we can check on her?"

"Maybe she just drove off somewhere," the guard said in defense of his actions.

"She couldn't have, that's her car right over there." Jason pointed in the direction of Jacqueline's car.

The guard glanced toward the main office to the complex as though looking for someone to bail him out of this dilemma.

"I'll take full responsibility for whatever happens. Come on, man, open the door." Jason shouted as well as pleaded with the guard.

The guard stared at Jason for a moment and then moved closer to the door. "Okay, but you stand back. I'll go inside and check it out."

"All right, whatever," Jason said. "Just open the door." Jason moved back away from the man. He watched the guard's every move. The guard found the right key and unlocked the door. He pushed it halfway open and stuck his head inside. "Hello, is anyone in there?" he shouted.

How dumb. Jason pounced forward and pushed the guard aside. He didn't look back as he shot up the stairs.

"Hey you come back here!" the guard shouted.

At the top of the stairs Jason shot a glance at the balcony. The door was open with the wind and rain pounding inside on the furniture and the floor. She wasn't out there so he turned and ran into the bedroom, then came to an abrupt stop. Jacqueline lay still with the covers pulled halfway up covering her body. She wore a blue negligee, with her hair down and makeup applied perfectly to cover the bruises from the beating. She had also placed a white carnation in her hair. Her eyes were closed, her arms folded across her body. She looked just as though she were asleep. She looked peaceful, content, and so beautiful. The empty pill bottle lay next to her with the top off.

"Oh no," Jason cried out. The tears blurred his eyes so that he could hardly see. He rushed over and placed her head in his arms. He felt for a pulse but she had none. No heartbeat either. Nothing, just a peaceful look. Jason began rocking her in his arms. "No, Jacqueline, no honey. No, baby, please wake up."

The security guard finally showed up at the door. Jason could hardly make him out; he was just a blur because of the tears. He continued to hold Jacqueline close. He finally said to the guard,

"Please call emergency. Please rush and call emergency. We can't lose her. We just can't lose her." He buried his head in her hair and thought about Hazel and just knew Jacqueline could not die. Not now and not this way.

Chapter 55

Theresa felt good watching her mother get ready to leave for the hospital. In fact, everyone seemed to be in a good mood. Even though later on that afternoon Tosha would know the results of her HIV test she smiled while sitting next to Cedric feeding the baby. This also was the happiest she'd seen Cedric in a long time. Theresa wondered did he miss his other life. And more important could he conquer his demons and get over all the animosity he felt toward his father and Jacqueline.

Her mood changed when she thought about how angry she felt yesterday when she talked with Jacqueline by phone. The entire family always supported her through her emotional roller coaster marriage and now when they called on her to show the same kind of loyalty and support to the family, she failed.

Hazel had just finished placing the breakfast dishes in the dishwasher when Cedric came bouncing into the room with Tosha and the baby close behind. He went over to Hazel, placed both arms around her waist and kissed her on the cheek.

"What's that for?" Hazel asked with a smile.

"I don't know, maybe just because you're such a sensational mother."

"Well thank you, honey," Hazel said as she patted him on the shoulder. "But let's get out of here and over to the hospital. Your father's going to be looking for all of us. Lord help us if something happens to either Jason or Jacqueline and they're not there this morning."

"Mama, please," Theresa said. "Nothing's going to happen to anyone."

"I know. But you know those two were after each other pretty badly and I don't trust Arthur at all," Hazel rejoined.

Theresa now began to get nervous simply because Hazel was. "Mama, why do you think something would happen?"

"I don't know. Just call it a mother's intuition." She turned on the dishwasher. "I'm not really worried about Jason. He's all right, but you know he's really close to his father and the fact that Jacqueline hasn't called is not good. For all her faults, I don't think she's gone over a day without calling me. God knows I'd be a real mess if something happened to that girl."

They all started for the front door. "What about the rest of us, Mama?" Cedric asked.

"You just be quiet," Hazel shot back. "You done earned all the worry points coming to you and all the other children." They laughed and exited the house on their way to the hospital.

u

In the waiting room the nurse briefed them on what to expect while in visiting with Big Casey. She informed them that only family members could visit with him, which meant Tosha and the baby had to stay there in the waiting room. Cedric decided that he would remain back with Tosha. Hazel agreed as long as he understood he'd have to be in the room with them when Jason and Jacqueline arrived at the hospital. He agreed and then Theresa and Hazel followed the nurse down the hall for their first visit with a conscious Big Casey.

Theresa stopped right in her tracks when she stepped into the room. The staff from the company had sent enough flowers to cover a medium-sized float in the Rose Parade. The room exuded joy and life. The doctors had just finished their examination of Big Casey. They turned and smiled at Hazel and Theresa.

"He is an amazing man," the doctor said. "He's doing well. All his vital signs are good and he should be able to eat regular food in a couple days. In fact he's doing so well we might let him out of here in a week or so."

Theresa came in view of her father and a big smile covered his face. She and Hazel moved in close to the bed.

"What happened?" he asked in a faint voice and then tried to smile.

"Don't you ever scare me like this again," Hazel said and then began to cry.

"Hey Daddy," Theresa said. "You really did give us a real scare."

"Why?" Big Casey said. "I wasn't going nowhere."

Hazel sat in one of the chairs close to the bed and continued to cry. Theresa remained standing but moved in closer to her father.

"Daddy, do you feel okay?" she asked.

"As good as I possibly can being stuck in this God-forsaken hospital. I heard that doctor say I'd have to be in here for another week. Ain't no way they going to keep me here that long." He tried to rise up but was unable to do so. He also tried to move his arms but there was no motion. "I'll be glad when this paralysis is gone so I can get around again. Doctor said it might take a while, but I know I'll be up and walking in no time. I have to get out of here and go home."

Hazel glanced over at Theresa and then looked back at Big Casey. "Don't be silly. You're going to stay in here as long as it takes to get you well."

"We'll see about that, 'cause I have to get back to the job. We're about to bid on a new project and I have to be there."

"Jason says that Howard is doing a good job in your absence." Hazel picked up a towel and wiped Big Casey's forehead. "So I don't want to hear it."

"Where is Jason?" Big Casey asked as he strained to look around the room. "And where is Jacqueline? And how is that idiot husband of hers doing at the job?"

"My, you're full of questions," Theresa said. "Jacqueline and Jason are probably on their way here right now. And Arthur is doing just fine." She looked at Hazel and slightly shrugged her shoulders. He need not know the truth right now and hoped Hazel would agree with her.

"What do you mean probably?" he asked and tried to rise up

in the bed to no avail. "Is there something you all are not telling me?"

"No, Daddy, everything is fine. Now lie back and rest."

"Guess what?" Hazel perked up with a smile. "Your baby boy is here to see you."

"Cedric's here? Where is he?"

"He's in the waiting room with the young lady that Theresa brought to your birthday party. He stayed back there with the girl and the baby. And they seem to be hitting if off quite well. You might have a couple additions to the family."

"What? But Jason said Cedric was a homosexual. What happened that fast to turn things around? Was it the stroke? If so, then the stroke was worth it."

"Daddy, please don't say that," Theresa admonished her father.

"I am who I am and I ain't going to change just because society wants to change."

"Okay that's enough," Hazel said as she got up from the chair. "Don't get excited."

"That's right," Theresa added. "You be any way you want to be. You're a wonderful father and that's all that counts."

Big Casey smiled and relaxed back on the bed. "The first thing I want to do when I get home is have another cookout for all the family. I want everyone there, even that knucklehead Arthur. This time with no arguments or no secrets. And I want Jason to bring that pretty girl he brought last time. Man, she is beautiful. In fact I might give him a run for his money with her." He smiled at Hazel.

"Old man, ain't no young woman wants you," Hazel said.

"You do and you're still my spring chicken."

"You all stop that mushy stuff." Theresa intervened and smiled at both her parents.

"It's that mushy stuff got you in this world," Big Casey faintly whispered as it was apparent he was tiring.

"All right, that's enough." Hazel looked at her watch. "Your brother should have been here by now." She turned and glanced at Theresa. "Go check the waiting room to see if they are here."

"Mama, they're not—"

"Theresa, go check the waiting room." She interrupted her daughter. "And if they are you bring them all down here including Cedric. I'll go and stay with Tosha. I want all his children here with him for a change."

"Do as your mother says," Big Casey added. "You know how stubborn she can be. Anyway I want a little private time with her so we can talk some more mushy stuff."

Theresa smiled, leaned down and kissed her father on his forehead. "You all be good," she said, then turned and left the room.

Walking down the corridor to the waiting room Theresa felt warm throughout her body. Just seeing her father with eyes open, smiling, and in his old joking mood made everything all right with her. There had been so many ups and downs in the Mitchell family over the past couple days, it was refreshing to know that it all would work out just fine. As far as she could tell Hazel had taken to Tosha and the baby, and Cedric firmly entrenched in their live made it even better. Strange how they came from completely separate worlds, yet understood each other so completely. There could be no barriers in the Black world. Theresa smiled as she swung the door open and saw Cedric holding the baby and Tosha sleeping on his shoulder. When she entered, Tosha straightened up.

"Don't move," Theresa said to her. "You all look good together."

"How's he doing?" Cedric asked.

"He's doing just fine. He's even talking about going home."

"No way," Cedric said.

"He's talking about it, but I'm sure the doctors will have something to say about it."

"Miss Theresa, me and the baby are ready to get the results of the test," Tosha said.

"I know you are, honey, but we're going to have to wait a little longer. I don't want to leave until Jason and Jacqueline get here."

"Everything was going fine until you mentioned her name," Cedric said sarcastically.

Theresa finally took a seat right next to where Cedric and Tosha sat. "Don't be like that," she admonished her brother. "Jacqueline loves you but has a difficult time relating to you right now. Once she sees you've changed, she'll be okay."

Cedric handed the baby to Tosha and sat straight up. "Theresa, I'm going to work real hard at this, but I don't know for sure if I've changed. I just have a lot of confusion right now."

"Take it one step at a time," Theresa rejoined.

"He's going to be all right," Tosha said. She snuggled close to Cedric. "Because we're going to be here to help each other."

"That's good." Theresa looked at her watch and then at the door. "I wonder where they are?" she whispered. "They should have been here by now."

"You think something's wrong?" Cedric asked.

"I don't know but I'm starting to worry."

Cedric put his arm around Tosha and smiled. "Don't worry, nothing's going to go wrong. In fact, I'll even be nice to Jacqueline just for you and Big Casey. We don't want him thinking there's strife in the family."

"That sounds just wonderful," Theresa rejoined and then grabbed her cell phone as it began to ring.

"It's about time you called," she said having recognized Jason's number. "Where are you guys?"

"Theresa," Jason spoke in a cracked voice. "Jacqueline has overdosed on some pills."

"Oh my God! Is she all right?" Jacqueline shrieked.

There was a long hesitation and Theresa could hear Jason's heavy breathing. She could hear him crying. This time she screamed, "My God, Jason, is she all right? Tell me she's all right?"

Finally from the other end. "She didn't make it. We've lost our sister. Theresa, honey, Jacqueline is dead."

Theresa's legs sagged and she felt herself losing consciousness. She dropped the cell phone and fell back into the chair. Deep inside she felt a burning sensation and finally screamed as loud as she possibly could.

"Theresa, what's wrong?" Cedric handed the baby to Tosha. Theresa's scream frightened the child and she started crying. Cedric got up and rushed over next to his sister. "Theresa, what's wrong, what's happened? It's Jacqueline, isn't it? What's happened to our sister?"

Theresa heard Cedric but was unable to respond. She couldn't speak and now couldn't move. Theresa temporarily felt paralysis throughout her body.

Cedric turned and looked at Tosha. "I'll be right back," he shouted. "I'm going to get a doctor." He shot out of the room and slammed the door.

Theresa sat there trying to actually comprehend what Jason had told her. It wasn't real. She hadn't answered the phone and he didn't just tell her that Jacqueline was dead. The past five minutes hadn't even occurred. She need only tell herself that and it would be true. But she glanced over at Tosha and Cedric wasn't there. He'd gone to get help and because he wasn't sitting next to Tosha smiling and holding the baby, it all had happened and now she must re-group. She must regain her senses, her composure, and her strength. She knew it had been too good to last. The crisis that started on Big Casey's birthday couldn't possibly go away. Now it had reached its apex and because it had, Theresa would have to again be that same person that Jacqueline had depended on in life and Hazel had called on in a crisis.

Finally the door swung open and Cedric rushed back in the room closely followed by the nurse. Cedric hurried over next to Tosha and put his arm around her while the nurse knelt down next to Theresa.

"Miss, are you all right?" the nurse asked.

"Cedric, Jacqueline's dead," Theresa said and now it was out and she knew it to be real. "My mother," Theresa whispered, "you can't tell my mother right now." She looked past the nurse at Cedric, who stood there in silence with a shocked look on his face. "We have to keep this quiet until we get home. Do you hear me, we have to keep this quiet?" Theresa rose up in the chair. "I'm all right," she said to the nurse. "I'll be just fine. I only need a few minutes."

The nurse moved away from Theresa and said, "I'll be at the desk if you need me." She then left the room.

"Theresa, you have to tell Mama," Cedric softly said.

"No, not right now, especially not in front of Daddy. He'll have another stroke and God knows we can't lose him too."

"What are you going to do, Miss Theresa?" Tosha asked.

Theresa managed to smile at Tosha but did not answer her. Instead she flipped open her cell phone and dialed Jason's number.

"Where are you and what's happening?" she asked Jason before he could speak.

"I'm at the Malibu Police Department answering a ton of questions," he said.

"Where's Jacqueline?"

"She's.....she's at the morgue."

"Jason, what are we going to do?"

"I don't know. Right now I can't really think."

"We have to tell Mama," Theresa said meekly. "But I can't do it alone. I'm going to wait until you get here."

"No, we can't do it at the hospital."

"We might need a hospital when she finds out."

"I know but you have to get her away from there. You have to get her home."

"How am I supposed to get her away from here?"

"I don't know," Jason snapped.

"How about Arthur, does he know?" Theresa asked.

"To hell with Arthur. If I see that son of a bitch I'll hurt him."

"Jason, don't do anything stupid. We don't need, in fact, we can't handle two tragedies. Somehow we'll get Mama back to the house. Meet us there and we'll tell her." Theresa began to cry as she imagined her mother's response.

"Theresa, this is so surreal. I can't believe it's happening."

Chapter 56

Jason didn't know if he could handle it. He felt weak, nervous, and unsure of himself at this point. He thought he was prepared for most things that life could deal him, even able to handle losing Dominique. But this one went beyond the pale. He had to tell his mother that she had lost her oldest daughter to suicide. The thought brought tears to his eyes and blurred his vision. Suicide was so final and no one, not even the person who committed the act, or all of the others that would do anything to turn it around, could change that finality. As he turned his BMW into the driveway and headed to the house to confront Hazel with the news, he'd do practically anything to make this go away. But it wouldn't and he had to overcome his weaknesses and do this.

They gathered in Big Casey's office. Hazel sat behind his desk, and Jason with Theresa in the chairs in front. Cedric had pulled a chair in from the other room and sat to the side of the desk. Tosha and the baby were upstairs. This was a family matter that only the three of them must deal with.

"What's wrong, why the long faces and where is Jacqueline?" Hazel asked bluntly. "Something has happened and I want to know what's going on?"

"Mama, we have some bad news," Theresa spoke up.

"Yes, what is it. Quit these games," Hazel's hands were shaking. "Has Arthur done something to my daughter? Is she in the hospital? Has she been hurt?" She leaned halfway across the desk. "Jason, tell me what's going on right now? Where in God's creation is my baby?"

"Mother, I swear I'd give anything not to have to tell you this, but Jacqueline..." Jason's words froze.

"Yes, what about Jacqueline? Where is my daughter, Jason? Is she hurt?"

"Mama, Jacqueline is dead. She committed suicide. Jason found her body in the townhouse when he went out there earlier today." Theresa blurted it out with as much detail as possible at that point so it would be over.

Hazel reared back in the chair, held her head toward the ceiling and breathed heavily. Total silence engulfed the room as no one dared say anything for fear it would be the wrong thing. Again tears filled Jason's eyes. He glanced over at Theresa and she also had tears running down her cheeks. Cedric buried his head between his hands. They all seemed to be waiting for a response from Hazel. The longer that response took, the more nervous Jason felt. She should show some emotion because by nature his mother was a very emotional person. She was the feisty one and always had something to say about everything. This deliberate silence was not her and that made him nervous.

"Where is my daughter now? Where do they have her?" Hazel asked in an emotionless tone. She reared up in the chair and crossed her arms.

"She's still in the morgue," Jason answered reluctantly.

"Morgue? What do you mean?" Hazel shouted as she finally began to show some emotions.

"Mama, they had to do an autopsy," Theresa said.

"Oh my God in Heaven!" Hazel wailed. "You mean they cut on my daughter?"

"Whenever there's a suicide—"

"Don't say that," Hazel shouted at Jason. "Don't you dare tell me that my daughter committed suicide! Just don't say that."

Jason and Theresa stared at each other and their thoughts seemed to merge. Hazel was about to explode and they both had to remain strong for what was coming.

"Why didn't the two of you help her?" Hazel asked between her crying. "You both knew she was weak and you should have helped her. You should have been there for her."

"Mama, we were," Theresa blurted out. "We did as much as we possibly could, Mama. But she loved him. No matter how rotten and no good he was she just plain loved him."

"Where is Arthur?" Hazel asked as she took a tissue from the box on the desk and wiped her eyes.

"We don't know," Jason lied.

"Can we do anything to him? Can we have him arrested for anything? I don't care what it is, can we hurt him? The same way he's hurt this family, can we hurt him?" Hazel shrieked. "Theresa, you work with all those hoodlums, can't you hire some of them to hurt him? I want him to suffer for what he's done."

"Mother, we can't do that," Jason said. "He's going to suffer eventually. He has to come back someday. That's just his nature. He's going to come crawling back and there will be nothing for him."

"That's not enough. I want him to hurt."

Theresa got up and hurried to the other side of the desk. She put her arm around her mother. "Mama, let's think about Jacqueline and what we have to do in the next couple days."

"What do you mean?" Hazel asked. She sounded confused. "We have to bring my baby home so she can get well. I want all my children here for when your daddy comes home. You all have to be here. Jason, you have to go and get your sister before Big Casey gets here. He has to see all his children or I don't know what he'll do. Go get Jacqueline and make her come with you."

"Mama, you have to pull yourself together. Jacqueline is not coming home." Theresa was stern and soft at the same time. "We can't leave her where she is. So we need to decide where you want her to go."

"Oh no," Hazel wailed again. "My baby's not coming home. She was such a sweet and pretty little girl. And she loved life so much. She can't be gone. Please, Jason, tell me she isn't gone?"

Hazel's tears and her words choked up Jason again and his eyes filled with tears. He looked at Theresa and she was still crying. He glanced at Cedric and his hands still covered his face. Jason knew he was also crying. You can't lose a sister and not feel the pain. His thoughts turned to Arthur, who he knew was oblivious to all this suffering. He had caused much of this and chances were excellent that he would escape unscathed.

Despite what he'd said earlier to Hazel, he now agreed with her. That was not enough. He didn't directly kill Jacqueline, but had to share much of the blame. By nature Jason was not a violent man, but nature had been pushed to its limits. For a moment his mind drifted to his manuscript. Slaves never fought back and they suffered for their pacifism. He didn't want to be weak and didn't want anyone, especially a piece of shit like Arthur, to think that he was weak. He stared over at Cedric and knew what had to be done. Undoubtedly it's what Big Casey would do and now he stood in his shoes.

"Cedric," Jason's tone was stern. "Get up."

Cedric looked up at him with a perplexed expression. Jason's abruptness caught Theresa's attention also. She looked at him and said, "Jason, you all right?"

"Hell no," Jason shot back at her. "I'm a long ways from being all right." He got up from his chair. "Mother, you're right," he continued, "someone has to make this right for Jacqueline. Long time ago I told her that if Arthur ever hurt her again he'd have to answer to me and Cedric." Jason hurried to the other side of the desk and opened the middle drawer. He removed Big Casey's pistol and jammed it inside his belt.

"Jason, no!" Theresa shouted. "You can't do this. Hasn't this family suffered enough? You can't do this."

"Mother's right. He can't just walk away from this." Jason turned and looked at Hazel. "Mother, I lied. I know where the bastard is and I think it's just fair that he know his wife is dead. And she died because of him."

Suddenly Cedric perked up. "What are we going to do?" he asked.

"We're going to let him know that the Mitchell family is a strong clan. Despite our differences we're a family and he's going to find that out."

"Mama, stop them. This is crazy."

"No!" Hazel answered abruptly. "You go let him know that this family will strike back. It's what your father would do and you are his sons."

Jason hurried over to Theresa and hugged her. "He has to know that he has some unpaid dues. And it's time for the Mitchell family to collect." Jason turned and Cedric followed him out of the room.

The emotional surge of anger rushing through Jason created a sensation he'd never experienced before in life. He'd been angry in the past, but nothing to match this level of anger. He found himself speeding across the 110 Freeway for the second time in a week, but with a different kind of anger this time and for a much more justifiable reason. Jason felt no concern for himself, and at that point, was willing to sacrifice everything for a piece of Arthur. He reached down and felt the gun snugly tucked inside his pants. He didn't know for sure how he'd handle the situation with Arthur, but the man had to accept some of the blame for his family's unnecessary pain. Jason glanced over at Cedric who had an apprehensive look all over his face.

"You okay?" Jason asked.

"Yeah, bro, I'm fine," Cedric answered.

From the boldness of his response Jason surmised that Cedric indeed would be up for this task.

"You up for this?" he still asked.

"Hey, the son of a bitch hurt my sister. You damn right I'm up for it." Cedric sat up in the car for emphasis. "Me and Jacqueline ain't ever got along and we probably never would have, but hell man she is still part of our family. So yeah I'm up for kicking this motherfucker's ass real good."

Jason glanced over at his brother somewhat surprised at his response. He noticed how muscular Cedric had become over the past years. He probably could take Arthur by himself. Being gay didn't mean he couldn't take care of himself. He smiled and felt good inside that he and his baby brother were about to teach this bastard a lesson about the Mitchell family.

Jason pulled up and parked directly in front of the apartment building. He glared over at Arthur's Mercedes still parked in the same spot from the other night. The son of a bitch probably hadn't left the apartment in a couple of days. His wife dead and he laid up with a lowlife getting high. Jason's blood rushed to the top of his head and he felt warm.

He opened the door and climbed out of the car. Without saying anything Cedric did the same. They started up the steps to the apartment and Jason felt for the gun still resting inside his pants. The two brothers reached the top of the stairs, stared for a moment at each other and then Jason banged his fist loudly against the door. Again he looked his brother in the eyes as he waited for a response. There was none so he banged on the door again. This time he just wasn't going to stand there and wait.

He shouted, "Arthur, Arthur Hannon! It's Jason and I know you're in there. Come on, man, open this door. It's an emergency. Something has happened to Jacqueline and the police may be looking for you." He again banged on the door. Cedric began to move from side to side like a nervous warrior about to strike. Finally he could hear someone stirring inside. He knew they were checking him out through the peephole in the door. The door flew open and Elizabeth stood there in jeans and a top.

"Why do you keep bothering Arthur all the time?" she scowled.

Jason pushed past her and headed for the bedroom. Cedric followed close behind. Elizabeth had closed both bedroom doors so Jason grabbed the door knob to the one closest to him and flung the door open. He snatched the gun out as he and Cedric started into the bedroom.

"Baby, did you get rid of them?" Arthur asked before turning to look at them.

"No, she didn't, you son of a bitch," Jason shouted. He rushed toward the bed.

Arthur, lying naked on top of the bed, grabbed the covers and pulled them up over his body. "What the fuck you think you're doing?" he shouted at Jason.

Jason signaled for Cedric to go to the other side of the bed. He knew Elizabeth had positioned herself right by the door. He could feel her presence in the room. He aimed the pistol right at Arthur's head.

"I ought to shoot your sorry ass."

Arthur moved back against the back board. "What the hell's wrong with you?" he shouted at Jason and then looked over at Cedric. "What the fuck is wrong with you, brother?"

"He's just a little upset," Cedric said smiling. "Wait until he gets real mad, then you're going to have something to worry about."

"What'd I do to you, man? And point that damn gun somewhere else."

"I'm not going to shoot you unless you force me to. I just want to make sure I have your attention. Don't get me wrong, I'd love to blast your ass into oblivion. But that wouldn't bring my sister back. If it would, you'd be one dead high yellow ass nigguh."

Arthur rose up in the bed, still holding the covers up over his chest. "What do you mean, something's happened to Jacqueline?" he asked in a rather subdued voice. "What's happened to Jacqueline? What do you mean if you could bring her back? What are you talking about?" Arthur's voice had now risen. "What's happened to my wife?"

"She's dead, you rotten son of a bitch," Jason shouted. "She overdosed this morning."

"No," Arthur screamed. "No, no, you're lying." He dropped the covers and lunged at Jason who moved to the side and watched him crash to the floor.

Cedric launched into action. He hurried to the other side of the bed and kicked Arthur right between the legs. Arthur screamed and doubled up in pain. He lay there in a fetal position. Elizabeth still stood back by the door frozen in place. Cedric dropped to his knees and punched Arthur in the face and the stomach. Jason could see blood rushing from his nose and mouth. He suddenly realized that this was not what he really wanted to do. Beating up on Arthur would not bring closure for the loss of Jacqueline. He watched as Cedric applied a couple more choice blows to Arthur's head and body, then grabbed his brother by the arm and pulled him off the beaten man. He glowered at Elizabeth and then down at Arthur.

"You'll never hold a decent job in this city ever again," he barked out. "You're a finished man, especially after the business world finds out you're responsible for Casey Mitchell's daughter's death. I'm going to make damn sure, in fact, I'll dedicate my life to making sure you're a miserable, finished low-life bastard."

Jason started toward the door. Cedric followed behind. They stopped in front of Elizabeth and Jason shouted at her.

"I'll give you five hours to get that son of a bitch out of your place. If I find out he's still here, then you're going to have some visitors. I'm sure you don't want that." The two brothers stormed out of the apartment and down to the car.

As Jason pulled away he knew he wouldn't carry through on his threat. But he wanted to frighten Elizabeth just enough that she would put Arthur out. He knew if he waited around long enough he would soon see Arthur's Mercedes leaving the parking lot.

u

Elizabeth hurried over to where Arthur lay on the floor. She grabbed him by the arm and tried to help him. Arthur could feel the burning from the pain throughout his body, but did manage to get up and sit on the side of the bed. He started to lie down, but Elizabeth held his body up.

"No, Arthur, you can't lie down. You have to get out of here." She grabbed his clothes from the chair and flung them on the bed. "You have to go."

He glared at her as she stood over him in order to make sure he didn't try to lie down. "I can't go anywhere right now," he cried out. "Damn, woman, I can hardly move."

"You heard what he said if you're not gone he's going to call the police. Now I need for you to go."

"Elizabeth, I can't go right now. I don't have a place to go to."

"Shit, Arthur, that's not my problem. Go get a motel," Elizabeth shouted. "I always told you I don't like trouble and I don't want drama. Well that was just a little too much drama for me, so you have to go."

"Listen, bitch, if I leave here I won't be coming back," Arthur shouted as he dressed.

"That's fine, because I don't want you to come back. That man said your wife's dead and it sounded to me like they're blaming you. So I definitely need to put some distance between you and me."

"What a piece of shit you are," Arthur continued to shout.

"No bigger than you. We live the same lifestyle only you think you're better than us 'cause you could always go back to your rich uppity wife. It sounds to me like you don't have that lifestyle no more and you sure don't have a wife."

Arthur lashed out and hit Elizabeth a hard blow to the head. She fell down on the floor, but before he could do anything more she sprang back up, rushed over to the night stand and pulled out a gun. Arthur froze in place.

"Your brother-in-law wouldn't shoot your ass. I will," she shouted at him. "I'm white and you're a nigger and I'll get away with it. So you take your Black ass on out of here and don't ever come back. If I even see you in the complex I'll blow your fucking brains out." She hesitated for a moment, took in a deep breath and released it. "That one blow was a gimme otherwise you'd be dead. Now get the fuck out of here."

Arthur wanted to launch out and beat her some more. But reason took over from anger. He grabbed his wallet, watch and keys from the night stand, headed out of the bedroom and the apartment. Arthur rushed to his Mercedes, jumped in and drove off. As he exited the apartment complex a large smile spread across his face. He had nothing to worry about. He would rebound from this setback and be settled in with some other woman in no time. No matter what Jason said about him getting another job, he knew he possessed the persuasive powers to always get what he wanted from the ladies. And if his persuasive powers didn't work, Arthur still had the magic weapon.

Chapter 57

Jason stood between Hazel and Theresa as they listened to the minister say his final prayer at the cemetery just prior to lowering the beautiful bronze casket containing Jacqueline's body into the ground. Most of the mourners from the funeral home had followed them to the cemetery. Jason's legs weakened as the casket was slowly lowered into the ground. But he had to regain his strength and maintain his composure for his mother, who had held up well. He knew she was at the point of exhaustion. He grabbed his mother by the arm and led her away from the burial spot before the dirt was thrown.

Hazel had been much stronger than Jason had expected. He knew that sometime in the future she would have to release her anguish, but not on this day. This had been very difficult for her to do without the support of Big Casey, whom the doctors had advised against telling for fear it would cause a relapse. But Jason knew that soon he would have to be told because very soon he would be looking for his oldest daughter. Even though he was recovering well the doctors told them it would be another two weeks before he could go home. And then the tedious recovery would begin.

It was good to know that Big Casey was going to make a partial recovery; but there lingered the question would this family ever recover from losing Jacqueline? Jason helped his mother back into the limousine and then went around and got in the passenger's seat up front. As they began to pull away it struck him that Forest Lawn did not look like a cemetery with all the grass, flowers and trees. They had left a ton of flowers at the gravesite so that Jacqueline would be surrounded with God's beauty. Hazel would keep it that way if she had to visit the site every day. With the funeral procession over, the cars that had followed them to the cemetery took off on their own. They would meet at the house for the traditional feast that followed Black funerals. Jason wasn't sure how long he'd stay at the house. He wanted to get home and be alone. Each of them had to work this out in their own way before they could make sense of it all.

It was quiet in the limousine and no one seemed to want to break the silence. Jason knew Theresa's heart was broken. She couldn't recover from the fact that she hung up on Jacqueline out of anger and that would always be her last memory of her sister. That was a terrible burden to bear. Hazel also had her burdens. Jacqueline had wanted to spend the night with her, but Hazel sent both her and Arthur home that night. All morning she'd muttered before the funeral that she should have kept her there with her. She should have recognized how fragile her daughter was and Arthur's volatile and irrational nature. She carried blame for the suicide and it would be a long while before she'd find closure.

Jason also had his burdens to bear and he felt them. He was probably the last one to see Jacqueline alive. He should have picked up on the utter desperation she projected that day and stayed there or taken her with him. His mind, pre-occupied with Dominique, failed to detect the warning signs all around Jacqueline that day.

It had been a couple of days since his confrontation with Arthur and they hadn't heard from him. Jason had returned to the townhouse and removed all the furniture and clothes, putting them in storage. Arthur couldn't go back there and Jason thought he probably was no longer with Elizabeth. He could only be back home with his mother or out wandering the streets. Jason's preference was for the streets.

The black limousine finally pulled into the driveway at the house in Altadena. After Jason got out and worked the combination to the gate, it opened, he got back in and the driver drove up to the front of the house. Jason had set the gate so that it would stay open. A long line of cars followed them up the driveway. He jumped out of the limousine and opened the door for his mother. She looked exhausted as she took his hand and forced her body out of the vehicle. For the first time in an hour she spoke.

"I don't know if I'll be able to stay here," she said while pausing to look at her home.

"Mother, you and Big Casey built this, so you can't think that way," Jason said. Theresa and Cedric walked up and stood beside them.

"What's wrong?" Cedric asked.

"Nothing, Mother's just tired," Jason answered.

"It's not that, Jason. It's just that it's not right. At some point I have to tell your father and I know he won't want to stay here."

"Mama, please, we've been through a lot. Let's not go through that right now," Theresa said. "Let's go in and get through the rest of the day."

Hazel hugged her children, and as the visitors approached, she turned and headed inside the house.

Chapter 58

At a little past midnight Jason stretched his body across the love seat in the apartment with his legs hanging over the side of the armrest. He felt more mentally exhausted than physically drained. This had been the longest and the most difficult day he ever encountered in his years on earth. It would take a great deal of time and space before he would adjust to what happened today. They actually buried Jacqueline and even though he knew sometimes the young do die early, it just couldn't be someone close to him. His thoughts momentarily slipped back to the time not so long ago when Jacqueline and Theresa showed up at his apartment. Theresa had berated Arthur because he'd hit her sister. Jason never imagined the culmination of that blow would be his sister's life. If they could only do it again he'd make sure the ultimate result would be different.

The silence in the room was much too penetrating for him. At that moment he could feel Jacqueline's presence. Jason was not much of a believer in spirits or any kind of meta-physical phenomenon. He got up and sauntered over to the CD player. There was only one person that could fulfill his needs at that moment. He located the Nina Simone CD, placed it in the player and returned to his original position on the couch. The silence was broken as Nina sang, "Here Comes the Sun," in her classic rendition. It was just the right pace for him. Momentarily he thought of Dominique and realized whenever he heard Nina Simone again he would have images of her all around him.

But at that moment the image of Jacqueline dominated him. He could clearly visualize her lying there in the bed when he found her. His visualization shifted to earlier that day when they all marched down the aisle of the church to the pew directly in front of the casket. He could have screamed while the others passed in front of the open casket for a final view of a very beautiful Black woman who still had so much life to live, but had given it up for such a wasteful reason. The minister talked about closure. His actual words still rang true, "Issues with no closure will linger and hang around as long as they can. You have to resolve them and let them go." Jason knew they would all have to follow his advice. Jacqueline was gone and he would have to let her go. They had to pick up their individual lives without her. At some point, Jason would get on with his life, but he would never totally give her up. It just wasn't that easy when you'd spent your entire life with someone as close as a sister. Jason needed to get his mind off the day's events.

He walked over to the counter, and practically unaware of what he was doing, began to look at the stack of mail he'd brought in that evening. It had been days since he'd checked his mail box, so looking through the mail was a convenient diversion. He stared at each piece and then tossed it back on the counter until he picked up a letter from the agent in New York. Immediately his mood changed. He eagerly tore open the envelope and took out the letter. "Mr. Mitchell, I really enjoyed your first three chapters. I'd like to read the entire manuscript before I make a decision, but I am seriously considering representing you." Jason read the letter again just to assure himself that he'd read it right the first time. He held it high in the air and smiled, then tossed it back down on the counter and balled his fist as a gesture of victory.

He had to share his good news with someone but didn't know where Elliott was on his tour so he couldn't call him. He'd always told him to get a cell phone, but Elliott complained that it was too yuppie and white. He could call Raquel and share his good news with her and then invite her out to dinner tomorrow night. Even though he was desperately in love with Dominique he still had to get on with his life. Jason sprang off the bar stool and hurried into the bedroom to call Raquel. It struck him as odd that he hadn't been in the bedroom since he got home and as he rushed into the room he spotted the red light flashing on the answering machine. He slowed his pace and his enthusiasm waned. No more bad luck, please, he whispered. It couldn't be about Big Casey. Not so soon after Jacqueline. There was no way his family could handle another tragedy.

With trepidation he hit the play button. "Jason, its Dominique and I hope you'll just listen to what I have to say." Her voice caused his heartbeat to race. He sat on the side of the bed and listened. "I did love you and I do love you. And for that reason I must leave Los Angeles so that my love will not become a hindrance to you or me. I also believe that you love me, but you will not ever be able to overcome your impression of a dancer who entertains other men for money. Jason, I became a dancer so that I'd never view men in any other light than what their behavior reveals in a club. But you caught me off guard. You broke the rule and also forced me to break my rule." Jason could hear her voice crack and her speech slowed. "As a young girl I lived with my mother and she was a drug addict. In order to satisfy her habit she would turn her back when her dealer raped me over and over."

Jason hit the stop button, took in a deep breath and slowly released it. He could hear Nina's voice in the background singing about a "New World Coming." It sounded peaceful and soothing. He hit the play button and Dominique continued. "I would cry all night after he left the room. The experience never made me hate men, but it made me want to use and humiliate them. I wanted them to leave the club destroyed because of their uncontrollable and insatiable need for sex. You may find this unbelievable but because of my earlier experience, for all intents and purposes, I was a virgin until you. The reason why I asked you to just hold me in Palm Springs is because I wasn't sure how I'd respond since my first and last experience had been with a man who was raping me at thirteen. When you agreed to just hold me I realized that I had found the exception to the rule with you. I knew I had to get beyond my fear and that it would be a positive experience with you."

Again Jason hit the stop button. He had to let this happen piecemeal. Again in the background Nina sang "My Way." It seemed appropriate to him. Now he understood why he felt an uncontrollable desire to protect her. They were more than lovers. She had taken them both to a higher plane. Her need to experience something good about a man had directed their relationship. He continued to listen. "I absolutely loved our first night together. Your penetration was ecstasy and made me feel like a woman. It made me feel good and clean. Thank you for allowing me to experience sex as a wonderful and beautiful act. For that I'll always be indebted to you. Jason, when you saw me meditating on the couch I was actually praying that you were for real. That you could handle the fact that I danced for a living because I believed that if you couldn't handle that, there was no way you'd be able to handle my past. Maybe someday I'll regret ending our relationship, but you just have to understand I had too much at stake to take the chance that ultimately you'd fail me and that would truly be something I would not be able to handle. Tonight is my last night at the club. I've decided to go back to East St. Louis and deal with my demons from the past. Please don't take this message as anything more than an explanation of why I may have behaved rather strangely to you. But I know that someday I'll pick up one of your novels and smile because I'll know just how much that will mean to you and just how much you meant to me. Good night, sweet man, and goodbye."

The machine cut off but Jason sat there not knowing what to feel. This day couldn't possibly drain him any more. The ups and downs were exhausting. Sorrow now turned to joy and he felt ashamed of himself. He'd just buried his sister and so there was no way he should find happiness in that message from Dominique. Wasn't it enough that he had found some joy in the letter from the agent asking for the rest of his manuscript? Was this some kind of test of his ability to mourn for his sister? He could still feel Jacqueline's presence in the room and it was all positive, something she'd never been in life. He thought back on the minister's words, "closure is the ability to let someone you love go." Suddenly it became clear to him. He must let Jacqueline go, but not Dominique. Despite her admonishing him not to look for her, that's not what she really wanted. She wanted the exact opposite and just like she needed to be held that night in Palm Springs, she now needed to be loved. And just loving her is all he wanted to do. He sprang from the bed, grabbed his keys and hurried out of the apartment.

u

Jason pulled into the parking lot at the Black Zebra and his biggest fear was that she wouldn't be there. Maybe she'd already left Los Angeles and he'd have no way to find her. He found an empty space close to the entrance and parked the car. He smiled and paid the cover charge, then rushed past the bouncer and into the club. Inside the club Jason knew exactly what he would do once he found her. He looked over at the third dance stage and she was there surrounded as usual by a large contingent of men. He didn't care about the other men because this was going to happen his way. He hurried over to the stage. She saw him coming and he could swear a slight smile appeared on the side of her mouth. That was all the encouragement he needed. He stood there staring at her and she stopped dancing and stared back. The men huddled around the stage looked back to see who had caught her attention. A number of the men mumbled some words and returned to their tables. That left an opening for him. Jason hurried up to the stage.

The song ended and Dominique moved away from the last man that gave her a tip. She stood in front of Jason but did not lean down.

"I listened to your message," he said.

"I thought I owed you at least an explanation."

"I want you to come with me."

"I can't go to the back room until my set is over. You know that, Jason."

"No, I don't care about a back room and I don't care about a set."

A new song began but Dominique did not move away from her position close to Jason. A few men gathered around the stage in anticipation of her entertaining them.

"Jason, I have to get back to work."

"Didn't you say this was your last night?"

"Yes, I'm leaving in the morning."

'No, you're leaving now. Get dressed, please."

"Come on, Dominique," one of the men holding a five dollar bill said.

"I'm sorry, she's not dancing anymore," Jason politely said to the man.

"What the fuck's going on?" the man asked, then turned and went over to another stage.

"I don't want to make a scene, but I want you to get dressed," Jason said. "We're leaving right now."

"Jason I can't—"

"What's wrong, Dominique?" the bouncer asked as he came up and stood next to the stage.

"Nothing."

"Well get to work. You're pissing off the customers."

"Let me take a break from this set," she said.

"Okay, but we can't have any trouble up in here." The bouncer turned and stared at Jason.

Jason ignored the man because nothing could interrupt what he had to accomplish. Dominique slipped on her clothes and came down from the stage. He took her by the hand and started toward the door. Everyone in the club was staring at them. The two girls dancing on the other stages stopped and stared.

"Jason, what are you doing?" Dominique asked as she reluctantly followed him. He held her hand tighter.

"I'll explain when we get out of this place."

"Jason, I don't have all my clothes."

"I have a shirt in the car that'll cover you up. When we get to an all night outlet I'll buy you something."

"What are you talking about? What are you doing?"

They were finally at the door. He swung it open and the two of them walked briskly right past the bouncer.

"Wait here and don't go back in there," Jason instructed her. He ran to his car, got in and pulled in front of the club. He jumped out and grabbed her hand, leading her to the car. She got in and after he got behind the wheel they drove off.

"Jason Mitchell, what are you doing?" Dominique asked again. "Where are we going?"

"Las Vegas." He turned and smiled at her.

"What are you talking about? I have to get my clothes. I told you I'm going back to East St. Louis."

"You can't go there."

"Why?"

"Because East St. Louis probably has a waiting period before you can get married. I can't wait, not another minute."

Dominique laid her head back on the headrest. "Is that a proposal?"

"You better believe it is."

"Well, my God, I'd better rest. I still have a lot of work to do with you."

"You sure do." Jason sped the BMW onto the 110 and smiled. "And I'm going to love every minute of it." He grabbed a CD and stuck it in the player, moved it forward to a specific song. Within seconds the sounds of Al Jarreau filled the space, as he sang, "We're in this love together, We got the kind that lasts forever. And like berries on the bind. It gets sweeter all the time."

Epilogue

Jason grabbed Dominique's hand and squeezed tightly as the Master of Ceremonies for the National Association for the Advancement of Colored People's Annual Image Awards Celebration opened the envelope to announce the winner for the Best New Novelist of 2006. The Mitchell family practically filled the entire front row. Big Casey's wheelchair rested at the far end of the row. When the NAACP called and informed Jason that he was a finalist for Jubilee's A'Comin', he was determined that the entire family would share in his joy. Over the past year they had grown larger with the addition of Dominique, and Cedric's marriage to Tosha. After the HIV test came back negative Cedric told the entire family they'd never have to worry about that again. He and Tosha both were clean and since they planned to marry and pledged their loyalty to each other there would be no way they could contract that dreadful disease. In a private moment with Jason, something they shared quite a bit, he did admit his confusion, but felt that a relationship with Tosha was best for him as well as her. Cedric, Tosha and the baby lived in the guest house and he worked for the company in Los Angeles. Howard, who still ran the company, had bid on and won a city project in Pasadena, which was scheduled to start in two weeks. He had named Cedric as the project manager. With he new position, he and Tosha could move into their own place. It seemed that Cedric now had all those things he craved in the past, someone to love, and someone who needed him.

Theresa had even agreed to dress up for the occasion. She sat between Tosha and Dominique. She had told Jason that she really missed her sister, but felt a very unique closeness with Dominique. Theresa hadn't lived quite the life Dominique had but, like her, she had been forced to carry a secret for a very long time, and now she shared this secret with Jason.

Hazel was the one they worried about most of all. She had not only to adjust to her oldest daughter's death, but to the fact that her husband would now be confined to a wheelchair for the rest of his life. Big Casey had been forced to give up the few amenities he enjoyed, that is a cigar and a glass of Scotch every once in a while. When Jason brought his father home for the first time from the hospital, the first thing Hazel did was make it clear that he would follow the doctor's instructions or he'd have hell on his hands. The hardest part of his coming home was when they told him about Jacqueline. He went into a depression and they all felt it might harm his recovery, but after a month he began to adjust, taking a closer interest in Tosha and the baby and of course Cedric.

Jason glanced at his daughter Julianne who clung to her grandmother and laid her head on Hazel's shoulder. Julianne had warmed up to Dominique since the marriage but still decided to sit next to Hazel. Jason offered Angela a ticket to the ceremony, but she had graciously turned it down. She did ask him, however, how much money she could expect in child support increase as a result of Jason's new found fame. Elliott had sent his congratulations from New York, where he now lived.

Hazel grabbed Big Casey's hand as the Master of Ceremonies glanced at the name on the paper.As the man adjusted the microphone to announce the winner, Jason looked down the row at his family and felt good. Regardless of the outcome, he knew they all were winners. He looked back up at the man and sighed. He really wished Jacqueline was there with them. She would, more than the rest, get great joy out of it all.

"It is my pleasure," the man said, "to announce this year's winner of the Best New Novelist Award for 2006. And it is Mr. Jason Mitchell for his outstanding novel Jubilee's A'Comin'."

Jason momentarily froze. He didn't know exactly what to do. Finally Dominique took the initiative. She leaned toward him and kissed him. That was his cue to get up. With a big smile, he rose from his seat and strolled to the stage. He turned and looked at an audience that was standing and applauding. He took the award and the Master of Ceremonies whispered to him, "Congratulations."

While the crowd continued to salute him, he could only stand there in awe. He looked up into the balcony and the image of Jacqueline, dressed in a beautiful black gown, hair down, flower over one ear, appeared high above the audience. He picked up her energy filled with pride for what he had accomplished. Through all the turmoil she had shown up. Without knowing what he was doing he held the award high in the air to give her a better view. He smiled and threw her a kiss. The applause waned and the audience finally sat down. It was his time to shine.

"I want to thank the National Association for this award. It means more than you could ever imagine, more than just an award, but an accomplishment for many people besides me. I accept it on behalf of myself, my family, and especially my sister who we tragically lost last year." He again looked up at her image still high above the others in the balcony. "Writing for me," he continued, "is not work but a joy. I guess you can say it's therapy. We as Black people need a lot more writers because we have one heck of a story to tell. And because we live this twoness, this double consciousness as Dr. Du Bois wrote over a century ago, it has to be us, my brothers and sisters, who boldly put pen to paper to tell our story." He paused and looked at Dominique who smiled at him. "As long as I write I will try to portray my people in the most honest way possible. I choose to write of positive images of our race because we are an absolutely positive people. I feel that you write as an artist, but also as a messenger of good news. And that news is that we as a people have given a lot and still have a lot to give. As novelists and poets we will reveal to the world a most beautiful race. We had the Harlem Renaissance and great writers who at that time captured our essence, and now we have the rebirth. Stand by because there is a lot more to come from a group of great and talented writers."

Jason ended his short acceptance speech and started off the stage. For some reason he stopped right at the top step. He